Rich People Problems

Kevin Kwan is the author of the international best-sellers *Crazy Rich Asians*, now a major motion picture, and *China Rich Girlfriend*. Born in Singapore, he has called New York's West Village home since 1995.

'Will make you both roll your eyes and chuckle . . . Pure entertainment. Think: Bravo's *Housewives* but with a lot more money and, as a result, a lot more drama.'

Nylon

'Kwan's satirical lance has become slightly more subtle, while no less deadly, over the course of the trilogy. The books are the essence of the beach read: lively plot(s), memorable characters, able to be read with adult beverages at hand.'

Minneapolis Star Tribune

'Readers who thought they didn't like to read about rich people will quickly lose all high-minded pretensions as they revel in the food, fashions, real estate, and art so lusciously strewn through this irresistible, knowing, and even sometimes moving story.'

Kirkus Reviews (starred review)

'Something for everyone . . . A smorgasbord of rich delights.'
New York Journal of Books

'Kwan creates a fictional universe so full, with language as well adorned as the lives of the glittering characters he paints.'
Town & Country Philippines

ALSO BY KEVIN KWAN

Crazy Rich Asians
China Rich Girlfriend

Rich People Problems

KEVIN KWAN

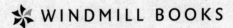

WINDMILL BOOKS

1 3 5 7 9 10 8 6 4 2

Windmill Books
20 Vauxhall Bridge Road
London SW1V 2SA

Windmill Books is part of the Penguin Random House group of companies
whose addresses can be found at global.penguinrandomhouse.com

Penguin
Random House
UK

First published in the United States by Doubleday, a division
of Penguin Random House LLC, New York in 2017
First published in Great Britain in paperback by Windmill Books in 2019

www.penguin.co.uk

A CIP catalogue record for this book is available from the British Library.

ISBN 9781786091086

Printed and bound in Great Britain by Clays Ltd, Elcograf S.p.A.

For my grandparents,

and for Mary Kwan

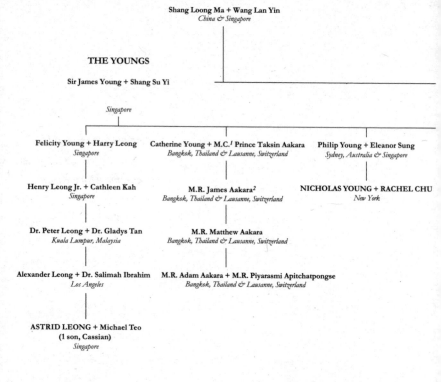

Shang Loong Ma + Wang Lan Yin
China & Singapore

THE YOUNGS

Sir James Young + Shang Su Yi
Singapore

Felicity Young + Harry Leong
Singapore

Catherine Young + M.C.[1] Prince Taksin Aakara
Bangkok, Thailand & Lausanne, Switzerland

Philip Young + Eleanor Sung
Sydney, Australia & Singapore

Henry Leong Jr. + Cathleen Kah
Singapore

M.R. James Aakara[2]
Bangkok, Thailand & Lausanne, Switzerland

NICHOLAS YOUNG + RACHEL CHU
New York

Dr. Peter Leong + Dr. Gladys Tan
Kuala Lumpur, Malaysia

M.R. Matthew Aakara
Bangkok, Thailand & Lausanne, Switzerland

Alexander Leong + Dr. Salimah Ibrahim
Los Angeles

M.R. Adam Aakara + M.R. Piyarasmi Apitchatpongse
Bangkok, Thailand & Lausanne, Switzerland

ASTRID LEONG + Michael Teo
(1 son, Cassian)
Singapore

---

[1] M.C. is the abbreviation for Mom Chao, the title reserved for the grandsons of King Rama V of Thailand (1853–1910) and is the most junior class still considered royalty. In English this rank is translated as "His Serene Highness."

[2] M.R. is the abbreviation for Mom Rajawongse, the title assumed by children of male Mom Chaos. In English this rank is translated as "The Honorable."

THE YOUNG, T'SIEN, & SHANG CLAN

(a simplified family tree)

THE SHANGS

Alfred Shang + Mabel T'sien

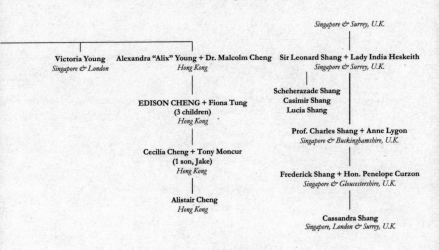

Singapore & Surrey, U.K.

Victoria Young
Singapore & London

Alexandra "Alix" Young + Dr. Malcolm Cheng
Hong Kong

Sir Leonard Shang + Lady India Heskeith
Singapore & Surrey, U.K.

Scheherazade Shang
Casimir Shang
Lucia Shang

EDISON CHENG + Fiona Tung
(3 children)
Hong Kong

Prof. Charles Shang + Anne Lygon
Singapore & Buckinghamshire, U.K.

Cecilia Cheng + Tony Moncur
(1 son, Jake)
Hong Kong

Frederick Shang + Hon. Penelope Curzon
Singapore & Gloucestershire, U.K.

Alistair Cheng
Hong Kong

Cassandra Shang
Singapore, London & Surrey, U.K.

THE T'SIENS

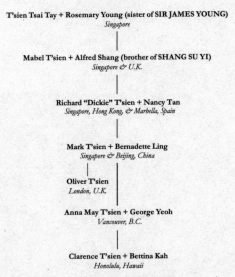

T'sien Tsai Tay + Rosemary Young (sister of SIR JAMES YOUNG)
Singapore

Mabel T'sien + Alfred Shang (brother of SHANG SU YI)
Singapore & U.K.

Richard "Dickie" T'sien + Nancy Tan
Singapore, Hong Kong, & Marbella, Spain

Mark T'sien + Bernadette Ling
Singapore & Beijing, China

Oliver T'sien
London, U.K.

Anna May T'sien + George Yeoh
Vancouver, B.C.

Clarence T'sien + Bettina Kah
Honolulu, Hawaii

RICH PEOPLE PROBLEMS

PROBLEM NO. I

*Your regular table at the fabulous restaurant on
the exclusive island where you own a beach house is
unavailable.*

HARBOUR ISLAND, THE BAHAMAS, JANUARY 21, 2015

Bettina Ortiz y Meña was not accustomed to waiting. A former
Miss Venezuela (and Miss Universe runner-up, of course), the
exceedingly bronzed strawberry blonde was these days the wife
of the Miami auto-parts tycoon Herman Ortiz y Meña, and at
every restaurant she chose to grace with her presence, she was
always greeted with reverence and whisked to the exact table she
desired. Today she wanted the corner table on the terrace at Sip
Sip, her favorite lunch spot on Harbour Island. She wanted to
sit on one of the comfy orange canvas director's chairs and stare
out at the gently lapping turquoise waters while eating her kale
Caesar salad, but there was a large, noisy group taking up the
entire terrace and they didn't seem in much hurry to leave.

Bettina fumed as she glared at the tourists happily savoring their lunch in the sun. Look how tacky they were . . . the women overly tanned, wrinkled, and saggy, none of them properly lifted or Botoxed. She felt like walking up to their table and handing out her dermatologist's business cards. And the men were even worse! All dressed in old rumpled shirts and shorts, wearing those cheap straw hats sold at the trinket shop on Dunmore Street. Why did such people have to come here?

This three-and-a-half-mile-long paradise with its pristine pink-sand beaches was one of the best-kept secrets in the Caribbean, a haven for the very very rich filled with quaint little wood houses painted in shades of sherbet, charming boutiques, chic oceanfront mansions turned into inns, and five-star restaurants to rival St. Barths. Tourists should have to take a style exam before being allowed to set foot on the island! Feeling like she had been patient long enough, Bettina stormed into the kitchen, the fringe on her crocheted Pucci caftan top shaking furiously as she made a beeline for the woman with a shock of pixie-cut blond hair manning the main stove.

"Julie, honey, what's the dealio? I've waited more than *fifteen minutes* for my table!" Bettina sighed to the owner of the restaurant.

"Sorry, Bettina, it's been one of those days. The party of twelve on the terrace showed up just before you did," Julie replied as she handed off a bowl of spicy conch chili to a waiting server.

"But the terrace is your prime spot! Why on earth did you let those *tourists* take up all that space?"

"Well, that *tourist* in the red fishing cap is the Duke of Glencora. His party just boated over from Windermere—that's his *Royal Huisman* you see moored off the coast. Isn't it the most handsome sailboat you've ever seen?"

"I'm not impressed by big boats," Bettina huffed, although secretly she was rather impressed by people with big titles. From the kitchen window, she surveyed the party assembled on the terrace with new eyes. These aristo British types were such a strange breed. Sure, they had their Savile Row suits and their heirloom tiaras, but when they traveled, they looked so painfully frumpy.

It was only then that Bettina noticed three tan, well-built men in fitted white T-shirts and black Kevlar pants sitting at the adjacent table. The guys weren't eating but sat watchfully, sipping glasses of seltzer water. "I assume that's the duke's security detail? They couldn't be more obvious! Don't they know that we're all billionaires here on Briland, and this isn't how we roll?"[*] Bettina tut-tutted.

"Actually, those bodyguards belong to the duke's special guest. They did a whole sweep of the restaurant before the party arrived. They even searched my walk-in freezer. See that Chinese fellow seated at the end of the table?"

Bettina squinted through her Dior Extase sunglasses at the portly, balding, seventy-something Asian man dressed in a nondescript white short-sleeved golf shirt and gray trousers. "Oh, I didn't even notice him! Am I supposed to know who he is?"

"That's *Alfred Shang*," Julie said in a hushed tone.

Bettina giggled. "He looks like their chauffeur. Doesn't he look like that guy that used to drive Jane Wyman around in *Falcon Crest*?"

Julie, who was trying to focus on searing a cut of tuna to per-

---

[*] A slight exaggeration, but this island—known affectionately as "Briland" to the locals—is home to twelve billionaires (at last count, and depending on who's counting).

fection, shook her head with a tight-lipped smile. "From what I hear, that chauffeur is the most powerful man in Asia."

"What's his name again?"

"Alfred Shang. He's Singaporean but lives mostly in England on an estate that's half the size of Scotland, so I'm told."

"Well I've never seen his name on any of the rich lists," Bettina sniffed.

"Bettina, I'm sure you know that there are people on this planet who are far too rich and powerful to ever appear on those lists!"

PROBLEM NO. 2

The twenty-four-hour on-call personal physician that you have on a million-dollar annual retainer is busy attending to another patient.

Sitting on the terrace overlooking Harbour Island's legendary beach, Alfred Shang marveled at the spectacular sight before him. *It's true—the sand really is pink!*

"Alfred, your lobster quesadillas are going to get cold!" the Duke of Glencora piped up, interrupting his reverie.

"So this is the reason you dragged me all the way here?" Alfred said, staring dubiously at the triangular wedges placed artfully before him. He didn't really care much for Mexican food, except when the chef of his good friend Slim in Mexico City was doing the cooking.

"Try it before you judge it."

Alfred took a careful bite, saying nothing, as the combination of semi-crisp tortilla, lobster, and guacamole worked its magic.

"Marvelous, isn't it? I've been trying to convince the chef at Wilton's to replicate this for years," the duke said.

"They haven't changed a thing at Wilton's in half a century—I don't think there's much of a likelihood they would ever put this on their menu." Alfred laughed, picking up a stray lobster chunk that had fallen onto the table with his fingers and popping it into his mouth. His phone began to vibrate in his trouser pocket. He took it out and stared at the screen in annoyance. Everyone knew that he was not to be disturbed on his annual fishing trip with the duke.

The screen read: TYERSALL UPSTAIRS SECURE.

This was his elder sister, Su Yi, the only person whose calls he would take no matter the hour. He picked up immediately, and an unexpected voice said in Cantonese, "Mr. Shang, this is Ah Ling."

It took him a few seconds to register that it was the housekeeper at Tyersall Park. "Oh . . . Ling Jeh!"*

"I was instructed by my lady to call you. She was feeling very unwell tonight and has just been taken to the hospital. We think it's a heart attack."

"What do you mean *you think*? Did she have a heart attack or didn't she?" Alfred's plummy Queen's English suddenly shifting into Cantonese in alarm.

"She . . . she didn't have any chest pains, but she was sweating profusely, and then she vomited. She said she could feel her heart racing," Ah Ling stuttered nervously.

"And did Prof Oon come over?" Alfred asked.

---

* Cantonese for "elder sister," often used as a term of familiarity for household help in the way that "boy" is sometimes used, as in Sonny Boy or Johnny Boy.

"I tried to reach the doctor on his cell phone, but it went straight to voice mail. Then I called his house and someone there said he was in Australia."

"Why are *you* doing all the calling? Isn't Victoria at home?"

"Mr. Shang, isn't Victoria in England?"

Alamak. He had completely forgotten that his niece—Su Yi's daughter, who lived at Tyersall Park—was at this moment at his house in Surrey, no doubt embroiled in some inane gossipfest with his wife and daughter.

"How about Felicity? Didn't she come over?" Alfred inquired about Su Yi's eldest daughter, whose house was nearby on Nassim Road.

"Mrs. Leong could not be reached tonight. Her maid said she was in church, and she always turns off her mobile phone when she's in the house of God."

Bloody useless, all of them! "Well, did you call an ambulance?"

"No, she didn't want an ambulance. Vikram drove her to the hospital in the Daimler, accompanied by her lady's maids and two Gurkhas. But before she left, she said you would know how to contact Professor Oon."

"Okay, okay. I'll take care of it," Alfred said in a huff, hanging up the phone.

Everyone at the table was staring at him expectantly.

"Oh my, that did sound rather serious," the duke said, pursing his lips worriedly.

"I'll just be a moment . . . please carry on," Alfred said, getting up from his chair. The bodyguards trailed after him as he strode through the restaurant and out the door to the garden.

Alfred hit another number on his speed dial: PROF OON HOME.

A woman picked up the phone.

"Is this Olivia? Alfred Shang here."

"Oh, Alfred! Are you looking for Francis?"

"Yes. I'm told he's in Australia?" *Why the bloody hell did they have this doctor on a million-dollar retainer if he was never available?*

"He just left an hour ago for Sydney. He's doing a triple bypass tomorrow on that actor who won an Oscar for—"

"So he's on a plane right now?" Alfred cut her off.

"Yes, but he'll be arriving in a few hours if you need to—"

"Just give me his flight number," Alfred snapped. He turned to one of his bodyguards and asked, "Who has the Singapore phone? Somebody get Istana* on the line right now."

Turning to another bodyguard, he said, "And please order me another of those lobster quesadillas."

PROBLEM NO. 3

Your airplane is forced to land before you can finish drinking your Dom Pérignon.

EAST JAVA, INDONESIA

The silk sheets had just been turned down in the first-class suites, the enormous double-decked Airbus A380-800 had reached a comfortable cruising altitude of thirty-eight thousand feet, and most of the passengers were comfortably ensconced in their seats, scanning through the latest movie offerings. Moments later, the pilots of Singapore Airlines Flight 231 bound for Syd-

---

* Malay for "palace." In this instance, Alfred is referring to Istana in Singapore, the official residence of the president.

ney received the most unusual instructions from Jakarta air traffic control as they flew over Indonesian airspace:

AIR TRAFFIC CONTROLLER: Singapore Two Thirty-one Super Jakarta.
PILOT: Singapore Two Thirty-one Super go ahead.
ATC: I have been instructed to have you turn around immediately and return to Singapore Changi Airport.
PILOT: Jakarta, you want us to return to Singapore Changi?
ATC: Yes. Turn the plane around and return immediately to Singapore. I have the amended route advise ready to copy.
PILOT: Jakarta, what is the reason for the course change?
ATC: I don't have that information, but this is a direct order from the Directorate General of Civil Aviation.

The pilots looked at each other in disbelief. "Should we really be doing this?" the captain wondered aloud. "We'll have to dump a quarter-million liters of fuel before we can land!"

Just then, the aircraft's selective-calling radio system lit up with an incoming message. The co-pilot read the message quickly and gave the captain an incredulous look. "*Wah lan!* It's from the minister of fricking defense! He says to get back to Singapore pronto!"

When the airplane made an unexpected landing at Changi Airport just three hours after it had departed, the passengers were disoriented and startled by the strange turn of events. An announcement was made over the intercom: "Ladies and gentlemen, due to an unexpected event, we have made an emergency diversion back to Singapore. Please remain in your seats with your seat belts fastened, as our flight to Sydney will resume immediately after refueling."

Two men in discreet dark suits came aboard and approached the man seated in suite 3A—Professor Francis Oon, Singapore's leading cardiologist. "Professor Oon? I'm Lieutenant Ryan Chen from SID.* Please come with us."

"We're leaving the plane?" Professor Oon asked, utterly baffled. One minute he was in the middle of watching *Gone Girl*, and the next minute the plane had landed back in Singapore. He hadn't even recovered from the film's jaw-dropping plot twist.

Lieutenant Chen nodded curtly. "Yes. Please gather up all your belongings—you won't be returning to this flight."

"But . . . but . . . what did I do?" Professor Oon asked, suddenly feeling uneasy.

"Don't worry, you didn't do anything. But we need to get you off this plane now."

"Am I the only one leaving?"

"Yes, you are. We are escorting you directly to Mount Elizabeth Hospital. You have been requested to attend to a VVIP patient."

At that moment, Professor Oon knew something must have happened to Shang Su Yi. Only the Shangs had the kind of influence to turn around a Singapore Airlines flight with four hundred forty passengers onboard.

---

* The Security and Intelligence Division, Singapore's equivalent of America's CIA or Britain's MI5, is so secretive that most people don't even know it exists. But yes, that man eating fish ball on a stick outside NTUC FairPrice could be the Singaporean James Bond, and you wouldn't even know it.

PART ONE

The only thing I like about rich people is their money.

—NANCY ASTOR, VISCOUNTESS ASTOR

CHAPTER ONE

DAVOS, SWITZERLAND

Edison Cheng stared up at the soaring honeycomb-structured ceiling in the vast white auditorium, feeling on top of the world. *I'm here. I'm finally here!* After years of Olympic-level networking, Eddie had at long last made it—he had been invited to attend the annual meeting of the World Economic Forum in Davos. Strictly by invitation only,* this prestigious event was the most elite schmoozefest on the planet.

Every January, the world's most important heads of state, politicians, philanthropists, CEOs, tech leaders, thought leaders, social activists, social entrepreneurs, and, of course, movie stars† would descend upon this secluded ski resort high in the Swiss Alps in their private jets, check in to their luxurious hotels, put on their $5,000 ski jackets and ski boots, and engage in meaningful dialogues about such urgent issues as global warming and rising inequality.

And now Eddie was part of this ultraexclusive club. As the recently appointed senior executive vice chairman of Private

---

* And if you happen to get invited, just know you're still obliged to pay the $20,000 attendance fee unless you are one of the people listed in the next footnote. (Beautiful people never have to pay for anything.)
† Leo, Brad, Angelina, and Bono have all attended.

Banking (Global) for the Liechtenburg Group, he now found himself standing in the middle of the futuristic auditorium at the Congress Centre, breathing in the rarefied air and catching slivers of his own reflection in the thin chrome leg of an auditorium chair. He was wearing his new bespoke Sartoria Ripense suit, which had been outfitted with an inner lining of ten-ply cashmere so that he never had to wear a ski jacket over it. His new Corthay squirrel suede chukkas had special rubber soles, so he would never slip on the slick Alpine streets. On his wrist was his newest horological acquisition—a rose gold A. Lange & Söhne Richard Lange "Pour le Mérite," peeking out the precise amount from his sleeve cuff so other watchophiles would see what he was wearing. But most important of all was what he wore over this sartorial splendor—a black lanyard at the end of which was attached a white plastic badge with his name printed in the middle: *Edison Cheng.*

Eddie fondled the slick plastic badge as if it were a jewel-encrusted amulet, personally bestowed on him by the God of Davos. This badge distinguished him from all the pee-ons at the conference. He wasn't some PR hack, journalist, or one of the common attendees. This white plastic badge with the blue line at the bottom meant that he was an *official delegate.*

Eddie glanced around the room at all the clusters of people in hushed conversations, trying to see which dictator, despot, or director he could recognize and connect with. Out of the corner of his eye, he spotted a tall Chinese man wearing a bright orange ski parka peeking in through the auditorium's side door, seemingly a little lost. *Wait a minute, I know that guy. Isn't that Charlie Wu?*

"Oy—Charlie!" Eddie yelled, a little too loudly, as he rushed over toward Charlie. *Wait till he sees my official delegate badge!*

Charlie beamed at him in recognition. "Eddie Cheng! Did you just get in from Hong Kong?"

"I came from Milan, actually. I was at the men's fall fashion shows—front-row seat at Etro."

"Wow. I guess being one of *Hong Kong Tattle*'s Best Dressed Men is serious work, isn't it?" Charlie quipped.

"Actually, I made it into the Best Dressed Hall of Fame last year," Eddie replied earnestly. He gave Charlie a quick once-over, noticing that he was wearing khaki pants with cargo pockets and a navy blue pullover under his bright orange parka. *What a pity—he used to be so fashionable when he was younger, and now he's dressed like every other tech-geek nobody.* "Where's your badge, Charlie?" Eddie asked, flashing his own proudly.

"Oh yes, we're supposed to wear them at all times, aren't we? Thanks for reminding me—it's somewhere buried in my messenger bag." Charlie dug around for a few seconds before fishing out his badge, and Eddie glanced at it, his curiosity morphing into shocked dismay. Charlie was holding an all-white badge affixed with a shiny holographic sticker. *Fucky fuck, this was the most coveted badge! The one they only gave to world leaders! The only other person he had seen so far wearing that badge was Bill Clinton! How the fuck did Charlie get one? All he did was run Asia's biggest tech company!*

Trying to mask his envy, Eddie blurted, "Hey, are you attending my panel—Apocalypse Asia: How to Secure Your Assets When the China Bubble *Really* Bursts?"

"I'm actually on my way to give a talk to IGWEL.* What time do you go on?"

---

* The acronym for Informal Gathering of World Economic Leaders, the most exclusive inner sanctum of the conference, so secretive that their meetings take place at an undisclosed location deep within the Congress Centre.

"Two o'clock. What's your talk about?" Eddie asked, thinking that he could somehow tag along with Charlie.

"I don't have anything prepared, really. I think Angela Merkel and some of the Scandinavians just wanted to pick my brain."

Just then, Charlie's executive assistant, Alice, walked up to join them.

"Alice, look who I found! I knew we'd bump into someone from back home sooner or later," Charlie said.

"Mr. Cheng, so nice to see you here. Charlie—could I have a quick word?"

"Sure."

Alice glanced at Eddie, who looked only too eager for her to continue while he was standing right there. "Er . . . would you mind coming with me for a moment?" she said diplomatically, guiding Charlie into a side reception room furnished with several lounge chairs and glass-cube coffee tables.

"What's up? Are you still trying to recover from sitting at the same breakfast table with Pharrell?" Charlie teased.

Alice smiled tensely. "There's been a developing situation all morning, and we didn't want to disturb you until we knew more."

"Well, spit it out."

Alice took a deep breath before beginning. "I just got the latest update from our head of security in Hong Kong. I don't quite know how to tell you this, but Chloe and Delphine are missing."

"What do you mean *missing*?" Charlie was stunned—his daughters were under round-the-clock surveillance, and their pickups and drop-offs were handled with military precision by his SAS-trained security team. *Missing* was not a variable in their lives.

"Team Chungking was scheduled to pick them up outside

Diocesan at 3:50 p.m., but the girls couldn't be located at the school."

"Couldn't be located . . ." Charlie mumbled in shock.

Alice continued, "Chloe didn't respond to any of her texts, and Delphine never showed up for choir at two. They thought maybe she sneaked off with her classmate Kathryn Chan to that frozen yogurt shop like she did last time, but then Kathryn turned up at choir practice and Delphine didn't."

"Did either of them activate their panic codes?" Charlie asked, trying to remain calm.

"No, they didn't. Their phones both appear to have been deactivated, so we can't trace them. Team 2046 has already spoken with Commander Kwok—the Hong Kong police have been placed on high alert. We also have four of our own teams searching everywhere for them, and the school is now reviewing all their security-camera footage with Mr. Tin."

"I'm assuming someone's talked to their mother?" Charlie's wife—from whom he was estranged—lived in their house on The Peak, and the children spent every other week with her.

"Isabel can't be reached. She told the housekeeper that she was meeting her mother for lunch at the Kowloon Cricket Club, but her mother reports that they haven't spoken all week."

Just then, the cell phone rang again and Alice quickly answered. She listened in silence, nodding her head every now and then. Charlie looked at her pensively. *This couldn't be happening. This couldn't be happening. Ten years ago his brother Rob had been kidnapped by the Eleven Finger Triad. It was like déjà vu all over again.*

"Okay. *Tor jeh, tor jeh,*"* Alice said, hanging up. Looking at

---

* Cantonese for "Thank you, thank you."

Charlie, she reported, "That was the leader of Team Angels. They now think that Isabel might have left the country. They spoke to the upstairs maid, and Isabel's passport is missing. But for some reason she didn't take any suitcases."

"Isn't she in the middle of some new treatment?"

"Yes, but apparently she didn't show up at her psychiatrist appointment this week."

Charlie let out a deep sigh. This wasn't a good sign.

CHAPTER TWO

Every month, Rosalind Fung, the property heiress, hosted a Christian Fellowship Banquet for three hundred of her closest girlfriends in the opulent ballroom of the Fullerton Hotel. An invitation to this occasion was highly coveted by a certain segment of Singapore society regardless of their religious affiliation as it was a seal of approval from the old guard (there wasn't a single Chindo or Mainlander in sight), and also because the food was *heavenly*—Rosalind brought in her personal chefs, who took over the hotel's kitchens for one day and prepared an enormous buffet feast consisting of the most mouthwatering Singaporean dishes. Most important—this biblical bacchanal was completely *free of charge* thanks to Rosalind's generosity, although guests were asked to contribute something to the offering basket immediately following the closing prayer.*

Having strategically chosen a table closest to the buffet area, Daisy Foo sighed as she watched Araminta Lee standing in line

---

* Most of the guests left five or ten dollars each, except Mrs. Lee Yong Chien, who never left anything. "I do all my giving through the Lee Family Foundation" was what she always said.

at the noodle station dishing out some *mee siam*. "*Aiyah*—that Araminta! *Bein kar ani laau!*"*

"She doesn't look old. She just doesn't have any makeup on, that's all. Those supermodel types look like nothing on earth without makeup," Nadine Shaw said as she tucked into her steaming bowl of *mee rebus* noodles.

Dousing her *mee goreng* with more chili oil, Eleanor Young commented, "It has nothing to do with that. I used to see her swim at the Churchill Club, and even when she was coming out of the pool dripping wet, she looked beautiful without a stitch of makeup on. Her face has just taken a turn, that's all. She has one of those faces that I always knew would age badly. What is she . . . twenty-seven, twenty-eight now? It's all over for her, *lah*."

At that moment, Lorena Lim and Carol Tai arrived at the table with plates piled dangerously high with food. "Wait, wait . . . who's aging badly?" Lorena inquired eagerly.

"Araminta Lee. Over at that table with all the Khoo women. Doesn't she look haggard?" Nadine said.

"*Alamak*, bite your tongue, Nadine! Didn't you know she just had a miscarriage?" Carol whispered.

The ladies all stared at Carol, mouths agape. "Again? Are you joking? Who told you, *lah*?" Daisy demanded, still chewing on her *mee pok*.

"Who else? Kitty, *lor*. Kitty and Araminta are the best of friends now, and ever since this latest miscarriage, she's been spending a lot of time at Kitty's house playing with Gisele. She's completely heartbroken."

"How often do you see Kitty and Gisele?" Lorena asked,

---

* Hokkien for "Gotten so old!"

dressed up like Christmas trees but just look at Astrid . . . hair in a sleek ponytail, ballet flats, not a drop of jewelry except that cross . . . is it turquoise? And *that outfit!* She looks like Audrey Hepburn on the way to a screen test," Daisy said approvingly as she fished around in her new Céline handbag for a toothpick. "Blah-dee-hell! See what my snobby daughter-in-law forces me to carry? She gave me this fancy handbag for my birthday because she's embarrassed of being seen next to me when I'm carrying my no-name purse, but I can't ever find anything in here! It's so damn deep, and there are so many damn pockets!"

"Daisy, will you please stop swearing? We are in the Lord's presence tonight, you know," Carol admonished.

As if on cue, the Christian Fellowship Banquet's hostess, Rosalind Fung, got up from her table and walked onto the stage. A short, plumpish woman in her mid-sixties with a frizzy spiral perm, Rosalind was dressed in what seemed to be the regulation uniform of every middle-aged old-money Singaporean heiress—a sleeveless floral blouse, probably purchased from the clearance rack at John Little, taupe elastic-waist pants, and orthopedic open-toe sandals. She smiled happily from the podium at her gathered friends.

"Ladies, thank you all for coming tonight to join in fellowship with Christ. A quick warning to everyone before we start: I'm told that the *laksa** is dangerously spicy tonight. I don't know what happened, but even Mary Lau, who everyone knows has to have extra chili with everything, told me that she *buey tahan†* the *laksa*. Now, before we continue to nourish our stomachs

---

* A spicy noodle soup dish served with cockles, fish cake, and thick rice noodles.
† Singlish for "cannot endure it."

and our souls, Bishop See Bei Sien will begin our program with a blessing."

As the bishop started one of his notoriously tedious prayers, bizarre noises could be heard coming from behind one of the ballroom's side doors. It sounded as if there was a heated argument going on outside, followed by a series of muffled bangs and scrapes. Suddenly the door burst open. "NO, I SAID YOU CANNOT GO IN!" a female attendant shouted forcefully, breaking the silence.

Something could be heard running along the side of the ballroom, wailing intermittently like an animal. Daisy prodded the woman at the next table who had stood up to get a better view. "What can you see?" she asked anxiously.

"Dunno, *lah*—it looks like . . . like some crazy homeless person," came the reply.

"What do you mean *homeless*? There is no such thing as a homeless person in Singapore!" Eleanor exclaimed.

Astrid, who was seated at the far end beside the stage, wasn't fully aware of what was happening until a woman with extremely disheveled hair wearing stained yoga sweats suddenly appeared at her table, dragging two young girls in school uniforms behind her. Mrs. Lee Yong Chien let out a gasp and clutched her purse tightly to her chest, as Astrid realized in astonishment that the two girls were Chloe and Delphine, Charlie Wu's daughters. And the deranged-looking woman was none other than Charlie's estranged wife, Isabel! The last time Astrid had seen Isabel, she had been exquisitely attired in Dior couture at the Venice Biennale. Now she was completely unrecognizable. What were they doing here in Singapore?

Before Astrid could properly react, Isabel Wu took her eldest daughter by the shoulders and turned her toward Astrid. "Here she is!" she screamed, spit forming at the corners of her mouth. "I want you to see her with your own eyes! I want you to see the whore that spreads her legs for your daddy!"

Everyone at the table gasped, and Rosalind Fung immediately made the sign of the cross, as if it would somehow protect her ears from absorbing the obscenity. The hotel's security guards came rushing up, but before Isabel could be properly restrained, she grabbed the nearest bowl of *laksa* and hurled it at Astrid. Astrid backed away reflexively, and the bowl ricocheted off the edge of the table, splashing scalding extra-spicy soup all over Felicity Leong, Mrs. Lee Yong Chien, and the Dowager Sultana of Perawak.

CHAPTER THREE

Patti Smith was in the middle of belting out "Because the Night" when Nicholas Young's cell phone began lighting up like a fire-cracker in his jeans pocket. Nick ignored the call, but when the lights came up after the concert's final encore, he glanced at the screen and was surprised to find one voice mail from his cousin Astrid, another from his best friend Colin Khoo, and five text messages from his mother. His mother never texted. He didn't think she even *knew* how to text. The messages read:

ELEANOR YOUNG:	4?Z Nicky#
ELEANOR YOUNG:	p lease cakk me at once! Where are y
ELEANOR YOUNG:	oy? Why don't you answered any of
your phines?	
ELEANOR YOUNG:	Ah Ma had a massive heat attack!
ELEANOR YOUNG:	C allhome now!

Nick handed the phone to his wife, Rachel, and sank into his seat. After the euphoric high of the concert, he felt like someone had suddenly knocked all the wind out of him.

Rachel read the text messages quickly and looked up at Nick in alarm. "Don't you think you'd better call?"

"Yeah, I guess I should," Nick replied. "Let's get out of here first, though. I need some air."

As the two of them exited Radio City Music Hall, they hurried across Sixth Avenue to avoid the crowds still milling under the famous marquee. Nick paced around the plaza outside the Time & Life Building to make his call. There was that familiar dead pause for a few seconds, usually followed by the distinctive Singapore ringtone, but today, his mother's voice abruptly came onto the line before he was ready for it.

"NICKY? Nicky, ah? Is that you?"

"Yes, Mum, it's me. Can you hear me?"

"*Aiyah*, why did you take so long to call back? Where are you?"

"I was at a concert when you called."

"A concert? Did you go to Lincoln Center?"

"No, it was a rock concert at Radio City Music Hall."

"What? You went to see those Rockette girls with the kicking legs?"

"No, Mum, it was a ROCK CONCERT, not the Rockettes."

"A ROCK CONCERT! *Alamak*, I hope you wore earplugs. I read that people are losing their hearing younger and younger now because they keep going to those rock-and-roll concerts. All those heepees with long hair are going stone-deaf. Serves them right."

"The volume was fine, Mum—Radio City has some of the best acoustics in the world. Where are you?"

"I just left Mount E. Ahmad is driving me to Carol Tai's—she's having a chili crab party. I had to get out of that hospital ward because it was getting too chaotic. Felicity is being her usual bossy mother hen—she said I couldn't go in to see Ah Ma because too many people had been to see her already and they had to start restricting the number of visitors. So I just sat out-side for a while and nibbled away on the buffet with your cousin Astrid. I wanted to show my face so no one would dare say I didn't do my duty as the wife of the eldest son."

"Well, how *is* Ah Ma?" Nick didn't want to admit it to himself, but he was rather anxious to know whether his grandmother was dead or alive.

"They managed to stabilize her, so she's okay for now."

Nick looked up at Rachel and mouthed, "She's okay," as Elea-nor continued her update: "They put her on a morphine drip so she's sedated at the moment in the Royal Suite. But Prof Oon's wife told me that it's not looking good."

"Prof Oon's wife is a doctor?" Nick asked, confused.

"No, *lah*! But she's his wife—she heard it straight from the horse's mouth that Ah Ma's not going to last long. *Alamak*, what do you expect? She has congestive heart failure and she's ninety-six years old—it's not like they can operate at this point."

Nick shook his head derisively—patient confidentiality was obviously not high on Francis Oon's list. "What is Mrs. Oon even doing there?"

"Don't you know Mrs. Oon is the niece of Singapore's First Lady? She brought along the First Lady, Great-aunt Rosemary T'sien, and Lillian May Tan. The entire floor at Mount E has been sealed off to the public—it's become a restricted VVIP floor because of Ah Ma, Mrs. Lee Yong Chien, and the Dowager Sultana of Perawak. There was a bit of a fuss over who would be put in the Royal Suite,* as the Malay ambassador insisted that

---

* The Royal Suite at Mount Elizabeth Hospital was originally built by the royal family of Brunei for their private use, but is now open to other VVIP patients.

the Dowager Sultana had to get it, but then the First Lady intervened and told the hospital's chief officer, 'This isn't even up for discussion. *Of course* Shang Su Yi must have the Royal Suite.'"

"Wait a minute, Mrs. Lee and the Sultana of Perawak? I'm not following you . . ."

"*Aiyoh*, you didn't hear what happened? Isabel Wu had a psychotic breakdown and kidnapped her children from school and flew them to Singapore and barged into Rosalind Fung's Christian Fellowship Banquet and threw a bowl of extra-hot *laksa* at Astrid but missed and it landed all over the ladies but thank God Felicity was wearing one of her *pasar malam** polyester dresses from that tailor of hers in Tiong Bahru so the soup did NOTHING to her and slid right off like Teflon but poor Mrs. Lee and the Dowager Sultana got drenched and are recovering from first-degree burns."

"Okay, you've completely lost me there." Nick shook his head in exasperation, as Rachel gave him a questioning look.

"I thought of all people you'd know. Isabel Wu accused Astrid of spreading her legs . . . I mean, having an affair with her husband, Charlie! Right in front of Bishop See Bei Sien and everyone in the banquet hall! *Aiyoh*, it's so shameful—now it's out in the open and all of Singapore is talking about it! Is it true? Is Astrid Charlie's mistress?"

"She's not his mistress, Mum. That much I can tell you," Nick said carefully.

"You and your cousin—always keeping secrets from me! Poor Astrid looked completely shell-shocked at the hospital, but

---

* Literally "night market" in Malay, the *pasar malam* is a traveling outdoor street market where many bargains are sold. In this instance, Eleanor is implying that Felicity Young's custom-tailored outfit looks like a cheap schmatta from an outdoor street market.

she was still trying to play the gracious hostess to all the visitors. Anyway, when are you coming home?"

Nick paused for a moment, before saying decisively, "I'm not coming back."

"Nicky, don't talk nonsense! You *must* come home! Everyone is coming back—your father is already on his way from Sydney, Uncle Alfred arrives in a few days, Auntie Alix and Uncle Malcolm are flying in from Hong Kong, and even Auntie Cat is coming down from Bangkok. And get this—supposedly all your Thai cousins are coming too! Can you believe that? Those high-and-mighty royal cousins of yours *never* deign to come down to Singapore, but I'm telling you"—Eleanor paused, glancing at her driver before cupping her hands over the cell phone and whispering rather indiscreetly—"*they all sense that this is the end.* And they want to show their faces at Ah Ma's bedside just to make sure they're in the will!"

Nick rolled his eyes. "Only you would say something like that. I'm sure that's the last thing on anyone's mind."

Eleanor laughed derisively. "Oh my goodness, don't be so naïve. I guarantee you that's the only thing going through *everyone's* mind! The vultures are all circling like mad, so get yourself on the next flight! This is your last chance to make up with your grandmother"—she lowered her voice again—"*and if you play your cards right, you still might get Tyersall Park!*"

"I think that ship has sailed. Trust me, I don't think I'll be welcomed."

Eleanor sighed in frustration. "You're wrong about that, Nicky. I know Ah Ma won't close her eyes until she sees you one last time."

. . .

Nick ended the call and quickly updated Rachel on his grandmother's condition and the Isabel Wu hot-soup incident. Then he perched on the edge of the plaza's reflecting pool, suddenly feeling drained. Rachel sat beside him and put her arm around his shoulder, not saying anything. She knew how complicated things were between him and his grandmother. They had once been extremely close—Nick being the adored only grandson who bore the Young surname and the only grandchild who had lived at Tyersall Park—but it had now been more than four years since they had last seen or spoken to each other. And it was all because of her.

Su Yi had ambushed them during what was supposed to be a romantic getaway in the Cameron Highlands of Malaysia, commanding Nick to end his relationship with Rachel. But Nick had not only refused; he had uncharacteristically insulted his grandmother in front of everyone—something that had probably never happened to this revered woman in her entire life. Over the past few years, the gulf had only widened as Nick defiantly married Rachel in California, leaving his grandmother and the majority of his large family off the wedding invitation list.

This girl does not come from a proper family! Rachel still vividly remembered Su Yi's condemnation, and for a moment, a slight chill went down her spine. But here in New York, Shang Su Yi's shadow didn't loom as large, and for the past two years, she and Nick had been blissfully enjoying married life far away from any family interference. Rachel had occasionally tried to see if anything could be done to mend the fences between Nick and his grandmother, but he had stubbornly refused to talk about it. She knew Nick wouldn't react so angrily if he didn't care about his grandmother so much.

Rachel looked Nick squarely in the face. "You know, as much

as it pains me to admit it, I think your mother's right—you should go home."

"New York is my home," Nick replied flatly.

"You know what I mean. Your grandmother's situation sounds really precarious."

Nick stared up at the windows of Rockefeller Center, still lit at this late hour, avoiding Rachel's eyes. "Look, I'm starving. Where should we go for a late supper? Buvette? Blue Ribbon Bakery?"

Rachel realized it was pointless to push him any further. "Let's do Buvette. I think their coq au vin is just what we need right now."

Nick paused for a moment. "Maybe we ought to avoid any place with hot soup tonight!"

CHAPTER FOUR

After five hours at the hospital's intensive care unit, alternately sitting beside her grandmother, managing the visiting dignitaries, managing her mother's nerves, and managing the caterers from Min Jiang that had set up a buffet* in the VIP visitors' lounge, Astrid needed a break and some fresh air. She took the elevator down to the lobby and walked out to the little grove of palm trees adjacent to the side entrance off Jalan Elok and began texting with Charlie on WhatsApp.

ASTRID LEONG TEO: Sorry I couldn't talk earlier. No phones allowed in the ICU.

CHARLES WU: No worries. How's your Ah Ma?

ALT: Resting comfortably at the moment, but the prognosis isn't good.

CW: So sorry to hear that.

ALT: Are Isabel and the kids all right?

---

* Yes, you can be sure Min Jiang's legendary wood-fired Beijing duck—with a first serving of crispy duck skin dipped in fine granulated sugar, wrapped in homemade pancakes with sweet sauce, shredded leeks, and cucumbers, followed by a second serving of the sliced duck in fried noodles—was part of the impromptu ICU buffet organized by Felicity Leong.

CW: Yes. Their plane landed a couple of hours ago, and thankfully Isabel's mother managed to keep her calm during the flight. She's been admitted to Hong Kong Sanatorium and her doctors are attending to her. The kids are okay. Bit shaken up. Chloe's glued to her phone as usual, and I'm lying here next to Delphine while she sleeps.

ALT: I have to tell you—they were such angels through it all. I could tell they were trying to stay composed during the whole ordeal. Delphine dashed to the side of Mrs. Lee Yong Chien while Chloe tried to help calm Isabel down as she was being restrained.

CW: I am SO SORRY for this.

ALT: Come on, it wasn't your fault.

CW: It IS my fault. Should have seen this coming. She was supposed to sign off on the divorce settlement this week, and my lawyers were pressuring her. That's why she snapped. And my security team totally screwed up.

ALT: Wasn't it the school that screwed up? Letting Isabel walk in and take them out of class in the middle of the school day?

CW: She apparently put on an Oscar-worthy performance. With the way she looked, they really thought there was a family emergency. This is what happens when you donate too much money to a school—they don't ever question you.

ALT: I don't think anyone could have anticipated this.

CW: Well, my security team should have! This was an epic fuckup. They never even saw Isabel and the kids exiting— they only had the front entrance under surveillance. Since Izzie went to Diocesan too, she knew all the secret ways to sneak out.

ALT: OMG I didn't think of that!

CW: She took them out through the laundry-room door and they hopped on the MTR straight to the airport. BTW, we discovered how she knew where to find you. Rosalind Fung tagged you in a Facebook pic from last month's Christian Fellowship event.

ALT: Really? I'm never on FB. Look at it about once a year.

CW: Isabel's mum is FB friends with Rosalind. She messaged her three days ago asking if you would be at this event, and Rosalind said yes and even told her you'd be seated at the table of honor!

ALT: So THAT'S how she knew how to find me in that crowd! I was so shocked when she started screaming at me.

CW: I guess the cat's out of the bag. Everyone must be talking about us now.

ALT: I have no idea. Probably.

CW: What did your mother say? Did she go ballistic when she found out about us?

ALT: Mum's said nothing so far. I'm not sure she even connected all the dots. When it happened she was too busy dabbing tissues on Mrs. Lee and the Sultana. And then in the midst of all that, Araminta Lee rushed up to us and said, "Haven't you heard? Your grandmother had a heart attack!"

CW: You've really had the day from hell.

ALT: Not compared to your kids. I'm sorry they had to go through this. Seeing their mother in that state . . .

CW: They've seen it before. It's just never been this bad.

ALT: I wanted to hug them. I wanted to get them out of there and fly them back to you myself but it was total chaos with everything happening all at once.

CW: YOU need a hug.

ALT: Mmm . . . would be so nice.

CW: I don't know how you put up with me and all the shit that keeps happening.

ALT: I could say the same myself.

CW: Your shit ain't half as crazy as mine.

ALT: Just you wait. With Ah Ma in the condition she's in, I don't know what's going to happen anymore. There's going to be a family invasion this week, and it's not going to be pretty.

CW: Is it going to be like *Modern Family*?

ALT: More like *Game of Thrones*. The Red Wedding scene.

CW: Oh boy. Speaking of weddings, does anyone know about our plans?

ALT: Not yet. But I think this might be the perfect opportunity to start prepping my family . . . letting some of my closer relatives know that I'm divorcing Michael, and there's a new man in my life . . .

CW: Is there a new man in your life?

ALT: Yes, his name is Jon Snow.

CW: Hate to break it to you, but Jon Snow is dead.[*]

ALT: No he's not. You'll see. :-)

CW: Seriously, I'm here if you need me. Do you want me to come down?

ALT: No, it's fine. Chloe and Delphine need you.

---

[*] In 2015, the world was most preoccupied about figuring out if the economy would continue to recover, how to keep the Ebola outbreak in Africa from becoming a global pandemic, where ISIS terrorists would strike next after the horrendous Paris attacks, how to help Nepal after its devastating earthquakes, who would be the front-runners in the next U.S. presidential campaign, and whether Jon Snow, Lord Commander of the Night's Watch and one of the heroes in George R. R. Martin's *Game of Thrones* television series, really died in the season finale.

CW: I need you. I can send the plane anytime.

ALT: Let's see how this week goes with my family and then we can really begin making some plans ...

CW: I'll be counting the minutes ...

ALT: Me too ... xoxoxo

CHAPTER FIVE

RUE BOISSY D'ANGLAS, PARIS

She stood on a raised mirrored platform in the middle of Giambattista Valli's elegantly appointed atelier, staring up at the glittering chandelier, trying to hold still as two seamstresses meticulously pinned up the hem of the delicate tulle skirt that she was modeling. Looking out the window, she could see a little boy holding a red balloon walking down the cobblestone street, and she wondered where he was heading.

The man with the string of baroque pearls around his neck smiled at her. "*Bambolina*, could you please turn for me?"

She twirled around once, and the women surrounding her all oohed and aahed.

"*J'adore!*" Georgina swooned.

"Oh Giamba, you were right! Just two inches shorter and look how the skirt comes alive. It's like a flower blooming right before our eyes!" Wandi cooed.

"Like a pink peony!" Tatiana gushed.

"I think for this dress, I was inspired by the ranunculus," the designer stated.

"I don't know that flower. But Giamba, you're a genius! An absolute genius!" Tatiana praised.

Georgina walked around the platform, scrutinizing the dress

from every angle. "When Kitty first told me that this couture dress would cost €175,000, I have to confess I was a little surprised, but now I think it's worth every cent!"

"Yes, I think so too," Kitty murmured softly, assessing the tea-length gown from its reflection in the rococo mirror leaning against the wall. "Gisele, do you like it?"

"Yes, Mommy," the five-year-old said. She was getting tired of standing there in the dress with the hot spotlight on her, and she wondered when she could get her reward. Mommy had promised her a big ice-cream sundae if she would stand very still during her fitting.

"Okay then," Kitty said, looking at Giambattista Valli's assistant. "We will need three of these."

"Three?" The tall, gangly assistant looked at Kitty in surprise.

"Of course. I buy everything in threes for myself and Gisele—we need one for each of our closets in Singapore, Shanghai, and Beverly Hills. But this one has to be ready for her birthday party in Singapore on March first—"

"Of course, Signora Bing," Giambattista cut in. "Now, ladies, I hope you don't mind if I leave Luka to show you the new collection. I have to rush off to an appointment with the fashion director of Saks."

The women exchanged air kisses with the departing designer, Gisele was sent off with her nanny around the corner to Angelina for ice cream, and as more Veuve Clicquot and café crèmes were brought into the showroom, Kitty stretched out on the elegant chaise lounge with a contented sigh. It was only their second day here, and already she was having the time of her life. She had come on this Parisian shopping spree with her Singaporean BFFs—Wandi Meggaharto Widjawa, Tatiana Savarin, and Georgina Ting—and somehow, things were so different on this trip.

From the moment she stepped off *Trenta*, the Boeing 747-81 VIP she had recently refurbished to look exactly like the Shanghai bordello in a Wong Kar-wai movie,* she was experiencing heretofore unprecedented levels of sucking up. When their motorcade of Rolls-Royces arrived at the Peninsula Paris, all of the hotel management stood in a perfect line to greet her at the entrance, and the general manager escorted her up to the impressive Peninsula Suite. When they went to dinner at Ledoyen, the waiters were bowing and scraping so frantically that she thought they were going to break into somersaults. And then during her Chanel couture fittings at rue Cambon yesterday, none other than *Karl Lagerfeld's personal assistant came downstairs with a handwritten note from the great man himself!*

Kitty knew that all this royal treatment was because she had arrived in Paris this time as MRS. JACK BING. She wasn't just the wife of some random billionaire anymore, she was the new wife of China's second-richest man,[†] one of the ten richest men in the world. To think that Pong Li Li, the daughter of sanitation workers in Qinghai, had achieved such great heights at the relatively young age of thirty-four (although she told everyone she was thirty). Not that any of this had been easy—she had worked nonstop her entire life to get to this place.

Her mother had come from an educated middle-class family, but she had been banished with her family to the countryside during Mao's Great Leap Forward campaign. But she had instilled in Kitty that getting an education was the only way out. All through her youth, Kitty studied extra hard to always be the

---

[*]   See Wong Kar-wai's *The Grandmaster*. I much prefer Wong's *In the Mood for Love* to this film, but the set design was amazing.
[†]   Or third or fourth or seventh richest, depending on which financial tabloid you trust.

top in her class, top in her school, top in her state exams, only to see her one chance at a higher education get snatched away when some boy with all the right connections was awarded the only slot to university in their entire district—the slot that was rightfully meant to be hers.

But Kitty didn't give up, she kept on fighting, moving first to Shenzhen to work at a KTV bar where she had to do unspeakable things, and then to Hong Kong, landing a bit part in a local soap opera, transforming it into a recurring role after becoming the director's mistress, dating a series of rather inconsequential men until she met Alistair Cheng, that cute, clueless boy who was much too sweet for his own good, going with him to the Khoo wedding and meeting Bernard Tai, running off to Vegas with Bernard to get married, meeting Jack Bing at Bernard's father's funeral, divorcing Bernard, and finally, at long last, marrying Jack, a man who was truly worthy of all her efforts.

And now that she had provided him with his first son (Harvard Bing, born in 2013), she could do anything she damn well pleased. She could fly to Paris on her own private jumbo jet with one French translator, two children, three fabulous girlfriends (all as toned and polished and expensively dressed as she was, and all wives of rich expats in Shanghai, Hong Kong, and Singapore), four nannies, five personal maids, and six bodyguards and rent out the entire top floor of the Peninsula Hotel (which she did). She could order the entire Chanel Automne-Hiver couture collection and have every piece made in triplicate (which she did). She could take a personal guided tour of Versailles with the chief curator followed by a special al fresco lunch prepared by Yannick Alléno at Marie Antoinette's hamlet (which was happening tomorrow, thanks to Oliver T'sien, who set it all up). If someone wrote a book about her, no one would believe it.

Kitty sipped her champagne and glanced at the ball gowns that were being paraded before her, feeling a little bored. Yes, it was so beautiful, but after the tenth dress, it was all beginning to look the same. Was it possible to overdose on too much beauty? She could buy up the whole collection in her sleep and forget she ever owned any of it. She needed something more. She needed to get out of here and look at some Zambian emeralds, maybe.

Luka recognized the look on Kitty's face. It was the same expression he had seen all too often in some of his most privileged clients—these women who had constant, unlimited access to everything that their hearts ever desired—the heiresses, celebrities, and princesses that had sat in this very spot. He knew he needed to change direction, to shift the energy in the room in order to reinspire his high-spending client.

"Ladies, let me show you something very special that Giamba has been toiling away at for weeks. Come with me." He pressed against one panel of the boiserie walls, revealing Giambattista's inner sanctum—a hidden workroom that contained only one gown displayed on a mannequin in the middle of the pristine space. "This dress was inspired by Gustav Klimt's *Adele Bloch-Bauer I.* Do you know the painting? It was purchased for $135 million by Ronald Lauder and hangs in the Neue Galerie in New York."

The ladies stared in disbelief at the artistry of the off-the-shoulder ball gown that transformed from ivory tulle at the bodice and into a shimmering gold column, with a cascading train-length skirt embroidered with thousands of gold chips, lapis lazuli, and precious gemstones, painstakingly scattered into a swirling mosaic pattern. It truly looked like a Klimt painting come to life.

"Oh my God! It's unbelievable!" Georgina squealed, running one of her long manicured nails over the gem-encrusted bodice.

"*Ravissement!*" Tatiana commented, mistakenly trying to show off her secondary-school French. "*Combien?*"

"We don't have a price on it yet. It's a special commission that's taken four full-time embroiderers three months to assemble so far, and we still have weeks of work to go. I would say that this dress, with all the rose-gold disks and precious stones, will end up costing more than two and a half million euros."

Kitty stared at it, her heart suddenly beginning to pound in that delicious way it did whenever she saw something that aroused her. "I want it."

"Oh, Madame Bing, I'm so sorry, but this dress is already spoken for." Luka smiled at her apologetically.

"Well, make me another one. I mean another three, of course."

"I'm afraid we cannot make you this exact dress."

Kitty looked at him, not quite comprehending. "Oh, I'm sure you can."

"Madame, I hope you will understand . . . Giamba would be happy to collaborate with you on another dress, in the same spirit, but we cannot replicate this one. This is a one-of-a-kind piece made for a special client of ours. She is from China also—"

"I'm not from China, I'm from Singapore," Kitty declared.[*]

"Who is this 'special client'?" Wandi demanded, her thick mane of Beyoncé-bronzed hair shaking indignantly.

"She's a friend of Giamba's, so I only know her by her first name: Colette."

---

[*] Kitty has only lived part-time in Singapore for two years, but like so many other immigrants from Mainland China has taken to referring to it as home.

The ladies suddenly fell silent, not daring to ask what they wanted to ask. Wandi finally piped up. "Er . . . are you referring to Colette Bing?"

"I'm not sure if that is her surname. Let me check the spec sheet." He turned over a leaf of paper. "Ah yes, it *is* Bing. *Une telle coïncidence!* Is she related to you, Madame Bing?" Luka asked.

Kitty looked like a deer caught in headlights. Was Luka kidding? Surely he must know that Colette was her husband's daughter from his first marriage.

Tatiana quickly jumped in. "No, she's not. But we know of her."

"Do we ever." Wandi sniffed, wondering whether she should tell Luka how Colette's bitch-from-hell video tirade had gone viral in China, logging more than thirty-six million views on WeChat alone, making her such a notorious poster child of *fuerdai*[*] bad behavior that she was forced to flee to London in disgrace. Wandi decided that it was better not to bring it up now.

"So this dress is for Colette," Kitty said, fondling one of the gossamer-like organdy sleeves.

"Yes, it's going to be her wedding dress." Luka smiled.

Kitty looked up at him, stunned. "Colette is getting married?"

"Oh yes, madame, it's the talk of the town. She's marrying Lucien Montagu-Scott."

"Montagu-Scott? What does his family do?" Wandi asked, since everything in her universe revolved around being part of an incredibly rich Indonesian family.

"I don't know anything about his *famille*, but I believe he's a lawyer?" Luka said.

---

[*]   Mandarin for "second-generation rich," this label is akin to "trust-fund kids" and carries all the scorn and envy it implies.

Tatiana immediately began googling his name, and read aloud from the first link that popped up: "Lucien Montagu-Scott is one of Britain's new generation of environmental lawyers. A graduate of the Magdalen College—"

"It's pronounced 'Maudlin,'" Georgina corrected.

"Maudlin College, Oxford, Lucien sailed across the Pacific on a catamaran made out of 12,500 reclaimed plastic bottles with his friend David Mayer de Rothschild to highlight the problem of global marine pollution. More recently, he has been involved in publicizing the environmental crisis in Indonesia and Borneo—"

"I think I'm going to fall asleep," Tatiana scoffed.

"He's a charming gentleman—comes with her to every fitting," Luka remarked.

"I can't imagine why Colette Bing of all people would end up settling for this guy. He's not even an M&A lawyer—his annual salary probably wouldn't even pay for one of her dresses! I guess she must be desperate to have mixed-race babies," Georgina said, glancing covertly at Kitty, hoping she wasn't too upset by the news. Kitty just stood staring at the dress, her expression inscrutable.

"Oooh . . . I want to have a beautiful mixed-race baby too! Luka, do you know any hot single French counts?" Wandi asked.

"I'm sorry, mademoiselle. The only *comte* I know is married."

"Married is fine . . . I'm married too, but I would dump my boring hubby if I could get a beautiful half-French baby!" Wandi giggled.

"Wandi, careful what you wish for. You never know what sort of baby you'll get," Tatiana said.

"No, if you have a baby with a Caucasian man, you're almost guaranteed it will be attractive. There's a ninety-nine percent chance it will look like Keanu Reeves. That's why so many Asian women are desperate to find white husbands."

"First of all, Keanu isn't half white. He's like three-quarters— his mother is only part Hawaiian and his father is American.[*] And not to burst your bubble, but I have seen some rather unfortunate-looking mixed-raced babies," Georgina insisted.

"Yes, but it's very rare. And soooo tragic when that happens! OMG—did you hear about that man in China who sued his wife because all their children came out looking so ugly? He had purposely married this beautiful woman, but it turns out she'd had tons of plastic surgery before she met him! So the children all looked like her before the surgery!" Wandi giggled.

"That story was a lie!" Tatiana insisted. "I remember when it went viral, but it turned out the newspaper made up the whole thing and did a fake photo shoot with two models posing with a bunch of ugly kids."

Finding the topic of unattractive children to be appallingly distasteful, Luka tried to steer the conversation in another direction. "I think Monsieur Lucas and Mademoiselle Colette will have beautiful children. She's so pretty, and he's very handsome, you know."

"Well, good for them," Kitty said in a merry tone. "Now, all this baby talk has made me want to look at some daytime outfits for Gisele. Can we do that? And do you have anything fun and unisex I can dress Harvard in?"

"*Oui, madame.*" As he headed back into the main showroom, Georgina took him by the arm. "Tell me, Luka, do you live on the second floor?"

---

[*] Actually, Keanu Reeves was born in Beirut, Lebanon, to an English mother and a father of Hawaiian, Chinese, and English ancestry.

Without missing a beat, Luka replied with a grin, "Yes, mademoiselle, I think you've seen me before."

Wandi and Tatiana stood by the doorway watching as Kitty lingered for a moment longer by the dress. As she turned to leave, she grabbed the back of the precious Klimt-inspired skirt and gave it one quick, forceful tug—ripping it clear down the middle.

CHAPTER SIX

Winding through the heart of Bukit Timah, Nassim Road was one of the few long, picturesque streets in Singapore that still retained a feel of graceful, Old World exclusivity with its parade of historic mansions converted into embassies, tropical modern bungalows on crisp manicured lawns, and stately Black and White houses left over from the colonial era. Number 11 Nassim Road was a particularly fine example of Black and White architecture, as it had only changed hands once since it had been built a century ago. Originally commissioned by Boustead and Company, it had been purchased by S. K. Leong in 1918, and every original detail had been preserved and lovingly maintained since then by three generations of Leongs.

As Astrid pulled up the long driveway lined with Italian cypresses to the home where she had grown up, the front door opened, and Liat, the majordomo, gestured for Astrid to come down. Astrid frowned—she was picking up her mother to visit Ah Ma at the hospital, and they were already running late for the morning briefing with Professor Oon. Astrid left her dark blue Acura in the arched porte cochere and entered the foyer, bumping into her sister-in-law Cathleen, who was seated on a rosewood stool lacing up her walking shoes.

"Morning, Cat," Astrid greeted.

Cathleen looked up at her with a strange expression. "They're still eating. Sure you want to show your face today?"

Astrid figured that Cathleen was referring to the Isabel Wu fiasco the other evening. With all the attention focused on her grandmother, the incident had gone unmentioned by her parents, but she knew that wouldn't last long.

"It's now or never, I guess," Astrid said, bracing herself as she walked toward the breakfast room.

"Godspeed," Cathleen said, grabbing her battered Jones the Grocer shopping bag[*] as she went out the door.

Breakfast at Nassim Road was always served in the glassed-in summer porch adjacent to the drawing room. Boasting a circular marble-top teak table from the Dutch Indies, wicker chairs cushioned in whimsical monkey-print chintz, and a profusion of hanging ferns from the Tyersall Park greenhouses, it was one of the loveliest rooms in the house. As Astrid entered, her elder brother, Henry, gave her a dirty look and got up from the table to leave. He muttered something under his breath as he passed by, but Astrid couldn't make out what he said. She glanced first at her father, who was sitting in his usual wicker chair methodically slathering a piece of toast with gooey Marmite, and then at her mother, who sat in front of an untouched bowl of porridge, clenching a wadded-up ball of tissue in her hand, her face red and puffy from crying.

---

[*]   Cathleen Kah Leong, the wife of Harry and Felicity Leong's eldest son, Henry, takes great pride in her thrift. A partner at Singapore's most esteemed law firm, she takes the public bus to work every day. A granddaughter of the late banking tycoon Kah Chin Kee, she uses a plastic bag from the local neighborhood gourmet grocers to transport her legal briefs when she could well afford to buy Goyard. (Not a nice Goyard leather tote bag—I mean Goyard, the company.)

"My God, did something happen to Ah Ma?" Astrid asked in alarm.

"Hnh! I think the question should be: 'Will you finish your grandmother off with another heart attack when she reads *this*?'" Felicity chucked a sheet of paper onto the marble-top table in disgust.

Astrid grabbed the sheet and stared at it in dismay. It was a printout from Asia's most popular online gossip column:

DAILY DISH FROM LEONARDO LAI

THE BEWITCHING HEIRESS AT THE CENTER OF THE ISABEL WU SOUPGATE INCIDENT!

For those of you who have been following the scalding *scandale* involving tech billionaire **Charlie Wu's** wife **Isabel** that almost caused an international incident between Malaysia and Hong Kong, fasten your seat belts, because boy do I have some shockers for you! We all know that Charlie and Isabel announced their separation in 2013, and informers tell me they've been privately negotiating the terms of their divorce ever since. At stake is a share of the Wu family fortune, their heritage mansion on Peak Road, and custodial rights of their two daughters. But a close friend of Isabel tells me, "It's been terribly hard for Isabel. She suffered her recent breakdown because of the emotional stress of the divorce and *that other woman* involved."

Yep, you heard that right. SHOCKER NUMBER ONE: Daily Dish can now confirm that *that other woman* is none other than **Astrid Leong Teo**, the model-pretty wife of hunka-licious Singaporean Venture Capitalist **Michael Teo** (who I think missed his calling as a Calvin Klein underwear model) and mother to a seven-year-old boy, **Cassius**. Yes, Charlie and Astrid have been having a torrid, secret affair for the past five years, and in fact, SHOCKER NUMBER TWO: that incredible **Tom Kundig**–designed house currently under construction in Shek O that everyone thought was **Leo Ming's** new private museum is actually going to be Charlie and Astrid's love pad once they can legally shack up! (Astrid and Michael Teo are apparently headed to divorce court too.)

The stunning seductress Astrid may be an unfamiliar name to Hong Kong readers, but she has an extraordinary backstory: According to my trusted Singapore insider, Astrid is the only daughter of **Harry Leong**, who officially is the chairman emeritus of the Institute of ASEAN Affairs. Unofficially, he's one of Singapore's most influential political power brokers who—my sources tell me—also happens to head S. K. Leong Holdings Pte Ltd, the secretive corporate behemoth that is rumored to own the Bank of Borneo, Selangor Mining, *New Malaysia Post*, and Palmcore Berhad, one of the world's largest commodity traders. And that's not all—Astrid's mother, **Felicity Young**, hails from one of Singapore's most pedigreed families. "The Youngs are in their own stratosphere. Cousins to the T'siens, the Tans, and the Shangs—they are related to practically everybody who's anybody, and Felicity's mother, **Shang Su Yi**, owns Tyersall Park, the largest private estate in Singapore," my insider reports.

Schooled in London and Paris, Astrid moves in the most rarefied circles and counts among her friends deposed European royals, A-list fashion designers, and celebrity artists. "How can Isabel compete with that? Izzie isn't some filthy-rich heiress—she has an important career as a legal advocate for Hong Kong's poor and downtrodden and is busy raising her two daughters, not jet-setting around the world, sitting in the front rows of fashion shows. No wonder she would suffer a breakdown! Of course Charlie would be swept up by the ultra-glamorous life of Astrid—he was seduced by her once before."

Which leads us to SHOCKER NUMBER THREE: Back in their college days, Astrid and Charlie *were actually engaged*, but the union was broken off by her family because the Hong Kong Wus weren't deemed worthy enough by those snooty Singaporeans! It seems like the star-crossed lovers have never gotten over each other, which has led to this big ugly mess. Stay tuned to Daily Dish for more shockers to come!

Astrid sank into a chair, trying to collect herself after reading the incendiary column. She was so upset, she didn't even know where to begin. "Who sent you this?"

"What does it matter who sent it? The news is everywhere now. Everyone knows your marriage is on the rocks, and that you are at fault!" Felicity moaned.

"Come on, Mum. You know it wasn't my fault. You know how careful and discreet I've been for the past couple of years as we've been working out the divorce. This article is nothing but a stream of inaccuracies and lies. When have I ever sat in the front row of any fashion shows? I'm always backstage helping out. Look, they even got Cassian's name wrong."

Her mother looked at her accusingly. "So you're denying everything? You're not having an affair with Charlie Wu?"

Astrid let out a deep sigh. "Not for the past five years! Charlie and I have only been together for about a year and a half—and this was *after* I left Michael and Charlie filed for divorce from Isabel."

"Then it is true! *That's* why Isabel Wu would go berserk and try to attack you! You broke up her marriage . . . you broke up her family!" Felicity muttered through her tears.

"Mum, Isabel Wu's marriage to Charlie has never been a happy one. I had nothing to do with their breakup. If you want to know the truth, *she* has been cheating on him for many years, with numerous men—"

"That still doesn't give you any excuse to be Anna Karenina! You're still being unfaithful! You're both still married to other people under the eyes of the law and God! Goodness me, what will Bishop See think when he gets wind of all this?"

Astrid rolled her eyes. She didn't give a rat's ass what Bishop See thought.

"So now what? You're going to move in to that 'love pad' with Charlie after the divorce and live in sin?"

"That's the other lie . . . it's *not* our love pad. Charlie started building that house long before we ever got together. He bought the land after his first separation from Isabel—four years ago!" Astrid took in a deep breath and steeled herself—it was the time to come completely clean with her parents. "But I suppose you should know that Charlie and I *do* intend to get married when our divorces are finalized, and I will likely be spending more of my time in Hong Kong."

Felicity looked at her husband in horror, waiting for him to react. "You *suppose* we should know? You're planning to get married this year and you only tell us now? I cannot believe you would actually marry Charlie after all this. Disgraceful . . . so disgraceful!"

"I really don't see what's so disgraceful about this, Mum. Charlie and I are in love. We've both acted entirely honorably throughout a very difficult time. It's just unfortunate that Isabel had another breakdown, that's all."

"That breakdown! Those obscene things she said about you in front of the whole world—I have never felt so humiliated in all my life! And those poor ladies! How can I ever look the Sultan of Perawak in the face again? We almost killed his poor mother."

"Auntie Zarah is just fine, Mum. You saw it yourself—her hijab was so encrusted with diamonds, hardly anything got through. She was more in shock because the *laksa* wasn't halal."

"That Charlie Wu—this is all his fault that our names are being dragged through the mud!" Felicity continued to rage.

Astrid sighed in frustration. "I know you've never liked Charlie or his family—that's why you broke us up in the first place all those years ago. But things have changed now, Mum. No one cares about their lineage and all that nonsense anymore. The Wus are no longer considered nouveau riche. They are an establishment family now."

"Establishment my foot! Wu Hao Lian's father used to sell soy sauce on a bicycle!"

"That may be how they started out, but they've come a long way since Charlie's grandfather's time. Charlie has created one of the most admired companies in the world. Look at your new phone—the screen, the casing, I'm sure at least half the components are manufactured by Wu Microsystems!"

"I *detest* this phone! I never know how to use this stupid thing! I swipe and swipe and instead of making a phone call, some silly video of an Indian granny singing 'Twinkle, Twinkle Little Star' keeps appearing on my screen. I have to ask Lakshmi or Padme to make every damn call for me!" Felicity was seething.

"Well, I'm sorry you still don't know how to use your smartphone. But that has nothing to do with how the Wus are perceived these days. Look how much money Mrs. Wu gives to that church on Barker Road—"

"Those Wus are frightfully common, and they prove it all the more by giving an obscene amount of money to that church. They think their dirty money can buy their way into heaven!"

Astrid just shook her head. "Stop being unreasonable, Mum—"

"Your mother is *not* being unreasonable," Astrid's father cut in, speaking up for the first time that morning. "Look at what's happened. Until today our family was able to enjoy the privileges of total privacy and anonymity. The Leong name has never appeared in the gossip columns, much less something as silly as this . . . this . . . I don't even know what to call this idiotic Internet thing."

"And you're blaming Charlie for this?" Astrid shook her head, not seeing her father's logic.

"No. I am blaming *you*. Your actions, however unconsciously, have led to this. If you had never gotten entangled with these people, our lives would not now be under the spotlight."

"Come on, Dad, you're making a mountain out of a mole—"

"SHUT YOUR MOUTH AND DON'T INTERRUPT ME WHEN I'M TALKING!" Harry banged his fist on the table, startling both Astrid and her mother. Neither of them could recall the last time he had raised his voice like this.

"You have completely exposed yourself! And you have exposed and compromised your family! For more than two hundred years our business interests have never been scrutinized, but now they will be. Don't you see how this affects you? I don't think you truly realize how much damage has been done, not just to us but to your mother's side. The Shangs were mentioned. Tyersall Park was mentioned. And all at the most inopportune time possible, when your grandmother is so ill. Tell me how you plan to face Uncle Alfred when he arrives this afternoon?"

Astrid was momentarily dumbfounded. She hadn't thought about the repercussions of this gossip site, but she finally said, "I will face Uncle Alfred myself if that's what you want me to do. I'll explain everything that happened."

"Well, you can thank your lucky stars you won't have to. This column and this whole ridiculous website have been taken down."

Astrid looked at her father, momentarily surprised. "This article is really gone?"

"Erased from the face of this planet! Although enough damage has been done—there's no telling how many people must have read this rubbish before it was taken down."

"Well, hopefully the exposure will be minimal. Thanks, Dad—thank you for doing this," Astrid muttered in relief.

"Oh I had nothing to do with this—thank your husband."

"*Michael* had it taken down?"

"Yes. He bought the company that owns this infernal website and put an end to all of the nonsense. It's probably the first useful thing Michael has ever done to protect you. Which is far more than I can say for Charlie Wu!"

Astrid sat back in her chair, feeling her face flush with anger. This was all Michael's doing. He must have alerted her parents to this gossip column in the first place, and of course he was only too happy to alert them that he'd saved the day. Hell, he was probably Leonardo Lai's "Singapore insider," relishing his chance to sabotage Charlie, to sabotage her.

CHAPTER SEVEN

Rachel was in her office suite at New York University, splitting a piece of German chocolate cake from Amy's Bread with her suitemate, Sylvia Wong-Swartz, when her mother called.

"Hey, Mom! How's Panama?" Rachel answered in Mandarin. Her mother was on a Chu family reunion cruise through the Panama Canal.

"I don't know. I haven't left the ship," Kerry Chu replied.

"You guys have been cruising for four days now and you haven't docked once?"

"No, no, the ship has docked but we've never gotten off. No one wants to leave the boat. Auntie Jin and Auntie Flora want to get their money's worth, so they just sit and stuff their mouths at the all-you-can-eat buffet all day long, and of course Uncle Ray and Uncle Walt aren't speaking to each other again. So they're both at the casino, but at opposite ends. Walt is at the black-jack tables, and supposedly Ray is losing his shirt at baccarat but won't stop playing."

"Well, Uncle Ray can afford it." Rachel chuckled. She was so glad she decided to skip this family reunion.

"Ha! Yes. You should see that wife of his! She changes outfits four times a day, and every night it's a different ball gown and different jewelry. I don't know where she thinks she is—this is a cruise ship, not the Oscars."

"Auntie Belinda is just doing what she loves, Mom."

"She's trying to rub it in all our faces, that's what she's doing! And of course, your cousin Vivian has to ask her what she's wearing every time, and Belinda always says something like, 'Oh, this one I bought in Toronto at Holt Renfrew, or this is a Liberace—I bought it on sale. It was $7,500, marked down to $3,000.'"

"Liberace? I don't think he ever designed clothes, Mom."

"You know that Italian designer, the one that got shot in Miami."

"Oh, you mean *Versace*."

"Hiyah, Liberace, Versace, it's all the same to me. If it's not on sale at Ross Dress for Less, I don't care what the brand is."

"Well, I'm sure Auntie Belinda appreciates Vivian's attention. She's *clearly* the only person on the cruise Auntie Belinda can talk to about high fashion." Rachel took a bite from her share of the cake.

"You and Nick should have come. All your cousins would have enjoyed spending time with you. You know this is the first holiday Vivian's taken since Ollie was born?"

"I would have loved to see everyone, Mom, but the dates just didn't work with my teaching schedule. I couldn't imagine Nick on a cruise ship, though—I think he'd jump overboard before the ship even left port."

"Hahaha. Your husband only likes those private yachts!"

"No, no—you got it all wrong. He'd much rather rough it than be on some luxury cruise—I could see him on some sort of expedition frigate going to Antarctica or on a fishing boat in Nova Scotia, but not on any kind of floating palace."

"A fishing boat! All these rich kids who grew up with every-thing just want to live like they are poor. How is Nick anyway?"

"He's fine. But you know what, his grandmother had a heart attack last week."

"Oh really? Is he going to go back to Singapore?"

"I don't know, Mom. You know how sensitive he gets about anything having to do with his grandmother."

"Nick should go back. You should convince him to go back—this might be his last chance to see the old lady."

Rachel's radar suddenly went off. "Wait a minute . . . you've been talking to Nick's mom, haven't you?"

Kerry Chu paused for a moment too long, before saying, "Noooo. We haven't spoken in ages."

"Don't lie to me, Mom. Only Eleanor calls Nick's grand-mother the 'old lady'!"

"Hiyah, I can't lie to you, you know me too well! Yes, Eleanor called. She's called a few times now and won't leave me alone. She thinks only you can convince Nick to go home."

"I can't talk Nick into doing anything he doesn't want to do."

"Did you know that Nick was supposed to inherit that house?"

"Yes, Mom—*I know*. I'm the whole reason she cut him out of her will. So don't you see I'm the last person to tell him to go back?"

"But his grandmother only has a few weeks to live. If he plays his cards right, he could still get the house."

"Jesus, Mom, stop parroting Eleanor Young!"

"Hiyah, no Eleanor! I'm speaking as your mother—I am thinking of *you*! Think about how this house could benefit your life."

"Mom, we live in New York. That house has no benefit to us except as one gigantic cleaning nightmare!"

"I'm not suggesting you should live there. You would sell it. Think of the windfall you'd have."

Rachel rolled her eyes. "Mom, we're already so fortunate compared to the rest of the planet."

"I know, I know. But imagine how your life could change *right now* if Nick inherits that house. It's worth *hundreds of millions*, so I'm told. That's like winning the Powerball lottery. This is crazy money, life-changing money, enough money so your poor mother doesn't have to work so hard anymore."

"Mom—you know you could have retired years ago, but you love what you do. You've been the top property agent in Cupertino three years running."

"I know, but I just wanted you to think about what it would be like to have that kind of fortune at your fingertips. I want to see all the good things that you and Nick can do with that money. Like that Chinese girl who's married to that Facebook fellow— they've given away billions. Think of how proud her parents must be of her!"

Rachel looked over at Sylvia, who was leaning back in her chair precariously as she stretched to reach for the cake on the coffee table.

"I can't talk about this now, Mom. Sylvia's about to fall over and break her neck."

"Call me back! We need to—"

Rachel hung up on her mother just as her friend had scraped a nice bit of chocolate-and-coconut frosting off with her finger and comfortably returned to her usual seated position.

"Way to go. Using me as an excuse to get off the phone with your mom." Sylvia cackled as she licked her finger clean.

Rachel smiled. "Sometimes I forget you can speak Mandarin."

"A lot better than you, banana girl! Sounds like she was in turbo nagging mode."

"Yeah, she was fixating on something and wouldn't let it go."

"If she's anything like my mom, she's going to call you back tonight and try the guilt angle."

"You're probably right. Which is why I need to see what Nick is up to for lunch."

A few hours later, Rachel and Nick were seated at their favorite window table at Tea & Sympathy. Nicky Perry, the owner, had been by to share a funny video of Cuthbert, her bulldog, and their lunches had just been placed on the table. It was a snowy January afternoon and the windows had fogged up inside the cozy restaurant, creating an even more inviting atmosphere for Rachel to enjoy the chicken-and-leek pie in front of her.

"This was the perfect idea. How did you know I was craving T&S for lunch?" Nick asked as he tucked into his usual English bacon, avocado, and tomato sandwich.

Taking advantage of his good mood, Rachel got right to the point. "So I spoke to my mom a little earlier. Apparently, our mothers have been talking—"

"Oh God, not the grandchildren talk again!"

"No, this time it was all about you."

"Let me guess . . . my mother has enlisted her help to convince me to return to Singapore."

"You're psychic."

Nick rolled his eyes. "My mother is so predictable. You know, I don't think she really cares about my grandmother dying—

she's just fixated on me getting Tyersall Park. It's her entire rai-son d'être."

Rachel broke the thick golden pastry crust of her chicken pie with a fork and let some of the steam escape. She took her first tentative bite of the piping-hot creamy sauce before speaking again. "What I've never really understood is why everyone thinks the house is supposed to go to you. What about your father, or your aunts? Don't they have more right to the house?"

Nick sighed. "Ah Ma, as you know, is an old-fashioned Chinese woman. She has always favored her son over her daughters—they were all just supposed to marry and be taken care of by their husband's families, while my father got Tyersall Park. It's this warped mash-up of archaic Chinese customs and the British rules of primogeniture."

"But that's so unfair," Rachel muttered.

"I know, but that's the way things are and my aunts grew up always knowing they would get the short end of the stick. Mind you, each of them is still going to inherit from Ah Ma's financial holdings—so no one's going to be hurting for cash here."

"So then how is it that you suddenly got to be first in line to inherit Tyersall Park?"

Nick leaned back in his chair. "Do you remember when Jac-queline Ling came to New York a couple of years ago and sum-moned me to lunch aboard her yacht?"

"Oh yeah, she had two Swedish blondes kidnap you in the middle of a lecture!" Rachel laughed.

"Yes. Jacqueline is Ah Ma's goddaughter, and they've always been extremely close. Jacqueline revealed to me that back in the early nineties, when my father decided to move to Australia pretty much full-time, it so angered my grandmother that she decided to change her will and disinherit him from Tyersall Park.

She skipped a generation and made me the heir to the property. But then after I married you, she supposedly changed her will again."

"Who do you think is currently in her favor to get Tyersall Park?"

"I honestly have no idea. Maybe Eddie, maybe one of my cousins in Thailand, maybe she's going to leave it all to her beloved guava trees. The point is, Ah Ma uses her fortune to control the family. She's always changing her will according to her latest whim. No one really knows what she's going to do, and at this point, I've stopped caring."

Rachel looked Nick straight in the face. "Here's the thing. I know that you don't care what happens to your grandmother's fortune, but you can't pretend that you don't still care for her. And that's the only reason why I think you should go back now."

Nick stared out of the fogged-up window for a moment, avoiding her eyes. "I dunno . . . I think part of me is still so angry at her for how she treated you."

"Nick, please don't hold on to this because of me. I forgave your grandmother long ago."

Nick looked at her skeptically.

Rachel put her hand on his. "I have. Truly. I realized it was a waste of time to be mad at her, because she never really got to know me. She never gave me a chance—I was this girl who came out of left field and stole her grandson's heart. But the more time passes, I find myself actually feeling grateful toward her now."

"Grateful?"

"Think about it, Nick. If your grandmother hadn't been so resistant to us being together, if she hadn't supported your mom in all her crazy shenanigans, I would never have found my real father. I would have never met Carlton. Can you imagine what my life would be like if I hadn't met them?"

Nick softened for a moment at the mention of Rachel's half brother. "Well, I can imagine what Carlton's life would be like if he'd never met you—he probably would have wrecked a dozen more sports cars by now."

"Oh God, don't even say that! The point I'm trying to make is, I think you need to find some way to forgive your grandmother. Because it's clearly an issue for you, and it's going to keep eating you up inside if you don't. Remember what that radio host Delilah always says? 'Forgiveness is a gift we give ourselves.' If you think you're able to let things go without ever seeing her again, more power to you. I'm not going to force you to get on a plane. But I think you need to see her in person, and I'm guessing she probably really wants to see you too but—like you—she's too damn proud to admit it."

Nick looked down at his cup of tea. The saucer was emblazoned with an image of Queen Elizabeth II, and seeing the gold patterning at the edge of the porcelain suddenly took him back to a memory of Tyersall Park, of sitting in the ornate eighteenth-century French pavilion overlooking the lotus pond with his grandmother when he was six years old, being taught how to properly pour a cup of tea for a lady. He could remember how heavy the Longquan celadon teapot felt in his hands, as he carefully lifted it toward the teacup. *If the butler doesn't notice that her cup needs to be refilled, you must do it for her. But never lift the cup away from the saucer when pouring, and be sure the spout is turned away from her,* his grandmother had instructed.

Emerging from the memory, Nick said, "We can't both take off for Singapore at the beginning of the semester."

"I wasn't saying we should both go—I think this is a trip you should make on your own. You're on sabbatical right now, and we both know you haven't made much progress on that book you were going to write."

Nick swept his tousled hair off his forehead with both hands with a sigh. "Everything's so perfect in our life right now, do you really want me to go back to Singapore and open another Pandora's box?"

Rachel shook her head in exasperation. "Nick, look around you. The box has been opened! It's been smashed open and gaping at you for the last four years! You need to go back and repair that box. Before it's too late."

CHAPTER EIGHT

His nails were like onyx. They were perfectly formed and lightly buffed so that there was just a hint of sheen. Su Yi had never before seen such beautifully manicured nails on a man, and couldn't help but stare as his fingers counted out rupees for the woman manning a cart piled high with brightly colored candles and strange wax figures, some in the shape of babies, some in the shape of houses, and others resembling arms and legs.

"What are these wax sculptures for?" Su Yi asked.

"People burn them as favors, in the hopes that their prayers will be answered. The babies are for people hoping for a child, the houses are for those that want a new home, and the sick choose a body part that corresponds to their ailment. So if you are looking to heal a broken arm, this is the one you'd get," he said, holding up a wax form of an arm with a clenched fist. "I bought two candles in pale red and blue—they were the closest colors I could find to represent the British flag."

"You must tell me what to do," she said hesitantly.

"It's very simple. We just place them in the shrine, light them, and say a little prayer."

As they walked up the hill with the lovely views of the Arabian Sea, Su Yi glanced at the imposing Gothic façade of Mount

Mary Church. "Are you sure they'll allow me to enter? I'm not Catholic."

"Of course. I'm not Catholic either, but everyone is welcome. If anyone asks us what we're doing, we can tell them that we're lighting candles for Singapore. Everyone is aware of what's happening there right now."

Stretching out his arm, he gestured gallantly at the arched front doors. Su Yi stepped into the church sanctuary, feeling self-conscious as her high-heeled shoes echoed against the black-and-white marble floor. It was her first time inside a Catholic church, and she stared in fascination at the vibrant frescos on the walls and the words painted in gold script against the majestic arch: *All Generations Shall Call Me Blessed*. The main altar reminded her of those in a Chinese temple, except that instead of a statue of Buddha, there was a beautiful small wooden one of the Virgin Mary dressed in gold-and-blue robes, holding an even smaller wooden baby Jesus.[*]

"I didn't know there were so many Catholics in India," she whispered to him, noticing the worshippers filling up the first four to five rows of pews, some kneeling in silent prayer.

"Bombay was a Portuguese colony during the sixteenth century, and they converted many Indians. This whole area—Bandra—is the main Catholic neighborhood."

Su Yi was impressed. "You've only been here a few months, but you've come to know the city rather well, haven't you?"

"I like to explore different areas. Mostly I wander around the city out of sheer boredom."

---

[*]   Called Moti Mauli, or "Pearl Mother" in Marathi, legend has it that the statue was brought to India in the sixteenth century by the Jesuits from Portugal but was stolen by pirates. One day, a fisherman had a dream in which he saw the statue floating in the sea, and this is how it was rediscovered.

"Has life been that boring?"

"Before you arrived, everything was boring," he said, gazing at her face intently.

Su Yi lowered her eyes, feeling her face begin to flush. They walked along the transept until they arrived at a side chapel where hundreds of burning candles flickered. He handed her the red candle and gently guided her hand as she placed its wick onto a flame. The whole ritual seemed strangely romantic.

"There. Now just find an empty slot for your candle. Anywhere you like," he said in a hushed voice.

She placed hers on the lowest rack, next to one that was almost burned out. As Su Yi watched the flame begin to brighten, she thought of the island she had been forced to flee. She still wished she could have defied her father and stayed on. She knew she should be feeling grateful rather than angry at her father, especially in light of the latest news. The Jurong-Kranji defense line had finally been breached yesterday morning, and invading Japanese soldiers were probably all over Bukit Timah now, swarming her neighborhood as they made their way to the city center. She wondered what was happening at Tyersall Park, if it had sustained any bomb damage, or whether the troops had discovered and pillaged the place.

Su Yi closed her eyes and chanted a little prayer for everyone who remained at Tyersall Park and for her cousins, her aunties and uncles, and her friends—everyone who couldn't get off the island in time. When she opened her eyes, James was standing right in front of her, so close she could feel his warm breath.

"My goodness, you startled me!" she gasped.

"Do you wish to confess?" he said, leading her toward a wooden booth.

"I'm not sure . . . should I?" Su Yi asked, her heart beginning to race. She wasn't sure she wanted to go into the dark box.

"I think it's time." He opened the latticework screen door for her.

She stepped inside the confession booth hesitantly, surprised by how comfortable the cushion on the seat was as she sat down. It was plush velvet, and it felt all of a sudden like she was seated in the Hispano-Suiza that her father had given to her for her sixteenth birthday. Every time she was driven into town, clusters of people would run after the car in excitement. The Anglos would look in curiously, wondering which dignitary was inside the grand automobile, and she loved seeing their stunned expressions when they realized it was a Chinese girl. Children would try to grab on to the car, while young suitors would attempt to throw roses through the window in the hopes of winning her attention.

The window to the confession booth slid open, and she could see that James was sitting on the other side, playing at being the priest.

"Tell me, my child, have you sinned?" he asked.

She didn't want to say anything, but suddenly, she felt her lips moving uncontrollably. "Yes I have."

"I can't hear you—"

"I have sinned. I have sinned against you." Again the words just pouring out even as she tried to keep her mouth closed.

"Speak up, dear. Can you hear me?"

"Of course I can hear you. You're sitting one foot away from me," Su Yi said, annoyed, as a bright flash of light coming through the latticework screen suddenly glared into her eyes.

"Can you hear me?" The voice sounded garbled as it morphed from English into Hokkien.

Suddenly it was all terribly bright, and she was no longer in the confession booth of Mount Mary in Bombay. She was in a hospital room, and her cardiologist was staring down at her.

"Mrs. Young, can you hear me?"

"Yes," she murmured weakly.

"Good, good," Professor Oon said. "Do you know where you are?"

"Hospital."

"Yes, you're at Mount Elizabeth. You had a cardiac episode, but we've managed to stabilize you and I'm very happy with the progress you're making. Do you feel any pain?"

"Not really."

"Good, you shouldn't. We have you on a constant dose of hydrocodone, so you should not have to feel any discomfort at all. Now, I'm going to send Felicity in. She's very eager to see you."

Felicity entered and tiptoed rather awkwardly to her mother's bedside. "Oh Mummy! You're finally awake. They've had you sedated for the past two days so that your heart could rest. How are you feeling? You gave us quite a scare!"

"Where are Madri and Patravadee?"

"Oh, your lady's maids are right outside. They've been with you all this time, but you haven't known it. Francis only allows one of us in at a time."

"I'm very thirsty."

"Yes, yes. It's this medication they have you on, and the oxygen tube in your nose. It really dries out your throat. Let's get you some water." Felicity looked around and found a water jug on a side table. "Hmm. I wonder if this is filtered or from the tap. Oh dear, they only have plastic cups. Do you mind? I'll have some proper glasses brought up as soon as possible. I don't understand why there are only plastic cups in here. I don't know if you can tell, but you're in the Royal Suite, built for the Brunei royals. We had it specially arranged for you. But dear me, they need proper cups."

"I don't care," Su Yi said impatiently.

Felicity poured some water into the cup and brought it over to her mother. She held the cup up to her mother's lips and began to tilt it forward, noticing that her hands were beginning to shake. "Oh, silly me, we need a straw. We wouldn't want to spill any of this on you."

Su Yi let out a sigh. Even in her delirious state, Su Yi noticed that her eldest daughter always brought along a certain frenetic energy. She was so eager to please, but in a cloying, obsequious way that Su Yi found so irritating. She had been like this even as a child. Where did she get it from?

Felicity found a cluster of straws on the side table and hastily jabbed one into the cup. "Here, that's much better." As she placed the straw up to her mother's lips, she glanced at the heart monitor and saw the numbers slowly begin to rise: 95 . . . 105 . . . 110. She knew she was agitating her mother, and her hands started shaking again. A few drops of water splashed onto her mother's chin.

"Hold still!" Su Yi hissed.

Felicity grasped the cup tightly, suddenly feeling like she was ten years old again, perched on the ottoman in her mother's bedroom as one of the Thai maids arranged her hair into an intricate braid. She would shift a little, and her mother would groan in annoyance. "Hold still! Siri is doing very delicate work here, and if you make one false move, you're going to mess it all up! Do you want to be the only girl at Countess Mountbatten's tea party with bad hair? Everyone will be looking at you because you're my daughter. Do you want to disgrace me by looking unkempt?"

Felicity could feel the veins in her neck beginning to throb at the memory. Where were her blood-pressure pills? She couldn't deal with Mummy like this. She hated even seeing her like this, dressed in a hospital gown with her hair out of place. Mummy must never look unkempt. Now that she was conscious, they must send over some of her own clothes and have Simon set her hair properly. And some jewelry. Where was the jade amulet she always wore against her chest? She stared at the heart monitor anxiously: 112 . . . 115 . . . 120. Oh dear oh dear. She didn't want to be responsible for causing another heart attack. She needed to leave the room now.

"You know, Astrid's been dying to see you," Felicity blurted out, appalled at her own choice of words. She pulled the cup away from her mother and fled out the door.

A few moments later, Astrid entered, the bright light from the doorway silhouetting her, and making her glow like an angel. Su Yi smiled at her. Her favorite granddaughter always looked so calm and collected, no matter the occasion. Today she was wearing a pale lilac dress with a low-waisted sash and delicate knife pleats all along the skirt. Her long hair was gathered into a loose bun at the nape of her neck, and the delicate locks on the side framed her face like Botticelli's Venus.

"*Aiyah*, how wonderful you look!" Su Yi said in Cantonese, the dialect she preferred to use with most of her grandchildren.

"Don't you recognize the dress? It's one of your Poirets, from the 1920s," Astrid said, sitting in the chair beside her bed and taking her hand.

"Ah yes, of course. It was my mother's actually. I thought it was terribly old-fashioned by the time she gave it to me, but it looks perfect on you."

"I wish I could have met Great-grandma."

"You would have appreciated her. She was very beautiful, like you. She always told me that it was unfortunate that I took after my father."

"Oh but Ah Ma, you're so beautiful! Weren't you the leading debutante of your day?"

"I wasn't ugly, but I didn't come close to my mother in looks. My older brother looked more like her." Su Yi sighed for a moment. "If only you could have met him."

"Great-uncle Alexander?"

"I always called him by his Chinese name, Ah Jit. He was so strikingly handsome and so kind."

"You've always said that."

"He died much too young."

"Cholera, wasn't it?"

Su Yi paused for a moment, before saying, "Yes, there was an epidemic in Batavia, where Father had sent him to manage our businesses. You know, things would have been so different for all of us had he lived."

"What do you mean?"

"He wouldn't have behaved like Alfred, for one thing."

Astrid wasn't sure what her grandmother meant, but she didn't wish to upset her by prodding any further. "Great-uncle Alfred is coming home, you know? He's due in on Thursday. Auntie Cat and Auntie Alix are on their way as well."

"Why is everyone coming down? Do they think I'm dying?"

"Oh, no, no. Everyone just wants to see you." Astrid laughed lightly.

"Hmm. Well, if that's the case, I want to be at home. Please tell Francis that I want to go home today."

"I don't think you can go home just yet, Ah Ma. You need to get a bit better first."

"Nonsense! Where is Francis now?"

Astrid pushed the button beside the bed, and within a few moments Francis Oon arrived in the room accompanied by his usual entourage of nurses. "Is everything okay?" he asked, looking a bit flustered. He always got flustered around her. Astrid noticed a spot of chili sauce at the edge of his mouth and tried to ignore it. She addressed him in English. "My grandmother wishes to be discharged."

Professor Oon leaned toward his patient and spoke in Hokkien. "Mrs. Young, we can't allow you to go home just yet. You need to get stronger first."

"I feel fine."

"Well, we want you to feel *even better* before we release you—"

Astrid cut in. "Professor Oon, I think my grandmother would be so much more comfortable at home. Can't we just have things set up for her at Tyersall Park?"

"Er, it's not that simple. Step outside with me for a moment, will you?" the doctor said a little uneasily. Astrid followed him out of the room, slightly annoyed by the ungracious way he had handled that. Now of course her grandmother would know they were discussing her condition.

Professor Oon found himself staring at Astrid. This woman was so blindingly pretty, it made him nervous just to be around her. He felt like he could lose control at any moment and say something inappropriate. "Er, Astrid, I must be very . . . um, blunt with you. Your grandmother's condition is extremely . . . touch and go . . . at the moment. There's been a tremendous amount of scarring on the heart, and her erection . . . I mean, her ejection fraction is up to twenty-seven percent. I know it looks like she's getting better, but you need to know that we are making monumental efforts to keep her alive. All those machines she's hooked up to . . . she needs them, and she requires nonstop care."

"How long does she really have?"

"Hard to say, but it's a matter of weeks. Her heart muscle is irreparably damaged, and her condition is worsening day by day. She could go at any moment, really."

Astrid let out a long exhale. "Well, it's even more essential that we get her home then. I know my grandmother would not want to spend her last days here. Why can't we simply move all the machines? Let's set up a medical suite just like this one for her at home. We can have you and the rest of her medical team stationed there."

"Something like that has never been done before. To set up a mobile cardiac intensive care unit in a private home with all the equipment we would need and round-the-clock doctors and nurses—it's a huge undertaking, and it would be extremely cost prohibitive."

Astrid cocked her head, giving him a subtly eviscerating look that said: *Really? Do we really need to go there?* "Professor Oon, I think I can speak for my entire family. The cost is not an issue. Let's just make it happen, shall we?"

"Okay, I'll get to work on that," Professor Oon replied, his face flushing red.

Astrid reentered the Royal Suite, and Su Yi smiled at her.

"All taken care of, Ah Ma. They will move you home as soon as possible. They just have to set up the medical equipment for you first."

"Thank you. You are much more efficient than your mother."

"Hnh! Don't let her hear you say that. Anyway, you shouldn't be talking so much. You should rest."

"Oh, I feel like I've rested enough. Before I woke up, I had a dream about your grandfather. Ah Yeh."

"Do you dream about Ah Yeh often?"

"Rarely. But this dream was very strange. Part of it felt so real, because it was a memory of something that really happened during the war, when I had been evacuated to Bombay."

"But Ah Yeh wasn't in Bombay, was he? Didn't you only meet him when you returned to Singapore?"

"Yes, when I went home." Su Yi closed her eyes and was silent for a few moments, and Astrid thought she had drifted back to sleep. Suddenly she opened her eyes wide. "I need you to help me."

Astrid sat up in her chair. "Yes, of course. What do you want me to do?"

"There are some things you must do for me at once. Very important things . . ."

CHAPTER NINE

The lid on the enamel kettle started rattling, and Ah Ling, the head housekeeper, reached for the kettle on the hot plate and poured some boiling water into her tea mug. She relaxed into her armchair and breathed in the earthy, musky scent of the *ying de hong cha* before taking her first sip. For the past two decades, her younger brother had been sending her a parcel of this tea every year from China, wrapped in layers of brown paper and sealed with old-fashioned yellow Scotch tape. These tea leaves were grown in the hills above her village, and drinking it remained one of her last connections to the place where she had been born.

Like so many girls of her generation, Lee Ah Ling left her tiny village on the outskirts of Ying Tak when she was just sixteen, taking a boat from Canton to an island far away in the Nanyang, the Southern Seas. She remembered how most of the other girls who were crammed into that stifling little cabin had wept bitterly every night on their voyage, and Ah Ling wondered if she was a bad person to be feeling not sadness but a sense of excitement. She had always dreamed of seeing the world beyond her village, and she didn't care if it meant leaving her family. She was leaving a difficult home—a father who died when she was twelve and a mother who seemed to have resented her since the day she was born.

Now at least she could do something to quell that resentment—in exchange for a modest sum of money that would enable her brother to go to school, she would go abroad, take the vow of celibacy that every black-and-white amah was asked to, and be tied to serve an unknown family in a strange new land for the rest of her life.

In Singapore, she had been brokered to work for a family called the Tays. They were a couple in their late thirties with two sons and a daughter living in a mansion more lavish and luxurious than she had ever dreamed was possible. Actually, it was a rather unspectacular bungalow off Serangoon Road, but to Ah Ling's untrained eyes, it might as well have been Buckingham Palace. There were three other black-and-white amahs like her in the household, but they had been there for years. Ah Ling was the new girl, and for the next six months she was assiduously taught the finer details of the domestic arts, which for her meant learning how to properly clean varnished wood and silver.

One day, the most senior maid announced, "Mrs. Tay thinks you're ready. Pack your belongings—we're sending you to the Youngs." It was only then that Ah Ling realized that her time at the Tay household had been a training ground, and she had passed some sort of unspecified test. Ah Lan, the junior maid who had been there ten years, said to her, "You are very lucky. You were born with a pretty face, and you've proven yourself good at polishing silver. So you get to work at the big house now. But don't let your head get too big over this!"

Ah Ling had no idea what she meant—she couldn't imagine a bigger mansion than the one she was already in. She soon found herself in the passenger seat of the Austin-Healey, with Mr. Tay at the wheel and Mrs. Tay in the backseat, and she would never forget that drive. They had entered what seemed like a jungle road, and at a clearing they pulled up to a grand wrought-iron gate painted light gray. She thought she was dreaming, to suddenly come upon this strange ornate gate in the middle of nowhere.

A fierce-looking Indian *jaga** wearing a crisp olive uniform and a bright yellow turban emerged from the sentry house and scrutinized them closely through the car window before ceremoniously waving them through the gates. Then they drove up a long winding gravel lane that had been cut through the thick trees, giving way to an avenue lined with majestic palm trees, until suddenly the most magnificent building she had ever seen came into sight. "What is this place?" she had asked, suddenly becoming afraid.

"This is Tyersall Park, the home of Sir James Young. You will be working here from now on," Mrs. Tay informed her.

"Is he the governor of Singapore?" Ah Ling asked in awe. She never knew a house could be this immense . . . it was like one of the grand old buildings on the Shanghai waterfront she had once seen on a postcard.

"No, but the Youngs are far more important than the governor."

"What does Mister . . . Sir James do?"

"He's a doctor."

---

* Hindi for "watchman," the term is used for any sort of security guard. The *jagas* at Tyersall Park were, of course, highly trained Gurkhas that could disembowel another man with just two strokes from their daggers.

"I never knew doctors could be so rich."

"He is a wealthy man, but this house actually belongs to his wife, Su Yi."

"A *lady* owns this house?" Ah Ling had never heard of such a thing.

"Yes, she grew up here. It was her grandfather's house."

"He was my grandfather too." Mr. Tay turned to Ah Ling with a smile.

"This is your grandfather's house? Why are you not living here, then?" Ah Ling asked, puzzled.

"*Aiyah*, stop asking so many questions!" Mrs. Tay scolded. "You will learn more about the family in due course—I'm sure the other servants will fill you in on all the gossip very fast. You will quickly see that it is Su Yi who rules over everything. Just work very hard and be sure that you never do anything to upset her and you'll do fine."

Ah Ling had done more than fine. Over the next sixty-three years, she rose from being one of twelve junior maids to become one of the Young family's most trusted nannies—having helped raise Su Yi's youngest children, Victoria and Alix, and then in the next generation, Nick. Now she was the head housekeeper, overseeing a staff that at its peak reached fifty-eight but for the past decade had remained at thirty-two. Today, as she sat in her quarters drinking tea and eating a few Jacob's Cream Crackers smeared with peanut butter and Wilkin & Sons red currant jam—one of the strange Western habits she had picked up from Philip Young—a round, smiling face suddenly appeared at her window.

"Ah Tock! My God, I was just sitting here thinking of your grandmother, and suddenly you appear!" Ah Ling gasped.

"Ling Jeh, didn't you know I had no choice but to come this

afternoon? Her Imperial Highness summoned me," Ah Tock reminded her in Cantonese.

"I had forgotten. My head is jumbled with a million things today."

"I can only imagine! Hey, I hate to make your life more difficult, but do you mind?" Ah Tock held up a Metro shopping bag full of clothing. "These are Mama's dresses—"

"Of course, of course," Ah Ling said, taking the bag. Ah Tock was a cousin of the Youngs through Su Yi's side,* and Ah Ling had known his mother, Bernice Tay, since she was a girl—she was the daughter of the couple who first took Ah Ling in "for training" when she arrived in Singapore. Bernice regularly smuggled some of her finer clothes to be cleaned at Tyersall Park, knowing there was a full team of launderers that washed every piece by hand, air dried them in the sun, and ironed them with lavender-scented water. There wasn't a finer laundering service on the entire island.

"Mama wanted me to show you this *sam fu* . . . the fastening hook came off."

"Don't worry, we'll have it sewn back for her. I know this vintage *sam fu*—Su Yi gave it to her years ago."

Out of another bag, Ah Tock produced a bottle of Chinese rum. "Here, from Mama."

"Hiyah, tell your mother she shouldn't have bothered! I still haven't finished the bottle she gave me a year ago. When do I have time to enjoy this?"

---

* Ah Tock is a great-great-grandson of Shang Zhao Hui, the grandfather of Shang Su Yi, but because he was descended from the second wife of the patriarch's five official wives, none of the children from her branch inherited any substantial fortune from the Shang empire and were considered lesser, "distant cousins" when they were in fact not so distant at all.

"If I had to run this place like you do, I'd be drinking every night!" Ah Tock said with a chuckle.

"Should we go up now?" Ah Ling gestured, getting out of her chair.

"Sure. How is Her Imperial Highness today?"

"Irritable, as always."

"Hopefully I can help fix that," Ah Tock replied cheerily. Ah Tock was a frequent presence at Tyersall Park, not because he was a beloved relation but because of his expertise in catering to the needs of his more privileged cousins. Over the past two decades, Ah Tock had smartly leveraged his family connections and founded FiveStarLobang.com, an exclusive luxury concierge service that serviced the most spoiled Singaporeans— from procuring that Beluga black Bentley Bentayga months before it hit the market to arranging covert Brazilian butt-lifts for bored mistresses.

Crossing the quadrangle that separated the servants' wing from the main house, they passed the kitchen garden, which was meticulously planted with rows of fresh herbs and vegetables. "Oh my. Look at those little red chilli padis—I'm sure they must be extra hot!" Ah Tock exclaimed.

"Yes. Burn-your-mouth hot. Let's not forget to pluck some for your mother. We also have too much basil right now—it's just gone wild. Do you want some of that too?"

"I'm not sure what Mama would do with that. Isn't it an *ang mor** herb?"

"We use it here for the Thai dishes. The Thais use basil a

---

*   The literal meaning in Hokkien is "red hair," but it's a derogatory colloquial term used to describe anything of Western origin, since to many of Singapore's older-generation Chinese, all Western people are considered *ang mor kow sai*—"redhaired dog shit."

lot in their cooking. And also sometimes Her Imperial Highness demands fancy *ang mor* food. She likes this disgusting sauce
called 'pesto.' It takes so many of these basil leaves just to
make one little batch of pesto sauce, and then she eats one tiny
plate of linguine with pesto and the rest gets thrown out."

A young maid walked past them, and switching to Mandarin,
Ah Ling ordered, "Lan Lan, can you pluck a big packet of the
chilli padis for Mr. Tay to take home?"

"Yes, ma'am," the girl replied shyly before darting off.

"Very cute. She's new?" Ah Tock asked.

"Yes, and she's not going to last long. Spends too much
time staring into her phone when she knows she's not allowed.
All these young China girls don't have the same work ethic as
my generation did," Ah Ling complained, as she led Ah Tock
through the kitchen, where half a dozen cooks sat around the
enormous wooden worktable, deep in concentration as they
meticulously folded little bits of pastry.

"*Shiok!** You're making pineapple tarts!" Ah Tock said.

"Yes—we always make a huge batch whenever Alfred Shang
comes to town."

"But didn't I hear that Alfred brought over his own Singaporean chef to England? Some Hainanese hotshot?"

"Yes, but Alfred still prefers our pineapple tarts. He complains
that it's not the same when Marcus tries to make it in England . . .
something about the flour and water being different."

Crazy rich bastard, Ah Tock thought to himself. Even though
he had been coming here for as long as he could remember, he
never ceased to be awed by Tyersall Park. He had of course been

---

*   Singlish slang that's equivalent to "cool" or "fantastic" or "amazing" in
Malay.

into many homes of the high and mighty, but nothing else came close to this. Even the kitchen was impressive beyond belief—a series of cavernous spaces with vaulted ceilings, walls covered in beautiful majolica tiles, and rows of shimmering copper pans and perfectly seasoned woks hanging over the gigantic Aga stoves. It looked like the kitchen of some historic resort hotel in the south of France. Ah Tock remembered a story his father had told him: *Back in the old days before the war, Gong Gong* loved *entertaining—there used to be parties for three hundred people every month at Tyersall Park, and we lesser children weren't allowed to attend, so we used to peer down at the guests from the upstairs balcony in our pajamas.*

Taking a service staircase to the second floor, they walked down another hallway leading into the east wing. There, Ah Tock found his cousin Victoria Young on the sofa of the study room adjoining her bedroom, going through stacks of old papers with one of her personal maids. Victoria was the only one of Su Yi's children who still lived at Tyersall Park, and in many ways she was even more imperious than her mother, hence "Her Imperial Highness," the nickname Ah Tock and Ah Ling used behind her back. Ah Tock stood in the room for several minutes, seemingly ignored. By now, he should be used to this kind of dismissive treatment, since his entire family had for three generations basically served as glorified help to these cousins, but he nevertheless felt a bit insulted.

"Lincoln, you're early." Victoria finally looked up for a moment to acknowledge his presence, calling Ah Tock by his English name as she riffled through a set of blue aerogram letters. "These can be shredded," she said, handing them off to the maid, who immediately fed them into the paper shredder.

---

* Cantonese for "grandfather."

Victoria's severe chin-length bobbed hair was looking frizzier and grayer than ever. Ah Tock wondered if she had ever heard of hair conditioner. She was wearing a white lab coat stained with paint marks over a polyester leopard-print blouse and what appeared to be white silk pajama pants. *If she wasn't born a Young, everyone would think she's an escapee from Woodbridge.** Fed up with waiting, Ah Tock tried to break the silence. "That looks like a ton of paperwork!"

"Mummy's personal papers. She wants everything destroyed."

"Er . . . are you sure you should be doing this? Wouldn't some historians be interested in Great-auntie Su Yi's letters?"

Victoria frowned at Ah Tock. "Precisely why I'm going through all of them. Some we'll save for the National Archives or the museums if there's anything relevant. But anything personal Mummy wants gone before she dies."

Ah Tock was taken aback by how matter-of-factly Victoria put it. He tried to change the subject to more pleasant matters. "You'll be pleased . . . everything is on schedule to be delivered. The seafood supplier is sending a big truck tomorrow. They promised me the very best lobsters, jumbo prawns, and Dungeness crabs. They've never gotten such a large private order before."

"Good." Victoria nodded.

---

* Officially known as the Institute of Mental Health, Singapore's first psychiatric hospital was founded in 1841 on the corner of Bras Basah Road and Bencoolen Street. It was first known as the Insane Hospital but was renamed the Lunatic Asylum in 1861 when it moved to a site near the old Kandang Kerbau Maternity Hospital. In 1928, a new building was built along Yio Chu Kang Road and after several more name changes—the New Lunatic Asylum and the Mental Hospital among them—it was renamed Woodbridge Hospital in an effort to shake off some of the stigma associated with its previous names. Yet for generations of Singaporeans, Woodbridge only means one thing: You've gone bat-shit crazy.

Ah Tock was pleased with the huge kickback he was getting from the seafood supplier, but he still found it hard to believe that the two Thai daughters-in-law of his cousin Catherine Young Aakara—Su Yi's second-eldest child—subsisted on a diet of shellfish and nothing else.

"And I managed to track down that mineral-water bottler in Adelboden," Ah Tock said.

"So they can have all the water here in time?"

"Well, it's coming from Switzerland, so it will take about a week—"

"Cat and her family arrive on Thursday. Can't you have it airfreighted?"

"It *is* being airfreighted."

"Well Lincoln, get them to put a rush on it. Or have some courier service do it if these people can't get it here fast enough."

"It's going to cost a fortune to have five hundred gallons of bottled water flown overnight!" Ah Tock exclaimed.

Victoria gave him a look that said: *Do I look like I give a damn how much it costs?*

In moments like these, Ah Tock couldn't believe he was actually related to these people. For the life of him, he could not imagine why the Aakaras needed to have special mineral water from some obscure spring in the Bernese Oberland flown in just for them. Wasn't Singapore tap water—rated one of the best in the world—good enough for these people? Or Perrier, for fuck's sake? Were these delicate Thai royals going to drop dead if they had to drink Perrier?

"How are things coming along with the room?" Victoria asked.

"The team will be here to install everything tomorrow morning. I've also rented two mobile-home units, which we can park behind the French walled garden. This is where the doctors and nurses can be based, since you don't want them in the house," Ah Tock reported.

"It's not that we don't want them in the house, but between Alix and Malcolm coming in from Hong Kong and the Aakaras bringing all their maids, there's just no room."

Ah Tock was incredulous. This was the biggest private house in Singapore—he had never been able to count how many bedrooms there actually were—and they couldn't even find space for the dedicated medical team that would be moving in to care for their dying mother?

"How many maids is Auntie Cat bringing?"

"She usually brings three of her own, five when Taksin joins her, but with all her sons and their wives coming, goodness knows how many of them will show up." Victoria sighed.

"The team from Mount E came earlier today to do their assessment, and they think that the best place to set up the cardiac care unit is in the conservatory," he said, trying to reason with his cousin.

Victoria shook her head irritatedly. "No, that won't do. Mummy will want to be upstairs in her own bedroom."

At this point, Ah Ling felt like she had to interject. "But Victoria, the conservatory is perfect. They won't have to transport her upstairs, not to mention all the machines and generators. It's secluded from any noise in the service wing, and they can set up all the machines in the adjoining dining room and have the wiring brought in right through the conservatory doors."

"It's no use arguing. Years ago when I suggested to Mummy that she move her bedroom downstairs so that she didn't have to keep climbing the stairs, she said to me, 'I will never sleep downstairs. The servants sleep downstairs. And the only members of my family who have ever slept downstairs have done so in their coffins.' Trust me, she will expect everything to be set up in her bedroom."

Ah Tock had to resist rolling his eyes. Even from her death-bed, Great-auntie Su Yi was still trying to control the whole world. And a little gratitude from Her Imperial Highness would have been nice—he had worked nonstop to make all this happen in record time, and Victoria hadn't uttered "thank you" even once.

Just then, a maid knocked softly on the open door and peered in.

"What is it?" Victoria asked.

"I have a message for Ah Ling," the maid said in a very soft voice.

"Well, come in here and tell it to her. Don't just stand there skulking by the door!" Victoria scolded.

"Sorry, ma'am," the maid said, glancing at Ah Ling nervously. "Um, the guardhouse called. Mrs. Alexandra Cheng and family are arriving."

"What do you mean *arriving?*" Ah Ling asked.

"They are pulling up to the house now."

"Now? But they aren't supposed to be here until Thursday like everyone else!" Ah Ling groaned.

"Oh for heaven's sake—did they give us the wrong dates?" Victoria fumed.

Ah Ling looked out the window and saw that it wasn't just Alix and her husband, Malcolm, getting out of the car. There were six cars, and the whole damn family was pouring out of them—Alistair Cheng; Cecilia Cheng Moncur and her husband, Tony, with their son, Jake; and who was that stepping out of the car in a white linen suit? Oh dear God. It couldn't be. She looked at Victoria in a panic and blurted out, "*Eddie* is here!"

Victoria groaned. "Alix didn't say he was coming! Where are we going to put him?"

"It's not just him . . . Fiona and the children are here too."

"Good God! He's going to kick up a fuss and demand the Pearl Suite again. And that's reserved for Catherine and Taksin when they arrive on Thursday."

Ah Ling shook her head. "Actually, Catherine's lady's maid in Bangkok called me to say that Adam and his wife should have the Pearl Suite."

"But Adam is their youngest son. Why on earth should he get the Pearl Suite?"

"Apparently Adam's wife is the daughter of some prince who ranks higher than Taksin. So they must have the Pearl Suite."

"Oh yes, I forgot about all that protocol nonsense. Well, Ah Ling, it will be your job to deliver the news to Eddie." Victoria smiled wryly.

CHAPTER TEN

Lined up in perfect military precision on the steps of the monolithic granite-and-concrete structure were six attendants. Back in the days when Colette Bing was the mistress of the house—thanks to her indulgent father, Jack—the staff had been clad in chic black T-shirts and black jeans from James Perse. But ever since Kitty Pong Tai Bing had taken over the grand residence at the heart of Porto Fino Elite Estates, she had outfitted the men in black-tie butler's uniforms and the women in classic black-and-white French maid outfits.

As the convoy of black Audi SUVs pulled up to the house, Kitty, her daughter, Gisele, her infant son, Harvard, and the children's nannies alighted from the car and the line of staffers bowed in unison before scurrying around to gather all the luggage.

"Oooh! It's good to be home!" Kitty squealed, kicking off her red Aquazzura suede fringe-and-tassel sandals as she entered the great hall, which was now reduced to a construction site with scaffolding against the walls, plastic tarp on all the furniture, and exposed wiring hanging from the ceiling. In an effort to remove every last reminder of Colette's taste, Kitty had spent the past year "collaborating" with Thierry Catroux—the celebrated interior designer who worked only with billionaires—to redesign every last square inch of the estate.

"Where is my husband?" Kitty asked Laurent, the estate manager she had poached from some tech mogul's estate in Kona to replace Wolseley, Colette's British butler, who had once worked for Princess Michael of Kent at Kensington Palace.

"Mr. Bing is having his daily massage, madame."

Kitty headed over to the spa pavilion and descended the steps to the subterranean swimming pool encircled with carved marble pillars. As she walked down the lacquered-cinnabar passageway leading to the treatment rooms, she smiled at the thought of all this coming down too—Colette's hammam-inspired Turkish spa was going to be transformed into a futuristic Egyptian fantasy spa inspired by the movie *Stargate*. It was her own idea!

Kitty entered the treatment room illuminated by scented candles and found Jack lying facedown on the massage bed. The scent of frankincense permeated the air, as Céline Dion played softly in the background. One of the female therapists[*] was doing reflexology on Jack's feet, while another walked precariously along his spine as if she were on a tightrope, grasping an elaborate lattice of poles affixed to the ceiling in order to ensure the precise amount of body weight on his aching muscles.

"Waaah! That's it! That's the spot!" Jack groaned through his face cradle, as the woman standing on his back dug the ball of her left foot into a muscle below his shoulder blades.

"Looks like someone's having a good time!" Kitty declared.

"Yea . . . aahh! Yessss! You're home!"

---

[*] Kitty also had the attractive eastern European therapists that Colette kept on staff replaced with middle-aged Chinese women who resembled Madame Mao.

"I thought I'd find you waiting to welcome me!"

"When I heard the plane was delayed coming in, I thought I'd . . . oooooh . . . get my massage first!"

"Those stupid French officials delayed our takeoff for two hours because of some idiotic bomb scare. They wouldn't even let me onto our plane, so I was stuck in that ghastly terminal with *the public*." Kitty pouted, as she stretched out on the plush chaise lounge next to Jack.

"I'm so sorry you had to be with the public, babylove. Did you have a good time in Paris?"

"I sure did! Do you know what happy news I heard while I was there?"

"Owwahhh! Gentle, gentle there! What?"

"You'll be pleased to know that your daughter is finally getting married," Kitty said, her voice dripping with sarcasm.

Jack let out a slow grunt. "Ummm . . . really?"

"Yes. And to an *Englishman*. But of course you already knew?"

"How would I? Colette hasn't spoken to me in almost two years—not since our wedding."

"You just don't seem overly surprised."

"Why should I be surprised? She was bound to get married at some point."

"But to an Englishman?"

"Well, Carlton Bao stopped talking to her, and Richie Yang wouldn't have her, so I think her options in China became quite limited. What is this fellow's story?"

"He's a nobody. Some nonprofit lawyer who's trying to save the planet. I suppose your ex-wife will have to support the both of them forever. Do you know what else I heard? Colette's wedding gown costs two million dollars."

"That's absurd. Is it made of gold?"

"Actually, there are gold chips sewn into it, and it's encrusted with precious stones. It's totally outrageous," Kitty said, as she sniffed a glass container of body lotion placed on the side table and began rubbing some on her arms.

"Well, I suppose she can do whatever she wants with her money."

"But I thought you cut her off completely?"

Jack went silent for a minute, then suddenly groaned. "AWWWWW! Why does that hurt so much?"

The therapist kneaded a point on his foot with her thumb and forefinger and sternly pronounced, "Sir, this is your gallbladder—it's totally inflamed. I think you must have consumed too much cognac and oily foods last night. Did you have those fried oysters and abalone noodles again when I told you not to?"

"Aww! Aww! Let go! Let go!" Jack screamed.

"Jack, answer me. What did you mean by *her money*?" Kitty pressed on, oblivious to his pain.

Jack sighed in relief as the therapist finally released his foot. "Colette receives income from a trust fund. It was part of my divorce settlement with Lai Di."

"Why is this the first time I'm hearing of it?"

"Well, I didn't want to bore you with the details of my divorce."

"I thought Lai Di only got two billion?"

"She did, but as a condition of her walking away and not making any more noise, I had to set up a trust fund for Colette."

"Oh really? And how much is that trust fund worth?"

Jack murmured something in a muffled tone.

"Speak up, honey, I can't hear you . . . you said what in U.S. currency?"

"About five billion."

"YOU GAVE YOUR DAUGHTER FIVE BILLION DOL-LARS?" Kitty bolted upright on the chaise lounge.

"I didn't *give* her five billion. She gets the income from a trust worth about five billion. It's all tied to shares in my companies, anyway, so her income fluctuates every year depending on the dividend yields. And it's only for her lifetime."

"And what happens *after* her lifetime?"

"It will go to any children she has."

Suddenly visions of Colette and her future half-white children began flooding into Kitty's mind. She could see Colette in a white summer dress, running barefoot through a field in the English countryside with laughing golden-haired kids. She began to seethe quietly as she calculated the figures in her head. Even if the trust was getting a measly one percent interest on five billion, this meant that Colette—who she always presumed was being supported by her poor mother who only had two billion dollars—would get at least *fifty million dollars in pure income every year!* And her unnaturally photogenic children, who wouldn't even know their Chinese grandfather, would also benefit from this!

"So where does this leave us?" Kitty said in a grave tone.

"What do you mean?"

"If you've set aside so much money for your darling daughter, who by the way won't even speak to you anymore, and her half-breed children, that haven't even been born yet, what are you doing for your other children and your poor wife?"

"I don't understand your question. What do *I* do for you? I work my balls off for you, and you have a fantastic life and get everything your heart desires. Didn't you just spend ten million dollars in Paris?"

"It was only nine point five—I'm a Chanel Privé preferred client, and they gave me a special discount. But say something happens to you? What happens to me?" Kitty demanded.

"Nothing's going to happen to me. But don't worry, you'll be well taken care of."

"What do you mean by *well taken care of*?"

"You'll also get a two-billion-dollar trust."

So, I'm not worth as much as your daughter, Kitty thought to herself, feeling her anger boil up. "And how much is Harvard getting?"

"Harvard is my son. He will get everything else of course, and let me remind you that's a great deal more than five billion dollars."

"And Gisele?"

"I don't see why I need to leave Gisele anything. She is going to inherit all the Tai billions one day."

Kitty stood up from the chaise lounge and walked toward the door. "It is *so interesting* to know all this. I can see where your true priorities lie now."

"What's that supposed to mean?"

"You're not really thinking of me . . . or our children," Kitty said, her voice shaking with emotion.

"Of course I am!"

"No, you're not! You're not thinking of us at all."

"Babylove, don't be unreasonable . . . ooohhwwhhh . . . not so hard there!" Jack yelled at the therapist who had climbed up on the massage table and was now kneading his ass with the full weight of her bare feet.

"Sir, you spend too much time sitting—that is why your buttocks hurt so much. I am barely stepping on them," the woman said in a soothing tone.

"I cannot believe you would give your daughter five billion dollars just like that! After all she's done to you!" Kitty cried.

"Ouch . . . aww . . . Kitty, you're not making any sense! Colette is my only daughter—why should it matter if she gets five billion, when I give you everything you want? Aii-yowwww!" Jack moaned.

"Stomp harder on his ass! And stomp on his saggy balls while you're at it!" Kitty shouted, fleeing the room in tears.

CHAPTER ELEVEN

HONG KONG

Chloe had finally fallen asleep after he had rubbed her back for half an hour, and Charlie tiptoed quietly up to his bedroom. He sat leaning against the foot of the bed, facing the floor-to-ceiling window with its panoramic view of Victoria Harbour and dialed Astrid's private line in Singapore. It rang a few times, and just as Charlie began to think he was calling too late, a sleepy-sounding Astrid picked up.

"Sorry, did I wake you up?" Charlie half whispered.

"No, I was reading. Did you just get home?"

"I've been in all night, but I was putting out a few fires."

"Isabel again?"

Charlie sighed. "No, nothing to do with her this time. Chloe had been bugging me for weeks to let her watch this movie, and I stupidly allowed her and Delphine to see it tonight . . . *The Fault in Our Stars.*"

"I don't know it."

"I thought it was for kids, but trust me, it's not. It's sort of like a modern-day retelling of *Love Story.*"

"Oh no. Young love, tragic ending?"

"You have no idea. When I began to realize where it was headed, I tried turning the movie off, but the girls screamed bloody murder, so I let them keep watching. Chloe's obsessed with the guy in the film, this goofy blond kid. But then in the end . . . oh God."

"In the end you had two weeping girls?"

"Sobbing uncontrollably. I think Delphine's traumatized for life."

"Charlie Wu! She's eight years old! What on earth were you thinking?" Astrid scolded.

"I know, I know. I was lazy, I saw the DVD cover and read the first two lines on the back. It looked harmless."

"You might as well have put on *A Clockwork Orange* for them."

"I'm a bad father, Astrid. That's why I need you in my life. The girls need you. They need a good, sensible influence around."

"Ha! I don't think my mum would agree with that statement."

"They're going to love you, Astrid. I just know it. And they're going to love Cassian too."

"We're going to be the Asian Brady Bunch, minus a few kids."

"I can't wait. By the way, I had a really good meeting with Isabel's lawyers yesterday. They don't have any more objections, thank God. You know, in a strange way the stunt Isabel pulled in Singapore has worked to our advantage. Her lawyers were so afraid that I'd try to get full custody of the girls that they've withdrawn most of their demands and are willing to settle now."

"That's the best news I've heard all week," Astrid said, closing her eyes for a moment. Slowly but surely, she was beginning to see her life with Charlie come into focus. She pictured herself cuddled up next to him on their new bed in their beautiful new house in Shek O, far from the crowds of Hong Kong or Singapore, bathed in moonlight and listening to the waves crashing against the rocks on the cliffs far below. She could picture Chloe and Delphine watching an age-appropriate movie in the media room with their new stepbrother, Cassian, passing a big pint of gelato amongst themselves.

Charlie's voice suddenly jarred her out of her daydream. "Hey, I'm going to India tomorrow. Visiting our new factories in Bangalore, and then I have to attend this charity polo match in Jodhpur that we're sponsoring. Why don't you come for the weekend?"

"This weekend?"

"Yeah. We can stay at the Umaid Bhawan Palace. Have you ever been there? It's one of the most gorgeous palaces in the world, and the Taj group now runs it as a very exclusive hotel. Shivraj, the future maharaja, is a good friend, and I'm sure we'll be treated like royalty," Charlie said.

"Sounds tempting, but there's no way I can leave Singapore right now with Ah Ma so sick."

"Isn't she feeling a bit better? And didn't you say that a million relatives have descended on Tyersall Park? They're not going to miss you for two or three days."

"It's precisely because so many relatives are in town that they'll need me. It's my duty to help entertain everyone."

"Sorry, I realize I'm being extremely selfish. You're a total saint for your family. I just miss you so much."

"I miss you too. I can't believe it's been more than a month since we've seen each other! But between my grandmother and everything going on with Isabel and Michael and our lovely legal teams, don't you think it's better for us to lay low and not to be seen together right now?"

"Who's going to know we're in India? I'm flying into Mumbai, you can fly straight to Jodhpur, and we'll be totally secluded at the hotel. In fact, if things go according to my plan, we're not going to ever leave our room the entire weekend."

"If things go according to your plan? Whatever do you mean, Mr. Grey?" Astrid teased.

"I'm not going to tell you, but it will involve chocolate mousse, peacock feathers, and a good stopwatch."

"Mmmm. I do love a good stopwatch."

"Come on. It'll be fun."

Astrid mulled it over. "Well, Michael's got Cassian this weekend, and I am supposed to represent my family at this royal wedding in Malaysia on Friday. I could maybe fly from KL after the big banquet—"

"I'll have the plane ready and waiting for you."

"Khaleeda, the bride, is a good friend. I know she'll cover for me. I could say I had no choice but to stay all weekend for the festivities. I was roped in."

"And I'm at the end of my rope. I *need* to see you," Charlie pleaded.

"You're such a corruptor. Even back when we lived in London during our uni days, you've always made me do bad things."

"That's because I've always known deep down you want to be a bad girl. Admit it, you want me to fly you to India, shower you with gemstones, and make love to you all weekend in a palace."

"Well, since you put it that way . . ."

CHAPTER TWELVE

CHANGI AIRPORT, SINGAPORE

As Nick pushed his luggage cart into the arrival hall of Terminal 3, he saw a familiar face holding up a sign that read PROFESSOR NICHOLAS YOUNG, ESQ, PHD. Most people at the airport would have figured the guy with the sign—clad in a faded yellow ACS tank top, navy blue Adidas jogging pants, and flip-flops—as some surfer bum hired to be a substitute driver and not the heir to one of Singapore's biggest fortunes.

"What are you doing here?" Nick said, hugging his best friend Colin Khoo.

"You haven't been back since 2010. I wasn't going to let you arrive without a proper greeting party," Colin said cheerily.

"Look at you! Tan as ever and rockin' that man bun! What does your father think of this look?"

Colin grinned. "He detests it. He says I look like an opium addict, and if this was the 1970s and I arrived at Changi Airport, Lee Kuan Yew would personally come down to Immigration, grab me by the ear, drag me to the nearest Indian barbershop, and have me shaved *botak!*"*

---

* Malay for "bald-headed." For some reason, the word has also become popular as a nickname for little boys with crew cuts.

They took the glass elevators down to Level B2, where Colin's car was parked.

"What are you driving these days? Is this a Porsche Cayenne?" Nick asked as Colin helped him to load his luggage into the back of the SUV.

"No, this is the new 2016 Macan. It's not actually out yet until March, but they let me have this special test driver."

"Sweet," Nick said, opening the passenger-side door. There was a cashmere wrap on the seat.

"Oh, just throw that in the back. That's Minty's. She freezes whenever she rides up front. She sends her love, by the way—she's in Bhutan at her mother's resort, doing a meditation retreat."

"Sounds nice. You didn't want to join her?"

"Nah, you know how my brain works. I'm totally ADHD—can't meditate for the life of me. My form of meditation these days is Muay Thai boxing," Colin said as he backed out of the parking spot at what felt like sixty miles per hour.

Trying not to flinch, Nick asked, "So it sounds like Araminta's been feeling better?"

"Um . . . getting there," Colin said haltingly.

"Glad to hear that. I know things have been rough lately."

"Yeah, you know how it is—depression comes in waves. And this miscarriage really pulled her under for a while. She's trying to be good to herself, doing all these retreats, and she's cut back on work. She's seeing a really great psychologist now, even though her parents aren't thrilled about that."

"Still?"

"Yeah, Minty's dad made her doctor sign this gigantic stack of NDAs, even though you know all psychologists are already bound by a confidentiality code. But Peter Lee needed assurance that the doctor would never even admit that Minty is a client of his, or that she would ever need something as shameful as therapy."

Nick shook his head. "It amazes me that there's still such a huge stigma about mental illness here."

"'Stigma' implies that something exists but society is prejudiced against it. Here, everyone's in denial that it even exists!"

"Well, that explains why you're not locked up," Nick deadpanned.

Colin punched Nick playfully. "It's so great to see you, to be able to say this stuff out loud!"

"Surely there are other people you can talk to?"

"Nobody wants to hear that Colin Khoo and Araminta Lee have any kind of problems. We're too rich to have problems. We're the golden couple, right?"

"You *are* the golden couple. And I've seen the pictures to prove it!"

Colin scoffed, remembering the infamous fashion shoot for *Elle Singapore* where he dressed up like James Bond and Araminta was painted in gold from head to toe. "Biggest mistake of my life was doing that photo shoot! I'm never going to live that down. You know, I was taking a piss at the bathroom at Paragon the other day when the guy at the next urinal suddenly looked at me and said, '*Wah lao!* Aren't you that Golden God?'"

Nick burst out laughing. "So did you give him your number?"

"Fuck you!" Colin replied. "Strangely enough, guess who's been a good friend to Minty lately? Kitty Pong!"

"Kitty! Really?"

"Yes, she was the one who connected Minty to her psychologist. I think it's because Kitty's not a local—she doesn't have the same sort of baggage that we have, and Araminta feels like she can speak frankly with her because she's completely removed from our tight little circle. She didn't go to Raffles, MGS, or SCGS,* and she's not a Churchill Club member. She hangs with that foreign billionaire crowd."

"It's only fitting. She's Mrs. Jack Bing now."

"Yeah, I feel a bit sorry for Bernard Tai. As much of an idiot as he used to be, he did become a good father, from what I hear. But he totally got burned by Kitty. I don't think he ever saw that Jack Bing thing coming. Hey, what ever happened to that daughter of his?"

"Colette? Hell if I know. After she had Rachel poisoned, we made sure to steer clear of her. I wanted to press charges against her, you know? But Rachel wouldn't hear of it."

"Hmm . . . Rachel sure is a forgiving person."

"That she is. And that's why I'm here. I'm under specific orders to come back and make peace with Ah Ma."

"And is that what you want to do?"

Nick paused for a moment. "I'm not sure, quite honestly. Part of me feels like all this happened a lifetime ago. Our daily lives are so removed from everything going on here. On the one hand, I can't ever forget the way Rachel was treated and how my grandmother couldn't trust me, but on the other hand, her acceptance is kind of irrelevant now."

"Everything ends up seeming irrelevant in the face of loss," Colin said as he sped onto East Coast Parkway. "So am I taking you straight to the house, or do you want to grab a bite first?"

"You know what, it's so late, I probably should go straight to the house. I'm sure there will be food for us there. With every-

---

* Singapore Chinese Girls' School, which we ACS boys used to call Sucking Co—uh, never mind.

one in town, I think Ah Ching's kitchen staff must be churning out food nonstop."

"No problem. Tyersall Park, coming right up! I'm just going to visualize a hundred sticks of satay awaiting me there. You know, not to push you in any way, but I like your grandmother. She's always been good to me. Remember how I ran away from home after my stepmonster threatened to ship me off to boarding school in Tasmania, and your grandma let us hide out in the tree house at Tyersall Park?"

"Yeah! And every morning, she would make the cook send a big basket full of breakfast goodies up to the tree," Nick added.

"That's what I mean! All my associations with your grandma revolve around food. I'll never forget the *chee cheong fun* and *char siew bao* delivered on those bamboo trays, and the freshly baked *roti prata*! We were feasting like kings up there! When I finally got sent home, I wanted to find any excuse I could to run away to that little tree house again. Our cook was nothing compared to yours!"

"Haha! I remember you ran away from home so many times."

"Yep. My stepmonster made life so miserable. You only ran away once, if I remember correctly."

Nick nodded as the memory began to unfurl in his mind, taking him back to when he was eight years old . . .

They had been in the middle of dinner, just the three of them. His father, mother, and him, eating in the breakfast room off the kitchen, as they did when his parents weren't entertaining guests in the formal dining room. He could even remember what they ate that night. Bak ku teh. *He had poured too much of the rich, aromatic broth over his rice, making it too watery for his liking, but his mother had insisted he finish his bowl before she would let him redo it. She was more irritable than usual—it seemed like both his parents had been so tense for days now.*

Someone came speeding up the driveway, too fast, and instead of park-ing by the front porch like all the guests would, the car kept going until it reached the back of the house, stopping just behind the garage. Nick looked out the window and saw Auntie Audrey, his parents' good friend, emerg-ing from her Honda Prelude. He liked Auntie Audrey, she always made the most delicious nyonya kueh. Was she bringing something yummy for dessert tonight? She came bursting through the back door, and Nick saw immediately that Auntie Audrey's face was puffy and bruised, her lip bleeding. The sleeve from her blouse was torn, and she looked totally dazed.

"Alamak, Audrey! What happened?" His mother gasped, as several maids came rushing into the room.

Audrey ignored her, staring instead at his father, Philip. "Look what my husband did to me! I wanted you to see what the monster did to me!"

His mother rushed to Auntie Audrey's side. "Desmond did this? Oh my dear!"

"Don't touch me!" Audrey cried out as she crumpled to the floor.

His father stood up from the table. "Nicky, upstairs now!"

"But Dad—"

"NOW!" his father shouted.

Ling Jeh rushed to Nick's side and steered him out of the dining room.

"What is happening? Is Auntie Audrey okay?" Nick asked worriedly.

"Don't worry about her, let's go to your room. I'll play dominoes with you," his nanny replied in her soothing Cantonese as she rushed him up the stairs.

They sat there in his bedroom for about fifteen minutes. Ling Jeh had laid out the dominoes, but he was too distracted by the sounds coming from downstairs. He could hear muffled shouts and a woman weeping. Was it his mum or Auntie Audrey? He ran out to the landing and overheard Auntie Audrey shouting, "Just because you are Youngs, you think you can go around fucking anyone you want?"

He couldn't believe his ears. He had never heard an adult use the f word like that. What did this mean?

"Nicky, come back into the room at once!" Ling Jeh yelled, pulling him back into his bedroom. She shut the door tightly and began rushing around, hurriedly shutting the jalousie windows and turning on the air conditioner. Suddenly the familiar tock, tock *sound of an old taxi could be heard laboring up the steep driveway. Nick rushed to the veranda and leaning out he could see that it was Uncle Desmond—Auntie Audrey's husband—stumbling out of the taxi. His father came outside, and he could hear the both of them arguing in the dark, Uncle Desmond pleading, "She's lying! It's all lies, I'm telling you!" while his father murmured something and then suddenly, forcefully, raised his voice. "Not in my house. NOT IN MY HOUSE!"*

At some point he must have fallen asleep. He woke up, not knowing what time it was. Ling Jeh had left the room, and the air conditioner had been turned off but the jalousie windows were still closed. It felt stiflingly hot. He cracked open the door carefully and saw across the hallway the line of light underneath the door to his parents' bedroom. Did he dare leave his room? Or would they be shouting at each other again? He didn't want to hear them fighting—he knew he wasn't supposed to hear them. He was feeling thirsty, so he walked out to the landing where there was a refrigerator that was always stocked with ice and a jug of water. As he opened the fridge and stood in front of it, feeling the cool draft against his body, he heard sobs coming from his parents' bedroom. Creeping over to their door, he could hear his mother suddenly scream, "Don't you dare! Don't you dare! You'll see your name splashed over the front pages tomorrow."

"Lower your voice!" his father shouted back angrily.

"I'm going to ruin your precious name, I tell you! What I've had to put up with all these years from your family! I'm going to run. I'll run off with Nicky to America and you'll never see him again!"

"I'll kill you if you take my son!"

Nicky could feel his heart pounding. He had never heard his parents this angry before. He rushed into his bedroom, stripped off his pajamas, and threw on a T-shirt and his soccer shorts. He took out all the ang pow *money he had saved in his little metal safe box—$790—and grabbed his silver flashlight, tucking it into the waistband of his shorts. He went out the door leading onto the veranda, where a large guava tree arched over the second floor. He grasped hold of one of the thick branches, swung onto the tree trunk, and quickly shimmied down to the ground, as he had done hundreds of times.*

Jumping onto his ten-speed bicycle, he raced out of the garage and down Tudor Close. He could hear the Alsatians at his neighbor's house begin to bark, and it made him cycle even faster. He sped down the long slope of Harlyn Road until he reached Berrima Road. At the second house on the right, he stopped in front of the tall steel electronic gate and looked around. The concrete fence had glass spikes at the top, but he wondered whether he could still climb it, holding on to the edges and propelling himself quickly enough that he wouldn't get cut. He was still out of breath from his escape. A Malay guard came out of the sentry box next to the gate, astonished to see a boy standing there at two in the morning.

"What do you want, boy?"

It was the night guard who didn't know him. "I need to see Colin. Can you tell him Nicky is here?"

The guard looked momentarily perplexed, but then he went into his sentry box and got on the phone. A few minutes later, Nick could see lights come on in the house, and the metal gate began to slide open with a quiet clang. As Nick walked down the driveway toward the house, the porch lights came on and the front door opened. Colin's British grandmother, Winifred Khoo, who always reminded him of a plumper version of Margaret Thatcher, stood at the doorway in a quilted peach silk robe.

"Nicholas Young! Is everything all right?"

He ran up to her and breathlessly blurted out, "My parents are fighting! They want to kill each other, and my mother wants to take me away!"

"Calm down, calm down. No one is going to take you away," Mrs. Khoo said soothingly, putting her arms around him. The tension that had been bottled up all evening came out, and he began sobbing uncontrollably.

Half an hour later, as he sat on a barstool in the upstairs library, enjoying a vanilla root beer float with Colin, Philip and Eleanor Young arrived at the Khoo residence. He could hear their polite tones as they talked to Winifred Khoo in the drawing room downstairs.

"Naturally, our boy overreacted. I think his imagination got away with him." He could hear his mother laughing, speaking in that English accent of hers that she put on whenever she was talking to Westerners.

"All the same, I think he should probably just spend the night here," Winifred Khoo said.

Just then, another car could be heard pulling up the front driveway. Colin turned on the television, which flickered a security-camera screen that revealed a stately black Mercedes 600 Pullman limousine arriving at the front door. A tall uniformed Gurkha jumped out and opened the passenger door.

"It's your Ah Ma!" Colin said excitedly, as the boys rushed to the banister to peek at what was going on downstairs.

Su Yi entered the house, with two Thai lady's maids trailing behind her, and Nick's nanny, Ling Jeh, suddenly also appeared, clutching three big boxes of mooncakes. Nick figured that Ling Jeh must have alerted his grandmother to what had happened at his house. Even though she now worked for his parents, her ultimate loyalty was always to Su Yi.

Su Yi, wearing her trademark tinted glasses, was dressed in a chic rose-colored linen pantsuit with a ruffled high-necked blouse, looking as if she had just come from addressing the UN General Assembly. "I must apologize for inconveniencing you like this," he heard his grandmother say to Winifred Khoo in perfect English. Nick had no idea his grandmother

*could speak English so well. He saw his parents standing off to the side
with stunned, chastened looks on their faces.*

Ling Jeh handed Winifred the towering stack of square tin boxes.

*"My goodness, the famous mooncakes from Tyersall Park! This is
much too generous of you!" Winifred said.*

*"Not at all. I am so appreciative of your calling me. Now, where's
Nicky?" his grandmother asked. Nick and Colin ran back into the
library, pretending they had heard nothing until they were summoned
downstairs by Colin's nanny.*

*"Nicky, there you are!" his grandmother said. She put her hand on
his shoulder and said, "Now, say thank you to Mrs. Khoo."*

*"Thanks, Mrs. Khoo. Good night, Colin," he said with a grin, as his
grandmother guided him out the front door and into the Mercedes. She
climbed in after him, and Ling Jeh also got in, sitting on the folding seat
in the middle row of the stretch limousine with the Thai lady's maids. As
the car door was about to shut, his father came rushing out. "Mummy, are
you taking Nicky to—"*

"Wah mai chup!" Su Yi said sharply in Hokkien, turning away
from her son as the guard shut the door firmly.*

*As the car pulled out of the Khoo residence, he asked his grandmother
in Cantonese, "Are we going to your house?"*

"Yes, I am taking you to Tyersall Park."

"How long can I stay there?"

"For as long as you want."

"Will Dad and Mum come to see me?"

*"Only if they can learn to behave themselves," Su Yi replied. His
grandmother reached her arm out, drawing him closer, and he remembered
being surprised by the gesture, by the softness of her body as he leaned*

---

* Hokkien for "I couldn't give a damn."

against her while the car rocked gently back and forth as it navigated down the dark leafy lanes.

And now in a flash Nick found himself on that same dark lane again, more than two decades later, with Colin at the wheel of his Porsche. As the car wound along Tyersall Avenue, Nick felt like he knew every curve and bump of the road—the sudden dip that put them eye level with the gnarled ancient tree trunks, the dense overhang of foliage that kept it cool even on the hottest day. He must have walked or cycled down this narrow lane a thousand times as a kid. He realized for the first time that he was excited to be home again, and that the hurt he had felt over the past few years was fading. Without quite realizing it, he had already forgiven his grandmother.

The car pulled up to the familiar gates of Tyersall Park, and Colin breezily announced to the approaching guard, "I'm delivering Nicholas Young."

The yellow-turbaned Gurkha peered in the front window of the car at the both of them and said, "I'm sorry, but we're not expecting any more visitors tonight."

"We're not visitors. This is Nicholas Young right here. This is his grandmother's house," Colin insisted.

Nick leaned toward the driver's seat, trying to get a better look at the guard. He didn't recognize the man—he must have started working for Tyersall Park after his last visit. "Hey, I don't think we've met before. I'm Nick—they are expecting my arrival up at the house."

The guard turned around and went back into the guardhouse for a moment. He returned with a brown paper log and began flipping through the pages. Colin turned to Nick and snickered in disbelief. "Can you believe this?"

"I'm sorry, but I don't see either of your names here, and we are under high alert at the moment. I'm afraid I'm going to have to ask you to turn around."

"Look, is Vikram here? Can you please call Vikram?" Nick asked, beginning to lose his patience. Vikram, who headed the guard unit for the past two decades, would quickly put an end to this absurdity.

"Captain Ghale is off duty right now. He returns at eight tomorrow morning."

"Well, call him, or call whoever the on-duty supervisor is."

"That would be Sergeant Gurung," the guard said, getting out his walkie-talkie. He began talking in Nepali into the device, and a few minutes later, an officer emerged from the darkness, having come from the main guardhouse up the road.

Nick recognized him immediately. "Hey, Joey, it's me, Nick! Will you tell your friend here to let us through?"

The burly guard in the starched olive fatigues walked up to the passenger-side window with a big smile. "Nicky Young! It's so good to see you! What has it been? Four, five years now?"

"I was last back in 2010. That's why your compadre over here doesn't know me."

Sergeant Gurung leaned against the car window. "Listen, we are under specific orders here. I don't quite know how to put this, but we're not allowed to let you enter."

CHAPTER THIRTEEN

TWENTY-FOUR HOURS EARLIER . . .

"Three, four, five," Eddie counted as he stood by the window in the upstairs foyer, looking down the driveway. There were five cars in the motorcade—four, really, if you didn't count the minivan transporting all the maids bringing up the rear. Auntie Catherine and her family had just flown in from Bangkok, and Eddie was surprised there were so few cars in their convoy. In the lead was a white Mercedes S-Class with diplomatic license plates, obviously provided by the Thai embassy, but the other cars were a random assortment: a BMW X5 SUV behind the Benz, an Audi that looked at least five years old, and that last car, he didn't even have a clue what it was—it was some non-European four-door sedan, something that didn't register on his list of acceptable vehicles to be seen in.

Yesterday, when he had arrived with his family from Hong Kong, his executive assistant, Stella, had arranged a fleet of six matching Carpathian Grey Range Rovers, making for an impressive entrance as the Cheng *famille* pulled up to the front door of Tyersall Park. Today he felt almost embarrassed for Auntie Catherine and her clan. Her husband, M.C. Taksin Aakara,* was one of the descendants of King Mongkut, and Eddie remembered every detail of his last visit to Thailand when he was nineteen as if it were yesterday: The sprawling compound of historic villas set in a garden paradise on the banks of the Chao Phraya River; the way his cousins James, Matt, and Adam had three servants *each* that would prostrate at their feet as if they were little gods, ready to attend to their every whim; the fleet of forest green BMWs idling in the front courtyard ready to take them to the polo club, the tennis club, or any of Sukhumvit's hottest dance clubs; and Jessieanne, that sexy cousin of theirs who went down on him in the upstairs toilet of a pizza parlor in Hua Hin one night.

So why were the Aakaras pulling up in such a ragtag bunch of cars? And wait a minute—what the hell was happening outside? Sanjit the butler and the entire household staff—including the Gurkha guards—were all dressed in their crisp uniforms and assembling along the front driveway! And Ah Ling and Auntie Victoria were also part of the greeting party! Fucky fuck, why hadn't they done this for his family when they arrived yesterday?

Eddie was annoyed to see that his parents had gone outside too, and he was determined that he would under no circumstances join them. Thank goodness Fiona had taken the kids to the zoo, otherwise they would surely want to be part of this idiocy and make the Aakaras feel like they were truly hot shit. He ducked out of view and hid in the service hallway, waiting for

---

* M.C. is an abbreviation for Mom Chao, which translates to "His Serene Highness" and is the title reserved for the grandchildren of the King of Thailand. Since King Chulalongkorn (1853–1910) had ninety-seven children by thirty-six wives and King Mongkut (1804–1868) had eighty-two children by thirty-nine wives, there are several hundred people still alive who can use the title of Mom Chao.

everyone to come upstairs, knowing it was always the custom at Tyersall Park for guests to be served iced longan tea in the drawing room when they first arrived. Two waiters passed by rolling cocktail trolleys filled with glassware and large silver samovars of tea, mystified by Eddie lurking in the hallway. He glared at them and hissed, "You didn't see me! I'm not here!"

When Eddie began to hear voices coming up the stairs, he ambled into the drawing room with his hands nonchalantly tucked into the pockets of his salmon-colored Rubinacci trousers. Auntie Cat was the first to arrive at the top of the grand staircase, chattering away excitedly with his mother in that distinctive convent-schoolgirl lilt of hers.[*] "What a surprise to see you and Malcolm out front! I thought you weren't arriving until this evening?"

"That was the plan, but Eddie managed to fly all of us down on a private jet yesterday."

"*Wah, gum ho maeng!*"[†] Catherine remarked, as a waiter approached them bearing a silver tray filled with tall glasses of iced longan tea.

Eddie studied his aunt for a moment as she sat down on a divan next to his mother, marveling at how different the sisters looked. Auntie Cat's stocky, athletic physique was enviable for a woman in her seventies, and in such contrast to his other aunties with their bony, aristocratically malnourished frames. Unfortunately, she *did* take after her sisters in her fashion sense—on

---

[*]   Catherine Young Aakara, like many of the girls of her generation and social standing, attended the Convent of the Holy Infant Jesus Girls' School in Singapore, where they were taught by British nuns and developed the curious distinctive accents that made them all sound like extras in BBC period dramas.

[†]   Cantonese for "Wow, what a good life."

a charitable day, Eddie might have politely described her style as "eccentric." Today, she just looked god-awful in that boxy purple silk pantsuit, obviously tailor-made and obviously several decades old, mud-colored Clarks open-toed walking sandals, and the same pair of Sophia Loren bluish-tinted bifocals he had seen her wear for decades.

Catching sight of him, Catherine exclaimed, "My goodness, Eddie, I hardly recognized you. You look like you've lost a bit of weight!"

"Thank you for noticing, Auntie Cat! Yes, I've lost about twenty pounds in the past year."

"Good for you! And your mother tells me you flew the whole family down yesterday?"

"Well, I was attending the World Economic Forum in Davos as an official delegate and my client Mikhail Kordochevsky— you know, one of Russia's richest men—insisted that I borrow his Boeing Business Jet when he heard about Ah Ma's heart attack. And you know, it's such a huge plane, I thought it was a pity that I was the only passenger. So instead of flying straight to Singapore, we made a detour to Hong Kong so I could pick up the whole family."

Catherine turned to her sister. "You see, Alix, I don't know what you keep complaining about—your son is so thoughtful!"

"Yes, very thoughtful," Alix added, trying to block out the memory of Eddie screaming at her over the phone yesterday: *You have two hours to get everyone to Hong Kong airport or I'm leaving without you! My special friend is doing us a very special favor by lending us his very special plane, you know! And for God's sake please pack some decent clothes and jewelry this time! I don't want you to be mistaken for a Mainland tourist when I'm with you in Singapore! Last time we got such bad service at Crystal Jade Palace because of the way you looked!*

"How did you all fly down?" Eddie asked, wondering what kind of private jet the Aakaras had these days.

"Well, Thai Airways was running a special just for today. If you buy three economy tickets, the fourth person flies for free. So it was quite a savings for our whole lot. But then when we got to the airport and they realized it was your uncle Taksin, they upgraded us to first class."

Eddie couldn't believe his ears. The Aakaras never flew commercial—not since Uncle Taksin had become a special attaché to the Thai Air Force back in the 1970s. Just then, Eddie spied his uncle entering the drawing room alongside his father. It had been years since he had last seen his uncle, but he appeared not to have aged one bit—he was older than his father but looked about a decade younger. His perpetually tan face was wrinkle-free, and he still had that ramrod-straight posture and robust gait of a man accustomed to seeing and being seen. If only his dad wasn't getting so stooped, and if only he dressed more like Uncle Taksin!

Eddie had always admired his uncle's dapper style, and on visits to Bangkok during his teens, he made a point of sneaking into his uncle's closet and checking out all the labels on his clothes—no small feat when there were so many pesky servants lurking everywhere. Today Uncle Taksin was decked out in an impeccably tailored pale orange dress shirt—judging from the Sea Island cotton it was most likely Ede & Ravenscroft—worn with a pair of navy blue chinos and a highly polished pair of monk strap loafers. Were they Gaziano & Girling or Edward Green? He would have to ask him later. And most important, what watch was Uncle Taksin sporting today? He glanced at his sleeve cuff, expecting to see a Patek, Vacheron, or Breguet, but was horrified to see an Apple Watch strapped to his wrist. Dear God, how the mighty had fallen!

Behind Taksin came his son Adam, whom Eddie didn't know all that well because he was more than a decade younger. The baby of the family, Adam was slightly built and had delicately chiseled, almost feline features. He looked like one of those Thai pop idols, and seemed to dress the part in his skinny jeans and a vintage Hawaiian shirt. Eddie was not impressed. But wait a minute, who was this sexy thing that he would definitely swipe right for? Sauntering up the stairs was a girl with alabaster skin and waist-length black hair. Here at last was someone with style—the girl was wearing a sleeveless ice-blue Emilia Wickstead jumpsuit, blue suede ankle boots, and casually slung on her shoulder was the sort of handbag that Eddie was sure had a three-year waiting list. This must be Adam's new wife, Princess Piya, whom his mother couldn't stop gushing about after she attended their wedding last year.[*]

"Uncle Taksin! So good to see you! And Adam—long time no see!" Eddie patted his cousin on the back enthusiastically. Adam turned to his wife and said, "This is Auntie Alix's eldest son, Eddie, who also lives in Hong Kong."

"Princess Piya, it is an honor to meet you!" Bending forward, Eddie grasped her hand and bowed to give it a kiss.

Adam snorted almost imperceptibly, while Piya burst into giggles at Eddie's ridiculously overblown gesture. "Please, it's just Piya. Only the children and grandchildren of the king use any sort of formal titles. I'm just a distant relation."

"I do believe you're being very modest. I mean, you've been given the Pearl Suite!"

---

[*] To his eternal chagrin, Eddie had not been invited to his cousin's wedding to M.R. Piyarasmi Apitchatpongse. Only his parents had been invited to the small, intimate destination wedding held at a private villa in the Similan Islands.

"What's that?" Piya asked.

Before Eddie could answer, Adam cut in, "It's this bedroom where all the walls are inlaid with mother-of-pearl. Really remarkable."

"Yes, it's this vast suite of rooms, perfect for families, really. My wife and three children usually stay in there when we visit," Eddie couldn't help adding.

"Which room are you in now?" Adam asked.

"We're in the Yellow Room. It's very . . . cozy."

Piya's brow furrowed. "Adam, this doesn't sound right to me. We must move in to another bedroom so Eddie and his family can have this larger suite."

"But you're our honored royal guest! You must have the Pearl Suite. I didn't mean to imply anything with my comment. Constantine, Augustine, and Kalliste are having loads of fun sharing the same bed, and Fiona even managed to get three hours of sleep last night."

"Oh dear, I wouldn't feel comfortable in the Pearl Suite knowing that. Adam, could you take care of this?" Piya insisted.

"Of course. I'll have a word with Ah Ling the minute I see her," Adam replied.

Eddie smiled graciously. "You are both too kind. Now, where are your brothers? I thought the whole family was coming today. There's an eighteen-wheeler full of seafood awaiting them."

Adam gave him a puzzled look. "Piya and I were the only ones who came down with Mum and Dad. Jimmy, as you know, is a doctor, so he can't get away from work so easily, and Mattie is on a skiing trip with his family in Verbier."

"Ah. I was just in Switzerland too! I was at Davos, as an official delegate at the World Economic Forum."

"Oh, I was at Davos two years ago," Piya said.

"Really? What were you doing there?"

"I was giving a talk to IGWEL."

Eddie looked momentarily stunned as Adam proudly explained, "Piya's a virologist based at WHO* in Bangkok—she specializes in mosquito-borne viruses like malaria and dengue fever, and she's become one of the leading authorities on tropical diseases."

Piya smiled bashfully. "Oh, Adam's exaggerating, I'm no authority—I'm just part of the team. Now that man over there looks like he's an authority."

Eddie turned to see Professor Oon, still in his surgical scrubs, enter the drawing room. Catherine got up from her divan and rushed up to him. "Francis! So good to see you. How is Mummy today?"

"Her vitals are stable at the moment."

"Can we go in and see her now?"

"She's in and out of consciousness. I will let four visitors in, but two at a time and only for five minutes each."

Alix looked at her sister. "Go on. Take Taksin, Adam, and Piya with you. I've already spent time with her this morning—"

"I haven't seen Ah Ma yet today," Eddie cut in. "Dr. Oon, surely one more visitor won't make any difference?"

"Okay, I'll let you go in for a few minutes after the rest have come out, but only for a few minutes. We don't want to add any more strain to her today," the doctor said.

"Of course. I won't say a word."

"Eddie, will you say a little prayer for Ah Ma when you're in the room with her?" Auntie Victoria suddenly asked.

---

* The World Health Organization is a specialized agency of the United Nations that deals with international public health issues. The South-East Asia Regional Office is located in Bangkok.

"Em, sure, I can do that," Eddie promised.

The five of them headed down the corridor to Su Yi's private quarters. The sitting room adjoining her bedroom had been transformed into a cardiac care unit, with half the room turned into a clinical prep area and the other half filled with various medical machines. Several doctors and nurses huddled over a bank of computer screens, analyzing every blip in their VVIP patient's vital signs, while Su Yi's Thai lady's maids hovered just by the doorway, ready to spring into action should their mistress bat an eyelash. The minute they saw Prince Taksin approach, they dropped to the floor, prostrating themselves. Eddie felt his gut tighten in a mixture of awe and envy as he noticed that his aunt and uncle walked right past the ladies, not even noticing the gesture. *Fucky fuck, why couldn't he have been born into that family?*

While Catherine and Taksin went into Su Yi's bedroom, Eddie waited in the hallway with Adam and Piya. Taking the seat next to Piya on a velvet Ruhlmann settee, he whispered, "So, I take it you had an IGWEL badge?"

Piya was momentarily confused. "I'm sorry, are you referring to Davos?"

"Yes. When you were at Davos two years ago, what kind of badge did they give you? The white one with the blue line at the bottom, or the plain white one with the hologram sticker?"

"I'm afraid I can't remember what it looked like."

"What did you do with it?"

"I wore it," Piya replied patiently, wondering why on earth her husband's cousin was so weirdly fixated on this badge.

"I mean, what did you do with your badge after the conference?"

"Er . . . I must have either thrown it away or left it in the hotel room."

Eddie stared at her in disbelief. His Davos badge was folded and placed in a special pouch along with his prized Roger W. Smith* watch and his precious sapphire-and-platinum cuff links. He couldn't wait to get it framed the minute he returned to Hong Kong. He was quiet for a few moments before turning his attention to Adam. "So what are you up to these days? Do you work or do you just live a life of leisure?"

Adam felt like grimacing, but he was too well brought up to show any reaction. Why did so many people assume that just because he had a royal title, he didn't have to work for a living? "I'm in F&B.† I have a restaurant at Central Embassy, which is the newest mall in town, and I also have a few gourmet food trucks that serve authentic Austrian *Würstelstand* snacks like bratwurst, currywurst, and Käsekrainer. You know, those Austrian sausages filled with cheese?"

"A sausage truck! You actually make a profit from that?" Eddie asked.

"We do quite well. We park the trucks in all the nightlife spots around the city. People love to get a snack late at night after they leave the bars and clubs."

"The sausages help to soak up the alcohol," Piya added.

"Hmm. Drunk-people snacks. How lucrative," Eddie said with a not-so-subtle hint of condescension. He sat waiting for Adam or Piya to ask him what he did for a living when his aunt

---

* One of the most sought-after bespoke watches in the world, each Roger W. Smith watch is made by hand, takes eleven months to complete, and there's a four-year waiting list for one (probably five years after this is published).
† An abbreviation for food and beverage, currently one of the hottest industries in Asia. All the CRAs that used to work in M&A want to get in to F&B these days.

and uncle came out of the bedroom. "She's asleep, but you can go in," Catherine said to her son.

Catherine sank down on the settee next to Eddie, suddenly looking totally deflated.

"How is she today?" Eddie asked.

"Hard to tell. Francis said that with the morphine drip, she wasn't in any pain. I've just never seen her look so . . . so frail," Catherine said, her voice cracking a little. Taksin placed a comforting hand on her shoulder as she continued to talk. "I should have come down in November like I meant to. And the boys. Why didn't we make them come down more often?"

"Auntie Cat, you should go to your room and rest for a little while," Eddie suggested in a gentle tone. He became uncomfortable whenever women got emotional around him.

"Yes, I think that's a good idea," Catherine said, getting up from the settee.

"I'm going to call Jimmy and Mattie. We'll get them to fly over immediately. There's not a moment to waste," Taksin said to her as they walked off.

Not a moment to waste, Eddie thought to himself. But Auntie Cat had done nothing but waste her time. She had spent so many decades away, and his cousins hardly knew their grandmother. And now that Ah Ma was dying, they were finally going to show their faces? It was too little, too late! Or could there be another motive behind all this? Were the Aakaras tight on money these days? Was this why they came down on a commercial flight? He couldn't imagine the humiliation. A Thai prince, flying in economy class! And they only brought five maids with them this time. And Adam had to run these pathetic little hot-dog trucks. It was all beginning to make sense. Was Uncle Taksin urgently summoning all his sons to Singapore so they could get their hands on

Tyersall Park? Everyone knew that Nicky had been disinherited, and that Ah Ma would never leave any of the Leong cousins Tyersall Park when they already owned most of Malaysia. The only contenders left were the Aakara boys; his brother, Alistair; and *him*. Ah Ma had never thought much of Alistair, especially after he tried to bring Kitty Pong home, but the Aakaras, she always had a soft spot for them because they were half Thai. She loved her Thai food and her Thai silks and her creepy Thai maids—everything from that goddamn country! But he wasn't going to let those Aakaras win. They lived their lavish snotty royal lives and only deigned to come for short visits every three or four years, while *he* made a point of visiting his grandmother at least once a year. Yes, he was the only one who deserved the deed to Tyersall Park!

Adam and Piya emerged from the bedroom, and Eddie immediately went in—there wasn't a moment of *his time* to waste. Su Yi's canopied bed with its ornately carved art nouveau headboard had been replaced by one of those state-of-the-art hospital beds with an electronic mattress that constantly shifted the patient's body weight to prevent bedsores. Aside from the oxygen tube at her nose and a few tubes coming out of various veins on her arms, she looked so serene lying there under her sumptuous lotus silk bedsheets. A heart monitor on a stand pulsed quietly by her side, its screen displaying her ever-changing heart rate. Eddie stood at the foot of the bed, wondering whether he should say a little prayer or something. It seemed slightly absurd, since he didn't really believe in God, but he did promise Auntie Victoria. He knelt down beside his grandmother, folded his hands, and just as he closed his eyes, he heard a sharp voice say in Cantonese, "*Nay zhou mut yeah?*" What on earth are you doing?

Eddie opened his eyes and saw his grandmother staring at him.

"Fucky fuh . . . I mean, Ah Ma! You're finally awake! I was about to say a prayer for you."

"*Nay chyee seen ah!** Don't you start on me. I'm so sick of all these people trying to pray for me. Victoria kept sending that Bishop See Bei Sien to drone his idiotic prayers every morning when I was at the hospital, and I was too weak to chase him out at the time."

Eddie laughed. "If you want, I can make sure Bishop See isn't allowed to see you ever again."

"Please!"

"Were you awake when Adam and Piya came in?"

"No. Adam is here?"

"Yes, and he brought his wife. She's pretty, in that Thai sort of way."

"How about his brothers?"

"No, they aren't here. I'm told Jimmy is much too busy working to come down. I guess since he's a plastic surgeon, there are too many urgent face-lifts and nose jobs that require his attention right now."

Su Yi smiled slightly at Eddie's comment.

"And do you know what Mattie is doing?"

"Tell me."

"He's on holiday with his family. *Skiing in Switzerland!* Can you imagine? I happened to be in Switzerland too, attending a very important conference with the world's most important businessmen, political leaders, and Pharrell, but I dropped *everything* and flew straight to Singapore the minute I heard you were ill!" Eddie looked up at her heart monitor and saw that it was accelerating from 80 to 95 beats per minute.

---

*   Cantonese for "Have you lost your mind?"

Su Yi let out a brief sigh. "Who else is here?"

"Our whole family came down from Hong Kong. Even Cecilia and Alistair."

"Where are they?"

"Everyone's at the zoo right now. Fiona, Constantine, Augustine, Kalliste, Cecilia, and Jake. Ah Tock got them special VIP tickets for that River Safari thing, but they will be back by tea time. Uncle Alfred gets in later tonight, and . . . um, I'm told that Nicky is arriving tomorrow."

"Nicky? Coming from New York?" Su Yi muttered.

"Yes. That's what I hear."

Su Yi remained silent, and Eddie observed that the heart rate number on her monitor was rising rapidly: 100, 105, 110 beats per minute.

"You don't want to see him, do you?" Eddie asked. Su Yi simply closed her eyes, a lone tear streaming down the side of her face. Eddie glanced uneasily at the monitor: 120, 130. "I don't blame you, Ah Ma. Showing up here like this now, after all he's done to betray your wishes—"

"No, no," Su Yi finally said. Her heart rate suddenly jumped to 145 beats per minute, and Eddie looked at her in alarm. When the number hit 150, the heart monitor began emitting a high-pitched beep, and Professor Oon rushed into the room along with another doctor.

"She's elevating too rapidly!" one of the doctors said in alarm. "Should we defibrillate?"

"No, no, I'm going to give her a slow bolus of digoxin. Eddie, please clear the room," Professor Oon ordered, as two nurses rushed in to assist.

Eddie backed out just as his aunt Victoria entered the sitting room. "Is everything okay?"

"Don't go in now. I think Ah Ma's having another heart attack! I mentioned Nicky and she began to freak out."

Victoria moaned. "Why on earth did you mention Nicky?"

"She wanted to know who was here and who was coming. I can tell you one thing, though—Ah Ma does not wish to see Nicky. She does not even want him to set foot in this house! It was the last thing she told me."

CHAPTER FOURTEEN

Astrid stood on the balcony, breathing in the luxuriant scent that wafted up from the rose gardens below. From her vantage point at the Umaid Bhawan Palace Hotel, she had a sweeping view of the city. To the east, an impossibly romantic-looking fort perched on a mountaintop, while in the distance the tight clusters of vibrant blue buildings that made up the medieval city of Jodhpur gleamed in the early-morning light. *The Blue City*, Astrid thought to herself. She had heard somewhere that all the houses here were painted this shade of cobalt because it was believed to ward off evil spirits. The color reminded her of Yves Saint Laurent and Pierre Bergé's estate in Marrakech—the Majorelle Gardens—much of which was also painted a distinctive shade of blue, the only house in an entire city of rose ochre allowed by decree of the king to be painted a different color.

Astrid stretched out on the chaise lounge and poured herself another cup of chai from the silver art deco teapot. This monumental palace had been commissioned by the present maharaja's grandfather in 1929 to give work to all the people during a great famine, so every detail retained its original art deco style—from the pink sandstone pillars in the rotunda to the blue mosaic tiles in the underground swimming pool built so that the maharani could swim in complete privacy. The place reminded her a bit of Tyersall Park, and for a moment, Astrid felt an intense pang of guilt. Her grandmother lay in bed attended by a team of doctors while she was here, enjoying a secret weekend rendezvous at a palace.

Her guilt faded slightly as she caught sight of Charlie padding out onto the balcony clad only in his drawstring pajama trousers. When did he become so built? Back in their university days in London Charlie had been positively scrawny, but now his lanky torso took on that distinctive V-shape and his abs looked more ripped than she had ever remembered. He stood behind her as she lay on the chaise lounge, bending over and kissing that tender spot on her neck. "Morning, gorgeous."

"Good morning. Did you sleep well?"

"Now I don't recall getting any sleep last night, but I'm sure glad *you* did," Charlie teased as he poured a cup of coffee from the samovar set up on the chrome-and-glass trolley. He took his first sip and murmured in satisfaction, "Mmm. How great is this coffee?"

Astrid smiled placidly. "Actually, I'm sure their coffee is great, but I brought these beans. I know how much you love your first cup, so I had them ground for you this morning. It's Ethiopian Yirgacheffe from Verve Coffee in LA."

Charlie gazed at her in appreciation. "That's it. I'm kidnapping you and not letting you go back to Singapore. I'm never going to let you leave my side for . . . well, the rest of eternity."

"Kidnap me all you want, but you'll have to contend with my family. I'm sure my dad will send out a SWAT team if I don't turn up for breakfast at Nassim Road on Monday morning."

"Don't worry, I'll get you back in time, and you can even show up with a big tray of these parathas for breakfast," Charlie said, taking a bite out of the buttery, still-warm Indian layered bread.

Astrid giggled. "No, no, it has to be something Malay, otherwise they'll suspect. It feels like I'm playing hooky, but I'm so glad you convinced me to do this—I really needed it."

"You've been spending so much time at your grandmother's bedside, dealing with the family circus, I thought you could use a break." Charlie perched on the balcony's edge, looking down at an ornately turbaned man sitting on a pile of pillows in the middle of the grand terrace, playing a soft melody on his bansuri while a flock of peacocks wandered behind him on the great lawn. "Astrid, you need to come check this out. There's a flute player on the terrace, surrounded by peacocks."

"I saw him. He's been out there all morning. It's absolute heaven here, isn't it?" Astrid closed her eyes for a moment, listening to the enchanting melody as she savored the warmth of the sun on her face.

"Well, just wait. We haven't even toured the city yet," Charlie said with a sly gleam in his eyes.

Astrid smiled to herself, enjoying his impish little-boy expression. What was Charlie up to? He looked just like Cassian did whenever he was trying to hide a secret.

After they had enjoyed a classic Indian breakfast of akuri-spiced scrambled eggs on laccha paratha, chicken samosas, and fresh mango pudding on their private balcony, Charlie and Astrid walked to the front entrance to the palace. As they waited for the maharaja's Rolls-Royce Phantom II to pull up to the front steps, the guards started showering compliments on Astrid. "Ma'am, we've never seen anyone look so beautiful in jodhpurs," they praised. Astrid smiled bashfully—she was wearing a white linen tunic tucked into the new pair of white jodhpurs that had just been tailored for her. But instead of a belt, she had wound a long hand-beaded Scott Diffrient turquoise necklace through the belt loops.

They were driven in the vintage convertible to the Mehran-garh Fort, an imposing red sandstone fortress perched on a dramatic cliff four hundred feet above the skyline of Jodhpur. At the foot of the hill, they transferred into a small jeep that sped them up the steep road to the main entrance, a beautiful arched gateway flanked by ancient frescos known as Jai Pol, the Gate of Victory. Soon they were strolling hand in hand through the interconnected network of palaces and museums that made up the fort complex, marveling at the intricately carved walls and expansive courtyards that afforded commanding views of the city.

"This is incredible," Astrid said in a hushed voice as they entered an elaborate chamber where the walls and ceilings were made entirely of mirrored glass mosaic tiles.

"Well, they don't call this the most beautiful fort in Rajasthan for nothing," Charlie said.

As they strolled through a reception hall where every surface—from the walls to the ceilings to the floors—was painted in dizzyingly colorful floral patterns, Astrid couldn't help but comment, "It's so empty. Where are all the tourists?"

"The fort's actually closed today, but Shivraj had the place opened just for us."

"How sweet of him. So this fort belongs to his family?"

"Since the fifteenth century. It's one of the only forts in India that's still controlled by the original ruling family that built it."

"Am I going to get the chance to thank Shivraj in person?"

"Oh, I forgot to tell you—we've been invited to the private residence at Umaid Bhawan for dinner tonight with his family."

"Great. I wonder if they are related to the Singhs—you know, Gayatri Singh, our family friend who throws those fabulous parties where she displays all her jewels? Her father was a maharaja of one of the Indian states . . . though I can't recall which one at the moment."

"Maybe. I think many of the royal families of India intermarried," Charlie replied a little distractedly.

"Are you okay?" Astrid asked, noticing his change of mood.

"Yeah, yeah, I'm fine. There's this amazing room that I'm trying to find for you—I know you'll love it. I think it's up these stairs." Charlie led her up a steep staircase that wound around in a teardrop shape, and at the top of the stairwell they arrived at a long narrow room flanked by arched windows along every wall. In the middle of the room was a collection of golden baby cradles, each more ornate than the other.

"Is this the nursery?" Astrid asked.

"No, this is actually part of the *zenana*, where the ladies of the palace were cloistered. This building is called the Peeping Palace, because the ladies would come here and peep down on the activities of the courtyard below."

"Oh, that's right. The royal wives and concubines could never be seen by the public, could they?" Astrid leaned out a window framed by a distinctive Bengali-style eave, peeking through the little star-patterned holes in the screened window. Then she opened the shutters completely, taking in the view below of the grand marbled courtyard surrounded on three sides by palace balconies.

"Hey, do you want to get your hands painted with henna?" Charlie asked.

"Ooh. I'd love to!"

"The concierge at the hotel told me there's a henna artist here who does the most incredible work. I think she's in the museum gift shop. Let me go get her."

"I'll come with you."

"No, no, stay here and enjoy the incredible view. I'll get her and be right back."

"Oh, okay," Astrid said, a little puzzled as Charlie rushed off. She sat on a bench in the room, contemplating what it would have been like to be married to a maharaja back in the time when they were absolute rulers of their kingdoms. It would have been a life of unfathomable luxury, but she wasn't sure she wanted to be part of a harem with dozens of queens and concubines. How could she ever share the man she loved with someone else? And were the women ever allowed to wander beyond the palace walls, or even to step onto the elegant courtyard below?

Astrid heard some laughter in the distance, and she spied several women emerging through an arched doorway in the courtyard. How pretty they looked in their red-and-white lehenga cholis. They were followed by another row of women in the same tightly cropped blouses and flowing embroidered skirts, and soon there were about a dozen of them in the courtyard. The women walked single file in a circle as the sound of drumming began to emanate from deep within the fort. Suddenly the women formed a straight line right below where Astrid was standing. They flung their hands in the air, jerked their heads up at her, and began stomping their feet in rhythm to the drumming.

From the archways on the lower floor beneath where Astrid was standing, a dozen men in white came running out between the women to the far side of the courtyard. A Hindi pop song began blasting through the air, and the men and women danced opposite each other in a seductive face-off. They were soon joined by another dozen female dancers in vibrant blue-and-purple saris, streaming in from the north and south gates of the courtyard, as the music got louder and louder.

Suddenly the song stopped abruptly, and the window shutters on the opposite side of the courtyard flung open, revealing a man in a gold embroidered sherwani. He extended his arms toward Astrid, singing a cappella in Hindi. Then the music resumed as the dancers continued to stomp and twirl. Astrid burst out laughing, delighted at the Bollywood spectacle unfolding before her. *Charlie must be behind all this! No wonder he's been acting weird ever since we got here*, she thought.

The man disappeared from the turret, only to appear moments later in the courtyard leading a band of musicians. The entire troupe danced to the beat of the music, moving in perfect formation. She looked down at the handsome lead singer outfitted in gold, realizing with a shock that it was none other than Shah Rukh Khan, one of India's biggest stars. Before she could even react properly, the sound of trumpets filled the air, followed by a strange roaring sound. Turning to the main archway into the courtyard, Astrid's eyes widened in surprise.

Coming through the gate was an elephant festooned with gemstones and vibrant pink-and-yellow patterns painted onto its head, being led by two mahouts dressed in the full regalia of the royal court of Jodhpur. On the elephant's back was an ornate silver howdah, and perched majestically on one of its seats, dressed in a midnight blue paisley sherwani with matching trousers and turban, was Charlie. Astrid's jaw dropped, and she ran out of the room onto the open veranda. "Charlie! What's all this?"

The elephant strode over to her veranda, and she was almost at eye level with Charlie as he sat on top of the elephant. The mahouts guided the elephant so that it stood alongside the balcony, and Charlie leapt off the howdah onto the terrace where Astrid stood.

"I wanted this to be a surprise. I haven't wanted to tell you until now, but Isabel signed our divorce papers last week."

Astrid let out a little gasp.

"Yes, I am a free man. Completely free! And I realized that in all the craziness of the past few years, we've just talked about getting married as though it was a done deal, but you know, I never properly proposed to you." Charlie suddenly got down on one knee and stared up at her. "Astrid, you are and have always been the love of my life—my angel, my savior. I don't know what I'd do without you. My dearest sweet love, will you marry me?"

Before she could answer, the elephant let out another roar, and then curled his trunk upward to grab something from Charlie's hand. The animal then extended its trunk toward Astrid, waving a red leather box in front of her face. Astrid took the box gingerly and opened it. Sparkling inside was a five-carat canary diamond solitaire, encircled in a delicate floral scrollwork of white gold. It was an unusual setting, unlike anything that a contemporary jeweler might design.

"Wait a minute . . . this . . . this looks like my grandmother's engagement ring!"

"It *is* your grandmother's engagement ring."

"But how?" Astrid asked, utterly confused.

"I flew down to Singapore last month and had a secret date with your grandmother. I know how important she is to you, so I wanted to be sure we had her blessing."

Astrid shook her head in disbelief as she stared at the precious heirloom ring, covering her mouth with her right hand as tears began streaming down her face.

"So how about it? Are you going to marry me?" Charlie looked at her plaintively.

"Yes! Yes! Oh my God, yes!" Astrid cried. Charlie got up and embraced her tightly, as the crowd of dancers and musicians cheered.

The two of them walked downstairs into the courtyard, and Shah Rukh Khan bounded toward them to be the first to offer his congratulations. "Were you surprised?" he asked.

"My goodness, I'm still in shock. I didn't think I could still be surprised at this point in my life, but Charlie really pulled it off!"

In the euphoria of the moment, no one noticed the series of bright flashes coming from the highest turret on the southern end of the fort. It came from the sunlight glinting off the telephoto lens of a Canon EOS 7D, the camera favored by paparazzi and private detectives.

And it was pointed straight at Astrid and Charlie.

PART TWO

I made my money the old-fashioned way.
I was very nice to a wealthy relative right
before he died.

—MALCOLM FORBES

CHAPTER ONE

Wandi Meggaharto Widjawa was in London with her mother, Adeline Salim Meggaharto, supposedly to watch her nephew Kristian compete in a fencing tournament, but secretly they were both there for their triannual visits to the clinic of Dr. Ben Stork on Harley Street, who was considered by the most discerning filler addicts to be the Michelangelo of Botox. So deft were his hands at plunging needles into fine lines, fragile cheekbones, and delicate nasolabial folds, even his patients with the thinnest skins never bruised, and so subtle was his artistry that every patient visiting his clinic departed with the guarantee that they would be able to close both eyelids completely should they ever choose to blink.*

As Wandi sat in the elegant Hollywood Regency–style waiting room of the clinic in her floral embroidered Simone Rocha dress, waiting for her mother to get her usual combo of Botox®, Juvéderm Voluma®, Belotero Balance®, Restylane® Lyft, and Juvéderm Volbella® injections, she paged through the latest issue of *British Tattle*. She always flipped to the back of the magazine

---

* Smiling, laughing, frowning, or arching of eyebrows is highly discouraged, though.

first to look at the Spectator section, which featured party pictures from the only parties that mattered throughout the realm. She loved scrutinizing all the English socialites from head to toe—the women looked like either chic swans or unmade beds (there was no middle ground).

This month's Spectator section was quite disappointing—nothing but photos from the twenty-first birthday bash of yet another kid named Hugo, the launch party for yet another Simon Sebag Montefiore book, and some boring country wedding. She could never understand why all these aristocrats loved getting married in decrepit little English country churches when they could have the most lavish nuptials at Westminster Abbey or St. Paul's Cathedral.[*] Suddenly Wandi's eyes zeroed in on the obligatory photo of the bride and groom. As was the custom with all the wedding shots in *British Tattle*, the couple was pictured posing underneath the stone archway of the modest rectory festooned with a few anemic sprigs of roses, sporting painful grins as rice was being pelted at them. But the thing that stood out to Wandi was that the bride was *Asian*, and this immediately triggered an alert.

Wandi was part of a particular breed of Chindocrat[†] that had been raised in a very specific manner—the only daughter of an Indonesian Chinese oligarch, she was a typical third-culture kid who had grown up all over the world. Born in Honolulu (for the

---

[*]   What Wandi doesn't know is that the only people who can be married in Westminster Abbey are members of the British royal family, Order of the Bath members and their children, or anyone living in the Abbey's precincts. St. Paul's only allows weddings for members of the Order of Saint Michael and Saint George, the Order of the British Empire, holders of the British Empire Medal, and members of the Imperial Society of Knights Bachelor and their children (but not their grandchildren).

[†]   Chinese + Indonesian × Aristocrat = Chindocrat

American passport), her early childhood was divided between her family's hospital-wing-size house in Singapore and the historic family *joglo* in Jakarta, where she attended kindergarten at the exclusive Jakarta International School (JIS). In the second grade, she was sent to the elite Singapore American School (SAS) before an unfortunate fake-Prada-backpack-trafficking incident in eighth grade led to her expulsion and swift enrollment into Aiglon, the boarding school of choice for privileged rebels in Chesières-Villars, Switzerland. After Aiglon, Wandi spent two years majoring in marketing at the University of California at Santa Barbara before dropping out and marrying the son of another Indonesian Chinese oligarch, shuttling between homes in Singapore and Jakarta, having her baby at Kapiolani Medical Center in Honolulu, and going through the existential crisis of trying to decide whether to send her firstborn son to JIS, SAS, or ACS.*

Like most of the women who made up Asia's jet set, Wandi had an innate radar for OAWS—Other Asians in Western Settings. Whenever she was traveling outside of Asia and happened to be, say, lunching at Tetsuya's in Sydney, attending the International Red Cross Ball in Monaco, or hanging out at 5 Hertford Street in London, and another person of Asian descent happened to enter the room, Wandi would notice that Asian well before any non-Asian did, and their face would immediately be run through the ten-point social-placement scanner in her brain:

1. **What kind of Asian is this?** In descending order of importance: Chindo, Singaporean, Hong Konger, Malaysian Chinese, Eurasian, Asian American living in New York or

---

* She knew by age three that Hugo was too dumb to get in to Raffles.

Los Angeles, Asian American working in private equity
in Connecticut, Canadian Asian from Vancouver or
Toronto, Australian Chinese from Sydney or Melbourne,
Thai, Filipino from Forbes Park, American-Born
Chinese, Taiwanese, Korean, Mainland Chinese, common
Indonesian.[*]

2. **Do I know this OAWS?** Specifically, is this a famous actor/
   pop singer/politician/social figure/social media star/
   doctor/celebrity without portfolio/billionaire/magazine
   editor. Add 50 points if royalty or Joe Taslim. If Joe Taslim,
   have bodyguard slip him my room key.

3. **Do I know any members of this OAWS's family?** Have
   I met/attended school/socialized/shopped/co-chaired a
   gala/blown/backstabbed anyone related to this person?

4. **How much is this OAWS or his/her family worth?**
   Evaluate actual net worth against published net worth.
   Add 25 points if they have a family office, 50 points if they
   have a family foundation, 75 points if they have a family
   museum.

5. **Have there been any juicy scandals in this OAWS's or their
   family's past?** Add 100 points if it involved bringing down
   an elected official, political party, or BFF at the Olivier Café
   in the Grand Indonesia Mall.

6. **Does this OAWS or their family happen to own some
   fabulous hotel/airline/spa resort/luxury brand/
   restaurant/bar/nightclub that I could potentially
   benefit from?** Add 25 points if family owns a private island,
   500 points for a major movie studio.

---

[*] If they happened to be Japanese, Vietnamese, or any other type of Asian
not mentioned on this list, abort scanner function. Totally inconsequential.

7. **How attractive and stylish is this OAWS in relation to me?** Body-scan assessment in this order:

    For Ladies: face, skin whiteness, physique, jewelry, watch, handbag, shoes, outfit, hairstyle, makeup. Subtract 50 points if any gauche brands are visible, or for an obvious cosmetic procedure.

    For Gentlemen: hair density, watch, shoes, physique, rest of outfit. Subtract 100 points if wearing an Hermès "H" buckle belt, which only looks good on French or Italian men with deep tans and/or titles.

8. **How attractive, well-dressed, important, or famous are the white people that this OAWS is with?** Subtract 20 points if it's a business occasion with Americans in corporate attire, add 25 points if European, add 50 points if French or Italian with deep tans and/or titles.

9. **How many bodyguards in this OAWS's security detail?** Evaluate intimidation level of bodyguards, factoring in muscle mass, uniforms, any visible weaponry, quality of earpieces, type of sunglasses, and how noticeable they are in the current space. The more they look like trigger-happy brick shithouses ready to unleash their Sig Sauers on the dinner crowd at Nobu Malibu, the better.

10. **When was this OAWS or their family last profiled in their local edition of *Tattle*, *Pinnacle*, or *Town & Country*?** Add 100 points if they've never appeared in any magazines but you *still* recognize them.

At this point in her life, Wandi's social-placement test was so finely calibrated, it could evaluate a new Asian face in a matter of nanoseconds, thus determining to what degree Wandi felt prettier, richer, or more important than this OAWS, and what appropriate overture she felt comfortable making—whether it be stealth eye contact, a nod of recognition, the slight smile, or actually greeting the person in close physical proximity.

Of course at the present moment the OAWS in question only appeared in a rectangular two-by-three-inch photograph, but it was so highly unusual for an Asian face to appear in this setting—an English country wedding worthy of being featured in the Spectator section of *British Tattle*—that Wandi couldn't help but take notice. The text block in the middle of the page simply read:

WINTER WEDDING WONDERLAND

The unexpected snowfall didn't deter England's grandest from dusting off their furs and braving the icy roads for the wedding of **Lucien Montagu-Scott** at St Mary's, Chipping Norton. Naturally, the **Glencoras** were out in full force along with the **Devonshires**, the **Buccleuches**, and a smattering of **Rothschilds** and **Rochambords** from both sides of the channel. Many a girl mourned that Lucien aka #TallDrinkofWater was off the market, but no one could fault the bride, **Colette Bing**, whose porcelain-doll complexion and ravishing smile could warm all the frigid chapels in the Home Counties put together.

Wandi couldn't believe her eyes as she stared at the picture of the couple again. There was no way the bride in the simple, almost monastic high-necked wedding gown was the same Colette Bing she had seen splashed over all of Asia's tabloids. What happened to the signature swath of black eyeliner and her matador-red lipstick? This girl's face bore no evident traces of makeup, her lips ghostly pale. Where was the spectacular gold Giambattista Valli dress that she had commissioned for her wedding? And most important, why wasn't she wearing some glittering tiara?

Wandi dug into her Mark Cross white python handbag for her phone, quickly snapped a photo of the page, and sent it via WhatsApp to Georgina Ting, who was at that very moment lounging poolside at the American Club in Singapore, not watching her daughter splash around in the deep end of the pool.

WANDI MEGGAHARTO WIDJAWA: Check this out!!!

GEORGINA TING: Badly dressed Brits?

WMW: No, check out the bride!!!!

GT: OMFG!!! Where did you find this???

WMW: British Tattle!

GT: Colette's wedding was in BRITISH TATTLE?!? Wow, she really hit the Holy Grail! Did you send to Kitty?

WMW: No!!! I didn't want to be the one to upset her.

GT: Good thinking. Messenger always gets blamed. You don't want to risk losing your spa privileges on her plane.

WMW: At least with me what you see is what you get—if I'm being a bitch, you know it's because I hate you. Kitty is so unpredictable! You remember what happened at Giambattista Valli's atelier in Paris—she was so calm and collected and then suddenly she attacked Colette's wedding dress!

GT: Yeah. No wonder she didn't wear it—they probably couldn't repair it in time.

WMW: Still, I can't believe the dress she chose instead. What the hell? She looks like Fräulein Maria at the convent. She's unrecognizable! Do you think she had her face rearranged in Seoul or Buenos Aires or London?

GT: I think that's just how she looks with no makeup. I know that style ... she's going for the posh Brit look now. They all want to look like freshly exfoliated virgins on their wedding day.

WMW: This guy she married looks like a true blueblood.

GT: I thought he was some science nerd?

WMW: No, lawyer.

GT: Didn't you google him when we were all in Paris?

WMW: Tatiana did.

GT: Has Tatiana seen this?

WMW: Not yet.

GT: Gimme a sec ...

Georgina forwarded the photo on to Tatiana Savarin, and then started doing a bit of googling on her own. A few moments later, Tatiana, who was holidaying on the island of Mustique, answered back.

TATIANA SAVARIN: THAT'S who Colette Bing married?!?!

WMW: Can you believe it?

TS: Hottie McHotpocket! Doesn't look like a boring suit at all!

GT: Tatiana, you suck as a private eye. I just did some googling, and look what I found. Check out this link, ladies ...

From RANKMYPEER.CO.UK

Lord Lucien Plantagenet Montagu-Scott, Earl of Palliser, is the eldest son of the Duke of Glencora. In 2013, Tattle *listed him as one of the ten most eligible bachelors in Britain. According to the* Sunday Times Rich List, *the Duke of Glencora is the fifth-largest landowner in England, with*

*holdings in Northamptonshire, Suffolk, and Scotland. But
the crown jewels of their portfolio are vast property holdings
in Central London. Next to the Dukes of Westminster and
Portland, the Glencoras are London's leading landlords, owning
huge swaths of prime Bloomsbury and Chelsea. Furthermore,
Lucien's mother, Liliane, hails from the French Rochambords.
C'est formidable!*

TS: This must be new! It didn't pop up when I did a search
on him!

WMW: Holy fuck!

GT: Colette the future Duchess of Glencora! Kitty's going to
shit gold bricks if she finds out about this.

TS: What do you mean IF? I just sent everything to her.

GT: You what?!?

Suddenly, all three women's phones started buzzing as a group
call was being initiated from a Shanghai number.

WMW: That's Kitty calling!

TS: Should we pick up? She can see that we're all on a group
chat.

"Tatiana, you silly bitch," Georgina muttered under her breath
as she swiped her phone to initiate the group call.

"Hi Kitty!" Wandi said in an overly cheery pitch.

"Hi everyone. What's this you sent me?" Kitty asked.

"Um, did you look at the picture or look at the link I just sent?
Check out the photo. Don't bother looking at the other links,"
Tatiana piped in urgently. There was a brief pause while Kitty
scrutinized the picture on the screen of her phone.

"What am I supposed to be looking at? There's a bunch of gray-haired women with yellow teeth."

"You don't see the bride?" Wandi asked.

"No—"

Georgina cut in. "Kitty, scroll down to the bottom of the page. Do you see the image of the bride and groom?"

There was silence for a few moments, as the girls all held their breath, not knowing how Kitty would react.

"How interesting," Kitty finally said in a frighteningly neutral tone.

"Colette looks awful, doesn't she? Without her usual makeup and jewelry, she's such a plain Jane—her common features really come out." Wandi sniggered.

"She looks like she's fallen on hard times," Tatiana remarked.

Kitty let out a little laugh. "I can assure you Colette hasn't fallen on hard times. She's just trying to appear modest to impress her new relatives. They look like the sort of people Corinna Ko-Tung is always trying to introduce me to. Well, good luck to her and her new English life."

Georgina was relieved that Kitty was taking it all so well. She was crossing her fingers, hoping to God that Kitty had completely missed the articles about the bridegroom when Kitty suddenly asked, "So do we know anything about the Rochambords?"

Damn, she's read everything, Wandi said to herself.

"I've never heard of them." Georgina sniffed.

"Hey, I'm at this house party on Mustique right now, and there's a girl here who might know," Tatiana offered, adding rather unnecessarily, "She comes from a high-society family in France, from what I'm told."

Tatiana padded out onto the terrace of the Balinese-style

villa, where the girlfriend of her husband's business partner sat sipping black coffee out of a bowl. "Lucie, I'm on the phone with some friends. Have you ever heard of a family in France called the Rochambords?"

"Which branch?" Lucie asked.

"Um . . . I don't know. We know someone who married a guy whose mother is a Rochambord. Here, let me put you on speakerphone . . ."

"The mother's name is Liliane Rochambord," Georgina offered.

Lucie's eyes widened. "*Liliane de Rochambord*? Are you talking about the mother of Lucien Montagu-Scott?"

"Yes! Do you know him?" Tatiana asked excitedly.

Lucie shook her head with a sigh. "I don't know him personally, but my God, every girl in France was madly in love with him. I mean, he's a future *duc*, and his mother is one of the *Bretagne* Rochambords, not the Paris branch that are the poorer cousins."

"But who are the Rochambords?" Georgina pressed on.

"Oh, they are an *ancienne famille de la noblesse* . . . how do you say . . . an ancient noble family that intermarried with the Bourbons, and their line goes back to Louis XIII. The Paris branch has all the vineyards—you know, Château de Rochambord—but the Bretagne Rochambords own one of the biggest military defense companies in France. They make all the submarines and ships for the French navy. So who's your friend that married Lucien?"

"Colette Bing. But she's not our friend exactly," Tatiana said awkwardly.

"She's a socialite and fashion blogger from Shanghai that—" Wandi began.

"She's a spoiled little cunt!" Kitty suddenly blurted out.

Everyone was too shocked to speak at first, but Georgina tried to turn it into a joke. "Haha, yes, she's famous for that spoiled rant that went viral, isn't she, Kitty?"

The line went silent for a few moments.

"Uh . . . I think Kitty hung up," Tatiana said.

CHAPTER TWO

RANAKPUR, INDIA

Su Yi placed her hand on the white marble pillar and with her fingers traced the intricate carving of a goddess, feeling every undulating curve of the figure, so cool to the touch. The entire pillar was carved with figures of dancing damsels from the ground all the way up to the soaring dome. Su Yi looked around the space and saw that she was surrounded in every direction by thousands of white pillars, so many of them that it was impossible to count.* And every one of them had been sculpted with deities, animals, love scenes, war scenes—each one so painstakingly carved it looked more like lacework than stone. She could hardly believe how exquisite it was.

Su Yi felt so grateful that the maharani had arranged this trip

---

* Actually, there are 1,444 pillars in the temple, which also boasts 29 halls and 80 domes in a 48,000-square-foot area. Built by a wealthy Jain businessman named Dharma Shah, construction of the temple began in 1446 and took more than fifty years to complete. If you are ever in Jodhpur, please do yourself a favor and head to this amazing place instead of wasting your time and money buying cashmere throws from charming merchants who claim they were "handwoven exclusively for Hermès" (or Etro, or Kenzo) "in a nearby village that employs 800 women." They really weren't, and Richard Gere wasn't just there last week buying a hundred scarves either.

for her to the Adinatha Temple, hidden in the remote Aravalli Range between Jodhpur and Udaipur. As she followed the marble passageway, she felt as though she were walking into a dream, and around another corner of the temple she came upon a beautiful tree growing in the middle of a serene stone courtyard. Underneath the tree was a young man in a simple saffron-colored robe, picking up stray leaves. He glanced up for a moment and smiled at her. Su Yi smiled shyly back at him before walking into yet another breathtakingly carved vestibule, this one depicting a deity entwined with hundreds of snakes.

"Excuse me, do you speak English?" a voice behind her suddenly asked. Su Yi turned around and saw that it was the young man. This time, she could see a faint gold dot painted in the middle of his forehead.

"I do," she replied.

"Are you from China?"

"No, I am from the island of Singapore. It is in the Straits Settlements—"

"Ah, yes, on the tip of Malaya. There are a few Jains in Singapore. Please allow me to introduce myself: My name is Jai, and I am a priest here. My grandfather is the high priest of this temple, and one day my father shall be high priest, and then it will pass on to me. But not for a long time."

"You are very fortunate. This is the most beautiful temple I have ever been to," Su Yi said.

"May I offer you a blessing?"

"I would be honored."

The priest guided her along to a quiet corner of the temple that was open to the view. They sat on the steps of a marble altar and looked out at the undulating hills as a cool breeze blew into the chamber. The monk smiled at her again. "We do not often get visitors from Singapore at the temple. I noticed you when you first entered the temple with your chaperone, because you were so beautifully dressed, but when you smiled at me, I sensed a great sadness in you."

Su Yi nodded, lowering her eyes. "I am away from my family, and my island is at war."

"Yes, I have heard about the war spreading through southern Asia. I do not understand this war. But I sense that your sadness comes from a deeper place . . ." He gazed intently at her, and Su Yi noticed for the first time that his irises had an almost bluish gray tint to them. Suddenly she found her eyes welling uncontrollably with tears.

"My brother," Su Yi said almost inaudibly, her throat choking up. "My elder brother has been missing for some time." She had told no one about this, and she wasn't sure why she was telling him now. She was about to reach into her purse for her handkerchief when the monk produced one, seemingly out of nowhere. It was a silk scarf with a deep-blue-and-purple paisley pattern, and it seemed incongruous with the rest of his austere appearance. Su Yi wiped away her tears and looked up at the priest, who suddenly appeared to be wearing wire-frame glasses just like the ones her brother wore.

"Yes, your brother Alexander wants to tell you something. Would you like to hear his message?"

Su Yi looked at him, not comprehending what he meant at first. Before she could answer, the priest began to unleash a torrent of Hokkien: *Seven. Eight. Nine. Coming ashore. Bloody hell, there's too many of them. This won't work. This won't work at all.*

A chill ran down her spine. This was her brother's voice coming out of the priest's mouth, and he was muttering the same nonsensical things he had said when he had been deliriously ill.

"What won't work? Ah Jit, tell me, what won't work?" Su Yi asked urgently.

"I can't take that many. It's too dangerous. We have to move very quickly, and we can't fight back?"

"Ah Jit, slow down, who's fighting back?" Su Yi wrung her hands in frustration, feeling them get sticky. When she looked down at the silk paisley handkerchief, she saw that it was covered in a strange weblike mucus mixed with blood. Suddenly her brother stopped his incoherent ranting and spoke to her in a clear, lucid tone. "I think you know what to do now, Su Yi. Trust your instincts. This is the only way we can atone for all that our ancestors have done. You can never tell anyone, especially not Father."

In an instant, she knew what her brother meant. "How am I going to do all this by myself?"

"I have no doubt in you, sister. You are the last hope now . . . are you awake? Mummy, are you awake?"

Su Yi felt a hand on her shoulder, and suddenly she was no longer in that exquisite temple in Ranakpur, and the priest with the bluish eyes was gone. She found herself waking up in her bedroom at Tyersall Park, the morning sun glaring into her eyes.

"Mummy, are you awake? I've brought Bishop See to see you," Victoria said chirpily.

Su Yi let out a low groan.

"I think she may be in pain," Bishop See said.

Su Yi groaned again. *This irritating daughter just interrupted me from one of the most vivid moments in my life. Ah Jit was speaking to me, Ah Jit was trying to tell me something, and now he's gone.*

"Let me call in the nurse," Victoria said in a worried tone. "She's pumped so full of hydrocodone, she really shouldn't be feeling anything. They said there might be hallucinations, that's all."

"I'm not in pain, you just woke me up so suddenly," Su Yi muttered in frustration.

"Well, Bishop See is here to say a prayer for you—"

"Please, some water . . ." Su Yi said, her throat as usual feeling so parched in the morning.

"Oh yes, water. Now, let me see. Bishop See, could you do me a favor and go into my mother's dressing room? There are some Venetian glasses on a tray beside her dressing table, lovely handblown glasses with dolphin stems from a wonderful shop near the Danieli. Just bring me one of those."

"*Aiyah*, there's a plastic cup right here." Su Yi gestured to the bedside table.

"Oh, silly me, I didn't see that. Ah, Bishop See, do you see a water carafe by that table behind you? There should be an insulated silver carafe, with an art nouveau motif of stephanotis flowers carved along the handle."

"Just get me the goddamn cup," Su Yi said.

"Oh dear, Mummy, *language*. Bishop See is in the room," Victoria said, trying to hand over the cup.

"Do you not see that my hands are tangled up in tubes? You need to help me sip the water from the straw!" Su Yi said in frustration.

"Here, do allow me." The bishop stepped in and took the cup from a frazzled Victoria.

"Thank you," Su Yi said gratefully after she had taken a few precious sips.

"Now Mummy, Bishop See and I were speaking earlier over breakfast, and I was reminded that you've never been baptized. The bishop has kindly brought with him a little vessel of holy water from the River Jordan, and I'm wondering if we might do a ritual baptism right here in this room."

"No, I don't want to be baptized," Su Yi said flatly.

"But Mummy, do you not realize that until you are baptized, you can never enter the kingdom of heaven?"

"How many times do I have to tell you I am not a Christian?"

"Don't be silly, Mummy, of course you are. If you're not a Christian, you won't be able to go to heaven. Don't you want to be with Daddy . . . and *all of us* in the future that is eternity?"

Su Yi could not think of a worse fate than to be trapped with her *eem zheem** daughter throughout all of eternity. She simply sighed, tired of having this conversation again.

"Er, Mrs. Young . . . if I might ask," the bishop began gingerly, "if you aren't a Christian, what do you consider yourself to be?"

"I respect every god," she replied softly.

Victoria rolled her eyes derisively. "My grandfather Shang Loong Ma's people were Buddhists, Taoists, Quan Yin worshippers, all that mishmash of religions . . . you know, in that old-fashioned *Chinese* sort of way."

The bishop adjusted his collar, looking slightly uncomfortable. "Well, Victoria, we really can't force your mother to be baptized, but perhaps we can pray that she will allow Jesus Christ into her heart. We have to let Jesus come into her softly, gently."

"I don't need Jesus to come into me," Su Yi said agitatedly. "I am not Christian. If I'm anything, I'm a Jain."

"Mummy, what on earth are you talking about? What is a Jane? Are you confused and talking about your friend Jane Wrightsman?" Victoria asked, looking up at the IV machine to make sure her mother wasn't being overdosed with some crazy opiate.

---

*   Cantonese for "difficult, persnickety."

"Jainism is an ancient religion that is an offshoot of Hinduism—"* Bishop See began to explain.

Victoria stared at her mother in horror. "Hinduism? You can't possibly be Hindu. My goodness, *our laundry maids are Hindu!* Don't say you are a Hindu, Mummy—it would absolutely break my heart!"

Su Yi shook her head wearily and pressed the buzzer in her right hand. Moments later, her lady's maids entered the room. "Madri, Patravadee, please show Victoria out," she ordered.

"Victoria, come, we can say a prayer together outside," the bishop urged, glancing up at Su Yi's heart rate monitor nervously.

"Mother, you can't just order me out of your room like this. Your soul is in peril!" Victoria shrieked, as Alix entered the bedroom amid all the commotion.

Su Yi glanced up at Alix pleadingly. "Please tell Victoria to leave. She is irritating me to death!"

"All right then," Victoria said in a quiet voice, as she turned swiftly and stormed out of the bedroom.

Patravadee turned to Su Yi with an attentive smile. "Madame, your usual porridge this morning?"

"Yes. And tell them to put an egg in it today," Su Yi instructed. As soon as her lady's maids left, Su Yi let out a long sigh.

"She means well, Mummy," Alix said diplomatically.

"Why does she always have to be such a nuisance? And I can't stand that fat little *lan jiau bin*† See Bei Sien. You know he only

---

*   Actually, Bishop See is wrong about that. While Jains and Hindus agree on the concept of karma, the cycle of life and death, and some other aspects of emancipation, liberation, and release, they are two distinct and separate religions.
†   Hokkien for "dick face."

wants money for his cathedral building fund. Victoria writes him so many checks every month her account is always going into overdraft."

"Victoria may have her irritating ways, but she has a good heart. She is the most generous person out of anyone I know."

Su Yi smiled at Alix. "And you are always the peacemaker. Even when you were a little girl, you were always the one to heal the rifts between your sisters. Will you be sure to keep the peace after I'm gone?"

"Of course, Mummy. But don't worry—Prof Oon assures me your heart is improving every day. Even Malcolm said he's so pleased with your progress."

"That may be the case, but I know I can't live forever."

Alix didn't know what to say. She simply busied herself by straightening her mother's bedsheets and smoothing them out.

"Alix, you don't have to be afraid for me. I have no fear of death—you have no idea how many times I've stared it in the face. I just don't wish to be in any pain, that's all."

"Prof Oon is making sure of that," Alix said matter-of-factly.

"Alix, will you do me a favor? Will you call Freddie Tan and tell him to come over?"

"Er . . . Freddie Tan, your lawyer?" Alix asked, unnerved by the request.

"Yes. It's very important that I see him as soon as possible. His number is in the address book on my dressing table."

"Of course. I'll go and call him right now," Alix said.

Su Yi closed her eyes, attempting to relax for a moment. She was still trying to forget the look of hurt she had seen on Victoria's face after she had snapped at her. *Stupid girl!* The words came echoing back to her, from a memory far back in time . . .

"You stupid, stupid girl!"

Her father had snarled angrily when Su Yi had appeared in the basement of the shop house at Telok Ayer Street. "Do you know the fortune I spent, the number of favors I had to call in, just to get you safely out of Singapore? Why are you here?"

"Did you think I could just sit in the Taj Mahal Palace Hotel while I got news every day about all the terrible things that were happening back here? All the bombings, all the people being tortured and killed?"

"Which is exactly why I got you out of Singapore! On the last frigate out!"

"I didn't know what was happening here, Pa. I got news about everyone else—Tan Kah Kee, Uncle SQ, Uncle Tsai Kuen, but there was never any news of you. When Chin Tuan came to India, he said he hadn't heard any news about you. That's when I thought you had been captured or maybe even killed somewhere!"

"I told you you weren't going to hear from me. I told you I would be fine!"

"Fine? Look at you—hiding in a hole in the ground, dressed in rags!" Su Yi said, tears in her eyes as she looked at her father in his stained singlet and trousers full of cigar ash. She had never seen her father out of his three-piece suit before. With his head shaved and his face smeared with dirt, he looked almost unrecognizable.

"Silly girl! Don't you see I'm dressed like this on purpose? The only way to survive is to be invisible. I made myself look like an illiterate dockworker. The Japanese soldiers don't even bother to spit in my direction! Now how the hell did you get back into the country without getting yourself raped or killed?"

Su Yi gestured at the Thai silk dress she was wearing. "I crossed from India to Burma on the train, and then came down through Bangkok as part of the Thai ambassador's entourage—I'm disguised as a lady's maid to Princess Narisara Bhanubhakdi."

Shang Loong Ma let out a phlegmy laugh as he looked over his daughter.

On the one hand, he was furious at her for coming back to a war-ravaged island, but on the other hand, he had to admire her resourcefulness. She knew how to be invisible too, and she had proved herself braver than her brothers. "What are we going to do with you, now that you're back? It's too dangerous for you to go to Tyersall Park, you know." He sighed.

"I'm going back to Tyersall Park whether you like it or not! I'm going to stay there and do everything I can to help anyone who is suffering and in danger."

Su Yi's father scoffed. "The Japanese control everything now. Where on earth did you get such an idea that you could actually be of help?"

"A priest told me, Pa. A young priest at the most beautiful temple on earth."

CHAPTER THREE

In all his years of working for the Young family as the head of security, Captain Vikram Ghale never had to deal with a situation quite like the one he now faced. Standing before him at the gates of Tyersall Park was Philip Young, the only son of Shang Su Yi. This was the man who had interviewed and hired him for the job thirty-two years ago, and this was the man who should have been his future boss had he not foolishly incurred his mother's wrath two decades ago by inexplicably moving to Australia and losing his rightful inheritance of the house he had grown up in.

Normally, Philip Young's hunter-green Jaguar Vanden Plas would have been waved through the gates without any hesitation, but the problem was the man sitting in the front passenger seat—Nicholas Young, whom Vikram had known since he was a little boy. Until about five years ago, Nicky was his grandmother's favorite and the presumptive heir of Tyersall Park. He was, for all intents and purposes, the young lord of the manor. But now Vikram was under the strictest of orders not to allow entry to Nicky.

Vikram knew he had to handle the situation as diplomatically as possible. Knowing how mercurial his mistress, Shang Su

Yi, could be, there was still a chance that she could change her mind at the last minute and reinstate Nicky or Philip as heir to the estate. For heaven's sake, Philip's initials formed the shape of the elaborate boxwood labyrinth in the gardens, and Nicky's bedroom was still left unoccupied and untouched—exactly as it had been the last time he stayed there. Either of these men could very soon be his boss, and he mustn't offend.

"I'm so sorry, Mr. Young. You must see how my hands are tied. Please don't take this personally," Vikram said earnestly, casting an embarrassed smile at Nick.

"I understand. Tell me, who gave the orders?" Philip's tone was polite, but his irritation was apparent.

Eleanor flung the car door open and climbed out angrily. "Vikram, what is all this nonsense? Don't tell me we can't go in!"

"Mrs. Young, as I was just explaining to Mr. Young, you are both more than welcome to enter. But I am under strict orders not to allow entry to Nicky. I checked again after he first arrived the other night while I was off duty. They said no, absolutely not."

"Who are *they*? Who gave you the orders? Su Yi is a living vegetable right now—she couldn't have said a thing to you!"

"Beg your pardon, Mrs. Young, but Mrs. Young is not a living vegetable!" Vikram sputtered.

Nick rolled down the window. "Mum, Dad, why don't you both just go in and I'll—"

"Shut up, *lah*!" Eleanor waved her hand in front of Nick's face dismissively. "Vikram, how much money have you made on my stock tips over the years? Sino Land, Keppel Corp, Silverlake Axis. Hnh! I swear to God I am never going to give you a single tip again. I made you a rich man, and this is how you repay us? *Mangkali kow sai!"**

Vikram sighed, as he tried to find a way out of this quagmire. "Why don't I call up to the house again, and perhaps you can speak to Miss Victoria directly?"

Philip had reached the end of his patience. "No, Vikram, I've had enough of this. This is my house too, and I will not take orders from my little sister! If my mother does not want to see Nicky, she can tell me herself. He won't go into her room unless he's asked for. But I will not have my son waiting by the gates like some sort of beggar. Call up to the house if you want to, but we are *all* going in."

Philip returned to the driver's seat and revved the engine. Vikram stood in front of the gray wrought-iron gates with his arms crossed, as Philip inched the sedan slowly toward the gates until the front bumper was almost touching the imposing guard's knees. The other guards stood by, not sure what to do.

Five, four, three, two, one. Vikram counted in his head. Have I let this go on long enough? Philip was a decent fellow, and he knew he wouldn't get in trouble with him. As far as he was concerned, there was no real security risk to letting the three of them in. It was just a family quarrel, and now that he had done his duty and put on a good show, he was going to get out of the way. He side-stepped the car in one easy stride and ordered his men, "Open the gates!"

Philip jammed his foot on the pedal angrily and zoomed up

---

* Hokkien for "Bengali dog shit." However, Eleanor is technically wrong in her swearing, since Vikram—being a Gurkha—is Nepali, not Bengali. But to her, there are only two types of Indians: rich ones, like her friends the Singhs, and poor ones, like everybody else.

the gravel driveway at top speed. As the road curved toward the main approach to the house, the most curious sight unfolded before them. Assembled on the front lawn were several rows of wrought-iron chairs shaded by colorful silk parasols. Most of the family members staying at Tyersall Park—Victoria Young, the Aakaras, and the Chengs—were seated watching a doubles badminton match along with a few invited guests like Bishop See Bei Sien, Rosemary T'sien, and the Thai ambassador. Behind the seats, an elaborate ice-cream bar had been set up alongside a table dominated by an immense crystal punch bowl brimming with icy fruit punch.

Eleanor shook her head disparagingly. "So shameful! Your mother lies on her deathbed while everyone is outside having a garden party!"

"What are they supposed to do? Kneel all day by her bedside and chant prayers?" Philip asked.

"Well, the bishop is here! At the very least he should be inside praying for her instead of eating an ice-cream sundae."

"Mummy detests that man. The only reason he's here is because Victoria is still infatuated with him. She's been like this since their NUS* days."

"Oh my God . . . how come I never knew this? This explains why she's always so bitchy toward Mrs. See."

"Mum, haven't you noticed that Auntie Victoria is a bitch to anyone who doesn't have a doctorate in divinity?" Nick chuckled.

As the Jaguar pulled up to the circular driveway in front of the house, Nick could see Eddie Cheng and his brother, Alistair, battling it out with Uncle Taksin and Adam Aakara. Taksin, Adam, and Alistair were casually dressed in shorts and polo tees, but

---

* National University of Singapore.

Eddie was dressed completely in white—from his long-sleeved white linen shirt and white linen pleated trousers to his white lace-up wing tips. Nick chuckled as he noticed that Eddie's wife, Fiona, and their three children were also sweating away under the afternoon sun in white linen outfits with beige cashmere sweaters tied around their shoulders, no doubt at Eddie's behest.

As Philip, Eleanor, and Nick emerged from their car, the match came to an abrupt halt as the group assembled on the lawn stared at the new arrivals. For a moment, Nick wondered if his relatives were going to treat him differently now that he had been officially banished from Tyersall Park. His cousin Alistair dropped his racket and bounded over immediately. "So glad you're here, man," he said, giving Nick a big hug. Nick smiled in relief—he could always count on good ol' Alistair.

Following behind him came Catherine. Of the four Young sisters, she was the one who had always been closest to Nick's father, since they were barely two years apart in age and had been sent away to boarding school in England together.

"*Gor Gor*,"* she said warmly, giving Philip a quick peck on the cheek. "Did you just get in?"

"Hi, Cat! I arrived earlier this morning. Is the whole family here?"

"Just Tak, Adam, and Piya for the time being. The other boys are making plans to come down."

"I see it's Thailand versus Hong Kong. What's the score?"

"Five to two. Advantage Thailand. Eddie suggested the match, but he's not carrying his own weight. Alistair's admirably trying to hold up his end, but I don't think he realizes that Tak used to play on the Thai Olympic team."

---

*   Cantonese for "brother."

"Bloody hell! No wonder he's kicking my ass!" Alistair groaned.

Catherine gave Eleanor a kiss before glancing over at Nick. "It's good to see you, Nicky. Been far too long. Is Rachel not here with you? I can't believe I still haven't met her."

"No, it's just me," Nick said, giving his aunt a hug. Catherine looked into his eyes, wanting to say something, but Victoria marched up to their little cluster before she could continue.

"*Gor Gor.*" Victoria nodded curtly at her brother while fanning herself furiously with a carved wooden fan. Then she glanced at Nick and said, "I'm afraid you can't come into the house. Please don't take this personally."

"How am I supposed to take it, then?" Nick said with a wry smile.

Eleanor spoke up. "This is ridiculous! Why can't Nicky go into the house? He just wants a chance to say he's sorry to Mummy."

Victoria winced visibly. Even after four decades, she had never gotten used to her sister-in-law calling her mother *Mummy*. "Eleanor, tell me what I'm supposed to do? You of all people should know what my mother is like. I'm just following her wishes."

Philip looked at his sister skeptically. "Mum *specifically* told you she didn't want to see Nick?"

"Actually, she told Eddie."

"Eddie! My goodness! You actually believe him? Eddie has been jealous of Nicky since they were children!" Eleanor scoffed.

Hearing his name come up among the chatter, Eddie sauntered over to the group.

"Uncle Philip, Auntie Elle, let me be very frank. Three days ago, when I was with Ah Ma in her bedroom, I told her that Nicky was on his way home. I thought it would soothe her to know that he was coming to make amends, but instead she got so upset that she went into cardiac arrest. Auntie Victoria was right there when it happened. We almost lost her that day."

"Well, that was three days ago. I'm going up to see my mother now. She can tell me to my face if she doesn't wish to see Nicky," Philip insisted.

"You're *really* going to put Ah Ma's life at risk again?" Eddie said.

Philip stared contemptuously at his nephew, who was drenched in sweat, his clammy skin showing through in large blotches on the most unflattering areas of his white outfit. What a ridiculous boy he was, all dressed up like he was playing in a cricket match at Lord's. He didn't trust him for one second. "Eddie, let me worry about my mother. Perhaps you should be more concerned about your own children at the moment."

"What do you mean?" Eddie swung around and saw his children standing by the ice-cream bar with their cousin Jake Moncur. Constantine, Augustine, and Kalliste were happily licking away at cones topped with double scoops of ice cream, oblivious to the ice cream melting down their hands and dripping all over their white linen outfits.

Eddie broke into a sprint toward them as he began screaming, "FI! FIONA! LOOK WHAT THE KIDS ARE DOING! I TOLD THEM NO ICE CREAM IN THEIR BRUNELLO CUCINELLI LINENS!"

Fiona Tung-Cheng, who was huddled in conversation with Piya Aakara and Cecilia Cheng Moncur, looked up for a brief moment. She rolled her eyes and went right back to talking with the ladies.

With Eddie urgently marching his three children off in search of Ah Ling and the head laundress, Nick took his place in the badminton game while his parents went into the house with Victoria. "She's really not supposed to have any more visitors today," Victoria muttered as she led Philip and Eleanor down the corridor toward Su Yi's bedroom-cum-hospital suite.

"I'm not a visitor—I'm her son," Philip shot back in annoyance.

Victoria fumed silently to herself. *Yes, I know you are her son. Her only son. Mummy's made this abundantly clear to me my entire life. Her precious only son gets special bird's nest soup prepared for him every week all through his childhood while we girls only get it on our birthdays. Her only son has all his clothes tailor-made on Savile Row while we have to sew our own dresses. Her only son gets his own Jaguar convertible the minute he returns from university while the girls have to share one miserable Morris Minor. Her only son gets to marry whomever he wants no matter how common she is while every man I ever bring home is deemed "unsuitable." Her only son abandons her to live out his Crocodile Dundee fantasies in Australia while I'm forced to stay here and take care of her in her old age. Her precious only son.*

When they arrived at her mother's sitting room, Victoria started interrogating the nurses while Philip and Eleanor went into the bedroom. Alix was sitting in the armchair by her mother's bedside when they entered. "Oh, *Gor Gor*, you're here. Mummy's just fallen asleep. Her blood pressure was fluctuating too wildly, so they gave her a sedative."

Philip looked down at his mother, suddenly shocked by her appearance. When he had last seen her at Christmas, barely five weeks ago, she was still climbing on the ladder to the top of her star-fruit trees. But now she seemed so small in the hospital bed, so lost in the tangle of tubes and machines surrounding her. All his life, she had seemed so strong, so invincible, he couldn't even begin to fathom the possibility of her not being around.

"I think I'll spend the night here with Mum," he said in a quiet voice.

"There's really no point. She's going to sleep right through the night, and besides, her lady's maids take turns to be with her all night long in case she wakes up. The nurses also come in to check on her every half hour. Come back tomorrow. She's usually conscious for a few hours in the morning," Alix said.

"It doesn't matter if she's asleep. I'll stay with her," Philip tried to insist.

"Are you sure? You look like you could use a little sleep yourself—" Alix began.

Eleanor agreed. "Yah, *lah*, you didn't sleep much on your flight, did you? You look so run-down—I can see all the bags under your eyes. Let's go home and come back early tomorrow."

Philip finally relented. "Okay. But Alix, can you do me a favor? If Mummy wakes up anytime soon, will you tell her I was here?"

"Of course." Alix smiled.

"And will you tell her Nicky was here too?" Philip pressed her.

Alix hesitated for a moment. She was concerned that any mention of Nicky would upset her mother again, but she also felt that her mother needed to mend her rift with him. It was the only way she would truly close her eyes in peace. "Let's see. I'll try my best, *Gor Gor*."

CHAPTER FOUR

Anyone lucky enough to be a guest at Harlinscourt should wake in time to watch the sun rise above the gardens, Jacqueline Ling thought as she sipped the orange pekoe tea that had just been brought to her bedside on an exquisite bamboo tray. Propped up against four layers of goose-down pillows, she had the perfect view onto the pure symmetry of the box parterres, the majestic yew hedges beyond, and the morning mist rising over the Surrey Downs. It was these quiet moments before everyone began to assemble downstairs for breakfast that Jacqueline relished most during her frequent visits at the Shangs'.

In the rarefied stratosphere inhabited by Asia's most elite families, it was said that the Shangs had abandoned Singapore. "They've become so grand they think they're British" was the common refrain. Though it was true that Alfred Shang enjoyed a lifestyle that surpassed many a marquess at his six-thousand-hectare estate in Surrey, Jacqueline knew it would be a mistake to assume that he had transferred all his allegiances to queen and country. The simple truth was that over the decades, his three sons (all Oxbridge educated, naturally) had one by one taken English wives (all from appropriately aristocratic families, of course) and chosen to make their lives in England. So beginning in the early eighties, Alfred and his wife, Mabel, were compelled to spend greater parts of the year there—it was the only way they would get to see their children and grandchildren regularly.

Mabel, being the daughter of T'sien Tsai Tay and Rosemary Young T'sien, was far more Chinese in her ways than her husband, who was an Anglophile even before his Oxford days in the late 1950s. At Harlinscourt, Mabel set about creating a decadent domain that indulged her favorite aspects of East and West. To restore the nineteenth-century Venetian revival–style house built by Gabriel-Hippolyte Destailleur, Mabel coaxed the great Chinese decorative-arts historian Huang Pao Fan out of retirement to work alongside the legendary British decorator David Hicks.[*] The result was a ravishingly bold mix of modern European furnishings with some of the finest Chinese antiquities held in private hands.

Harlinscourt soon became one of those great houses that everyone talked about. At first, many of the Burke's Peerage crowd talked about how terribly vulgar it was for a Singaporean to buy one of the finest houses in Britain and try to run it "in the old way" with its mind-numbing number of staff and all the trimmings. But the landed gentry accepted their invitations anyway and after their visits grudgingly had to admit that the Shangs hadn't mucked it up. The restoration was splendid, the grounds were even more splendid, and the food—well, that was utter heaven. In the decades that followed, guests the world over began to covet their invitations because word got out that Harlinscourt's chef Marcus Sim—a Hong Kong–born prodigy who had trained with Frédy Girardet—was a genius in both classic

---

[*] The interiors were given a marvelous face-lift in the mid-1990s by David Mlinaric, coinciding with Mabel's own (much less marvelous) face-lift.

French and Chinese cuisine. And it was the thought of breakfast this morning that made Jacqueline reluctantly get out of bed.

She walked into the dressing room adjoining her bedroom and discovered a fire already burning in the fireplace, a vase of freshly cut Juliet roses arranged on the dressing table, and the outfit she had selected for the morning already hanging against the copper warming rack. Jacqueline slipped on her figure-hugging cream fit-and-flare sleeveless dress with iconic pointelle knit trim, marveling at how it had been warmed to the perfect temperature. She thought of weekends at other English estates, where the bedrooms felt like iceboxes in the morning and her clothes felt just as frozen when she put them on. *I don't even think that the queen lives this well,* Jacqueline thought, recalling that before Alfred and Mabel had moved in, her godmother, Su Yi, had sent a team over from Tyersall Park to help train the British staff properly. Asian hospitality standards were fused with English manor-house traditions, and even her boyfriend Victor had been impressed the last time he visited. Holding up his Aubercy dress shoes one evening as they dressed for dinner, he said in astonishment, "Honey, they fucking ironed my shoelaces!"

This morning, it was the chef's eggs that most astonished Jacqueline as she sat at one end of the immense dining table in the Grade II Heritage-listed breakfast room. "Ummmm. How is it that only Marcus can make scrambled eggs like this?" She sighed to Mabel as she savored another forkful.

"Doesn't your chef do good eggs?" Mabel asked.

"Sven's omelets are fabulous, and he can poach perfectly. But there is something about these scrambled eggs that are absolutely *divine*. Fluffy, creamy, and just the right amount of runny. I look forward to every visit because of them. What is the secret?"

"No idea—I never touch the eggs. But you must try some of this *yu zhook*.* It's made with Dover sole that was caught just this morning," Mabel said.

"It's the cream. Marcus uses the top cream made from our Guernsey cows in the scrambled eggs," twelve-year-old Lucia Shang piped up from the far end of the table.

"At last—*she speaks!* That's the first peep I've heard out of you all morning, Lucia. Now, what's this book you're so engrossed in? You're not still reading those *Hunger Games* vampire novels, are you?" Jacqueline asked.

"*The Hunger Games* isn't about vampires. And I stopped reading them ages ago. I'm reading *Siddhartha* now."

"Ah, Hesse. He's quite good."

"It sounds Indian," Mabel said, scrunching up her nose at her granddaughter.

"It's about the Buddha."

"*Aiyah*, Lucia, what are you doing reading about Buddha? You're a Christian, and don't forget that we come from a very distinguished long line of Methodists."

"Yes, Lucia, on your great-grandmother Rosemary's side— the Youngs—your ancestors were actually the first Christians in southern China," Jacqueline agreed.

Lucia rolled her eyes. "Actually, if it wasn't for missionaries running amok in China after England won the Opium Wars, we'd all be Buddhists."

"Shut up, *lah*! Don't talk back to Auntie Jacqueline!" Mabel admonished.

"It's fine, Mabel. Lucia's just speaking her mind."

---

* Cantonese for "fish porridge."

Mabel wouldn't let it go, muttering to Jacqueline, "*Neh gor zhap zhong syun neui; zhan hai suey toh say!*"*

"Ah Ma, I understand every word you're saying!" Lucia said indignantly.

"No you don't. Shut up and read your book!"

Cassandra Shang, Mabel's daughter (and better known by those in her circle as "Radio One Asia"), entered the room, cheeks still flush from her morning ride. Jacqueline did a double take. Cassandra's hair, normally parted down the middle and pulled into a tight coil at the nape of her neck Frida Kahlo–style, was rather uncharacteristically braided intricately along the sides but flowing free down her back. "Cass, I haven't seen your hair down like this in ages! This is a throwback to your Slade days. Looks marvelous!"

Mabel peered at her daughter through her bifocals. "*Chyee seen, ah!*† You're not a young girl anymore—it looks ridiculous."

Cassandra felt tempted to tell her mother that you could begin to see the face-lift scars through the thinning hair in her scalp, but she resisted. Instead, she chose to acknowledge Jacqueline's compliment. "Thanks, Jac. And you look ridiculously perfect as always. New dress?"

"No, *lah*! I've had this old rag for ages," Jacqueline said deprecatingly.

Cassandra smiled, knowing full well Jacqueline was wearing a one-of-a-kind Azzedine Alaïa. Not that it even mattered what she wore—Jacqueline had the sort of beauty that made anything she put on look drop-dead chic. Cassandra headed to the side-

---

*   Cantonese for "This half-breed granddaughter will be the death of me."
†   Cantonese for "so crazy."

board, where she helped herself to a single toast point, a dollop of Marmite, and some fresh prunes. As she took her seat opposite Jacqueline, a footman approached, deftly placing her morning cappuccino (made with small-batch, single-origin beans) and iPad next to her.

"Thank you, Paul," Cassandra said, switching on the device and noticing that her e-mail in-box was unusually full for this early in the morning. The first message came from her cousin Oliver in London:

> OTSIEN@CHRISTIES.COM: Have you seen the photos yet? Oy vey! I can already imagine what your mother must be saying…
>
> CASSERASERA@GMAIL.COM: Which photos?

While she waited for his response, an instant message came in from her sister-in-law India Heskeith Shang. Cassandra looked up from her iPad and announced to everyone, "India just messaged me—apparently Casimir has an opening for his photography at Central Saint Martins tonight and he didn't tell anyone. She's wondering if we want to go and surprise him? Lucia, your mother wants to know if you want to go up to London to see your brother's latest photos?"

"If it's going to be more pictures of his friends vomiting curry outside of pubs, I'm not interested," Lucia replied.

"*Aiyah*, don't talk like that! It's fine art. Casimir won an award for his photography last year," Mabel told Jacqueline, in defense of her favorite grandson.

Cassandra realized that Oliver must be talking about Casimir's photographs. "Well, I think these photos are going to be quite . . . daring. I just got an e-mail from Oliver, and apparently he's already seen them."

"Oh. Oliver's back in London? Is he going to come to the show too?" Mabel asked.

"I'm not sure, but India is now saying that Leonard can pick us up in the helicopter on his way from Southampton. We can all go to the opening together and then dinner at Clarke's."

"*Alamak*, another tasteless English dinner." Mabel groaned.

Cassandra checked her Facebook wall and let out a sudden gasp. "*Oh. My. God.*" She clasped her hands over her mouth, staring at the photos that flashed through on her iPad. Oliver wasn't talking about Casimir's silly little exhibit after all. *These* were the photos he was talking about.

"What are you looking at now? Another piece of dirty gossip from one of your unreliable *kang taos*?"* her mother asked derisively.

"Jacqueline, you need to see this!" Cassandra said, handing her the iPad. Jacqueline peered at the screen and saw an image of Astrid standing on a turret next to an elephant.

"I don't get it. What's the big deal?" Jacqueline asked.

"Oh, you're on the last photo. Scroll up. There's a whole series of photos."

Jacqueline waved her hand over the screen, her eyes widening as she scrutinized the images. "Are these real?"

"Looks pretty real to me," Cassandra chuckled.

"Dear me . . ."

"What is it?" Mabel asked.

Jacqueline held up the iPad, and from across the table, Mabel could see the blaring headline:

---

* Hokkien slang for "contacts" or "connections."

EXCLUSIVE PICS OF TECH TITAN CHARLES WU'S
LAVISH PROPOSAL TO GIRLFRIEND ASTRID LEONG—
BUT SHE'S STILL MARRIED!

"*Alamak!* Let me see! Let me see!" Mabel demanded excitedly. A footman wordlessly appeared at Jacqueline's side. She handed the iPad to him and he dutifully walked it over to the other side of the table where Mabel was seated. Lucia, clearly not as engrossed in *Siddhartha* as she pretended to be, rushed over to peer at the pictures with her grandmother, reading aloud:

"The ink hasn't even dried on Hong Kong tech titan Charles Wu's divorce papers yet, but this apparently didn't stop him from orchestrating an over-the-top marriage proposal to his gorgeous girlfriend Astrid Leong. The million-dollar proposal involved renting out the fairy-tale Mehrangarh Fort in Jodhpur, hiring more than a hundred musicians and dancers, and having Bollywood superstar Shah Rukh Khan serenade them while an elephant helped to deliver the ginormous diamond ring. Looking at the pictures, Astrid has obviously said yes, but there's one small problem—as far as we know, this highborn beauty is STILL MARRIED to Charlie's arch rival, the Singapore tech wünderkind Michael Teo."

Mabel squinted at the picture. "*Aiyah, hou sau ga!*[*] When were these taken?"

"Last weekend, it looks like," Jacqueline said.

---

[*] Cantonese for "so shameful."

"Last weekend? But isn't Astrid in Singapore with the rest of the family?"

"Obviously she snuck out of town with Charlie. My God, can you imagine how furious Felicity and Harry are going to be when they see this?" Cassandra said, shaking her head.

"Not only that, but this is a disaster for her divorce case. Michael's going to have so much new ammunition now. Poor Astrid!" Jacqueline sighed.

Mabel huffed, "Poor Astrid my foot! She should be at her grandmother's bedside instead of splashed all over the news! How dare that Charlie Wu propose to her again! The cheek of him . . . still trying to invade *our family*! I thought Felicity got rid of him years ago!"

"Oh Mother, those two have been in love since day one. If Felicity had let it happen the first time around, the whole Michael Teo disaster would never have happened!" Cassandra said.

"Felicity was right to put a full stop to that nonsense. Those Wus were completely unacceptable! That ghastly vulgar mother of his—I'll never forget what she did to me!"

"What did Irene Wu do to you?" Jacqueline asked.

Cassandra rolled her eyes. "That's ancient history, Mum. Please don't bring it up again!"

"That! Woman! Tried! To! Steal! My! Seamstress! I found this girl, Minnie Pock, who did the most wonderful tailoring. She had a little shop next to Fitzpatrick's on Dunearn Road, soooo convenient, and she could replicate all the Nina Ricci, Scherrer, and Féraud dresses I loved so perfectly."

"My goodness, Mabel, those Louis Férauds were fakes? They looked like they came straight from his Paris boutique!" Jacqueline lied.

Mabel nodded indignantly. "Yes, I had everyone fooled. But

then that Irene Wu came along and tried to hire the girl to work in their tacky 'mansion' full-time! So then I had to go and hire her full-time!"

"So you won?" Jacqueline asked.

"Yes, but it should never have happened. I had to pay Minnie Pock *almost fifteen percent* over what Irene offered to pay her!"

"It was 1987, Mum. Time to get over it," Cassandra said.

"People like the Wus . . . they never know when to stop. And now look what's happened? Once again they are dragging our family name into the mud. Who sent this article to you anyway?"

"Mrs. Lee Yong Chien posted it to her Facebook page," Cassandra replied.

"*Mrs. Lee Yong Chien is on Facebook?* I don't believe it! The old lady can't even draw her own eyebrows!" Mabel exclaimed.

"Rosie, that adopted daughter she treats like a slave, does everything for her! Ever since Mrs. Lee discovered Facebook, she's been posting like a fiend. Every other day there's either annoying photos of her grandchildren winning some award or pictures of some funeral she's attending."

"*Aiyah*, if Mrs. Lee knows about this, then the whole of Singapore will soon know. All her mah-jongg *kakis** will find out about this!" Mabel surmised.

"Ah Ma, I don't think you understand—this is on *Facebook*. The whole world can already see this," Lucia informed her.

Mabel tut-tutted sadly. "Then I truly feel sorry for Su Yi! This is happening at the worst time. I thought Astrid was her last hope, but one by one all her grandchildren have disgraced her.

---

* Malay slang for "mates" or "buddies." Although, should you really be calling the cheating scoundrels who try to screw you at every mah-jongg game your buddies?

How is she ever going to close her eyes in peace? No wonder she changed her will yet again!"

"*Really?*" Jacqueline and Cassandra gasped in unison.

Jacqueline sat bolt upright in her chair. "Is this why Alfred rushed back to Singapore?"

Mabel looked a bit flustered. "*Aiyah*, I'm not supposed to say anything."

"Say what? What did Dad tell you?" Cassandra prodded, leaning forward in anticipation.

"Nothing, nothing!" Mabel insisted.

"Mum, you are so bad at lying. You clearly know something. Come on, spit it out!"

Mabel stared down at her bowl of porridge, looking conflicted.

"Oh well, there's no use trying to force her. After all these years, your mother still doesn't trust us. So sad." Jacqueline sighed, giving Mabel her seductive, sideways stare.

"See what you've done? You've insulted Jacqueline!" Cassandra scolded her mother.

"Hiyah! You two! I know you are both such big mouths. If I tell you, you must promise not to say anything, okay?"

The two ladies nodded in unison like obedient schoolgirls.

Mabel, who had grown up surrounded by staff and usually spoke in her unfiltered manner with no thought to their presence, did the rare thing of making eye contact with George, the head footman, who immediately recognized her signal for privacy. George gestured quickly to the four other footmen, and they made a discreet exit from the morning room.

As soon as the door closed, Mabel said in a hushed tone, "I know your father had a big meeting with all the lawyers from Tan and Tan two days ago. Very hush-hush. And then Freddie Tan went off to see Su Yi. *By himself.*"

"Hmmm," Jacqueline said, digesting this intriguing new tidbit.

Cassandra winked at Jacqueline. "Don't worry—I'm sure you're still in the will!"

Jacqueline laughed lightly. "Come on, I am the *last* person to expect to be in Su Yi's will. She's already been so generous to me over the years."

"I wonder what she did this time?" Cassandra mulled.

"Well, until these pictures leaked, I actually thought Astrid might have a chance at inheriting Tyersall Park," Jacqueline theorized.

"Astrid? Never, *lah*! Su Yi is so old-fashioned, she would never leave that house to *a girl*! She might just as well leave it to her own daughters!" Mabel insisted.

"Then if it's just the boys, my bet is on Eddie. I hear that he's *really* been working overtime to be the number one grandson. He apparently won't leave her side!" Cassandra reported.

"I'm not sure it will be Eddie. Su Yi told me herself that she can't take him seriously," Jacqueline said.

"Well then she's running out of contenders. No way she would ever let one of the Leong boys get ahold of the house, but maybe one of the Aakaras?" Mabel wondered.

Cassandra snorted. "That would be too ironic for words! Would she really spite Philip and Nicky—the only true Youngs left—in favor of those foreign grandsons getting Tyersall Park? I think not."

"Maybe she's had a change of heart, then. Don't you think Nicky might have been reinstated?" Jacqueline said.

"Definitely not. He's still banned from the house! My sources tell me that he goes over there every day groveling on his knees, hoping to see her, but he still can't get in. Why would she suddenly give him Tyersall Park now?" Cassandra argued.

Mabel scrunched her face. "That stupid boy. Giving everything up for that ugly girl."

"Come on *lah*, Mabel, she's not ugly. She's quite pretty, actually. She's just . . . not the kind of beauty one would have expected for Nicky," Jacqueline remarked diplomatically.

"I know what you mean. Rachel is pretty, but in a very conventional way. Her lack of style doesn't do her any favors, either," Cassandra said.

Jacqueline smiled. "I wish I could tell her that she needs to grow out her hair by another four inches. That medium-long length is just so *American*."

Cassandra nodded in agreement. "And her nose is a bit too rounded. Her eyes could be a bit bigger too."

"And have you seen the way she sits? So frightfully common." Mabel sniffed.

"Uggh! I can't bear to listen to any more of this!" Lucia shrieked in anger, pushing her chair back dramatically. "You're all talking about Rachel as if she was some kind of show dog! What does it even matter what she looks like, as long as they love each other? Uncle Nicky gave up everything to be with her. I think that's sooooo romantic! I can't wait to meet her. And you're all wrong—I know what's going to happen to Tyersall Park, and it's certainly not what any of you think!"

"Shut up, Lucia! Stop making up stories!" Mabel scolded.

"Ah Ma, you and Auntie Cassie just chatter on and on about so much rubbish but none of you have a clue what's really going on! Do you ever listen to what Grandpa and Daddy talk about?" With that, Lucia stormed out of the breakfast room, the ladies staring openmouthed after her.

"What utter nonsense!" Cassandra scoffed.

Mabel shook her head gravely. "Can you believe how rude

that girl has become? I knew Bedales would be all wrong for her—those teachers do nothing but keep encouraging her confidence! My goodness, back in my day at the Convent,* if I had talked like that, the nuns would have beat me blue-black with a wooden ruler! *Neh kor suey neui moh yong, gae!*"†

Jacqueline's eyes narrowed. "On the contrary, Mabel—I don't think she's useless at all. I think you have a very smart little girl on your hands. Smarter than I ever realized . . ."

---

* Mabel, like many other well-born women of her generation, attended Singapore's venerable Convent of the Holy Infant Jesus. These days, the nuns have long since retired, and by most accounts, corporal punishment is no longer practiced.

† Cantonese for "This lousy girl is useless." (A refrain heard by Cantonese daughters since the beginning of time.)

CHAPTER FIVE

Godfrey Loh, the esteemed Supreme Court justice, could not believe what he was hearing in the stall next to his in the men's room of the Pulau Club.

"Yeah, that's so hot. Fucky fuck! I need a close-up. Send me a close-up, pleeeease."

What in God's name was happening?

"Wait a minute. The pic is still downloading—Wi-Fi's terrible in here. Oh my God . . . I'm looking at it now. *Phwoar!* So . . . fucking . . . sexy!"

Someone is looking at dirty pictures on his phone right next to me! But who is it? Sounds like a Hong Kong accent. No wonder, all the men in Hong Kong are perverts. That's what you get from a country when you can buy filthy magazines right in the airport!

"Looks like it's dripping wet. It's so beautiful I want to lick it all over! Come on, come on, I'm ready for it now!"

Is this creep actually engaging in phone sex in the next stall? Godfrey had heard enough. He emerged from the cubicle hurriedly and went over to the sink, washing his hands furiously with twice the amount of soap he would normally use. He felt dirty all over just listening to that heavy breather in the stall.

"I want to slip my whole foot inside."

He wants to do WHAT with his foot? This man should be arrested. Godfrey banged his fist against the stall door and said loudly, "You are a degenerate! A complete disgrace to this esteemed club! Take your dirty business elsewhere! Not in our toilets!"

Inside the cubicle, Eddie looked up from his phone, completely mystified. "Sorry, I have no idea what that was about. Some ranting weirdo—Singapore's full of them. Anyway, when will this last coat dry? Stop teasing me, Carlo. I need these shoes now!"

"Just a few more days. We are waiting for this latest coat of varnish to dry, and then we're going to add one more. Once the patina is perfect, we can overnight them to you in Singapore," Carlo replied.

"My uncle Taksin—you know, he's a Thai prince—I can't wait for him to see me in these. Taksin started wearing bespoke Lobbs when he was five years old. Nobody else will appreciate them like he would," Eddie said as he gazed longingly at the picture of his new custom-made Marini shoes. These tasseled loafers were glazed a deep lapis blue, a process that took up to four weeks to achieve in Marini's Rome atelier, and the shoemaker, Carlo, had been sending him teaser photos of the progress all through the month.

"You will have them by this weekend," Carlo promised.

Eddie ended his call, pulled up his pants, flushed the toilet, and walked back to the Lookout—the casual eatery with sweeping views of the nature reserve where Singapore's oldest and most exclusive country club was situated.* Returning to the table where members of his extended family had gathered for a luncheon hosted by his aunt Felicity, he asked his wife, Fiona, "Did you order me the beef satay and the chicken rice?"

---

* If you assumed that Eddie did not wash his hands, you would be correct.

"No one's ordered yet," Fiona replied, giving him a strange frown. It was then that Eddie noticed that no one at the table was talking, but all eyes were on Felicity. Her eyes were red and swollen with tears, and his mother, Alix, was busily fanning her with a menu.

"What happened? Is it Ah Ma?" Eddie whispered to Fiona.

"Hiyah! Ah Ma's fine, but Auntie Felicity just received some news that's quite upsetting."

"What news?" Eddie asked, irritated that he had only been in the toilet for barely ten minutes and somehow missed the whole first act.

His auntie Cat was now speaking in a low, soothing tone to Felicity. "If you ask me, this is all much ado about nothing. It's a slow news week, and the press just had to pounce on something."

"Just watch, Felicity, this will all blow over in a few days," Taksin agreed.

Eddie, who was seated in the middle of the long table, cleared his throat loudly. "Will someone please tell me what's going on?"

Alistair handed a cell phone over to him, and Eddie eagerly scrolled through the paparazzi pictures of Astrid and Charlie Wu in India, feeling his pulse begin to race. Oh boy oh boy oh boy. His always-perfect, goody-goody cousin had really stepped in shit at long last! What would Ah Ma think when she found out? One by one, all his cousins were falling from grace, and he was the last man standing. He stared at the hundreds of comments left by viewers of the leaked photos:

Wah! So beautiful. This is my dream engagement!
—AngMohKioPrincess

What a fucking waste! Outrageous that CRAs spend this much on one day when 75 million Indians still don't have access to clean water!—clement_desylva

Astrid is babelicious. Charlie Wu is the man of the hour! —shoikshoik69

Suddenly, those words sparked something in Eddie's mind that hadn't quite occurred to him until this moment. *Man of the hour*. Earlier in the week, his grandmother's lawyer, Freddie Tan, a senior partner at Singapore's most prestigious law firm Tan and Tan, had paid an unexpected visit to Tyersall Park. Aside from Bishop See, he had been the only nonfamily member allowed into the private sanctum of his grandmother's bedroom, and the distinguished white-haired gentleman had arrived with a smart-looking Dunhill briefcase and spent a rather long time behind closed doors with Su Yi. At some point during their meeting, Professor Oon and his associate doctor were summoned into the bedroom. Could they have been witnesses to the signing of a new will?

Eddie naturally hovered around outside her bedroom like a dog eager for scraps, and when Freddie Tan emerged, he studied Eddie from cravat to wing tips and said, "You're Alix Young's eldest boy, right? I haven't seen you since you were a teenager, and now look at you—man of the hour!" Freddie then proceeded to spend the next ten minutes chatting with Eddie, asking after his wife and which schools his children attended. At the time, it didn't occur to Eddie why a man who had never paid him any attention before was suddenly chatting him up like he was his biggest client. But now it dawned on him . . . did his grandmother make him the heir to Tyersall Park? Was this why Freddie was calling him the *man of the hour*?

As this epiphany was still settling in Eddie's brain, he suddenly heard Alistair saying, "You know, you really can't blame Astrid for this. How would she know that the paparazzi would be there? I'm sure she meant for this to be a very private moment."

Fucky fuck! Eddie thought irritatedly. What the hell was Alistair doing defending Astrid? Didn't he realize that they all needed to play this to their advantage, especially now when he stood to inherit the whole kit and caboodle. Eddie quickly cut in, drowning out his brother. "Auntie Felicity, I am so sorry you had to be put through this horrible scandal. What a disgrace!"

Alix scowled at her son, as if to say, *Don't make this any worse than it is!*

Victoria spoke up. "Actually, I rather agree with Eddie. This is a complete disgrace. I can't believe Astrid would be so careless."

Felicity pulled another piece of tissue out of her Jim Thompson silk pouch and sniffed into it dramatically. "My hopeless daughter! We have spent all our lives protecting her from the press, spent so much money protecting her from unwanted attention. And now look how she's repaid us!"

At the other end of the table, Piya Aakara whispered into her husband's ear, "I don't understand what the big deal is. Her daughter just got engaged, and the pictures look wonderful. Shouldn't she be happy for her?"

"I don't think Auntie Felicity approves of this fellow. And my family just doesn't like to see themselves in the press—ever," Adam explained.

"Not even *Tattle*?"

Overhearing Piya's comments, Victoria suddenly piped up, "Especially not *Tattle*. My God, that ghastly magazine! You know,

I wrote a few pieces for them back in the 1970s. But then one day the editor said my stories were too 'cultural'—yes, I believe that's the word he used. He said to me, and I'll never forget it, 'We don't need any more stories on emerging Chinese artists. We thought you were going to write about your relatives. That's why we hired you.' And that's when I gave my notice!"

Eddie continued to fan the flames. "It's one thing to be in *Tattle* or *Town & Country*—I'm featured in those magazines all the time. Full disclosure, Piya—Fiona and I have been on the cover of *Hong Kong Tattle* once, and I alone have been on the cover three times. But it's another thing to see Astrid's photos popping up on these *cheap gossip websites*. As if she's some actress or, even worse, a porno star. Like that Kitty Pong girl Alistair dated for half a minute."

Alistair was indignant. "For the millionth time, Kitty was not a porn star! It was some other girl who just looked like her!"

Eddie ignored his brother and kept on talking. "The thing I can't believe is that Astrid would dare to leave Singapore when Ah Ma is so sick. I mean, here we all are, spending every precious moment we have with her."

"She was supposed to be in Malaysia, representing us at Prince Ismail's wedding. I can't believe she deceived us like this! Running off to India, of all places. Getting engaged on an elephant! Who on earth does Charlie Wu think he is? A maharaja?" Felicity sniffed angrily.

"So vulgar. Those Wus are all the same—they haven't changed in all these years." Victoria tut-tutted, shaking her head. "Did you know that that horrid Wu woman tried to steal Mabel Shang's seamstress? Imagine the cheek! Thank goodness Mabel rescued that talented girl from her clutches! She made me several nice silk jacquard blouses, perfectly copying the style of this Liz Claiborne blouse Lillian May Tan brought back for me from America. I gave one to Mummy, which she loves, and didn't I give you one too, Cat, when I came to visit you in 1992?"

Catherine looked like a deer caught in headlights for a moment. "Oh yes, that's right . . . lovely!" she said, remembering that she had immediately passed on the hideous blouse to one of her maids.

Eddie furrowed his brow and tried to sound terribly concerned. "I saw Charlie Wu at Davos. You know, he didn't even have the decency to wear a proper suit and tie to the most important conference in the world! My God, what if Astrid and Charlie are on their way back to Singapore now? What if she wants him to meet Ah Ma? Or worse, to introduce his mother to Ah Ma? Can we risk upsetting Ah Ma when her condition is so fragile?"

"She wouldn't dare bring that man to Tyersall Park! Or his seamstress-snatching mother!" Victoria sniffed.

"She's not going to have the chance. I'm going to make sure that girl doesn't show her face anywhere near Tyersall Park!" Felicity angrily decreed.

Eddie tried to hide his satisfied smirk by looking at the view of the golf course for a moment. Nicky was banned from Tyersall Park, and now his biggest ally Astrid was banished as well. Things could not be working out any better if he had planned it himself. And let's not forget, his sexy-as-fuck bespoke Marinis were on their way too.

CHAPTER SIX

The fountain-blue Bentley Mulsanne pulled up by the front steps and a bodyguard jumped out of the passenger side to open the back door. As Araminta Lee Khoo emerged from the car in a sculptural ballerina-pink silk strapless Delpozo dress with a contrasting oversize yellow bow and pink sequined miniskirt, the paparazzi began clicking away furiously at her showstopping look.

"Araminta! Araminta! Look over here!"

"Can we have a fashion pose, please, Araminta?"

Araminta paused for a moment, pivoted expertly toward the photographer with one hand on her hip, her other hand showing off her exquisite Neil Felipp Suzy Wong minaudière, before proceeding up the red-carpeted steps.

Waiting at the freshly lacquered front doors of their mansion were Kitty and Jack. Kitty wore an explosion of powder-blue feathers courtesy of Armani Privé, and chose this occasion to debut her new diamond and antique Burmese cabochon sapphire earrings from Chaumet. Jack squirmed uncomfortably beside her in skinny black jeans and a shawl-collared white tuxedo jacket by Balmain that was made-to-measure but looked two sizes too small.

"Minty! You made it!" Kitty leaned over and gave her an air

kiss, as another set of photographers stationed by the front doors clicked away.

"My yoga retreat is practically right next door to you in Moganshan, so I thought it could do no harm to sneak away for just one night!" Araminta replied.

"I'm so glad you did. And now you finally get to meet my husband. Jack, this is my best friend from Singapore—Araminta Lee, er, I mean Khoo."

"Thank you for coming," Jack said stiffly.

"Fabulous to meet you! I feel like I know you already!" Araminta tried to give Jack an air kiss, but he tilted back reflexively as he saw the glossy red lips coming at him. Kitty prodded him sharply with an elbow and he quickly straightened up just in time to collide heads with Araminta.

"*Aiyoh!*" Jack groaned. Araminta appeared to see stars for a second, but quickly recovered and laughed it off.

"Please forgive my husband. He's just excited to meet you—he gets excited whenever he's around famous supermodels," Kitty gushed apologetically.

Araminta moved along into the house, while Kitty shot daggers at her husband with her eyes. "Don't you know how to do a perfect Euro-fashionista triple-cheeked air kiss? You almost gave her a concussion!"

Jack muttered under his breath, "Tell me why we're doing this again?"

"Honey, we were specially chosen by *Vogue China* to host the most exclusive party of Shanghai Fashion Week! This is the party all the most important *lao wais** are attending! Do you know how

---

* A derogatory term for Caucasians; in Mandarin it translates as "foreign/white/Caucasian."

many people would sell their servants' organs for this opportunity? Please stop complaining."

"What a waste of time . . ." Jack muttered under his breath.

"Waste of time? Do you even know who my friend is?"

"Some silly model."

"She's not just a model—she's the wife of Colin Khoo."

"No idea who that is."

"Oh come on, he's the heir to the Khoo empire of Singapore. And besides, Araminta is also the only daughter of Peter Lee. I'm sure you know who that is—he was the first Chinese billionaire in U.S. dollars."

"Peter Lee's old news. I'm worth exponentially more than him."

"You may have more money, but the Lees have more influence. Don't you realize I'm introducing you to the most influential people in the world?"

"These people make clothes. How are they influential?"

"You have no idea. These people control the world. And the cream of Shanghai society wants to be around them. Just think of who has showed up so far—Adele Deng, Stephanie Shi. And now the First Lady is about to arrive—"

"And it looks like Mozart came with her."

"Oh my God, that's not Mozart, that's Karl Lagerfeld. He's a very, very, *very* important man! He's the Kaiser of fashion."

"What the fuck does that even mean?"

"He is so powerful, he could simply flare one of his nostrils and have me banned from Chanel forever and I might as well be dead. Please, *please* be polite."

Jack snorted. "I'll try not to fart in his general direction."

After all the VVIP *lao wais* had been greeted, Kitty made her grand entrance into the house while Jack fled to his screening room until it was time for dinner. ("As long as you show up for my toast and tell Peng Liyuan how much you adore her singing at some point during the banquet, I don't care what else you do," Kitty had told him.) The whole party was actually an excuse for Kitty to show off the redesign of the house, and she stood on the top step of the former great hall—which she had renamed the Salon Grande—surveying the scene.

Gone was Colette's Zen-like Puli Hotel–inspired decor, and in its place, Thierry Catroux had created a look he called "Ming emperor meets Louis-Napoléon at Studio 54." Ming dynasty urns mingled with rare Aubusson carpets against sixties-mod Italian leather-and-Lucite furniture, while the monochromatic Shikumen gray brick walls were now covered in Tibetan yak hair dyed in shimmering shades of persimmon. The eighty-foot-long east wall had been covered with purple-and-crimson latticework screens—in homage to the Hall of Dispelling Clouds at the Summer Palace in Beijing. Colette's prized collection of black-and-white Wu Boli calligraphy scrolls had been banished to the museum wing, and in its place were enormous paintings of vibrantly colored canvases by Andy Warhol, Jean-Michel Basquiat, and Keith Haring in antique rococo gilt frames. Kitty's guests flocked to her side, gushing about the radical transformation.

"It's unbelievable, Kitty," Pan TingTing praised.

"So . . . original, Kitty," Adele Deng demurred.

"You've *really* put your stamp on the house," Stephanie Shi said and smiled.

"It's such a trip, all that's missing are the quaaludes!" Michael Kors[*] said.

---

[*]   Michael, *Project Runway* just hasn't been the same without you. Pleeeeeeeeease come back.

At some point during the social swirl, Araminta appeared at her side with a glass of champagne. "I thought you could use this. I can see you've been circulating nonstop."

"Oh thank you. Yes, everyone has been soooo nice, except for that awful Englishman over there talking to Hung Huang."

"Philip? But he's usually so charming!" Araminta furrowed her brow in surprise.

"Charming? Do you know what that snob said to me? When I asked him what he did, he actually dared to say, 'I'm a millionaire!'"

Araminta clutched Kitty's arm and doubled over in laughter. Trying to catch her breath, she said, "No, no, you're mistaken!"

Kitty continued her tirade, "So I said to him, 'Well, I'm a *billionaire*!'"

Wiping the tears of laughter away from her eyes, Araminta explained. "Kitty, that man is Philip Treacy. He's not a millionaire, he's a *milliner*—a hat designer. I'm sure that's what he told you. He's one of the best milliners there is—Perrineum Wang is wearing one of his hats right over there."

Kitty gazed at the young Shanghai socialite, who was sporting a gigantic flesh-colored disk with a bejeweled starfish of pink rubies in the middle that covered eighty percent of her face. "No wonder he gave me a strange look."

"Oh Kitty, you can always crack me up!" Araminta was still laughing when a pair of hands reached out from behind her and covered her eyes.

"Oh, who's this?" Araminta giggled.

"Three guesses," a man whispered into her ear in an extremely affected French accent.

"Bernard?"

"*Non.*"

"Er . . . Antoine?"

"*Non.*"

"Surely it can't be Delphine? I give up!" Araminta whipped around and saw a patrician-looking Chinese man in a three-piece suit and small round tortoiseshell glasses grinning back at her.

"Oliver T'sien, you rascal! You had me fooled with that ridiculous accent." Araminta giggled. "Oliver, have you met the chatelaine of this . . . er . . . magnificent estate, Kitty Bing?"

"I was hoping you'd introduce me," Oliver purred.

"Kitty, this is Oliver T'sien. He's an old friend from Singapore . . . and . . . aren't we somehow related now through Colin? Oliver is related to practically everyone who's anyone in Asia, and he's also the consultant at large for Christie's."

Kitty shook his hand politely. "It's a pleasure to meet you. You work for Christie's, the auction house?"

"Indeed I do."

"Oliver is one of the top specialists in Asian art and antiquities," Araminta continued.

"Hmm . . . there's a little horse sculpture in the library I would love to show you. My husband is convinced it's from the Tang dynasty, but I think it's a fake. His ex-wife bought it," Kitty said derisively.

"I am at your service, madame," Oliver said, extending an arm. They walked into the library, and Kitty led him to a magnificent Macassar and Gabon Boulle armoire in one corner. She pressed against the tortoiseshell-and-gilt-bronze marquetry doors, which opened to reveal a hidden entryway into Jack Bing's private cigar lounge.

"Well, this is quite splendid!" Oliver exclaimed, looking around the decadently upholstered room.

As soon as the doors closed behind them, Kitty sank into one of the tasseled velvet Louis-Napoléon smoking chairs and breathed a sigh of relief. "I'm so glad we're finally alone! How do you think it's going?"

Unbeknownst to any of her guests, and especially to friends like Araminta, Kitty knew Oliver rather well—he had been secretly advising her for the past couple of years and had been instrumental in helping her acquire *The Palace of Eighteen Perfections*, a set of prized Chinese scrolls that had broken auction records two years ago to become the most expensive Chinese artwork ever sold.

"You have nothing to worry about. Everyone is most impressed. Did you notice that Anna actually took her sunglasses off for a moment to scrutinize your Qianlong dragon vessel?"

"No, I missed that!" Kitty said excitedly.

"It happened so quickly, but it happened. I also spoke to Karl and—fingers crossed—I think you're getting front row at next season's show in Paris."

"Oliver, you're a miracle worker! You'd think spending nine million dollars a year at Chanel would be enough to get you a front-row seat at the damn fashion show."

"You'll be front row dead center next season! See? You have nothing to worry about. We should head back to the party before anyone suspects anything. We've been gone too long to look at one Tang horse. Which, by the way, is not fake but is frightfully common. Every drawing room on Park Avenue has at least one collecting dust on top of a stack of coffee-table books. Just throw it away, or give it to Sotheby's to auction off—some philistine will buy it."

As Oliver and Kitty were about to emerge from the hidden

cigar lounge, a trio of ladies entered the library. Oliver peeked through the crack in the armoire door and whispered to Kitty, "It's Adele Deng, Stephanie Shi, and Perrineum Wang!"

Stephanie could be heard saying, "Well, Kitty has certainly succeeded in removing every trace of Colette from the house. What do you think of this Picasso over the desk?"

"I'm so sick of seeing Picassos—every starter billionaire in Beijing has one. You know that in the last two decades of his life, the man was doing four paintings a day like some desperate whore? The market is flooded with mediocre Picassos. Give me a good Gauguin any day—like the one in my father's museum," Adele Deng said with a sniff.

"Colette's vision for this house was utter perfection, and now it's been ruined," Stephanie lamented.

"I don't care what anyone says—to me this will always be Colette's house," Perrineum chimed in.

Adele walked up to the Boulle armoire, tracing over the marquetry with her fingers. "This is actually a nice piece, but what the hell is it doing here in the corner? If you ask me, Kitty's trying so desperately to impress. Every single object in this house is a museum showpiece. Everything is screaming, 'Look at me! Look at me!' Kitty wouldn't understand the meaning of subtlety if it hit her on those fake breasts. As Marella Agnelli might say, 'It will take her another lifetime to understand wicker.'"

"Hiyah, what do you expect from a porn star? She will never have Colette's taste—you have to be born with it," Perrineum decreed, readjusting her gigantic hat for the millionth time.

"I wonder if we can sneak over to her bedroom wing. I want to see what she did with the space," Stephanie suggested.

"She probably put mirrors on the ceiling," Perrineum cracked.

"Louis XIV mirrors. Stolen from Versailles!" Adele cackled, as she followed the ladies out the door.

Perched in the corner of the cigar lounge, Kitty couldn't hide her look of devastation. "My breasts are *not* fake!" she cried.

"Don't listen to them, Kitty."

"Adele Deng told me the house was 'so original.' Why would she lie to my face like that?"

Oliver paused for a moment, thinking that Adele was right on one score—Kitty certainly didn't pick up on the subtler cues. "They're just jealous of all the attention you're getting. Ignore them."

"You know, it's not so easy to ignore those ladies. Adele Deng and Stephanie Shi—they rule the scene here. If this is what they're really thinking, I'll never be able to compete."

"Kitty, look—you've already conquered the world stage. These women aren't your competition anymore, don't you see?"

"I realize that, but I also realize something else. No matter what I do, this will always be known as Colette's house. And this will always be Colette's town, even though she's gone. She was born here—these are her people. I will always be an outsider in Shanghai, no matter what I do. Why did I even bother spending two years redecorating this house? I should be where people appreciate me."

"I couldn't agree more. You have houses all over the world, you can be anywhere you want to be, creating your own social universe. Honestly, I don't know why you don't live in Hong Kong full-time. It's my favorite city in Asia."

"Corinna Ko-Tung tells me it will take at least one generation for me to break into Hong Kong society—Harvard might have a chance if I enroll him in the right kindergarten, but it's already too late for Gisele. You know, the only place where Chinese people have ever treated me well is Singapore. Look how nice Araminta Lee has been. And my friends Wandi, Tatiana, and Georgina live there part-time too."

Oliver didn't want to remind Kitty that Araminta was actually born in Mainland China, and that neither Wandi, Tatiana, nor Georgina were native Singaporeans, but he began to see a new opportunity arise. "You know, you already own one of the most historic houses on one of the best streets in Singapore. I had assumed you'd spend more time there after you acquired it."

"I thought I would. But then I got pregnant with Harvard and Jack insisted that I give birth in the United States. And after that we just somehow spent more time in Shanghai because I needed to redo this house."

"But your poor Frank Brewer estate in Singapore is completely neglected. It's only half decorated. Think of what you could accomplish there if you focused your attention on it. Think of all the accolades you would receive from architectural preservationists if you truly restored it to its former glory. My God, I'm sure my friend Rupert would insist on doing a feature story for *The World of Interiors*."

The wheels in Kitty's head began turning. "Yes, yes. I could transform that little house. Make it even more spectacular than this cursed place! And it will be *one hundred percent mine*! Will you help me?"

"Of course. But you know, aside from the house, I do think it's time for *you* to undergo another radical transformation as well. You need a new look that will launch you into Singapore society properly. My God, the *Tattle* crowd will love you. Let's get you a photo shoot and feature story. Hell, I'm sure I can wrangle you the cover."

"You really think so?"

"Absolutely. I can see it already ... we'll get Bruce Weber to shoot it. You, Gisele, and Harvard, romping through your historic heritage property in Singapore surrounded by a dozen golden retrievers. All wearing Chanel! Even the dogs!"

"Um ... can we get Nigel Barker to shoot it instead? He's soooooo dreamy!"

"Of course, dear. Whoever you want."

Kitty's eyes lit up.

CHAPTER SEVEN

RESIDENCES AT ONE CAIRNHILL, SINGAPORE

The cook had brought home the most scrumptious Singaporean breakfast delicacies from the market. There was *chwee kueh*—delicately steamed rice-flour cakes topped with salty radish pickle and chili sauce; freshly grilled *roti prata*—crisp, buttery Indian bread served with a curry dipping sauce; *chai tow kuay*—daikon radish cakes pan-fried with egg, shrimp, and spring onions; and *char siew bao*—sweet barbecued-pork buns. As Eleanor and Philip gleefully unwrapped the brown waxed-paper packets of food, Nick entered the white Calacatta-marble-clad kitchen and padded toward the elegant diner-style banquette that had been glassed in so Eleanor's guests could enjoy a "chef's table" experience without having to worry about getting any of the smoky aromas on their expensive outfits or in their perfect coiffures.

"Oh good, you're up. Come, come, eat while it's still hot," Eleanor said, dipping a piece of her *roti prata* into the spicy coconut chicken curry.

Nick stood at the table, not saying anything. Eleanor looked up at him and saw the grimace on his face. "What's wrong? Are you constipated? I know we shouldn't have gone to that Italian restaurant last night. So overrated, and so awful."

"I rather enjoyed my linguine with white truffles," Philip commented.

"*Aiyah*, nothing special, *lah*. I could open a can of Campbell's Cream of Mushroom Soup and pour it over some noodles and you wouldn't even know the difference! Not worth the money, even if Colin did pay, and all that cheese always clogs up the system."

"I just can't believe you sometimes." Nick pulled out a chair and sat down at the banquette.

"What don't you believe? Eat a ripe banana, or I have some Metamucil if that doesn't work."

"I'm not constipated, Mum, I'm annoyed. I just got off the phone with Rachel."

"Oh, how is she?" Eleanor asked in a merry tone, as she spooned a heaping portion of *chai tow kuay* onto her Astier de Villatte plate.

"You know exactly how she is. You spoke to her yesterday."

"Oh, she told you?"

"She's my wife—she tells me everything, Mum. I can't believe you actually asked her what kind of birth control we use!"

"What's wrong with that?" Eleanor asked.

"Have you gone completely mental? She's not some Singaporean girl you can interrogate about every bodily function. *She's American*. They don't discuss things like that with just anyone!"

"I am not just anyone. I am her mother-in-law. I have a right to know when she's ovulating!" Eleanor snapped.

"No you don't! She was so appalled and embarrassed, she didn't even know what to say."

"No wonder she hung up so quickly." Eleanor giggled.

"This whole grandchildren business has to stop, Mum. We won't be pressured into having kids just because you want us to."

Eleanor banged down her chopsticks irritatedly. "You think I'm pressuring you? Hiyah, you don't know the meaning of pressure! When your father and I came back from our honeymoon, your darling Ah Ma commanded her maids to ransack our luggage! When she found our French letters,* she got so upset, she said that if I wasn't pregnant within six weeks, she would throw me out of the house! Do you really want to know what it took for me to get pregnant? Your father and I had to—"

"Stop, stop! Boundaries, please! I don't need to know any of this!" Nick groaned, waving his hand in front of his mother's face frantically.

"Believe me, I'm not trying to pressure you to have a child. I'm only trying to help you!"

"Help me how? By trying to ruin my marriage again?"

"Don't you see? I thought if we caught Rachel at the right time in her cycle, we could just fly her to Singapore. Auntie Carol already offered to loan her new Gulfstream G650—it's very fast and Rachel can be here in eighteen hours. She can even come this weekend. And my *kang tao* at Capella Resort can get me a nice ocean-view suite."

"And then what?"

"*Aiyah*, you do your job and get her pregnant, and we can announce it immediately. And then maybe, just maybe, Ah Ma will agree to see you!"

Nick looked at his father incredulously. "Can you believe this?"

Philip simply put a *char siew bao* on Nick's plate in a silent show of commiseration.

"Believe what? I am trying to do anything I can to get you into

---

* Women of Eleanor's generation—especially God-fearing MGS girls like Eleanor—were brought up using this quaint term for condoms.

that damn house! Your best chance now is to get Rachel pregnant. We need to prove to Su Yi that you can actually produce the next heir to Tyersall Park."

Nick sighed. "I don't think that's going to matter at this point, Mum."

"Hnh! You don't know your grandmother—she's so old-fashioned. Of course it will matter to her! It will restore you into her good graces. She will have no choice but to see you!"

"Listen to me, Mum. Rachel is *not* going to get pregnant just so I can see Ah Ma. That's the most ridiculous plan I've ever heard. You should stop all your ploys trying to get me into Tyersall Park. It's only going to make things worse. I've actually made my peace with the whole situation. I came to Singapore, I offered to visit Ah Ma. If she doesn't want to see me, I'll get over it. At least I tried."

Eleanor wasn't listening to him. Instead, her eyes narrowed as a new thought entered her head. "Don't tell me . . . hmm . . . Nicky, are you . . . how do they say it . . . robbing banks?"

Nick furrowed his brow in confusion. "Robbing banks? What do you mean? I do all my banking online these days, Mum."

"*Aiyah*, when was the last time you went to see the doctor? Do you have a good urologist in New York?" Eleanor demanded.

Philip chuckled, realizing what his wife was talking about. "She means *shooting blanks*, Nicky."

"Yes, yes, shooting blanks! Have you ever checked your sperm count? You used to play around with so many girls when you were younger, maybe you used all your good sperm up."

"Oh my God, Mum. Oh my God." Nick put his hand to his forehead and shook his head, completely mortified.

"Don't 'oh my God' me. I'm dead serious," Eleanor said indignantly as she chewed.

Nick got up from the table in a huff. "I'm not going to answer any more of these questions. It's so weird and inappropriate! And don't you dare bring any of this up with Rachel either. Have some respect for our privacy!"

"Okay *lah*, okay *lah*. Don't be so sensitive. I wish we hadn't sent you to school in England, I don't know what kind of man they turned you into over there. Everything is so private-private with you, even medical issues. You're my son—I've watched your nannies change your diapers, you know! Now, aren't you going to eat any of the food we bought? The *chwee kueh* is extra good today," Eleanor said.

"Not only have I completely lost my appetite but I'm going to meet Astrid for breakfast."

"*Aiyah*, that poor girl. Did you read the latest gossip this morning?"

"No, Mum. I don't pay attention to silly gossip," Nick replied as he stormed out.

CHAPTER EIGHT

EMERALD HILL, SINGAPORE

Since separating from Michael, Astrid had moved in to one of the heritage shop houses on Emerald Hill Road that she had inherited from her great-aunt Mathilda Leong. As Nick strolled down the street toward her place, he couldn't help but stop along the way and admire some of the ornamental friezes, timber-framed windows, and elaborate entrance gates on the beautifully restored Peranakan-style terrace homes that made this street so unique.* No two façades were alike—each one blended different elements of Chinese baroque, late-Victorian, and art deco details.

When Nick was a child, many of these shop houses where old Peranakan families lived and worked had fallen into neglect and the street had an air of faded grandeur, but now that real estate prices had shot up to absurd levels and the neighborhood had

---

* Originally an area of orchards and nutmeg plantations during the colonial era, Emerald Hill was developed into a residential neighborhood for Peranakan families in the early twentieth century. These Peranakans—or Straits Chinese, the term that was used for them in the era—were English educated (many of them at Oxford and Cambridge) and intensely loyal to the British colonial government. Serving as the middlemen between the British and Chinese, they grew rich and powerful as a result, as was clearly evidenced in the opulent shop houses they built.

been designated a conservation area, these houses had become highly coveted properties going for tens of millions. Many of them had been turned into hip bars or sidewalk cafés, leading some of Nick's snootier relatives to derisively refer to Emerald Hill Road as "that street where all the *ang mor kow sai* go to *leem tzhiu*,"* but Nick found it all rather charming. Arriving at a handsome white shop house with smoky gray shutters, he stopped and rang the doorbell.

A blond girl in her early twenties peered over the *pintu pagar*—an ornately carved wooden half door that was a typical feature of such houses—and asked in a heavy French accent, "Are you *Nicolas*?"

Nick nodded, and she slid the lock open to allow him to enter. "I'm Ludivine, Cassian's au pair," she said.

"*Salut, Ludivine. Ça va?*" Nick said with a smile.

"*Comme ci, comme ça,*" Ludivine replied coquettishly, wondering why she'd never met madame's hottie French-speaking cousin before.

Stepping into the front foyer, Nick could see that the room had been painstakingly restored to its original style. The floor was an elaborate mosaic of ceramic tiles painted in a William Morris–esque floral pattern, and intricately carved gilt wood screens created a partition between the front room and the rest of the house beyond. The centerpiece of a typical Peranakan front room was the ancestral shrine, and Astrid had honored the tradition by installing an elaborate Victorian altarpiece against

---

* Although the Hokkien phrase literally translates to "redhaired dog shit go to drink alcohol," it can be interpreted as "that street where the Eurotrash go to get drunk."

the back wall. But instead of placing pictures of dead relatives or porcelain gods within the altar, she had cheekily hung a small Egon Schiele drawing of a nude male figure inside.

Ludivine led Nick from the front foyer through a darkened antechamber into the *chimchay*—the open courtyard exposed to the sky that provided the natural ventilation and lighting essential to these long, narrow shop houses. Here, Astrid had departed from tradition and completely transformed the space: The roof had been glassed in and the entire space air-conditioned, while the usual concrete floor was now covered in obsidian black tiles, making it shimmer like a pool of black ink.

But the pièce de résistance was the east wall of the courtyard, where Astrid had worked with the pioneering French landscape architect Patrick Blanc to install a vertical garden that soared three stories high. Creepers, ferns, and other exotic palms seemed to grow out of the wall, defying gravity. Against this dramatic fresco of flora was a sleek arrangement of sculpted bronze divans covered in soft pillows of blindingly white linen. There was a verdant, monastic stillness to the space, and in the midst of it all, Astrid perched cross-legged on a divan, nestling a cup of tea on her lap, Zenly attired in a black tank top and a voluminous black skirt.[*]

Astrid stood up and gave Nick a tight hug. "I've missed you!"

"Same here! So this is where you've been slumming it."

"Yeah, you like it?"

"It's incredible! I remember coming here as a kid for one of

---

[*] Deceptively simple, as it turns out—Astrid was wearing a perfectly constructed ribbed jersey tank from The Row over a vintage Jasper Conran black silk skirt in a festive tiered rah-rah design.

your great-aunt's *nyonya* feasts—I can't believe what you've done with it!"

"I moved in here thinking it would just be temporary, but I ended up falling in love with the place so I figured I'd do some work on it. I can feel my great-aunt all around me here." Astrid gestured for Nick to take a seat next to her on the divan, and she began to pour him some tea out of a cast-iron teapot. "This is a Nilgiri from the Dunsandle Tea Estate in South India . . . I hope you like it."

Nick took a sip of the tea, savoring its delicate smokiness. "Hmmm . . . fantastic." He gazed in wonder at the ocular-patterned skylight far above. "You've really outdone yourself with this space!"

"Thanks, but I can't take any credit for it—Studio KO, this amazing Parisian duo, designed everything."

"Well, I'm sure you inspired them much more than you let on. I don't think I've ever been in a house quite like this—it feels like Marrakech two hundred years from now."

Astrid smiled and gave a little sigh. "I wish I could be in Marrakech two hundred years from now."

"Yeah? I get the feeling it hasn't been all that great a morning. What's this latest gossip I hear?" Nick asked, sinking down into the plush sofa.

"Oh, you haven't seen it?"

Nick shook his head.

"Well, I'm *very* famous now," Astrid said self-mockingly as she handed him the newspapers. It was the *South China Morning Post*, and on the front page, the headline screamed:

MICHAEL TEO SEEKS RECORD $5 BILLION DIVORCE
SETTLEMENT FROM HEIRESS ASTRID LEONG

SINGAPORE—For the past two years, billionaire venture capitalist Michael Teo, 36, has been mired in divorce proceedings with Singapore heiress Astrid Leong. What was supposed to be an amicable divorce has taken a new twist, as Mr. Teo's legal team is now demanding a $5 billion settlement in light of recent developments.

Last week, pictures of Ms. Leong, 37, went viral on international gossip sites. The images purport to show Ms. Leong being proposed to by Hong Kong tech tycoon Charles Wu, 37, at the Mehrangarh Fort in Jodhpur, India. Surrounding them were 100 classical Indian dancers, 20 Sitar players, two elephants and Bollywood superstar Shah Rukh Khan, who reportedly serenaded the couple with a Hindi version of the Jason Mraz love ballad "I'm Yours."

Mr. Teo is now accusing Ms. Leong of "intolerable cruelty and adultery" in his latest divorce filings. He claims to have incontrovertible evidence that his wife has been having an affair with Mr. Wu "since as early as 2010." It is a sad ending to what was once a romantic Cinderella story in reverse: Mr. Teo, the son of two schoolteachers, grew up in middle-income housing in Toa Payoh, met Ms. Leong, an heiress to one of Asia's largest fortunes, at the birthday party of one of his army friends. After a whirlwind courtship and wedding, the ridiculously photogenic couple married in 2006.

It was a union that took many in Asia's society circles by surprise. Ms. Leong is the only daughter of Henry Leong, the president of S. K. Leong Holdings Pte Ltd, the secretive conglomerate said to be the world's leading supplier of palm oil. Before she married Mr. Teo, she had previously been engaged to Charles Wu and also linked to a Muslim prince and several members of European nobility. Like her family, Ms. Leong is an exceedingly private individual who has never granted an interview and has no social media presence. The Heron Wealth Report has ranked the Leong family number three on a list of Asia's richest families, and estimates Ms. Leong's personal fortune to be "in excess of $10 billion."

Now, half of Ms. Leong's fortune is at stake, along with custody of their seven-year-old son, Cassian. "My client is a self-made billionaire—this is not about the money," claims Mr. Teo's lawyer Jackson Lee of the esteemed firm Gladwell and Malcolm. "This is about the principle of it all. Michael Teo, a loyal and devoted husband, has been humiliated on the world stage. Imagine how you would feel if the woman you were still married to was proposed to by another man, in such a public and disgustingly showy manner."

Singapore legal experts feel that Mr. Teo's legal maneuvers are unlikely to succeed, due to Ms. Leong's assets being tied up in the labyrinthine S. K. Leong Trusts. But this latest filing has already done its damage. An insider to Singapore's social scene comments, "The Leongs do not ever like being in the news. This is a huge embarrassment for them."

"Bloody hell," Nick said, throwing the newspaper on the floor in disgust.

Astrid smiled at him wanly.

"How does the *Post* get away with publishing this? I've never read so much bullshit in all my life."

"You're telling me. Self-made billionaire my ass."

"And if you're really worth ten billion, there's this David

Bowie limited-edition box set I want for my birthday. It's $89.95 on Amazon."

Astrid laughed for a moment, and then shook her head. "All my life, I've done everything to avoid being in any newspapers, but it seems like these days, the harder I try, the more I end up becoming front-page news. My parents are apoplectic with rage. They were angry enough when the pictures first leaked, but this just put them over the edge. My mother has taken to her bed and is mainlining Xanax, and I've never heard my father scream so loud as he did this morning when he came by with the newspaper. The blood vessels were bulging out of his temples so hard, I thought he was going to have a stroke."

"But can't they see that none of this is your fault? I mean, surely they know that Michael set this all up?"

"It seems pretty obvious to me, but of course, it doesn't matter to them. I'm the naughty girl who snuck off to India. I mean, I'm a thirty-seven-year-old mother, and I still need to ask my parents' permission to go away for the weekend. It's all my fault. I'm the one who's 'exposed' the family, I'm the one who's disgraced the family name for a thousand generations."

Nick shook his head in commiseration, cracking his knuckles as something else came to his mind. "You gotta give Michael some credit ... he *knew* that the Singapore papers wouldn't touch this story, so he purposely had it leaked to the *South China Morning Post* in Hong Kong."

"It was a well-played move. He's trying to do maximum damage to Charlie and to our future life there."

"I'll bet you anything he's behind those paparazzi pictures too."

"Charlie seems to think so. He's got his whole security team trying to figure out how Michael's had me under surveillance."

"I know this is going into Jason Bourne territory, but is there any way Michael could have put some sort of tracking device on you before you went on your trip? I mean, he *did* hack your cell phone once upon a time."

Astrid shook her head. "I haven't seen Michael in almost a year. We only communicate through our lawyers now—and that's his doing, not mine. Ever since he hired this Jackson Lee fellow, who I'm told is a mad legal genius, things have gotten more and more acrimonious."

"How often does Michael see Cassian?"

"Technically, he gets him three days a week, but Michael rarely lives up to his end of the deal. He takes Cassian for a meal once a week or so, but sometimes he goes two or three weeks before he sees him. It's like he's forgotten he even has a son," Astrid said sadly.

A maid entered the courtyard and set a breakfast tray down on the coffee table.

"Kaya toast!" Nick exclaimed happily at the sight of the perfectly toasted triangles of bread smeared with a thick layer of kaya coconut jam. "How did you know I was craving that this morning?"

Astrid smiled. "Don't you know I can read your mind? This is Ah Ching's homemade kaya from Tyersall Park, of course."

"Brilliant!" Nick said.

Astrid noticed the glint of sadness that played across his eyes as he took his first bite of the crisp yet fluffy white bread. "Listen, I heard about how you've been banned from Tyersall Park. It's so ridiculous. I'm sorry I haven't been able to help, but now that I'm back, I'm going to try to figure something out."

"Come on, Astrid, you've had so much to deal with. Don't

worry about it. Do you know the stunt my mother's been trying to pull? She wants me to get Rachel pregnant, pronto, and then she'll announce the news to Ah Ma in the hopes that she will want to see me."

"You can't be serious!"

"She called Rachel and demanded to know where she was in her cycle. She had Carol Tai's plane all lined up to whisk her to Singapore this weekend specifically so that I could impregnate her. She even had a honeymoon suite ready at her friend's resort in Sentosa."

Astrid clasped her mouth in laughter. "Jesus! And I thought I had a crazy mother!"

"No one is crazier than Eleanor Young."

"Well, at least she's still trying to look out for you. She'll do anything for you to get back in Ah Ma's good graces."

"For my mother, everything's about the house. But you know I just want to see Ah Ma. It's taken me a while to get there, but I realize I do owe her an apology."

"That's big of you, Nicky. I mean, she was pretty horrendous to you and Rachel."

"I know, but I still shouldn't have said the things I said. I know how much it hurt her."

Astrid reflected on this, staring into her teacup for a moment before looking up at her cousin. "I just don't understand why Ah Ma suddenly doesn't want to see you. I sat by her bedside for a whole week while she was at Mount E. She knew you were on your way back, and she never mentioned a thing about not wishing to see you. Something's up. I think Auntie Victoria or Eddie or somebody's been influencing her while I've been out of the picture."

Nick looked at Astrid hopefully. "Maybe you can find a way to bring it up with her . . . delicately. You've always had a way with her that no one else has."

"Oh, didn't you know? I'm persona non grata at Tyersall Park too. My parents don't want me to show my face at the house, or anywhere in public for that matter, until this scandal blows over a bit."

Nick couldn't help but laugh at the whole situation. "So we've both been excommunicated, as if we were the devil's spawn."

"Yep. We're the friggin' Children of the Corn. But what can we do? Mum doesn't want anything at all to risk upsetting Ah Ma right now."

"I think Ah Ma would be more upset that you're not there by her bedside," Nick said indignantly.

Astrid's eyes brimmed with tears. "We're losing precious time with her, Nicky. Every day, she's fading away more and more."

CHAPTER NINE

Eddie walked down the east corridor on the way to his grandmother's bedroom, admiring the cluster of old photographs that had been hung salon-style over a damask-covered settee. In the center was a framed oversize print of his great-grandfather Shang Loong Ma posing next to several enormous elephant tusks and a jewel-turbaned maharaja after a safari in India. Next to that hung a studio portrait of his grandfather Sir James Young in the late thirties, looking every inch the matinee idol in his houndstooth jacket and white fedora, and improbably clutching a Norwich terrier in his arms. *How dapper he looked! Who made that blazer for him? Could it be Huntsman, or Davies & Son?* Eddie wondered. *I wish I had known him back then. Of all his grandsons, I'm obviously the only one who inherited his style.*

Lower down on the wall was a long, rectangular photo of his grandmother Su Yi wearing a tea dress, sprawled elegantly on a picnic blanket in what looked like the Jardin du Luxembourg. Next to her were two French ladies, and each of them clutched intricate lace parasols that appeared to be straining against a gust of wind. The two ladies were laughing, but Su Yi stared straight into the camera, perfectly composed. How beautiful she had been in her youth. Eddie scrutinized the signature that had been scrawled at the bottom of the print: J. H. Lartigue. *Holy fuckballs, did the great French photographer Jacques Henri Lartigue really take this picture of Ah Ma? Jesus, this is priceless. I must have it for my office. It could go right next to my Cartier-Bresson print of the boy holding the wine bottles. No one else would appreciate this photograph like I would. If I took this photo and replaced it with one of the others hanging on the other wall, would anyone notice?*

Eddie looked around the corner to see if any of the maids were skulking nearby. There were so many goddamn maids everywhere, no one had any privacy to steal a thing in this house. That's when he heard the slow, deep moan. *Ooaahhh!!! Ooooaaaahhh!* It was coming from a door halfway down the hallway that had been left slightly ajar. Eddie quickly realized it was the suite where his cousin Adam and Piya Aakara were staying. He knew that Thais could be kinky, but would they really leave the door ajar like this while they were having their morning nooky? Anyone coming down this corridor could hear them. Then again, if that sexy Piya was his wife, he'd ride her into next week and not give a damn if the whole house could hear.

Eddie crept closer to the door, and a woman's voice could be heard giggling. Suddenly, another guttural voice could be heard moaning over the first one. *Gwaahhh! Gwaahhh!* Wait a minute, there were *two guys* in the room. And then the second male voice moaned, *Oh yeah, right there! Go deeper! Gwaaaaahhh!* Eddie's eyes widened as he recognized that voice. It was his brother, Alistair. What the fucky fuck was happening? Was Alistair having a ménage à trois with his Thai cousins *right under his grandmother's roof, while she lay dying?* The sacrilege! Whenever he came to visit his grandmother, he always had the common decency of checking his latest mistress in to the Shangri-La Hotel nearby. He would *never think* of sleeping with anyone that wasn't his wife in his dear Ah Ma's house.

Eddie barged into the room in a self-righteous fit. "WHAT IN GOD'S NAME DO YOU THINK YOU'RE DO—" he began, and then he stopped in surprise. Piya was seated on the chaise lounge sipping her morning cappuccino, coolly elegant in a sleeveless kelly green silk faille top with matching faille pencil pants from Rosie Assoulin. Eddie swung around and discovered the most curious sight. Sitting at the foot of the silver-enameled four-poster bed was Alistair, stripped to the waist, and leaning over him was Uncle Taksin, digging his elbows deep into Alistair's shoulders. Adam lay facedown naked on the bed while his mother straddled his thighs, massaging his lower back with coconut oil.

"Ooaahhh!" Adam groaned, as Piya continued to giggle.

"I told you boys to do some stretches before your badminton match, but you didn't listen, did you?" Catherine chided, as she rubbed Adam's lower back vigorously.

"Duuude, Uncle Taksin is giving me the best Thai massage on the planet! You really should try it," Alistair said.

Eddie stared at the scene in disbelief. He couldn't believe that the Thai prince was giving his brother a massage. "Um, shouldn't your maids be doing this?"

"No . . . Mummy's the best." Adam sighed through his pillow.

Piya laughed. "All the Aakara boys have been spoiled by their parents giving them massages since they were little. Adam doesn't even like it when I try to massage him—only Mummy will do."

Catherine looked up at Eddie, her chin smeared with a drop of coconut oil as she kneaded her fingers deep into Adam's butt muscles. "Do you want a massage? I'm almost done here."

"Er... no, I'm fine, thanks. I'm not sore—I... I... only played the first set, remember?" Eddie stuttered, uncomfortable at seeing his auntie touch her own son *down there*.

"You don't know what you're missing." Alistair sighed contentedly.

"I'm just on my way to see Ah Ma," Eddie said, backing out of the room as fast as he could. Those Aakaras were such strange people. Imagine, giving their children massages when they had a posse of prostrating servants at their beck and call! He could hardly believe that Auntie Cat and his mother were sisters—they were such polar opposites. His mother was always so poised and ladylike, while Cat was this no-nonsense woman with tomboyish ways. Her arms, her face—practically the whole front of her body was smeared with coconut oil as she gave her son a massage. His mother didn't even like putting moisturizer on her own hands. How the hell did Cat ever manage to snag a prince? Of all the sisters, his mother had clearly made the worst match, not including old maid Auntie Victoria, of course.

He entered his grandmother's private study and saw his father huddled in conversation with Professor Oon. Malcolm Cheng was one of Asia's most respected heart surgeons, and had only recently retired as the chief of the Cardiology Centre at Hong Kong Sanatorium. Professor Oon was one of his protégés, and he was obviously keeping close tabs on Su Yi's condition.

"How's the patient doing today?" Eddie said cheerily.

"Don't interrupt when I'm talking!" His father scowled at him, turning back to Professor Oon. "And I'm really not happy with the fluid buildup in her lungs."

"I know, Malcolm," Professor Oon murmured worriedly.

Eddie went into the bedroom, where he found his mother rearranging the vases of flowers that had been sent to Su Yi.

Every day, several dozen new arrangements were delivered to the house, along with cases upon cases of Brand's Essence of Chicken.

"Mummy hates hydrangeas. Who sent them?" Alix said, opening the creamy thick envelope to look at the card. "Oh God, it's from the Shears. Well, I suppose we have to keep the flowers here until Mummy wakes up to see them. She was so close to Benjamin. He was the doctor who delivered me, you know?"

"Oh look, I think she's awake now!" Eddie said excitedly, as he ran over and crouched beside her. "Dear Ah Ma, how are you feeling today?"

Su Yi's throat was too dry to talk, but she managed to mutter, "Water . . ."

"Yes, yes of course. Mother, Ah Ma needs some water now!"

Alix looked around and grabbed the nearest pitcher. "Tsk, why is this empty?" she said irritatedly, as she ran into the bathroom to refill it. She came back out and started to pour some of the water into the plastic cup with the sippy straw attached.

"Is that tap water? Are you trying to kill Ah Ma?" Eddie snapped at his mother.

"What do you mean? Singapore tap water is perfectly safe!" Alix argued.

"Ah Ma should only drink sterilized water in her condition. Where's that damn Swiss water that the Aakaras have been guzzling nonstop? Why isn't any of it in here? And where are her goddamn lady's maids when you need them?"

"I sent them to prepare her breakfast."

"Well, call down and get them to bring up some of the Swiss water too," Eddie ordered.

Su Yi sighed, shaking her head in annoyance. Why were all her children so incapable of fulfilling this simple request?

Alix could see the look of frustration on her mother's face and quickly decided to override her son. "Step aside Eddie, let me give her this water now."

"No, no, let me," Eddie insisted, grabbing the cup from her hands and leaning down at his grandmother while mustering his best Florence Nightingale expression.

When Su Yi was hydrated and feeling more revived, she gazed around her bedroom, as if searching for something. "Where's Astrid?" she asked.

"Er . . . Astrid isn't here at the moment," Alix said, not wanting to mention anything about the unfolding scandal surrounding her niece. She made eye contact with Eddie, silently warning him not to say anything.

"Astrid went to India," Eddie announced with a smirk.

Alix glared at her son in dismay. Why was he trying to agitate his grandmother like this?

"Oh good. She went," Su Yi said.

Eddie couldn't hide his surprise. "You knew about this? You know about Charlie Wu's proposal?"

Su Yi said nothing. She closed her eyes, her lips curling into a slight smile. Suddenly she opened her eyes again and looked questioningly at Alix. "And Nicky?"

"Um, what about Nicky?" Alix asked carefully.

"Isn't he supposed to be back by now?"

"Do you mean you want to see Nicky?" Alix asked, trying to clarify.

"Of course. Where is he?" Su Yi said.

Before Alix could answer, Eddie cut in. "Ah Ma, Nicky unfortunately had to cancel his trip at the last minute. Something came up with work, and he couldn't make it back just yet. You know how important that history professor job is to him. He had to deliver a lecture on the Intergalactic Wars."

"Oh," Su Yi said simply.

Alix stared at her son, amazed by his bold-faced lie. She was about to say something when Su Yi's lady's maids entered with the breakfast trays.

"Mummy—" Alix began, when she suddenly felt Eddie grab her arm forcefully from behind and pull her into Su Yi's dressing room. From there, he took his mother onto the balcony and shut the glass door firmly behind them.

"Eddie, I don't know what's gotten into you. What was that nonsense about Nicky? What kind of game are you playing this time?" Alix demanded, squinting at him under the glare of the morning sun.

"I'm not playing any games, Mother. I'm just letting nature take its course."

Alix stared her son in the eye. "Eddie, I want the truth: Did Ah Ma *really* tell you that she didn't want Nicky in the house?"

"She . . . she almost went into cardiac arrest when I mentioned his name!" Eddie sputtered.

"Then tell me why she just asked for him?"

Eddie paced around the balcony, looking for a shady spot to stand. "Can't you see that Nicky only wants to see Ah Ma so that he can beg for her forgiveness?"

"Yes, and I'm all for it. Why shouldn't he be allowed to patch things up with her?"

"Are you crazy or what? Do I really need to spell it out for you? I'm fighting for what's rightfully mine!"

Alix threw up her hands in exasperation. "You're delusional,

Eddie. Do you really think my mother is going to change her will and leave *you* Tyersall Park?"

"She already has, Mother! Didn't you see how Freddie Tan acted the other day after he came to visit Ah Ma?"

"He seemed his usual friendly self to me."

"Maybe he's always been friendly to you, but to me, he behaved in a way that he never has. The man has hardly exchanged two words with me over the past thirty years, but the other day, he spoke to me as if I was his biggest client. He told me I was the 'man of the hour.' And then he spent an inordinate amount of time talking to me about my watch collection. What does that tell you?"

"Only that Freddie Tan is a watch lunatic like you."

"No, Mother, Freddie Tan was trying to give me a hint about being the *man of the hour* in Ah Ma's new will! He's already sucking up to us, can't you see? Now, do you want to ruin all that and see Ah Ma give Nicky this house? The house you grew up in?"

Alix gave a weary sigh. "Eddie, this house is already supposed to be his. We have all known since the day Nicky was born that it was meant for him. He's a *Young*."

"That's right, he's a Young, he's a Young! All my bloody life people have been telling me he's a Young and I'm just a Cheng. This is all your fault!"

"My fault? I don't understand you half the time—"

"Why the hell did you have to marry Dad, a complete nobody from Hong Kong? Why couldn't you marry someone else, like an Aakara or a Leong? Someone with a respectable surname? Didn't you think of how it would affect your children? Didn't you realize how it has fucked up my whole life?" Eddie seethed.

Alix looked at her son's petulant expression and for a moment felt the urge to slap him. Instead, she took a deep breath, sat down on one of the wrought-iron chairs, and said through gritted teeth, "I'm glad I married your father. He may not have inherited an empire or been born a prince, but for me he is far more impressive. He built himself up from nothing to become one of the world's leading cardiologists, and his hard work has sent you to the best schools and given us a lovely home."

Eddie laughed mockingly. "A lovely home? Oh my God, Mum, your flat is a disgrace!"

"I think ninety-five percent of the population of Hong Kong would beg to differ. And don't forget, we even bought you your first flat when you graduated from university to help you get started—"

"Ha! Leo Ming was given a hundred-million-dollar tech company when he graduated."

"And where has that gotten him, Eddie? I don't see that Leo has accomplished much in his life except expand his number of ex-wives. We gave you the support to become successful on your own terms. I can't believe you fail to see all the advantages your father and I tried to give you. How did we manage to raise you to be so ungrateful? I don't hear Cecilia or Alistair complaining about their lives or their surname."

"They're both underachieving losers! Cecilia is so obsessed with her horses, you should have named her Catherine the Great! And Alistair and his film-production bullshit—who in Hong Kong has ever seen any of those strange art-house movies that his director friend makes? *Fallen Angels*? It should have been called 'Fallen Asleep'! I'm the only one of your children who has ever accomplished a damn thing! Do you really want to know what having the surname Cheng has done for me? It meant that I didn't get to go to Robbie Ko-Tung's birthday party at Ocean Park when we were in Primary Two. It meant that I didn't get picked for the debate team at Diocesan. It meant that I didn't get asked to be a groomsman at Andrew Ladoorie's wedding. It meant that I knew I would never get a cushy no-show job at one of the Hong Kong banks and had to spend half my life licking the balls of everyone at Liechtenburg Group in order to claw my way to the top!"

"I never realized you felt this way." Alix shook her head sadly.

"That's because you never bothered to get to know your own children! You've never really had time to care about our needs!"

Alix got up from her chair, finally losing her patience. "I'm not going to sit here in the hot sun and listen to you whine about being a neglected child, when you jet around the world and hardly ever make time for your own kids!"

"Well, that's fitting, isn't it? Dad spent most of my childhood flying to medical conferences in Sweden or Swaziland while you were always off buying up properties in Vancouver. You've never listened to me! You've never once asked me what I truly wanted! YOU'VE NEVER EVEN GIVEN ME A BUTT MASSAGE!" Eddie wailed, as he collapsed onto one of the balcony chairs, his body suddenly wracked with sobs.

Alix stared at her son, thinking that he must have temporarily gone mad.

Eddie wiped away his tears and glared at his mother. "If you truly care about your children, if you truly love us as you say you do, you will say NOTHING to Ah Ma about Nicky. Don't you see what a perfect opportunity this is for us? We need to make sure he never gets to see her, and we need to keep reinforcing to Auntie Felicity that Astrid is still not welcome here! We can tell Uncle Philip that Ah Ma is too weak to see anyone. I will plant myself outside Ah Ma's bedroom at all times—nobody is going to get in or out without my approval!"

"This is insane, Eddie. You can't restrict other family members from seeing Ah Ma like this."

"This is not insane!" Eddie screamed. "YOU'RE insane if you allow us to lose this opportunity. This could be our only chance to get Tyersall Park. Yes—*OUR*. You see, I'm always thinking of what's best for our family! I'm not doing this just for me, but for Alistair and Cecilia and all your precious grandchildren. If we are the new owners of Tyersall Park, no one can ever say that the Chengs aren't as great as the Youngs or the Shangs. Please don't ruin everything for us now!"

CHAPTER TEN

"Which bottle?" Jiayi asked in Cantonese as she stood on the third-highest step of the wooden rolling ladder.

"Um . . . look for any bottle from before 1950," Ah Ling instructed.

The maid squinted her eyes at the ancient yellowing labels affixed to the front of the large glass canisters, looking at the dates. She remembered going to a fancy herbal shop in Shenzhen when she was a teenager and seeing one precious golden tin of *yen woh* in a locked glass cabinet in the pride of place behind the cash register. Her mother had explained that the container was full of edible bird's nest—one of the most expensive delicacies in China. Now she was looking at an entire shelving unit lined with them. "I can't believe that all these bottles are filled with *yen woh*. It must be worth a fortune!"

"That is why we keep this larder under lock and key," Ah Ling said. "All of these bottles came from Mrs. Young's father. Mr. Shang owned a company that supplied the finest *yen woh* in Asia, taken from the most prized caves in Borneo."

"Is this how they became so rich?"

"Hiyah, you can't build a fortune like the Shangs' on *yen woh* alone. This was just one of the many companies Mr. Shang owned."

The maid climbed down from the ladder hugging a huge bottle almost as big as her entire torso. She stared through the musty glass at what looked like dried white husks, marveling at the precious treasure inside. "Have you ever tried it?"

"Of course. Mrs. Young always has a bowl prepared for me on my birthday."

"What does it taste like?"

"I can't quite describe it . . . it's like nothing you've ever had. It's more about the texture . . . it's sort of like snow fungus, but much more delicate. But here, Ah Ching makes it into a dessert soup. She cooks it in a double boiler with dried longan and rock sugar for forty-eight hours, and then puts shaved ice over it. It's marvelous. Now, third rack from the bottom on that shelf over there. Get me three cups of dried longan," Ah Ling instructed, as she carefully marked the amount of bird's nest she had taken out of the canister in a ledger book.

"Whose birthday is it now?" Jiayi asked.

"Nobody's. But Mrs. Young's brother Alfred Shang is coming over for Friday-night dinner. And we know how much he likes *yen woh.*"

"So he gets to have it whenever he wants?"

"Of course! This used to be his house too, you know."

"Life is so unfair . . ." Jiayi muttered as she strained to open the lid of the bottle of dried longans.

There was a knock on the door, and Vikram, the head of security, poked his head in and smiled at Ah Ling. "There you are! Ah Tock said you were down in the larder, but he didn't say which one. I searched two other larders before finding you!"

"I only ever come to the dried-goods larder, because only I have the key. The other larders I never bother with. What do you need?"

Vikram eyed the young maid scooping out the dried longans into a bowl and said to the housekeeper, "May I have a few minutes of your time after you're done with this?"

Ah Ling looked over at Jiayi. "Take everything up to Ah Ching now. And maybe if you are very nice to her, she will let you have a little taste of the *yen woh* on Friday."

As soon as the maid had left the room, Ah Ling asked in a slightly weary tone, "What is the problem today?"

"Well, I've been going through something in my mind for the last couple of days," Vikram began. "You know how Joey's been out on leave since his mother's surgery? Well, I took over his patrol schedule myself, and the other day while I was on the roof, I overheard something rather interesting coming from Mrs. Young's balcony."

Ah Ling's ears perked up. "What was so interesting?"

"It was Eddie Cheng talking to his mother. From what I could gather, it sounds like Mrs. Young never said she didn't want to see Nicky. I think Eddie made it all up."

Ah Ling cracked a smile. "I suspected this all along. Su Yi has never banned anyone from the house before, and surely not Nicky of all people."

"I felt it was wrong too, but what could I say? Clearly Eddie has an agenda of his own, and he's the one who has instigated this ban on Nicky. And Victoria has fallen for his ploy."

"What did Alix have to say? I'm surprised she's going along with it—mother and son are usually at loggerheads."

"She didn't say much. He was so busy screaming at her, the poor woman could hardly get a word in. Apparently Eddie has held a grudge against his mother for a very long time because she won't massage his buttocks."

"Whaaaat?" Ah Ling made a face.

Vikram couldn't help but chuckle a bit. "Yes, I know, strange family. What can you expect—they're Hong Kongers. Anyway, Alix tried to reason with Eddie, but he's determined to make sure Nicky doesn't get to see Mrs. Young at all. He's gotten it into his fat head that he alone will inherit Tyersall Park—that's why he's been planting himself outside her bedroom for the past two days like a Doberman. He's not letting anyone in who will ruin his plan!"

"*Sek si gau!*"* Ah Ling muttered angrily.

Vikram peeked out of the larder door for a moment to see if there was anyone within earshot before continuing in a lower voice. "Now, from what I understand, Mrs. Young thinks that Nicky had to cancel his trip because of the Intergalactic Wars. She has been kept completely in the dark, and has no idea he's even back on the island. Astrid is being kept away too, and you know none of those daughters are going to tell her anything. We need to do something about this!"

Ah Ling let out a long sigh. "I don't know if we can interfere. This is a family matter. I don't like to get mixed up in their quarrels. And I especially don't want either of us to get in trouble for this . . . after Su Yi is gone."

"Mrs. Young isn't . . . going anywhere!" Vikram sputtered.

"Vikram, we both have to face it . . . I don't think Su Yi is going to last much longer. I see her waning day by day. And we have no idea who's going to get control of Tyersall Park. God forbid, it could be Eddie. We need to be extra careful, especially now. I've seen what has happened before in this family. You weren't around when T'sien Tsai Tay passed away. My God, the drama!"

---

* Cantonese for "shit-eating bastard."

"I think there's going to be drama no matter what. But you practically raised Nicky—don't you want to see him get the house?"

Ah Ling gestured for Vikram to follow her to the back of the larder. "Of course I do," she whispered.

"We both know it would be ideal if Nicky is the new master of Tyersall Park. He is our best hope to keep things just the way they are. That's why we have to do what we can to make sure he gets to see Mrs. Young."

"But what can we do? How are we going to get Nicky into the house and into her bedroom without the whole family knowing about it? Without losing our jobs?"

Vikram felt a lump in his throat, but he continued to speak. "Ah Ling, I swore an oath—a Gurkha's oath—to protect and serve Mrs. Young with my life. I feel like I would be betraying her if I didn't see that her wishes are followed. You just confirmed that she wants to see Nicky, right?"

Ah Ling nodded. "I have a feeling she's hanging on to see him."

"Well, it's my duty to make sure that happens. Even if I lose my job."

"You are an honorable man," Ah Ling said as she sat down on a wooden stool, momentarily lost in a thought. She gazed up at the rows and rows of glass bottles containing the world's rarest foods—wild mountain ginseng, preserved abalone, caterpillar fungus—precious herbs that had been stored here since before World War II, suddenly remembering one afternoon back in the early eighties . . .

Su Yi had taken out a leather box from the vault filled with old medals that she wanted Ah Ling to polish with extra care. Most of them were honors given over the years to Su Yi's husband—his Order of the British

Empire badge, a medal from the Knights of Saint John of Jerusalem, various decorations from Malay royals—but one medal stood out: an eight-point Maltese cross made of pewter, and at its center was a large amethyst.

"What did Dr. Young receive this medal for?" Ah Ling asked, holding up the translucent gemstone to the light.

"Oh, that wasn't his. This was given to me after the war by the queen. Don't bother to polish that," Su Yi answered.

"How come I never knew you were honored by the queen?"

Su Yi huffed dismissively. "It wasn't very significant to me. Why would I care what the Queen of England thinks? The British abandoned us during World War II. Instead of sending more troops to defend the colony that helped to make them rich, they retreated like cowards and wouldn't even leave us with real weapons. So many young men—my cousins, my half brothers—died trying to hold back the Japanese."

Ah Ling nodded her head gravely. "So what did you get this medal for?"

Su Yi gave her a wry smile. "One night during the height of the occupation, I got careless. I was in the Botanic Gardens with a small group of friends, and none of us should have been there. The island was under curfew, and the gardens were locked up in the evenings—they were especially out of bounds. A patrol of Kempeitai—the vicious Japanese military police—came out of nowhere and surprised us. Now, a few of my friends couldn't risk getting caught by the Japanese—they were already on the wanted list—so I let them flee and allowed myself to be caught. I had protection papers, you see. Our family friend Lim Boon Keng had gotten me a special badge that was marked 'Overseas Chinese Liaison Officer,' and this meant that I could go about the island unmolested by the soldiers.

"But these soldiers didn't buy my story—I told them that we were all just good friends out on a lark, but they still arrested me and took me to their commanding officer. When I saw I was being taken to a certain house on Dalvey Estate, I remember getting very anxious—this colonel was known for his brutality. He once shot a young boy on the street just because

the boy didn't salute him in the correct manner. And here I was about to face him after committing a big offense.

"When we got to the front door, some soldiers were coming out carrying a body that was covered by a bloody sheet. I thought it was all over for me then, that I was about to be raped or shot, or maybe both. My heart was racing a mile a minute. They dragged me into this sitting room, where I came upon the most unexpected sight. The colonel was this tall, elegant man sitting at the grand piano playing Beethoven. I stood there just watching him perform the entire piece, and when he had finished, for some reason I decided to speak first, something you were never supposed to do. I said to him, 'The Piano Concerto No. 5 in E-flat major is one of my favorites.'

"The colonel turned and gave me this piercing stare and said in perfect English, 'You're familiar with this piece? You know the piano? Play something for me.'

"He got up from the stool, and I sat down at the piano absolutely petrified, knowing what I chose to play could mean the difference between life and death. So I took a deep breath and thought, if I'm about to die, this is what I want to play. Debussy's 'Clair de Lune.'

"I played my heart out, and when I finished, I looked up from the piano and saw that there were tears in his eyes. It turns out that before the war, he had been in the diplomatic corps in Paris. Debussy was his favorite. He let me go, and twice a week for the next year, he made me come over to his house and play the piano for him."

Ah Ling shook her head incredulously at the story. *"You were very lucky to get away like that. How did you and your friends get in to the Botanic Gardens in the first place?"*

Su Yi gave her a sphinxlike smile, as if she was trying to decide whether or not to let her in on something. And then she shared her secret.

. . .

Emerging from the memory of Su Yi's story, an idea began to form in Ah Ling's mind. She looked up at Vikram and said, "There is a secret about this house that even you don't know. Something from the war times."

Vikram looked at her in surprise.

Ah Ling continued, "Now, don't you have connections in the Khoo household?"

"Sure, I know their head of security very well."

"This is what I need you to do . . ."

. . .

Nick and Colin were spending the afternoon hanging out at Red Point Record Warehouse on Playfair Road, where they had spent countless hours listening to obscure records back when they were teenagers. As Nick flipped through the meticulously organized bins, he called out to Colin, "Did you know that the Cocteau Twins collaborated with Faye Wong?"

"No way!"

"Take a look at this," Nick said, handing him a record. While Colin read the liner notes to a rare EP recorded by the Hong Kong diva titled *The Amusement Park*, his phone buzzed with a text message. He glanced at the screen and read a message from Aloysius Pang—the head of his family's security team—summoning him to his father's house to pick up a package ASAP. Colin wondered what this was all about, as it was highly uncharacteristic of Aloysius to summon him like this.

"Hey Nick, I need to run over to my dad's place to pick up something that's apparently quite urgent. Do you want to stay here or come with?"

"I'll come along. If I stay any longer I'll just end up buying the whole store," Nick replied.

The two of them sped over to Colin's father's house on Leedon Road, a stately Georgian mansion that looked like it had been transported straight out of Bel Air, California.

"Jeez, it's been years since I've been here," Nick remarked as they entered the house through the front door. A grandfather clock ticked loudly in the circular foyer, and all the curtains in the formal living room had been closed to block out the afternoon sun. "Is anyone home?"

"My dad and stepmom are on a safari in Kenya at the moment," Colin answered, as a Filipino maid appeared from the corridor.

"Is Aloysius here?"

"No, but there's a package for you, Sir Colin," the woman replied. She went into the kitchen and returned moments later with a large padded envelope that didn't bear the markings of any courier service.

"Who dropped this off?" Colin asked.

"Sir, Mr. Pang, sir."

He ripped open the envelope, and inside was a smaller manila envelope that was stamped PRIVATE & CONFIDENTIAL. There was a Post-it affixed to the front of it. Colin looked up at Nick in surprise. "This package isn't for me—it's for you!"

"Really?" Taking the package, Nick saw that the Post-it note read:

Please give this letter by hand to your friend Nicholas Young.
It is imperative that he receives it by tonight.

"Well this is convenient! I guess whoever sent this knows I'm crashing at your place," Nick said as he began tearing into the sealed envelope.

"Wait! Wait! Are you sure you want to do that?" Colin said.

"Why not?"

Colin glanced suspiciously at the package. "I dunno . . . what if there's anthrax or something in there?"

"I don't think my life is as exciting as that. But here, why don't you open it?"

"Fuck no."

Nick laughed as he continued to open the envelope. "Has anyone told you that you have an overactive imagination?"

"Dude, I'm not the one getting mysterious packages delivered to my best friend's house!" Colin said, taking a few steps back.

CHAPTER ELEVEN

28 CLUNY PARK ROAD, SINGAPORE

Nigel Barker had photographed some of the most famous and beautiful women in the world, from Iman to Taylor Swift. But he'd never had a subject fly him halfway around the world in their personal Boeing 747-8I VIP before, and he had never gotten a lymphatic drainage massage and a seaweed exfoliating body wrap in a private spa on a private jet. Naturally, when he arrived at Kitty Bing's gracious heritage bungalow on 28 Cluny Park Road with his team of four photo assistants, there was yet another never-before-witnessed drama unfolding.

A Chinese man wearing a deconstructed black Moroccan djellaba was standing on the front driveway, screaming, "CHUAAAAAAAAAAN! Where the fuck did you put the Oscar de la Renta? If you didn't pack it, I'm going to fucking skin you alive! CHUAAAAAAAAAAN!" As he yelled, he bounced several inches off the ground, looking like a deranged Jedi.

Twenty feet from the main house, a huge tent had been set up, and Nigel could see dozens of fashion assistants in white lab coats rushing from the house to the tent with various bits of clothing, while another set of assistants within the tent were going through the rolling racks filled with hundreds of ball gowns straight from the Paris catwalks. A guy in a white denim zip-up jumpsuit came running out of the tent. "We're still steaming it! It just arrived from New York thirty minutes ago!"

"*Ka ni nah!* I need the dress now, you good-for-nothing *goondu!*"[*]

Nigel approached the ranting Jedi warily. "I'm assuming this is the location for the *Tattle* photo shoot?"

"*Wah laooooo!*" The man gasped, putting his hands to his mouth. He suddenly stood ramrod straight, his face went from manic to Zen in a nanosecond, and his speech took on a pseudo-English-meets-Eurotrash accent. "Nigel Barker, it's really you! *Merde!* You are even more dashing in person! How is that possible? I'm *Patric*, the couture consultant. I'm styling the shoot today."

"Pleasure to meet you," Nigel replied in a real English accent.

Patric kept staring Nigel up and down. "It's an honor to be working with you! I've worked with Mert and Marcus, Inez and Vinoodh, Bruce and Nan, Alexis and Tico, I've worked with them all! Now come with me. We're having a minicrisis at the moment, but I think your presence will help calm things down!"

They entered the house, which was filled with more staffers rushing around frantically at full speed. "As you know, Mrs. Bing has spared no expense on this shoot. Oliver T'sien flew in the top hairstylist from New York, the top makeup artist from London, and the top set designers from Italy for this shoot. Everyone's a top, and we're having to compete for space with all these tops. It's not how I usually like to work," Patric said with an

---

[*] Don't quote me on this, but I believe a *goondu* is the Malay cousin of a *goondusamy* (India), which is in turn distantly related to a *goombah* (Jersey Shore and certain suburbs of Long Island).

arched eyebrow. Climbing up the beautiful Arts and Crafts–style wooden staircase, he led Nigel to the door of the library.

"Brace yourself," Patric warned as he cracked open the door slowly.

Inside, Nigel could see a woman seated in a hairdresser's chair in front of a bank of lighted mirrors, her face streaked in tears, surrounded by half a dozen stylists.

"Kitty . . . Kitty . . . I have a little treat for you . . ." Patric cooed.

Kitty looked in the mirror and saw them approaching. "Nigel! Nigel Barker! Oh no, this isn't how I wanted you to meet me for the first time. Look at my hair! Look what they've done! It looks terrible, doesn't it?"

Nigel glanced at the floor quickly and saw that they had lopped off about ninety percent of her hair. Kitty now had a pixie hairstyle that actually looked incredibly chic. "Kitty, it's a pleasure to meet you, and I think you look wonderful."

"See? We wanted a radical change, and this is a terrific look for you. It's very gamine," Oliver tried to reassure her in a calm voice.

"You look like Emma Watson. Wait till we do the color," Jo the hairstylist said.

"No, no, I'm not desirable anymore. I look like . . . *a mother*! Nigel, what do you think? Would you ever want to make love to me looking like this?" Kitty swiveled her chair around dramatically and gave him a piercing stare.

Nigel hesitated for a moment.

"Now, don't make things awkward for Nigel! He's a married man," said a blond woman with a British accent.

"Hello, Charlotte, I didn't know you'd be here," Nigel said, giving the makeup artist a quick hug.

Patric continued to reassure her. "Kitty, by the time Jo Blackwell-Preston is done with your hair color, Charlotte Tilbury is done with your makeup, I'm done pouring you into an amazing gown, and Nigel works his magic, you will look like the very definition of MILF! All the husbands and teenage boys who see you in these photos will want to take the magazine into the bathroom with them, trust me."

"Kitty, remember what we discussed," Oliver said. "The entire point of this photo shoot is to reposition your image. You're not supposed to look like a high-fashion temptress anymore. You're going to look like a supremely elegant hostess who's not trying too hard to impress. A cultural force and a rising civic leader. Charlotte, think of those photos by Skrebneski of Jacqueline de Ribes in her Paris apartment. Or C. Z. Guest bending down to pet her poodle. Or Marina Rust on her wedding day. We want young, regal, comme il faut."

"Ollie, we're going to comme-il-faut the hell out of her! Kitty, dry your tears. We need to give your face one of my emergency hyaluronic acid boosters right now, before it gets too puffy," Charlotte commanded.

"And then we're going to add the subtlest sun-kissed highlights to your hair. You'll look like you just came back from a summer in the Seychelles!" Jo proclaimed.

Two hours later, Kitty was posed on a Regency settee in front of *The Palace of Eighteen Perfections*, the magnificent Chinese scroll painting she had purchased two years ago for a record-breaking $195 million. She was dressed in a pale pink Oscar de la Renta off-the-shoulder ball gown, the billowing duchesse satin skirt pooling gloriously around her, and on her head was a delicate Edwardian pearl headband.

Gisele, in an adorable Mischka Aoki cornflower blue dress

with feathers and cascading ruffles was positioned lying on the settee, one leg dangling and her head resting on her mother's lap. Harvard stood on the other side of his mother with his arms around her neck, looking precious in a white sailor suit with navy blue piping from Bonpoint and white socks that went up to his knees. At the foot of the settee lay a gleaming pair of Irish setters.

Nigel had imagined Kitty's cover shot as a sort of modern-day re-creation of a Watteau portrait, and to achieve this he had brought all the way from New York the enormous Polaroid 20 x 24 camera. There were only six of these unique handmade cameras in the entire world, and so precious were the prints that every frame Nigel shot would cost $500. But the camera was somehow able to achieve an indescribable alchemy, creating images that were remarkably crisp and yet otherworldly. To go along with this concept, Nigel had confected an extraordinary blend of natural light fused with massive studio lights to create the sort of dappled, late-afternoon northern light straight out of an eighteenth-century atelier.

"Gisele, you have the prettiest smile," Nigel remarked as he stared into his viewfinder. Harvard was distracted by the dogs and kept reaching down to try to pet them. "Harvard, give your mommy a kiss!" Nigel encouraged, and then at the precise moment, just as Gisele was relaxing into her smile, Harvard was planting kisses on his mother's cheek, and the sunlight was hitting the painting at just the right angle, Nigel asked, "Kitty, what are you thinking?" Her expression suddenly took on a faraway look, and Nigel clicked the shutter, knowing he had just captured the defining shot.

Minutes later, the giant Polaroid was ready, and Toby, the first assistant, carefully placed the print on a special easel at the back of the room for all to see.

"Oh that's the shot! It looks like a Sir Joshua Reynolds come to life! Isn't this the most perfect tableau you've ever seen?" Oliver said to Patric.

"If only Nigel could join them in the photo. And take his shirt off. Then it would be perfect," Patric whispered back.

"I'm speechless! It's sooooo gorgeous I can hardly believe it. Nigel, this is going to be our best cover ever!" gushed Violet Poon, the editor in chief of *Singapore Tattle*. "Oliver, I'll admit I thought you were out of your mind when you said you wanted to cut all her hair off. But it was a stroke of genius! Kitty looks so soigné! Like Emma Stone! She's positively regal now. I can already see the headline on the cover: *Princess Kitty!* I'm going to take a picture of this glorious print for my friend Yolanda, since she so kindly allowed us to borrow her Irish setters for the shoot!"

Violet snapped a picture on her phone and immediately sent it out in a text. Minutes later, she excitedly reported, "Yolanda is absolutely crazy about the photo!"

"Would this be Yolanda Amanjiwo you're referring to?" Oliver asked.

"The one and only!"

"This is the woman who's so pretentious, she put a Picasso in her powder room right above the toilet so everyone has no choice but to notice it while they pee?"

"She's really not like that, Oliver. Haven't the two of you met?"

"I'm not sure she'd ever deign to meet me, since I don't have a title or my own plane."

"Oh come on, Oliver. You know Yolanda would love to meet you. She's throwing one of her famous dinners tonight. I'll see if you can come," Violet said as she continued to text at warp speed. A few moments later, she looked up at Oliver. "Guess what? Yolanda wants to invite everyone to her dinner. You, Nigel, and especially Kitty."

"No doubt she's heard about Kitty's three planes," Oliver quipped.

"Oliver T'sien, don't be like that!" Violet scolded.

Oliver approached Kitty, who was now posing languidly Madame Récamier–style in a vintage emerald-green-and-white-striped Anouska Hempel ball gown as Nigel and his team rearranged the lighting for a more dramatic evening look. "Do you think this pose works?" Kitty asked.

"It's gorgeous. So, guess what they are going to put on the cover of *Tattle* as a headline to your photo? 'Princess Kitty.' "

Kitty's eyes widened. "Oh my God I love it!"

"Annnnd . . . guess who has just invited you to dinner tonight? Yolanda Amanjiwo."

Kitty couldn't believe her ears. "This is that lady *Tattle* calls the Empress of Entertaining?"

"The very one," Violet said excitedly. "I sent her a pic from your photo shoot and she's absolutely bonkers to meet you. See, your photo shoot isn't even out yet, and already you're the toast of the town, Princess Kitty! Please say you'll come tonight!"

"Of course. I'll change my plans," Kitty said. She had planned a moonlight dinner cruise alone with Nigel, but this, she felt, was more important.

"Splendid! Eight o'clock sharp, white tie."

"White tie? In *Singapore*?" Oliver frowned.

"Oh yes. You'll see. Yolanda does things on a grand scale. She entertains like no one else I know."

. . .

Several hours later, Oliver, Nigel, and Kitty found themselves in Yolanda Amanjiwo's drawing room, a vast space with black travertine floors that felt more like the lobby of a resort hotel than a home. Half the room was comprised of a reflecting pool that extended outdoors into an even larger pool, and from the middle of the pool rose an immense Jeff Koons gold *Balloon Dog*.

Yolanda and her husband, Joey, stood at the far end of the room in front of a wide marble block that displayed a collection of ancient Apulian vases. As Kitty was led to the receiving line, she knew she had made the right choice by wearing a black off-the-shoulder vintage Givenchy gown with white satin gloves and her not overly flashy necklace of graduated diamonds ending in a teardrop canary diamond of forty carats. As she approached her hosts, flanked by her debonair escorts in their white-tie tuxedos, a butler announced in a high, nasal tone, "The Honorable Oliver T'sien, Mr. Nigel Barker, and Mrs. Jack Bing."

Yolanda was a tall, thin woman with a gravity-defying bouffant hairdo, clad in a dramatic strapless scarlet column gown that Kitty recognized to be Christian Dior couture. She had obviously chosen her plastic surgeon with meticulous care, since she possessed one of those faces that looked perfectly taut and sculpted, but not a single muscle moved when she spoke. Which was a pity, since she spoke in an exceedingly warm, rapid-fire Indonesian accent. "Oliver T'sien we meet at last I am such an admirer of your family and of course your grandfather was such a great man so revered Nigel Barker how lovely to meet you my God what a beauuuuuuutiful set of pictures you took today can I commission you to please do a portrait of my Irish setters?"

"Actually, I did take some pictures of just the two of them. I'm having them printed as a gift to you."

"Oh my goodness Joey did you hear that Nigel Barker did a portrait of Liam and Niall and we didn't even have to pay him a million bucks!" Yolanda prodded her husband frantically, who looked like he was in the midst of waking from a long coma.

"Ummm" was all the short, paunchy man said, his eyelids heavy.

"And you must be the divine Kitty Bing I have heard so much about you and my God what a divine dress it must be a classic Givenchy and that party you threw during Shanghai Fashion Week ooh la la I wish I had been there Karl Lagerfeld told me your new villa is to die for and your plane the big one has a spa in it my God what a genius idea I must visit I absolutely must!"

"Thank you. Of course you'll have to visit my spa—we call it the mile-high spa."

"Hahahehe mile-high spa you're too funny oh my goodness Kitty I know we are going to be dear dear friends."

As the Amanjiwos continued to greet the arriving guests, Kitty broke into a big smile as she spotted Wandi Meggaharto Widjawa arriving.

"Kitty!" Wandi screamed from across the room, as the two ladies ran to hug as though they hadn't just seen each other yesterday.

"What are you doing here?" Kitty asked excitedly.

"Joey's my cousin. I always get invited to these dinners because Yolanda needs me to sit beside him to keep him awake. Look at you! I love the new hairstyle. You look like Emma Thompson! How did the shoot go today?"

"It was fantastic. I couldn't be happier."

"Well I'm so happy to see you here! We're going to have such a good time! You know, Joan Roca i Fontané is the celebrity chef tonight. He has the top restaurant in the world right now—El

Celler de Can Roca. It's so hard to get a reservation, you have to murder someone to get on the list. I wonder who else Yolanda invited? Oh look who's here—it's the First Lady of Singapore!"

Kitty looked over and saw Oliver greeting the First Lady as if they were both embarrassed to be seeing each other at the party.

"You are among the crème de la crème of Singapore now, Kitty. These parties are so exclusive that no photographers are ever allowed," Wandi said, just as a roving photographer dressed in a black tuxedo flashed his camera at them.

"That's Yolanda's personal documentarian. It's not for the public," Wandi quickly explained. "Oh look, here come the footmen—this means we are adjourning to the dining room!"

A set of grand double doors were opened, and as Kitty walked through the arched doors, her eyes widened in wonder. She felt as if she had been transported back to a royal banquet in eighteenth-century France. The room was a mirrored chamber decorated with baroque gold boiseries, gilt bronze mirrors stretching from floor to ceiling, and dozens of candlelit crystal chandeliers. An immense dining table that seated thirty stretched along the middle of the room, heaving with Meissen china, gilt silverware, and towering gold birdcage centerpieces filled with white doves. The room sparkled under the light of thousands of candles, and footmen with powdered white wigs and dressed in black-and-gold livery stood behind every Amiens tapestry-covered chair.

"Hashtag madamedefuckingpompadour!" Oliver muttered under his breath.

"Yolanda had this dining room rescued from an old crumbling palace in Hungary and transported here piece by piece. It took three years to restore it to its former glory," Wandi proudly announced.

"Can we do this at my house? Find an old palace and transport the dining room over?" Kitty whispered to Oliver.

Oliver cast Kitty a disapproving look. "Absolutely not! Alexis
de Redé would be projectile vomiting in his grave if he saw this
travesty."

Kitty didn't have a clue what he meant, but she was only too
thrilled to be shown to her seat by a handsome footman, where
her place card was a small antique gilt mirror with her name
etched in glass. As she was about to sit down, the man beside her
grabbed her arm. "Madame, not yet. We don't sit until the First
Lady has been seated. Yolanda follows the official court proto-
cols here," he said in a Scandinavian accent.

"Oh, sorry, I had no idea," Kitty said. She stood by her seat,
watching everyone stand at their places. Finally, the butler standing by the double doors announced, "The Honorable First Lady
of the Republic of Singapore!"

The First Lady entered and was shown to her seat. Kitty's
five-inch Gianvito Rossi heels were beginning to kill her and
she couldn't wait to sit down, but the First Lady perplexingly
remained standing by her seat near the head of the table. Why
the fuck was everyone still standing?

The butler entered the room again and called out in a booming voice, "The Earl and Countess of Palliser!"

Kitty's eyes widened in shock as a tall blond man entered the
room, dressed casually in a button-down shirt, khaki chinos, and
a rumpled navy blazer. By his side was Colette, dressed in a long
white cotton eyelet dress with her hair pulled into a casual ponytail. She didn't appear to be wearing any makeup, and her only
jewelry was a pair of pearl-and-coral drop earrings.

After reacting to the shock of seeing her nemesis in Singapore, Kitty wanted to laugh out loud at how inappropriately

Colette was dressed. This stepdaughter of hers was a complete disgrace. Did Colette even know where she was?

And then, to Kitty's horror, the First Lady of Singapore performed a deep curtsy. Yolanda Amanjiwo and all the other guests in the room quickly followed suit—the men bowing low and the women dropping curtsies as the Earl and Countess of Palliser were led to the place of honor.

CHAPTER TWELVE

BOTANIC GARDENS, SINGAPORE

It was still dark when Colin and Nick entered the grounds of the Botanic Gardens.[*] They followed to a tee the instructions in the mysterious letter that Nick had received—parking in the Gleneagles Hospital parking lot and crossing Cluny Road to enter the gardens through a little-known side gate. Just as the letter had said, the gate had been left unlocked.

As they walked down the tree-lined pathway, monkeys could be heard chattering and leaping through the bushes, no doubt alarmed by the sudden presence of humans in this secluded part of the garden. "God, it's been years since I've been here," Nick commented.

"Why would you come here? You had your own private botanic gardens right next door!" Colin said.

"Sometimes my dad and I would go on walks here, just for a

---

[*] Declared a UNESCO World Heritage Site in 2015, the Singapore Botanic Gardens is cherished by locals in the same way Central Park is by New Yorkers or Hyde Park is by Londoners. A verdant oasis in the middle of the island filled with amazing botanical specimens, colonial-era pavilions, and one of the most amazing orchid collections on the planet, it's no wonder that so many Singaporeans want to have a tiny bit of their ashes scattered here. In secret, of course, since it's highly illegal. (No one escapes the law in Singapore, not even the dead.)

change, and I only wanted to go to the lake with the two islands in the middle. I called it my 'secret island.' Wait a minute, let's check the instructions again," Nick said, unfolding the map that had been placed inside the envelope. Colin held his iPhone up to provide some lighting, while Nick peered at the map intently.

"Okay, the animal topiaries are over on the right, so I think we're supposed to cut through this grove of trees right here."

"There isn't any path," Colin said.

"I know, but the arrow points down this way."

Lit only by the light of their phones, they ventured into the thick of the forest, Colin feeling a little creeped out. "It's pitch-black in here. Why do I feel like I'm suddenly in *The Blair Witch Project*?"

"Maybe we'll run in to a *pontianak*,"[*] Nick joked.

"Don't joke—a lot of people say that parts of the Botanic Gardens are haunted, you know. I mean, the Japanese tortured and killed people all over the island."

"Good thing we're not Japanese," Nick said.

---

[*] If you read *China Rich Girlfriend*, you'd already know what a *pontianak* is. But just in case you haven't (and why the hell haven't you?), allow Dr. Sandi Tan, the world's foremost pontianakologist, to elucidate you: "A tropical female vampire-slash-dryad combo, often assuming the form of a comely, sarong-draped maiden, who inhabits the darker corners of the Southeast Asian jungle. Her metamorphosis into her true form will reveal: putrefying gray flesh, mucho teeth, many claws, accompanying unpleasant odors. Her traditional prey is the unborn fetus of a pregnant woman, consumed in situ, though during severe hunger pangs, any living person—even flatulent, stringy grandpas—would suffice. She can be summoned by tying a white string between two adjacent banana trees and intoning a chant of your own choosing, but she is more than capable of being an independent operator. Must not be confused with her inelegant country cousins, also female bloodsuckers, the *penanggalan* (bodiless flying she-demon with long, unwashed hair and a meaty chandelier of entrails) and the *pelesit* (an all-purpose slave, horrendously and pathetically devoted to her conjuror, with no agency of her own)."

Soon the trees gave way to a trail, and after following it for a few minutes, they came upon a small concrete hut under an enormous casuarina tree.

"I think this is it. It's some sort of pump room," Nick said, trying to peer in through the darkened windows.

Suddenly a dark figure darted out from behind the tree.

"*Pontianak!*" Colin yelled, dropping his iPhone in panic.

"Sorry, it's just me," a female voice said.

Nick flashed his iPhone in the direction of the figure and suddenly before them, illuminated in the white blue light, appeared Astrid in an audaciously large Vetements hoodie with super-long sleeves and tight camouflage pants.

"Jesus, Astrid! I almost shit myself!" Colin exclaimed.

"Sorry! I was scared for a moment when you first walked up, and then I realized it was you guys," Astrid said.

Nick smiled in relief. "I'm assuming you got the same note I did about seeing Ah Ma?"

"Yes! It was all rather mysterious. I was at my parents' watching Cassian swim in the pool. I must have dozed off in my deck chair for a moment, because when I got up, there was a tray of iced tea and pandan cake by my side, and the envelope was under the cake. Cassian swears he didn't see who put it there."

"How curious. Are you okay?" Nick asked.

"I'm fine. It didn't really spook me." Just as Astrid said this, a light came on inside the pump room and the three of them jumped a little in shock. The steel door could be heard being unlocked from the inside, and as it opened with a loud rusty creak, a turbaned silhouette could be seen peeking out.

"Vikram!" Nick said excitedly.

"Come quickly," Vikram instructed, ushering them all in.

"What is this place?" Astrid asked.

"This is the pump room that controls the intake for the two ponds," Vikram said as he led them toward the back of the space, which was cramped with machinery. Behind a large round pipe going into the ground, a barely discernable panel opened to reveal a dark gaping void. "This is where we're going. Each of you take turns—there are ladder rungs against the inner wall of this pipe."

"Is this what I think it is?" Nick said in astonishment.

Vikram smiled. "Come on, Nicky, you go first."

Nick hauled himself into the small crawl space and climbed down what seemed like a dozen or so rungs. After landing on solid ground, he helped Astrid find her footing as she descended the steps. When the four of them finally made it down, they found themselves in a small steel-walled vestibule. An old sign nailed against one wall read in English, Chinese, and Malay:

DANGER! NO OUTLET!

CHAMBER WILL FLOOD DURING VALVE RELEASE!

Vikram pushed against one of the wall panels, and it opened to reveal a well-lit tunnel. Nick, Astrid, and Colin entered with mouths agape, stunned by the existence of such a space.

"No. Fucking. Way!" Colin exclaimed.

"This tunnel leads to Tyersall Park, doesn't it?" Nick asked excitedly.

"It goes right under Adam Road and puts us within the grounds of the house. Let's go, we don't have much time," Vikram said.

As they made their way through the tunnel, Nick looked around in wonderment. There were spots of mold along some of the concrete walls and the ground was caked in a layer of dirt, but overall the tunnel was remarkably well preserved. "When I was a little kid, my father used to tell me stories about how there were secret passages in Tyersall Park, and I just thought he was pulling my leg. I begged him to show me one, but he never would."

"Did you always know this was here?" Astrid asked.

"Not until yesterday," Vikram said. "Ah Ling told me about it. Apparently this tunnel was used during the war by your great-grandfather Shang Loong Ma. That's how he got in and out of the property and was never once caught by the Japanese."

"I've heard there are tunnels similar to this. There's supposedly one that leads from Uncle Kuan Yew's house on Oxley Road to the Istana," Astrid commented. "I just never imagined Tyersall Park would have one too."

"Incredible! I can't believe this whole elaborate plan—just to see your grandmother!" Colin remarked to Nick.

"Yes, apologies for all the cloak-and-dagger. Ah Ling and I needed to devise a way to get messages to the both of you without incriminating ourselves. Tyersall Park has been on complete lockdown for the past few days, as you are well aware," Vikram said with a grin.

"I'm so grateful, Vikram." Nick smiled back at him.

They arrived at the end of the tunnel and faced another set of rungs. Nick went first, and when he was out of the shaft, he looked down at Astrid as she climbed up. "You'll never believe where we are!"

Astrid climbed out of the shaft and found herself standing in the middle of hanging orchid plants. They were in their grandmother's orchid conservatory, and the large round stone table carved with griffins at its base in the middle of the conservatory rolled to the side to reveal the entrance into the tunnel.

"I've spent countless hours sitting at this table, having afternoon tea with Ah Ma!" Astrid exclaimed.

Standing on lookout at the door of the conservatory was Ah Ling. "Come, come, let's get in before it gets light and people start waking up."

When they were all safely ensconced inside Ah Ling's room in the servants' quarters, she wasted no time in explaining her plan. "Colin, you should stay here in my room, out of sight. I will take Astrid and Nicky up to Su Yi's bedroom. I know a special route that will let us enter from the balcony outside her dressing room, and Astrid, you should go in alone first and be with her when she awakes. She will usually wake up after you draw the curtains open. She'll be pleased to see you, and then you can tell her that Nicky is outside waiting to see her. This way she won't get a shock if she wakes up and sees Nicky standing right there."

"Good thinking," Nick said.

"Madri and Patravadee know about the plan. They are stationed right outside her door in the sitting room. Usually the nurses will check on her every fifteen minutes, but today they will block the nurses from entering. Professor Oon usually does his first check-in at seven thirty. Now, Astrid, I am counting on you to be outside Su Yi's bedroom at seven thirty to intercept him. I've seen how he defers to you."

Astrid nodded. "Don't worry, I'll deal with Professor Oon."

"The other thing is Eddie. These days he likes to be the first to visit Su Yi in the morning. But I got Ah Ching to make his favorite crepes with Lyle's Golden Syrup this morning, so I will tell him he needs to eat them while they are hot. I'll try to keep him at breakfast as long as possible."

"Maybe you can slip a sedative into his crepe batter," Nick suggested.

"Or something to give him explosive diarrhea," Colin said.

They all laughed for a moment, and then Ah Ling got up from her chair. "Okay, everyone ready?"

Nick and Astrid proceeded up the servants' staircase to the second floor, following quietly behind Ah Ling as she expertly guided them through the service hallways until they found themselves on the balcony outside Su Yi's dressing room. Astrid opened the door as quietly as she could and tiptoed in. The cool, mosaic-tiled space adjoining Su Yi's bedroom smelled of jasmine and lavender water. She stood by the doorway, peeked into her grandmother's bedroom, and saw Su Yi's lady's maids silently prepping the room for the morning. Madri was spritzing a beautiful pot of orchids with water, while Patravadee was tidying up the nurses' station.

The minute they saw Astrid, they nodded at her and pulled the curtains open. Then the two ladies slipped out of the bedroom, closed the door behind them, and stood guard diligently outside. A nurse could be heard behind the door asking, "Is Mrs. Young awake yet? Are you getting her breakfast?" One of the lady's maids replied, "She wants to sleep a little longer today. We will send for her breakfast after eight."

Astrid headed first to the side table, opened a bottle of Adelboden water, and refilled one of the cups. Then she took it over to Su Yi's bedside and sat down in the chair beside her.

Su Yi's eyelids fluttered open, her eyes hazily registering Astrid beside her.

"Good morning, Ah Ma," Astrid said cheerily. "Here, drink some water."

Su Yi accepted the water gratefully, and after satiating her parched throat, she looked around the room and asked, "What day is it today?"

"It's Thursday."

"Did you just return from India?"

"Yes, Ah Ma," Astrid fibbed, not wanting to cause her grandmother any undue concern.

"Let me see your ring," Su Yi said.

Astrid held her hand up to show her grandmother her engagement ring.

Su Yi studied it carefully. "I knew it would look perfect on you."

"I don't know how to thank you for this, Ah Ma."

"Did everything go according to plan? Did Charlie manage to surprise you?"

"Yes, I was so stunned!"

"Were there elephants? I told Charlie he needed to arrive on an elephant. That's how my friend the Maharaja of Bikaner proposed to his queen."

"Yes, there was an elephant." Astrid laughed, realizing just how involved her grandmother had been in helping to plan the whole affair.

"Are there any pictures?"

"No, we didn't take any . . . oh, wait a minute." Astrid took out her phone and did a quick google search for the paparazzi photos that had been leaked of her private moment. She never imagined how useful they would be until this moment. As she showed a few of the snapshots to her eager grandmother, she thought how ironic it was that the rest of her family was so upset by what was one of the happiest moments in her life.

Su Yi sighed. "It looks beautiful, I wish I could have been there. Charlie looks so handsome in his outfit. Tell me, is he in Singapore now?"

"Actually, he'll be coming to town tomorrow. He comes to visit his mother every month."

"He's a good boy, that one. I knew from the moment I met him that he will always take good care of you." Su Yi stared at the grainy shot of Charlie putting the ring on Astrid's finger. "You know, of all the jewelry I own, this ring is the most special to me."

"I know, Ah Ma."

"I never got the chance to ask your grandfather if he bought it."

"What do you mean? Who would have bought this engagement ring, if not him?"

"Your grandfather did not have that much money when I first met him. He was just a recent medical graduate. How on earth would he have been able to afford this canary diamond?"

"You're right. It would have cost a fortune at the time," Astrid said.

"I always suspected that Uncle T'sien Tsai Tay was the one who bought it, since he helped to broker the marriage. The quality of the stone isn't perfect, but when I wore it, it always reminded me of how life can surprise you. Sometimes, the thing that at first appears flawed can end up being the most perfect thing in the world for you."

Su Yi was silent for a few moments, and then she looked at her granddaughter with a sudden intensity. "Astrid, I want you to promise me something."

"Yes, Ah Ma?"

"If I die before your wedding day, please don't go into all that mourning nonsense for me. I want you to have your wedding just as you planned in March. Will you promise me you'll do that?"

"Oh Ah Ma, nothing's going to happen. You're go . . . going to be sitting in the front row of my wedding," Astrid stammered.

"I'm planning on it, but I wanted to say this just in case."

Astrid looked away, trying to hold back her tears. She sat there holding her grandmother's hand for a few quiet moments, before she said, "Ah Ma, you know who's back in Singapore to see you? Nicky."

"Nicky's home?"

"Yes, he's here. In fact he's right outside. Do you want to see him now?"

"Send him in. I thought he was going to be here last week."

Astrid got up from her chair and was about to head for the dressing room when her grandmother said, "Wait a minute."

Astrid stopped in her tracks and turned around. "Yes?"

"Is his wife here as well?" Su Yi asked.

"No, it's just him." Astrid paused for a second, anticipating another question from her grandmother. But Su Yi was now fidgeting with the bed controls, raising the incline of her bed to the exact angle she wanted. Astrid proceeded to the balcony, where she found Nick sitting pensively at the wrought-iron table.

"Is she awake?" he asked.

"Yes."

"How is she?"

"She's okay. A lot better than I was expecting, actually. Come on, your turn."

"Um . . . she really wants to see me?" Nick asked trepidatiously.

Astrid smiled at her cousin. For a moment he looked like he was six years old again. "Don't be ridiculous. Of course. She's ready for you now."

CHAPTER THIRTEEN

Oliver had just boarded his flight to London and was in the process of stealing an extra pillow from the seat behind him when Kitty called.

"Morning, Kitty," he said cheerily, steeling himself for the barrage he knew was about to come. "Did you sleep well?"

"Are you fucking kidding me? That was the worst night of my entire life!"

"I know several billion people who would have happily traded places with you, Kitty. You got to attend one of Yolanda Amanjiwo's legendary dinners. The world's most acclaimed chef prepared a twelve-course tasting menu for you. Did you not enjoy that? I thought the langoustines were superb—"

"Ugh! That so-called genius chef from that de la cellar place should be locked in his own cellar and they should throw away the key!"

"Come on, aren't you being a bit harsh? Just because you don't appreciate deconstructed surrealist Catalan fusion cuisine doesn't mean you should sentence him to the gallows. I could have eaten ten more plates of that *jamón ibérico* flash-frozen fried rice."

"How could I possibly appreciate the food when I was being

tortured? I've never been more humiliated in my life!" Kitty seethed.

"I don't know what you mean, Kitty," Oliver said lightly as he took the stack of in-flight magazines out of the seat pocket and shoved them into the pocket adjacent to him before the passenger arrived. Anything for the extra legroom.

"Everybody at the dinner curtsied to Colette! That snotty Swedish ambassador guy next to me glared at me when I didn't move, but I'll be damned if I curtsy to my own stepdaughter!"

"Well, Thorsten obviously did not know who you were. And Kitty, that whole curtsying thing was a complete farce. I don't know which edition of *Debrett's* Yolanda Amanjiwo is reading, but she was absolutely incorrect. A British earl does *not* have precedence over the First Lady of the country where he is nothing more than a visitor. They should have been bowing to *her*. But these Singaporeans are so awed by any *ang mor* with a two-bit title that they just bow and scrape away like subservient little toadies. I remember a time when the Countess of Mountbatten came to visit Tyersall Park, and Su Yi wouldn't even come downstairs to receive her!"

"You're missing the point. Everyone treated Colette like royalty all through the dinner. They were dressed like peasants and the people were still sucking up! That idiot on my right wouldn't even lift his fork until Colette lifted her fork. And then the minute she was done with her dinner, we all had to stop. That Carolina Herrera–perfumed flan was the first thing I was actually enjoying, but then dinner abruptly ended and the royal couple was off."

"The last thing I thought I'd ever wanted to eat was a dessert that tasted like Carolina Herrera, but it was superb, wasn't it? Well, aren't you at least glad the dinner passed with no incident? Colette didn't try to insult you or cause a scene."

"No, what she did was worse—she didn't even acknowledge my presence! And I'm married to her father! The man who pays all her bills even though she won't talk to him anymore! Do you know how hurt he feels? That ungrateful, spoiled little beast!"

"Kitty, I wouldn't take it so personally if I were you. There were thirty of us in that ghastly room, sixty if you count the ridiculous footmen, and Yolanda was dominating every minute of Lucien and Colette's time. Trust me, I was right opposite from them. You were on the other end of the table hidden behind those ridiculous birdcage centerpieces—I honestly don't think she even saw you."

"Colette saw me, I can assure you. She doesn't miss a thing. Why was she even in Singapore anyway?"

"Lucien is an environmentalist, and they are going to be based in Singapore for the next month, that's all. They're on their way to Sumatra to observe the orangutan situation."

"What orangutan situation?"

"Oh, it's quite a tragedy. Thousands of orangutans are dying because of deforestation in their natural habitats. Colette's become quite involved in orangutan orphan rescue."

"That's what you talked about? There was no mention of me? Of her father?"

"Kitty, I can assure you that the only people that were mentioned by name happened to be orangutans."

"So she doesn't know you and I have a connection?"

"She doesn't. But what would it matter anyway? Why didn't you just come over and say hi? Be the bigger person and welcome her to Singapore? That would have been the smart move," Oliver said as he struggled to tuck his leather valise under the seat next to him.

"Hnh! I am her stepmother! She should introduce herself to *me*, not the other way around!"

"Wait a minute . . . are you saying you've never met Colette?" Oliver was genuinely shocked.

"Of course not! I told you, she hasn't seen her father since she found out about our affair. And she wouldn't come to the wedding. She hasn't set foot in China in more than two years. She told him that he . . . that he was marrying a whore."

Oliver could hear the tears in her voice, and he began to see the situation in a whole new light. No wonder Kitty had been traumatized when Colette made her grand entrance last night. In China, Kitty had been eclipsed by Colette in absentia, and here in Singapore, she had been eclipsed again in an even more dramatic fashion. A flight attendant gestured to Oliver. "Kitty, my flight to London is about to take off now, so I have to put away my phone."

"Oh really? I thought no one cared if you use your phone in first class."

"Well, you don't know this, but I'm one of those aviation geeks that actually likes to watch the safety demonstration."

"I didn't know you were off to London again. You should have told me—I would have lent you one of my planes."

"That's very kind of you. Kitty, I'm going to spend the next fourteen hours on this flight coming up with a plan. I promise you, Colette will never humiliate you again."

"You promise?"

"Absolutely. And look on the brighter side . . . you have so much to look forward to. Your *Tattle* cover is coming out next month. You will be an absolute sensation, I tell you! And you're besties with Yolanda Amanjiwo now. This is just the beginning for you, Kitty. Colette has to head back to some drafty old manor in England, while we are designing you the most spectacular house Singapore has ever seen."

Kitty sighed. Oliver was right. There was so much to look forward to. She put down her phone and looked in the small gilt mirror that was given to her as a party favor last night. She did look a bit like Emma Watson, that actress who played Hermione Granger. And Oliver with his big round spectacles looked a bit like Harry Potter. Oliver really was a kind of wizard. And now he was going to wave his wand and bring even more magic into her life.

On the SQ 909 flight to London, Oliver turned off his phone and tucked it into the seat pocket. A flight attendant suddenly leaned into his row. "Excuse me? Is that an extra pillow I see? I'm afraid I'm going to need that," she said with an apologetic smile.

"I'm sorry, I didn't even see it," Oliver lied.

"And is that your leather bag? I'm also going to have to ask you to tuck it under your own seat. Make sure the straps are tucked in completely. We have a very full cabin here in economy class today," the stewardess said.

"Oh, of course," Oliver said, as he bent down to retrieve his bag, cursing silently. It was going to be a very long flight.

CHAPTER FOURTEEN

The morning light filtering through the windows made the mahogany art deco furniture in Su Yi's bedroom glow like amber, and Nick was shocked for a moment to see how tiny and frail his grandmother looked in the middle of her hospital bed, the machines clustered around her like an army of invading robots. It had been almost five years since he had seen her, and now a tremendous sense of remorse descended over him. How had he let so much time pass? He had lost five precious years because of a quarrel, because of his pride. As Nick approached her bed, he was temporarily at a loss for words.

Astrid stood by Nick's side for a moment, and then she announced in a gentle voice, "Ah Ma, here's Nicky."

Su Yi opened her eyes and gazed up at her grandson. *Tien, ah. He looks more and more like his grandfather every day*, she thought to herself. "You look even handsomer than before. I'm glad you haven't put on any weight. Most men put on weight after they get married—look how bloated Eddie has become."

Nick and Astrid both laughed a little, breaking the tension in the room. "I'll be back in a while," Astrid said, quietly slipping out through the bedroom door. No sooner had she closed the door behind her than Professor Oon entered Su Yi's sitting room.

"Good morning, Professor Oon," Astrid said cheerily, blocking his way.

The doctor was momentarily taken aback. It had been more than a week since he had seen Astrid, and he couldn't believe how she was dressed today. Holy Annabel Chong! She looked even sexier than he could have possibly imagined in this skater punk outfit and those bootylicious camouflage pants. It was better than any Japanese-schoolgirl porn site. Was she wearing a sports bra under that big hoodie? Her body was a work of God. Recovering himself, Professor Oon put on his blasé, clinical tone. "Ah, Astrid. Welcome back. I was just about to run the morning vitals on your grandmother."

"Oh, don't you think that can wait for a moment? Why don't you give me an update first, since I've been away? Ah Ma seems rather well this morning. Could her condition be improving?"

Professor Oon frowned. "It's possible. We put her on a new cocktail of beta-blockers, and she's benefited from a sustained period of rest."

"I'm soooo grateful for all you've done," Astrid said warmly.

"Um, yah. After I look at her latest EKG, I'll be able to give you a more accurate prognosis."

"Tell me, doctor, have you heard of a specialist at St. Luke's Medical Center in Houston named David Scott? Dr. Scott has developed an experimental new treatment for congestive heart disease," Astrid continued, not letting him off the hook.

Wow, beauty and brains. A woman who can talk so seductively about heart disease, Professor Oon thought. That damn Charlie Wu was one lucky prick. If only Astrid came from another family, if only she wasn't so bloody rich, she could be his mistress. He would set her up at his secret apartment at The Marq and watch her do laps, naked, in the pool all day.

. . .

Inside the bedroom, Nick was wondering what precisely to say to his grandmother. "*Nay ho ma?*"* he said, and then immediately wondered why he had asked her such a stupid question.

"I haven't been too well. But today I'm feeling better than I have in many weeks."

"I'm so glad to hear that." Nick crouched beside Su Yi and looked her squarely in the face. He knew that the moment had come for him to deliver his apology. As much as he had been hurt by her, and as much as he felt that she had wronged Rachel, he knew that it was his duty to ask for her forgiveness. He cleared his throat and began, "Ah Ma, I'm so sorry for the way I behaved. I hope that you can find it in your heart to forgive me."

Su Yi looked away from her grandson and let out a long slow exhale. Nicky was home. Her dutiful grandson was by her side again, kneeling at her feet and asking for redemption. If only he knew how she truly felt. She was quiet for a few moments, and then she turned to face him again. "Are you comfortable in your bedroom?"

"My bedroom?" Nick asked, momentarily confused by her question.

"Yes, has it been made up nicely for you?"

"Um, I haven't been staying here. I've been at Colin's."

"On Berrima Road?"

"No, Colin's family sold that house a few years ago. He's living in Sentosa Cove now."

"Why on earth are you staying there and not here?"

It dawned on Nick at that moment that his grandmother

---

* Cantonese for "How are you?"

didn't have a clue that he'd been back for over a week. She obviously had nothing to do with banning him from Tyersall Park! He wasn't sure what to say at first, but then quickly recovered himself. "There are so many people visiting at the moment, I didn't think there would be room for me."

"Nonsense. No one is supposed to be in your bedroom." Su Yi pushed a button beside her, and within a few seconds Madri and Patravadee were by her bedside.

"Please tell Ah Ling to have Nicky's rooms made up. I have no idea why he is staying at some godforsaken place instead of here," Su Yi instructed her lady's maids.

"Of course, ma'am," Madri replied.

At that moment, Nick realized that this was his grandmother's tacit manner of forgiving him. He felt suddenly lighter, as if a gigantic boulder had been lifted off his back.

As Su Yi's lady's maids stepped out of the bedroom, Adam and Piya walked into the sitting room and for a few seconds before the bedroom door closed saw their cousin Nick crouched by his grandmother's side.

Astrid waved from the settee where she was seated talking with Professor Oon. "Adam! It's so good to see you!"

"Oh Astrid, I'm sorry, I didn't see you over there. Piya, this is my cousin Astrid. She's Auntie Felicity's daughter."

"I've heard so much about you," Piya said with a smile.

"Was that Nicholas I saw in there with Ah Ma? We were just going to have a quick look-in before breakfast," Adam said.

"Nicholas Young?" Professor Oon said in alarm. "He's in the bedroom? But we are under strict orders not to—"

"Francis, hold that thought for one minute," Astrid said, placing her hand on his lap, her fingers almost grazing his inner thigh. The doctor trembled at her unexpected touch and immediately went mute. Astrid turned to Adam and Piya and said, "I'm sure Ah Ma would love to see you in a little while. She's doing much better this morning. Why don't you head down to breakfast first? I hear that Ah Ching is making her famous crepes."

"Ooh, I do love a good crepe," Piya said.

"Me too. And Ah Ching makes a special sauce of Belgian chocolate and Lyle's Golden Syrup to drizzle over them. Professor Oon, have you ever had chocolate-infused golden syrup drizzled over your crepes?"

"Er, no," the doctor said, sweat beginning to bead around his temples.

"Well you must. In fact why don't you join us right now? Let's all go down for some crepes. I'm sure the whole family would love to have an update from you about Ah Ma," Astrid said, getting up from the settee.

The three of them stood there, waiting for the doctor.

"Um, give me a minute," Professor Oon said sheepishly. He knew that there was no way he could stand up at that moment.

Back in the bedroom, Su Yi had instructed Nick to go to the top drawer of her bureau and fetch something for her. "Do you see the pale blue box?"

"Yes."

"At the bottom of the box are some silk pouches. Please bring me the yellow one."

Nick unfastened the metal clasp on the blue embossed leather box and flipped open the lid. Inside was an assortment of objects and curiosities. Vintage tortoiseshell combs and coins of varying currencies mixed in with letters and faded old photographs. He came upon a small stack wrapped with a piece of ribbon and realized that it was every picture he had ever sent to her from his boarding-school days in England. At the bottom of the box were several jewelry pouches, the kind made of padded silk that one saw in Chinatown trinket shops all over the world. He found a small yellow pouch and returned to his grandmother's bedside.

Su Yi unzipped the pouch, took out a pair of earrings, and placed them in the palm of Nick's hand. "I want you to have these. For your wife."

Nick felt a lump in his throat as he realized the enormous significance of her gift. His grandmother was acknowledging Rachel as his wife for the very first time. He glanced at the earrings in his palm. They were simple pearl studs set on old-fashioned gold posts, but the luminosity of each pearl was stunning—they seemed to glow from within. "Thank you, Ah Ma. I know Rachel will love these."

Su Yi looked her grandson in the eye. "My father gave these to me when I escaped Singapore before the war, when the Japanese soldiers had finally reached Johor and we knew all was lost. They are very special. Please look after them carefully."

"We will cherish them, Ah Ma."

"Now, I think it's time for my morning pills. Will you call Madri and Patravadee in?"

In the breakfast room, Ah Ching had set up a cooking station at the end of the long dining table. Rather unusually, she eschewed the use of a crepe pan to make her beloved recipe. Instead, she cooked them on her trusty wok, expertly tilting and twisting the large black wok to create the perfect round thin pancakes.

Eddie had woken up Fiona and the kids for this special treat, and his mother, Victoria, Catherine, and Taksin were assembled in the room as well, eagerly awaiting their custom-made crepes.

"Can I have mine with some ham and cheese?" Taksin asked. "I prefer savory ones to sweet ones, especially in the morning."

"Uncle Taksin, you're missing out if you don't try the fabulous sauce that Ah Ching makes," Eddie said.

"I want mine with ice cream," young Augustine said.

"Augie, you will eat them exactly as I instruct you to!" Eddie barked at his son.

Catherine exchanged glances with Alix, who simply rolled her eyes and shook her head.

As the family began tucking into the first round of crepes, Astrid entered the dining room with Adam, Piya, and Professor Oon.

"What are you doing here?" Eddie said, startled by his cousin's sudden appearance at the house. He thought she had been ordered to stay away by her parents since the India engagement scandal.

"I'm having crepes, just like you," Astrid replied breezily.

"Well, I suppose *some of us* don't have any shame," Eddie muttered under his breath.

Astrid chose to ignore her cousin and went over to greet her aunties with pecks on their cheeks. Victoria stiffened visibly as Astrid kissed her and asked, "How is your mother? I hear she's been bedridden for the past two days." Implicit in her disapproving tone was that Astrid was the one responsible for making her mother sick.

"Considering the fact that she managed to play bridge for five hours yesterday with Mrs. Lee Yong Chien, Diana Yu, and Rosemary Yeh, I think she's doing just fine," Astrid replied.

Alix wondered what the doctor was doing at their breakfast

table, but ever well mannered, she smiled graciously at her old classmate and said, "Francis, how good of you to join us."

"Er, Astrid insisted I try some of Ah Ching's famous pancakes."

"You've been upstairs already?" Eddie said in alarm, wondering if she had told Ah Ma that Nicky was in town.

Astrid looked him straight in the eye. "Yes, I've spent a little time with Ah Ma. She wanted to see photos of my engagement, since she helped to plan it. Such a wonderful stroke of luck that there was someone there to capture the occasion."

Eddie looked at her openmouthed.

"Congratulations on your engagement, Astrid," Fiona said.

"Yes, congratulations," Catherine and Alix both chimed merrily.

Victoria was the only aunt not to offer any wishes, turning instead to Professor Oon. "How is my mother faring this morning?"

"Well, I haven't had the chance to look in on her yet, as Nicholas is with her at the moment."

"WHAAAAT? Are you telling me that Nicky is upstairs with my grandmother?" Eddie exclaimed loudly.

"Calm down, Eddie," Fiona chided.

Astrid smiled sweetly at her cousin. "Precisely what is your issue with Nicky seeing Ah Ma? When did you become her bouncer?"

"He's been banned from the house!" Eddie said.

"Who banned him, exactly? Because if you ask me, Ah Ma was certainly quite overjoyed to see him a few minutes ago," Astrid said, calmly pouring some of the chocolate golden syrup onto her crepe.

"Are you sure about that?" Victoria said indignantly.

"Yes, I was in the room when Ah Ma specifically requested to see him."

Eddie shook his head angrily, bolting up from his chair. "If nobody is going to do anything about this, I am! Nicky's going to give her another heart attack!"

"Give *who* a heart attack?"

Eddie spun around to see his grandmother sitting in a wheelchair as Nick pushed her into the breakfast room. Trailing them were her oxygen tank and several other medical devices, dutifully being guided along by her Thai lady's maids. Behind them followed a cluster of nurses and the on-duty associate cardiologist.

"Mummy! What are you doing down here?" Victoria shrieked.

"What do you mean? I wanted to have breakfast in my own breakfast room. Nicky told me that Ah Ching was making her delicious crepes."

The young associate looked at Professor Oon rather helplessly, but handed his boss several computer printouts. "Prof, she insisted on coming downstairs, but I managed to run some diagnostics first."

Professor Oon scanned the morning's reports, his eyes widening. "My goodness . . . Bravo, Mrs. Young—I am amazed you are feeling so well this morning!"

Su Yi ignored the doctor, her eyes instead focusing on Eddie. "What an interesting place for you to sit," she said mischievously.

"Oh, sorry," Eddie said, getting flustered as he hastily got up from his chair at the head of the table, while Nick dutifully rolled Su Yi's chair into place.

"Come, sit next to me," Su Yi said to Nick, patting the table. One of the maids swiftly produced a chair, and as Nick took his seat beside his grandmother at the head of the table, he couldn't help but grin from ear to ear. For the first time since he had arrived in Singapore, he felt like he was home again.

Ah Ling entered the breakfast room and placed a cup and saucer in front of Su Yi. "Here's your favorite *da hong pao** tea."

"Splendid. I feel like I haven't tasted tea in ages. Ah Ling, did you get my message to see that Nicky's room is made up? For some reason he's been staying in Sentosa, of all places!"

"Yes, Nicky's bedroom is all ready for him," Ah Ling announced, trying to suppress a giggle as she noticed the veins in Eddie's neck beginning to twitch.

"Is my little brother coming over tomorrow for Friday-night dinner?" Su Yi asked.

"Yes. We're making Mr. Shang his favorite *yen woh*."

"Ah, good. Astrid, be sure to invite Charlie tomorrow night."

Astrid's heart soared. "I'm sure he would love to come, Ah Ma."

"Has everyone seen Astrid's engagement ring?" Su Yi asked.

Catherine, Alix, and Victoria craned their necks to study the diamond on Astrid's finger, realizing with a start that they were staring at their mother's old engagement ring.

Alix, who had absolutely no interest in jewelry, quickly went back to devouring her crepe, but Victoria couldn't hide her look of disappointment—she always thought that this ring would be hers one day.

"Astrid, it looks lovely on you," Catherine offered, before adding, "Are you planning on having an engagement party?"

Su Yi cut in enthusiastically, "What a good idea. Ah Ling, will

---

* Grown in the Wuyi Mountains of China's Fujian Province, *da hong pao*—which translates to "big red robe"—is one of the world's rarest teas. It's priced at $1,400 per gram, which makes the tea worth thirty times its weight in gold.

you call the T'siens and the Tans to come over tomorrow night? Let's have a party!"

"Of course," Ah Ling said.

"Mummy, I don't think you should have so much excitement when you're just beginning to feel better. You should rest," Victoria said officiously.

"Nonsense, I'll rest when I'm dead. Tomorrow, I want to see everyone. Let's celebrate Astrid's engagement and Nicky's homecoming!" Su Yi decreed.

Fiona noticed that Eddie was turning purple. Elbowing him in the ribs, she said, "Eddie, loosen your ascot so the air can get in. And breathe, darling. Breathe deeply."

CHAPTER FIFTEEN

"Your IC, please," the security guard said sternly as Astrid rolled down the window of her car. Astrid dug into her purse for her wallet, took out her Singapore Identity Card, and handed it to the guard. He held the card up to his eye level to compare the semi-pixilated photograph to her face, squinting at every detail.

"It was a bad-hair day," Astrid joked.

The guard didn't crack a smile, but took her IC into the guard-house and began to scan it through his computer system.

Astrid had to resist rolling her eyes. This particular Mainland Chinese guard already knew her—how many times had she been here in the past few months? It made her understand how the Wus came to develop a particular reputation among Singapore's establishment when Charlie's father, Wu Hao Lian, first made his fortune in the early 1980s. The Wus did seem pretentious—there was no avoiding that fact.

At a time when the moneyed crowd preferred to populate elegant bungalows tucked away in the leafy enclaves of Districts 9, 10, and 11, Wu Hao Lian had bought a large parcel of land off one of Singapore's busiest thoroughfares and built a sprawling family compound right there for all the world to see. He had erected a tall white stucco wall around the property, and at the top of the wall, sharp red-glazed tiles undulated up and down like the scaley curves on a dragon's back, ending at the main gates with twin carved dragon heads in bronze. Rectangular gold plaques placed in niches at thirty-foot intervals around the wall were engraved in an ornate calligraphy script with the words:

Wu Mansions

To ordinary Singaporeans—the ninety percent who lived in public-housing apartments—it seemed like the Wus were the richest family in the land. The family was seen being driven around in a fleet of ever-changing Rolls-Royces, always accompanied by security guards in a Mercedes wherever they went. They were one of the first families on the island to flaunt their private jet, and spent all their holidays touring Europe, where Irene Wu and her daughters developed a voracious appetite for haute couture and haute jewelry. Whenever Irene appeared in public, she was always clad in the most ornately festooned frocks and laden with so much jewelry that all the other socialites nicknamed her "Christmas Tree" behind her back.

But all this was so long ago, Astrid thought as the tall steel gate embossed with the ornate W seal began to slide to one side and she sped up the short driveway to the Palladian-style house with a white columned portico covered in bougainvillea. The Wus had receded into the background, especially after Charlie's father passed away and a new generation of brash billionaires burst onto the scene in the early 2000s, building even more ostentatious pleasure domes and vying for visibility in the society pages. Only Charlie's mother remained in Singapore these days, reluctant to give up her house.

Astrid pulled up behind a gray Mercedes SUV already parked underneath the portico. She saw Lincoln Tay, her distant cousin, emerge from the driver's seat and walk around to the trunk of the car. "Ah Tock! Fancy seeing you here," Astrid said as she got out of her car.

"What can I tell you? You're always hanging around the rich and famous, and I just work for them," he joked. "Now Astrid, tell me why are you still driving that old Acura? Does it even pass inspection anymore?"

"This is the most reliable car I've ever owned. I'm going to drive it until I'm forced to scrap it."

"Come on *lah*, you are so loaded, at the very least you should upgrade to the ILX. Or maybe Charlie can buy Acura the company for you and have them design you a car from scratch."

"Ha-ha, very funny," Astrid said. It occurred to her that every time she saw this distant cousin, he would make some sort of reference to her money.

"Hey, come and see something very special," Ah Tock said, as he opened the trunk of the SUV. A large Igloo cooler was strapped to one side of the spacious rear, and Ah Tock carefully lifted out a large plastic bag that had been inflated with oxygen. Inside was a dragon-like fish about two feet in length.

"Oh, it's an arowana," Astrid said.

"Not just any arowana. This is Valentino, Mrs. Wu's prized super red arowana. It was worth at least $175,000 and now it will be worth $250,000, minimum."

"Why's that?"

"I just took Valentino to his plastic surgeon. He was beginning to develop a droopy eye, so we gave him an eye lift. And he even got a very slight chin job. See how handsome he looks now?"

"There's a plastic surgeon for *fish*?" Astrid asked incredulously.

"The best in the world, right here in Singapore! He specializes in arowanas."[*]

Before Astrid could properly soak in this fabulous bit of trivia, the front door opened and Irene Wu came running out. A round-faced woman in her early seventies, she was dressed in a bright orange Moroccan-style tunic top embroidered with tiny mirrored glass pieces and sequins, white capri pants, and fluffy white bedroom slippers embroidered with the Four Seasons Hotel logo. On her fingers sparkled an emerald ring; another ring consisting of three interlaced bands of diamonds set in white, yellow, and rose gold; and a pear-cut diamond ring that was nearly as big as the real fruit itself.

"How is he? How's my baby Valentino?" Irene asked breathlessly, rushing toward Ah Tock and the plastic bag.

"Mrs. Wu, he's doing very well. The surgery was a success, but he's still a bit sluggish at the moment from being drugged. Let's get him acclimated back in his tank."

"Yes, yes! *Aiyah*, Astrid, I didn't even see you. Come in, come in. Sorry-ah, I am so *kan jyeong*[†] today because of Valentino's procedure. My goodness, don't you look lovely. Who are you

---

[*] The Asian arowana is the world's most expensive aquarium fish, especially coveted by collectors in Asia who will pay hundreds of thousands for a fine specimen. Known in Chinese as *lóng yú*—dragon fish—this long fish plated with large shimmering scales and with whiskers jutting from its chin resembles the mythological Chinese dragon. Aficionados believe that the fish brings good luck and fortune, and there have even been tales of arowanas sacrificing their lives by leaping out of their tanks in order to warn their owners of imminent danger or bad business deals. No wonder lovers of this fish are willing to shell out thousands to get their precious pets eye lifts, fin tucks, or chin jobs. No word on arowana Botox yet, but that can't be far behind.

[†] Cantonese for "panicky, anxious."

wearing today?" Irene asked, admiring Astrid's floral kimono-inspired wrap dress.

"Oh, this is a dress that Romeo Gigli made for me years ago, Auntie Irene," Astrid said, leaning in to give her a peck on the cheek.

"Of course it is. So pretty! And don't you think it's high time you started calling me Mama instead of Auntie Irene?"

"Come on, Mum, lay off Astrid!" Charlie said, standing at the front door. Astrid beamed at the sight of him and rushed up the steps to give him a tight hug.

"*Aiyah*, I'm going to tear up and ruin my mascara. Look at my two lovebirds!" Irene sighed happily.

As the group entered the house, Charlie steered Astrid toward the sweeping *Gone with the Wind*–style double staircase instead of the living room.

"Where are you two going?" Irene asked.

"I'm just taking her upstairs for a little while, Mum," Charlie said in a slightly exasperated tone.

"But Gracie has spent all day making so many types of *nyonya kueh*. You must come and have tea and *nyonya kueh* with me in a little while, okay?"

"Of course we will," Astrid said.

As they climbed the stairs, Charlie said in a low voice, "My mum is getting more and more needy every time I see her."

"She just misses you. It must get rather lonely for her now that none of you are around in Singapore."

"She's surrounded all day by her staff of twenty."

"It's not the same and you know it."

"Well, she has a house in Hong Kong—she could spend all her time there if she wants, but she insists on staying here," Charlie argued.

"This is where most of her memories are. Just like yours," Astrid said as she entered Charlie's bedroom. The space had been redecorated several years ago in cool, masculine tones with shagreen-covered walls and custom-designed contemporary wood furnishings from BDDW in New York, but Charlie had kept one reminder of his childhood in the bedroom: The entire ceiling had been installed with a mechanized mural depicting all the constellations in the sky, and as a kid, Charlie would go to sleep every night staring at the glowing ceiling of stars as they rotated daily according to the zodiac.

Today, he wasted no time in pulling Astrid onto the bed and smothering her with kisses. "You have no idea how much I've missed you," Charlie said, kissing the tender area right above her collarbone.

"Me too," Astrid sighed, as she put her arms around him, feeling the ripple of muscles down his back.

After spending some time making out, they lay entwined in each other's arms, staring up at the sparkling night sky together.

"I feel like a teenager again." Astrid giggled. "Remember how you used to sneak me up here after MYF* on Saturdays?"

"Yeah. I still feel like I'm doing something naughty having you in here right now."

"The door's wide open, Charlie. We haven't done anything R-rated," Astrid said with a laugh.

"I'm so happy to see you in such a good mood," Charlie said, running his fingers through her hair.

"I feel like the storm's finally lifted. You have no idea how amazing it felt to be in the breakfast room yesterday when my grandmother came downstairs."

---

* Methodist Youth Fellowship.

"I can only imagine."

"She made everyone look at my engagement ring. It's like she was daring the rest of the family to challenge us."

"Your grandmother is one cool lady. I'm looking forward to seeing her tonight. She invited my mum too, you know?"

"Really?" Astrid looked at him in surprise.

"Yeah, an engraved invitation was delivered this morning. My mother could hardly believe it. She never thought the day would come that she would be invited to Tyersall Park. I think she's going to frame the card."

"Well, it's going to be quite a party. I can't wait to see the looks on certain faces when I walk into the drawing room with your mother!"

"Which ones?"

"Oh, you know, one or two of my aunties are snottier than others. And there's one cousin in particular who's going to lose his shit!"

"Rico Suave, the Best Dressed Man in Hong Kong?" Charlie teased.

"Best Dressed Hall of Fame, he'll tell you." Astrid laughed. "Come on, let's go back downstairs before your mother thinks we're doing something nasty up here."

"I *want* her to think I'm doing something nasty."

They got out of bed reluctantly, straightened their clothes, and strolled down the gracious curving stairway hand in hand. Passing through the archway underneath the staircase, they entered the grand living room, which was handsomely decorated in French Empire style intermingled with museum-quality Chinese antiques. In the middle of the cavernous space was a large free-form pond, where a grove of tropical trees grew out of the water, reaching almost to the top of a glass-domed cupola. Big koi swam in the gurgling pond, but the focal point of the living room was the main wall, which featured a two-hundred-gallon fish tank painted pitch-black that was recessed into the wall.

"Valentino looks happy to be home!" Charlie said excitedly as the two of them went up to look at him. Inside the tank, Irene's precious super red arowana undulated happily all alone, the pink fiber-optic light making his body glow an even brighter iridescent red. Astrid looked down at the coffee table, which was groaning with a colorful array of *nyonya* dessert cakes on navy-and-gold-rimmed Limoges plates.

"*Kueh lapis*, my favorite!" Charlie said, plopping down on the plush gold-brocade sofa and picking up one of the buttery pieces of cake with his fingers.

"Don't you think we should wait for your mum?"

"Oh, she'll be out in a minute, I'm sure. Let's get started. You don't ever have to stand on ceremony here—you know how down-to-earth my mother is."

Astrid began to pour tea into Charlie's cup from the silver tea service. "That's what I've always loved about your mother. She doesn't put on any airs—she's such a warm and simple lady."

"Yeah, tell that to the folks at Bulgari," Charlie snorted, as Ah Tock entered the living room. "Lincoln! Are you going to join us for some tea? Where's my mum?"

"Um, she's in her bedroom. She went to lie down," Lincoln said as he fidgeted with his cell phone.

"Why is she lying down?" Charlie asked.

Astrid looked up from pouring her tea. "Is she not feeling well?"

"Er, no . . ." Ah Tock stood there with a funny look on his face. "Astrid, I think you better call home."

"Why?"

"Um . . . your grandma just passed away."

PART THREE

The man who dies rich, dies disgraced.

—ANDREW CARNEGIE, 1889

CHAPTER ONE

MADRI VISUDHAROMN

Lady's Maid to Su Yi Since 1999

Madame usually has a bowl of congee in the morning, sometimes with a fresh raw egg cracked into the steaming-hot congee, sometimes with just a few *ikan bilis*. Today she asked for Hokkien *ma mee*, which was a highly unusual request for breakfast. The noodles Ah Ching prepares for her are done in a very specific way, using a hand-pulled flat yellow noodle, which she likes stir-fried in a thick oyster sauce gravy with a dash of brandy. For lunch, madame just wanted me to bring her some fresh star fruits and guavas from her trees. She asked for the whole fruit—she didn't want them sliced or anything, and sat up in her bed, staring at her fruits and holding them in her hands but not eating anything. That's the moment I realized that something was terribly wrong.

PHILIP YOUNG

Only Son

I saw Mummy after breakfast. For the first time in as long as I can remember, she wanted to know how I spent my days in

Sydney. I told her about how I drive down to my favorite café in Rose Bay every morning for my flat white, and then there are always errands to run, something in the house that needs fixing, or I'll have lunch in the city at one of my clubs or play a round of tennis with a friend. In the late afternoons I like to sit at the end of my dock and do a spot of fishing... that's when the fish are always biting. For dinner I often eat whatever I've caught. Mickey our chef will always do something terrific with the fish—grilled and served over risotto, made into a tartare, or steamed Chinese-style with rice or noodles. Sometimes I'll just go down to the local and have a pub dinner. (Mummy shook her head in a mixture of sadness and disbelief—the thought of me sitting in a pub eating a burger by myself like a common laborer is too much for her to fathom.) But I love eating very simply when Eleanor isn't around. If she's in town, Eleanor keeps Mickey very busy cooking twelve to fourteen courses for her dinners. Then Mummy said something rather surprising. She asked me if I had forgiven Eleanor. I was a bit shocked for a moment; in all these years, Mummy had never brought it up. I told her that I had forgiven my wife a very long time ago. Mummy seemed happy about this. She looked at me for a long time and said, "You are just like your father after all." I told her I was going to meet up with a few of my ACS old boys for drinks at the Men's Bar in the Cricket Club, but I would be back before our dinner guests arrived. As I left her bedroom, there was a part of me that sensed she didn't want me to leave. I wondered for a moment if I should cancel the meet-up and stay by her bedside, but then I thought, Philip, you're being ridiculous. You'll be back in two hours.

LEE AH LING

Head Housekeeper

At around 4:30 p.m., I went upstairs to give Su Yi a final update on tonight's menu for the party. When I went into the bedroom, Catherine was sitting by her bedside and I noticed that someone had opened all the windows and curtains. Su Yi usually prefers the curtains drawn in the afternoons, to protect her antique furniture from the setting sun, so I began to close them. "Leave them," Catherine said. I looked over at her and began to ask why, and that's when I realized that Su Yi was gone. You could just see that her spirit had left her body. I was so shocked, I panicked at first and asked, "Where are the doctors? Why didn't the alarms go off?" "They did. The doctors came in and I sent them all away," Catherine said in an unnaturally calm voice. "I wanted to be alone with my mother one last time."

PROFESSOR FRANCIS OON, MBBS, MRCP (U.K.), MMED (INT MED), FRCP (LONDON), FAMS, FRCP (EDIN), FACC (USA)

Personal Cardiologist

I had been entertaining Debra Aronson, the publisher of Poseidon Books, at home in my wine cellar when the call came. You see, I collect contemporary Chinese art, and Poseidon has been trying to woo me into doing a coffee-table book on my collection. When my associate Dr. Chia called with the urgent news from Tyersall Park, I immediately said, "Do *not* resuscitate." I knew it would be hopeless. There's been so much scarring to her heart, it would be pointless to try and revive her. It's her time to go.

None of this came as a surprise to me. In fact, after looking at her stats the previous morning during that fabulous crepe breakfast, I was surprised that she was even able to get out of bed. Her heart rate, her blood pressure, her ejection fraction—everything was off the charts. But you know, I've seen this happen time and again. In the day or two before a patient passes, they can experience a sudden spurt of energy. The body rallies, as if it knows that this will be the last hurrah. The minute I saw Su Yi appear at the breakfast table, I surmised that this was happening. After all this time, with all the medical advances we've made, the human body is still an unfathomable mystery to us. The heart most of all.

ALEXANDRA "ALIX" YOUNG CHENG

Youngest Daughter

I was in the library with Fiona and Kalliste, showing Kalliste my Enid Blyton first editions, when the dogs started howling. It must have been around half past three in the afternoon. It wasn't just our pack of Alsatians that patrol the grounds, but it seemed like every dog within a two-mile radius was making restless, high-pitched yelps. I gave Fiona a look and she knew exactly what I was thinking. She left the library without a word and went upstairs to check on Mummy. By now the howling had stopped, but I remember feeling enveloped by a sense of dread. My heart was beating a mile a minute, and I kept staring at the door. I was somehow willing Fiona to not come back through those doors. I didn't want to hear any bad news. I was trying to focus on Kalliste, who wanted to know if she could have the entire Malory Towers series—they were her favorites too when she was younger. Then Fiona came back in and I just froze until she smiled. "All's well. Auntie Cat is with her," she whispered to me. I was so relieved, and we went back to the stacks. About an hour later, Ah Ling came rushing into the library to tell me to get upstairs. The look on her face told me everything. You see, the dogs knew all along. They could sense it coming.

CASSANDRA SHANG

Niece

I was in bed at Harlinscourt, reading the latest Jilly Cooper novel when my phone began to vibrate on silent mode. I recognized the number immediately—it was Deep Throat, my spy at Tyersall Park. (Of course you knew I had an inside source at that house. It would be so foolish of me not to.) At first, Deep Throat simply said, "*Boh liao*."* I said, "What do you mean *boh liao*?" Deep Throat was overly excited, but she managed to get it out: "Su Yi just died. Big fight upstairs right now. I must go." So of course the first thing I did was call my father. I said, "Are you at Tyersall Park?" He said, "Er, no." I think I caught him at his mistress's apartment—he was very out of breath. So I said, "You better head over there now. Something just happened to your sister."

LINCOLN "AH TOCK" TAY

Distant Cousin

Great-uncle Alfred called me. I think he was on his way to Tyersall Park. He said to tell everyone on my side of the family that

---

* Hokkien for "No more."

Su Yi had just passed. But he didn't want any of us at the house tonight. "Tell your father to stay home, and I'll let you all know when to come. Tonight is just for the family." As if we're not part of the family, fucking bastard! Then he said, "Better start ordering the tents and folding chairs. We're going to need a lot of them." I was still at Irene Wu's house trying to acclimate the damn fish back into the tank, so I told her the news and she started to lose it. "Oh no! *Alamak!* How to face Astrid?" she cried, fleeing to her bedroom. I went back into the living room and when I saw Astrid sitting there pouring tea like Princess Diana, I realized the spoiled bitch didn't have a clue that her grandma had just kicked the bucket. *Kan ni na*, I had to be the one to tell her. Of course she was in total shock, but I don't feel sorry for her one bit. She's now instantly a million times richer than she already is.

VICTORIA YOUNG

Third Daughter

The first thing that came into my mind when I saw her lying there with Eddie crying over her body hysterically was: *Thank you Jesus, thank you Jesus, thank you Jesus. She has been released, and so have I. I'm free at last. Finally free.* I numbly put my hand on Alix's back, and tried to rub it soothingly while she stood looking at Mummy. I thought I might cry, but I didn't. I looked over at Cat, who was sitting in the armchair still holding Mummy's hand, and she wasn't crying either. She was just staring out the window with a rather odd look on her face. I suppose we must have all looked rather odd that day. I started to consider the curtains—Mummy's curtains with the *point d'Alençon* lace trim, and I began to imagine how they would look in the front windows of the town house I would buy in London. I could really see myself moving to one of those lovely town houses in Kensington, perhaps on Egerton Crescent or Thurloe Square, just a stone's throw from the Victoria and Albert. I would use the V&A's glorious library every day, and go for afternoon tea at the Capital Hotel or the Goring. I'd attend All Souls Church every Sunday, and maybe even start my own Bible-study fellowship. I could endow a chair in theology at Trinity College, Oxford. Maybe I could even convert an old rectory in some charming town in the Cotswolds. Someplace with a particularly smart and handsome clergyman like that Sidney Chambers in *Grantchester*. Goodness me, one look at him in that stiff clerical collar and I go weak in the knees!

MRS. LEE YONG CHIEN

Chairwoman Emeritus of the Lee Philanthropic Foundation,
Su Yi's Mah-jongg Kaki

I was at my Friday-afternoon mah-jongg game at Istana with the First Lady, Felicity Leong, and Daisy Foo when Felicity got the call. She didn't say anything to us at first—she just started rummaging through her Launer handbag, saying she needed to find her blood-pressure pills. Only after she had swallowed her pills did she say, "Ladies, I'm terribly sorry to leave like this in the middle of a game, but I must go. My mother has just passed." My goodness, the First Lady became so overcome I thought she was going to faint right there at the table! After Felicity left, the First Lady said she should go upstairs to the office to tell the president the news, and Daisy said, "*Alamak*, I should call Eleanor! She didn't call me, so I bet you she doesn't know yet!"

When the ladies all returned, we decided to toast Su Yi. After all, she was a mah-jongg maven par excellence. We all knew never to bet serious money when Su Yi was at the table. Now that she has left us, my money market account won't feel the loss, but I know her family will. Su Yi was the glue that held them all together. Those children of hers are a disgrace. Philip is a simpleton, Alix is a useless Hong Kong *tai tai*, Victoria is a spinster, and the one that married the Thai prince, I never really knew her, but I always heard she was very stuck up, like most Thais I've met. They think just because they've never been invaded they are the best. Only Felicity has any sense, because she was the eldest. But all those grandchildren are also good-for-nothings. This is what happens when too much money falls on people who are too attractive. That Astrid, so pretty, but her only talent is spending more than the GDP of Cambodia on her clothes. Look at my grandsons. Four of them are doctors, three are lawyers—one is the youngest judge ever to be appointed to the Court of Appeal, and one is an award-winning architect. (Let's not mention the grandson living in Toronto who is a hairdresser.) So sad for Su Yi, she can't brag about any of her descendants. Just you watch, everything is going to go down the toilet now.

NICHOLAS YOUNG

Grandson

I had only just arrived at Tyersall Park and was unpacking my suitcases when I heard the commotion outside my bedroom. Maids were running down the corridors everywhere like a fire alarm had gone off. "What's going on?" I asked. "Your Ah Ma!" one of them shouted frantically as she passed me. I immediately ran up the back stairs to Ah Ma's bedroom. When I got there, I couldn't see anything. There were too many people blocking the way, and someone was wailing uncontrollably. Victoria, Alix, Adam, and Piya were hovering around the bed while Uncle Taksin was embracing Auntie Cat, who was still sitting in the armchair beside Ah Ma. Ah Ling was closest to me by the door, and she turned toward me, her face swollen with tears. As Adam and Piya moved aside to make room for me, I could see that Eddie was lying in bed with Ah Ma, holding her body, shaking violently as he whimpered like a tortured animal. He caught my eye and suddenly, he leapt out of bed and started screaming, "You killed her! You killed her!" Before I knew what was happening, he's on top of me and we're both on the ground.

HER SERENE HIGHNESS *MOM RAJAWONGSE* PIYARASMI AAKARA

Granddaughter-in-law

What an odd family I've married into. Adam's aunties are like characters straight out of a Merchant Ivory film. They go rattling around this huge palace, dressed like underpaid civil servants, but then they start speaking and they all sound like Maggie Smith. Auntie Felicity clucks about like a mother hen, criticizing everyone, while Auntie Victoria seems to be an expert on everything even though she hasn't worked a day in her life. She even tried to challenge me on the origin of the hantavirus! Then there are the Hong Kong cousins—Alistair Cheng, who is very sweet but . . . how do I put it politely . . . not the sharpest tool in the box, and his sister, Cecilia, and Fiona Tung-Cheng, both perfectly polite but sooooooooo stuck up. Why do all Hong Kong girls think the sun shines out of their asses? They just chatter away to each other in Cantonese and go off on foodie adventures every day with their kids. I suspect they only came to Singapore to eat. Every time they are around I feel like they are assessing me from head to toe. I don't think Cecilia approves of Balmain. And then there's Eddie. What a crazy fuck. Grandma has just died, and all her daughters stand there staring at her body without a single tear in their eyes. The only people who seem to be crying are the maids, the Sikh guard, and Eddie. OMFG I have never seen a grown man sob like that. Crawling into bed and cradling his dead grandmother. Dressed in a velvet smoking jacket! And then Nick—the only halfway normal person in the whole house—enters the room and Eddie lunges at him. The aunties start to scream but really, it's a pretty pathetic fight, because Eddie hits like a girl and Nick simply rolls him off and pins him to the ground. "Calm the fuck down!" Nick says, but Eddie's screaming, kicking, thrusting, and finally Nick has no choice but to sock him right in the nose, and blood just goes EVERYWHERE. Especially all over my brand-new Rick Owens toad-skin boots. And now I'm told we have to spend at least another week with these people. Kill me now.

CAPTAIN VIKRAM GHALE

Head of Security, Tyersall Park

Ah Ling called me in a panic. "*Aiyah*, come quick! They are fighting! Eddie is trying to kill Nicky!" I rushed upstairs with two Gurkhas but by the time I got to the room, it was all over. Eddie was sitting at the foot of the bed, blood all over his face. He kept saying, "You broke my nose! You are going to fucking pay for my nose job!" Nicky just stood there, looking stunned. Alix smiled at me as if nothing had happened and said, in the calmest voice ever, "Ah, Vikram, you're here. I'm not sure what the procedure is. Who do we call? Do we call the police now?" I was confused at first and said, "You want to report this fight?" She said, "Oh no, not that. My mother has passed away. What are we supposed to do now?" In all the confusion, I hadn't even noticed that Mrs. Young was dead. I couldn't help myself—I burst into tears right there in front of everyone.

FELICITY LEONG

Eldest Daughter

No matter how old you are, no matter how ready you think you are, nothing quite prepares you for the loss of a parent. My father passed away years ago, and I still haven't quite recovered. People have been saying to me all week long, "At least your mother lived to this ripe old age, and you got to spend all these years with her." And I just want to spit in their faces. I want to scream at them, *Shut up, all of you!* My mother died. Please don't tell me how lucky or fortunate I am that she lived this long. She has been here on this earth my entire life and now suddenly in the blink of an eye she's gone. Gone, gone, gone. And I am an orphan now. And even though she was a difficult woman, even though she drove me crazy half the time and I was never ever quite good enough for her exacting standards, my heart is broken. I will miss her every day and every hour for the rest of my life. My only regret was that I wasn't there with her at the moment of her passing. Cat was the only one in the room with her, and I kept asking her what happened. But Cat seems too distraught to speak. She won't tell me a thing.

. . .

A small, discreet, one-column death notice was published in the obituary section of *The Straits Times*:

SHANG SU YI, Mrs. James Young

(1919–2015)

Beloved wife and mother

Son—Philip Young

Daughters—Felicity Young, Catherine Young,
Victoria Young, Alexandra Young

Sons-in-law—Tan Sri Henry Leong,
M.C. Taksin Aakara, Dr. Malcolm Cheng

Daughter-in-Law—Eleanor Sung

Grandchildren and Their Spouses—Henry Leong Jr.
(m. Cathleen Kah), Dr. Peter Leong (m. Dr. Gladys
Tan), Alexander Leong, Astrid Leong, M.R. James
Aakara (m. M.R. Lynn Chakrabongse), M.R. Matthew
Aakara (m. Fabiana Ruspoli), M.R. Adam Aakara
(m. M.R. Piyarasmi Apitchatpongse), Nicholas Young
(m. Rachel Chu), Edison Cheng (m. Fiona Tung),
Cecilia Cheng (m. Tony Moncur), Alistair Cheng

Great-grandchildren—Henry Leong III, James Leong,
Penelope Leong, Anwar Leong, Yasmine Leong,
Constantine Cheng, Kalliste Cheng, Augustine Cheng,
Jake Moncur, Cassian Teo

Brother—Alfred Shang (m. Mabel T'sien)

Visitations begin tonight at Tyersall Park
by invitation only.

Funeral at St. Andrew's Cathedral, Saturday at
2:00 p.m. by invitation only.

No flowers please. Donations may be made to the
St. John's Ambulance Association.

CHAPTER TWO

Goh Peik Lin turned to Rachel from the driver's seat of her Aston Martin Rapide. "How do you feel?"

"Well, I didn't manage to sleep a wink on the plane, so it's 7:30 a.m. New York time for me right now and I'm about to crash the funeral of a woman who didn't approve of me marrying her grandson and meet all of her possibly hostile relatives that I haven't seen in five years. I feel *great*."

"You're not crashing the funeral, Rachel. You're part of the family and you're here to support your husband. You're doing the proper thing," Peik Lin tried to assure her. Peik Lin was her closest friend from their Stanford days and had always been such a pillar of support.

Sitting beside Rachel in the backseat of the sports sedan, Carlton squeezed her hand in a show of support. Rachel leaned her head against her brother's shoulder and said, "Thanks for flying down from Shanghai. You really didn't have to do this, you know."

Carlton made a face. "Don't be daft. If you were going to be anywhere in this hemisphere, did you think I could stay away?"

Rachel smiled. "Well, I'm glad I get to spend a few moments with you both before I get sucked into the matrix. Thanks so much for picking me up, Peik Lin."

"Don't even mention it. Poor Nick, I know he wanted to come get you but he's totally trapped at the night visit," Peik Lin said.

"So what is this night-visit thing, exactly?" Rachel asked.

"Night visits are like sitting Shiva, Singapore-style. It's officially for family and close friends to come to the house to pay their last respects, but really, it's a chance for all the *kaypohs** to get in on the family gossip and start scheming. I guarantee you everyone at Tyersall Park is furiously speculating about what's going to happen to the house now that Shang Su Yi has dearly departed, and there are plenty of shenanigans going on in every corner."

"Unfortunately I think you may be right," Rachel said with a slight grimace.

"Of course I'm right. When my grandfather died, all my uncles and aunties came out of the woodwork and crept around his house during the night visit, putting stickers with their names behind paintings and under antique vases so they could claim that he had given it to them!" Peik Lin said with a chuckle.

Soon they found themselves in bumper-to-bumper traffic as the line of cars snaking up Tyersall Road to the estate's gates were stopped at a security checkpoint. Glancing at the policemen peering into the cars ahead of them, Rachel felt her stomach begin to knot up.

"There's so much security—I think the president or prime minister must be here," Peik Lin noted. After passing through all the checkpoints, the car sped up the long driveway, and as they rounded the last curve, Tyersall Park finally came into view.

"Bloody hell," Carlton said, impressed by the scene before him. The great house was ablaze in lights, the front driveway

---

* Hokkien slang for "busybody."

resembled a parking lot lined with fancy cars, many with diplomatic plates. Uniformed Gurkhas and policemen were stationed everywhere, trying to manage the traffic flow.

As the three of them got out of the car, a large black military helicopter swooped into sight over the house and descended gracefully onto the manicured lawn. The doors slid open, and a portly Chinese man in his early eighties dressed in a black suit with a deep purple tie was the first to get out. A woman in a black cocktail dress with art deco patterned jet beading followed behind him.

Rachel turned to Peik Lin. "Is that the president and First Lady?"

"No. I have no idea who they are."

Then a middle-aged man in a black suit emerged, and Carlton exclaimed, "Well that's the president of China!"

Peik Lin looked awestruck. "Oh my God, Rachel, the *president of China* has come to pay his respects!"

Much to their surprise, the next person to emerge was a tall, lanky college-age kid with long, messy shoulder-length brown hair, dressed in tight black jeans, steel-tipped black boots, and a black tuxedo jacket. A Chinese man in a pinstripe suit and a blond middle-aged lady in a black dress with a pale green shawl draped around her shoulders emerged next, followed by a cute fair-haired girl of about twelve.

"Stranger and stranger," Peik Lin said.

A small crowd had clustered outside the house to observe the arriving dignitaries, and as Rachel walked up, she saw Nick's cousin Alistair waving at her.

Alistair greeted Rachel with a big bear hug before excitedly hugging Carlton and Peik Lin as well. "Peik Lin, I haven't seen you since Rachel's wedding! I love your new red hair! I'm so glad

you guys are finally here—it's been soooo lame inside . . . all anyone wants to talk about is 'Who's getting the house?' And now
things are about to get *even* stuffier," he said, gesturing to the
arriving VIPs.

"Who *are* those people with the president of China?" Rachel
asked.

Alistair looked momentarily surprised. "Oh, you haven't met
them yet? Those people are the Imperial Shangs. The old farts
are my uncle Alfred and auntie Mabel. The younger farts are my
cousin Leonard and his very posh wife, India, who's apparently
descended from Mary Queen of Scots or something like that,
and those are his kids, Casimir and Lucia. Doesn't Cass look like
Harry Styles from One Direction?"

Everyone laughed.

"I think Harry's shorter," Peik Lin quipped.

"So they all just came from China?" Rachel asked, still
confused.

"No, the Shangs just had dinner with the president at the
Chinese embassy. The president's only here because of Uncle
Alfred. He never knew Ah Ma, of course."

"I believe my father knows him," Rachel remarked.

"They've been good friends since their university days, and
Dad serves on his standing committee," Carlton chimed in.

"Of course, I keep forgetting your father is Bao Gaoliang,"
Alistair said.

"One last question . . . who is *that girl*?" Carlton asked.

Stepping out last from the helicopter was an astonishing
Eurasian beauty in her early twenties. She had waist-length, sun-
streaked hair and wore a long, sleeveless black linen Rochas dress
and gold sandals from Da Costanzo, looking like she had just
stepped in from a beach party on Majorca.

"I think I've just met my future wife," Carlton declared as he watched the girl's hair billow around her sensationally under the draft of the helicopter rotors.

"Best of luck, mate! That's my cousin Scheherazade Shang. She's working on her dissertation at the Sorbonne. Brains *and* beauty. You know, I've heard there's another dude that's been trying to get her number for years with absolutely no success. His name's Prince Harry."

. . .

As the Shangs retreated into the house with the president of China, Rachel, Carlton, and Peik Lin followed a few paces behind. In the grand foyer, they ran into Oliver T'sien staring disapprovingly as hordes of people passed through, navigating past the hundreds of floral wreaths—some bigger than Michelin tires—that now invaded the space.

"Rachel! Wonderful to see you! Isn't this awful?" Oliver whispered in her ear. "Singaporeans just love sending these ghastly funeral wreaths." Rachel glanced at the card on the nearest wreath: GREAT EASTERN LIFE ASSURANCE OFFERS CONDOLENCES ON THE DEATH OF MADAM SHANG SU YI.

As they continued past the dining room where an enormous dinner buffet had been set up, Rachel could see guests standing in a long queue that snaked out the terrace doors, waiting to devour the delicacies at the various food stations. A little boy dashed past Rachel, shouting, "Auntie Doreen wants more chili craaaaab!"

"Whoa!" Rachel said, narrowly dodging the boy who was precariously clutching a heaping platter of crustaceans.

"Not what you were expecting?" Peik Lin said with a laugh.

"Not quite. It's all so . . . festive," Rachel remarked.

"It's the funeral of the year!" Oliver quipped. "Don't you know everyone who's anyone wants to be here? A little earlier, a rather pushy young socialite named Serena Tang tried to take a selfie with Su Yi's coffin. She got thrown out, of course. Here, let's take a shortcut." He directed them through a side door and the atmosphere changed completely.

They found themselves in the magnificent Andalusian Cloister, an enclosed courtyard surrounded by carved columns open to the sky. Rows of chairs with white slipcases had been arranged around the reflecting pool in the center of the courtyard, and the guests who gathered here murmured quietly amid the sound of the trickling water. Antique silk lamps had been placed in each of the arched alcoves surrounding the courtyard, the flickering candles within each lamp adding to the monastic stillness of the space.

At the far end of the courtyard, in front of the carved lotus blossom fountain, Su Yi's simple black teakwood casket rested on a marble dais surrounded by orchids. In a nearby alcove, Nick, his parents, and many members of the extended Young clan stood in an informal receiving line. Nick was dressed in a white button-down shirt with black trousers, and Rachel noticed that all the men present—Nick's father, Alistair Cheng, and a few other men she didn't recognize—were dressed in the same manner.

"Rachel, why don't you go to Nick first. We don't want to disrupt your reunion," Peik Lin suggested. Rachel nodded and descended the few steps into the courtyard toward the receiving line, feeling her stomach tense up in a sudden wave of anxiety. Nick was hugging Lucia Shang and was just about to be introduced to the president of China when he saw her approach. He quickly stepped out of the receiving line and dashed to her.

"Darling!" he said, sweeping her into an embrace.

"Oh my, did you just dis the president of China?" Rachel asked.

"Did I? Oh well, who cares? You're far more important." Nick laughed, and taking Rachel by the hand, led her to the receiving line and announced proudly, "Everyone—my wife has arrived!"

Rachel immediately felt every eye in the room turn to take her in. Philip and Eleanor welcomed Rachel and the avalanche of introductions began. Nick's uncles, aunts, and cousins from all the various branches greeted her far more warmly than she had expected, and suddenly Rachel found herself face-to-face with the president of China. Before she could say anything, Nick stepped forward and announced in Mandarin, "This is my wife. I believe her father, Bao Gaoliang, serves on your standing committee?"

The president looked momentarily startled, and then he broke into a wide grin. "You're Gaoliang's daughter? The economics professor from New York? It's a pleasure to meet you at last. My God, you look just like your brother, Carlton."

"He's right over there," Rachel replied in perfect Mandarin, waving her brother over.

"Carlton Bao, you seem to be everywhere these days! Didn't I just see you at my daughter's birthday dinner two nights ago? I hope you're flying on air miles," the president said in mock seriousness.

"Of course, sir," Carlton replied. He beamed at the gathered group, making sure to catch Scheherazade's eye.

Alfred Shang, who had observed the whole scene silently, looked at Rachel and Carlton with a newfound curiosity.

Rachel turned to Nick and said in a quiet voice, "Can I pay my respects to your grandmother?"

"Of course," he said. They walked up to the casket, which was surrounded by exquisite orchids in delicate celadon pots. "My grandmother was most proud of her prizewinning orchids. I don't think I ever saw her happier than the day the National Orchid Society named one of her hybrids after her."

Rachel peered into the casket a little hesitantly, but she was surprised by how splendid Su Yi looked. She lay majestically swathed in a robe of shimmering yellow silk intricately embroidered with flowers, and her hair was crowned by the most spectacular Peranakan headpiece made of gold and pearls. Rachel bowed her head for a moment, and when she looked up at Nick, she saw that his eyes were brimming with tears. Placing her arm around his waist, she said, "I'm so glad you got to see her before she passed. She looks very peaceful."

"Yes, she does," Nick said, sniffing quietly.

Rachel noticed something glistening between Su Yi's teeth. "Um, what's that in her mouth?"

"It's a black pearl. It's an old Chinese custom . . . the pearl ensures a smooth transition into the afterlife," Nick explained. "And do you see the Fabergé case beside her?"

"Yeah?" Rachel noticed a small rectangular bejeweled box next to the pillow.

"Those are her glasses, so she can have perfect vision in her next life."

Before Rachel could make another comment, a strange, whimpering sound could be heard echoing from one of the alcoves. They turned to see Alistair and his father, Malcolm, holding up a frail man as he limped toward them slowly. Rachel realized with a start that the man was Nick's cousin Eddie, and behind him walked his wife, Fiona, and their three children, all dressed in matching black linen and silk bespoke outfits.

"Kaiser Wilhelm has arrived," Oliver pronounced, rolling his eyes.

Eddie collapsed into a heap dramatically at the foot of the casket and began to convulse and emit deep, hacking sobs.

"Ah Ma! Ah Ma! What will I do without you now?" he wailed, flailing his arms wildly, almost knocking over one of the orchid pots.

Felicity Leong whispered to her sister Alix, "He better not break any of those vases! They're worth a fortune!"

"What a devoted grandson!" the president of China observed.

Hearing this, Eddie cried out even more bitterly, "How can I go on living, Ah Ma? How will I survive?" Tears poured down his face, mixing with lines of dangling snot as he continued to prostrate himself beside his grandmother's casket. Eddie's two younger children, Augustine and Kalliste, knelt on either side of their father and began to rub his back soothingly. He elbowed the kids quickly, and they started to cry on cue.

Standing at a distance, Alistair whispered to Peik Lin, "I guess we didn't need to hire any professional mourners."[*]

"Well, your brother can certainly do this professionally! The kids are doing a great job too."

---

[*] If you're looking to make some extra cash, many families in Singapore will hire you to cry at the funerals of their loved ones. Because the more mourners there are at a funeral, the more impressive it looks. Professional mourners usually come in groups, and they offer a variety of packages (i.e., normal crying, moaning hysterically, foaming at the mouth, and collapsing in front of the coffin).

"I'm sure they were forced to rehearse a million times," Alistair said.

Eddie suddenly turned around and glared at his other son. "Constantine, my firstborn! Come! Give your great-grandma a kiss!"

"No fucking way, Dad! I don't care how much you say you'll pay me, I'm not going to kiss a dead body!"

Eddie's nostrils flared in rage, but since everyone was staring at them he simply gave his son a big you're-gonna-get-your-ass-wupped-later smile and sprang up from the ground. He smoothed out his Mandarin-collared linen suit and announced, "Everyone, I have a surprise in honor of Ah Ma. Please follow me."

He led the group of relatives out to the walled rose garden that bordered the east wing of the house. "Kaspar, we're ready!" he shouted. Suddenly, a bank of floodlights illuminated the darkened garden, and everyone gasped. In front of them was a three-story structure made out of wood and paper. It was an intricately constructed scale model of Tyersall Park, with every pillar, eave, and awning painstakingly replicated down to the last detail.

"Kaspar von Morgenlatte, my personal decorator, had a whole team of artisans working on this for weeks," Eddie proudly announced, bowing to the crowd that had by now gathered in front of the house replica.

"I am not a decoratur! I am an interieur arkitect und art konsultant!" declared a tall, exceedingly thin man with slicked-back white-blond hair, dressed in a white turtleneck sweater and high-waisted white linen trousers. "Ladies und gentlemen, pleazzze pay attention! The interieur of this maknificent schloss opens up . . ."

Four equally blond assistants scurried out from the shadows. They unfastened a few hinges along the side columns, allowing the entire front façade of the house to open and reveal interior rooms that had been decorated to excruciating detail, but unfortunately *did not* replicate the real interiors of Tyersall Park.

"The walls are twenty-four-carat gold leaf, the fabrics are all Pierre Frey, the crystal chandeliers are Swarovski, und the furnishings are hand-krafted by the same people that did the set designs for Wes Anderson's *Graaand Hotel Budapeshhhhhhht*," Kaspar continued.

"Good God, what an insult to Wes. This looks more like a Ukrainian bordello," Oliver whispered to Rachel. "Thank God it's about to be set on fire."

Rachel laughed. "I know you don't care for it, but don't you think that's a bit extreme?"

"Rachel—Oliver's not joking," Nick cut in. "This is a paper tomb offering. People burn these at funerals as gifts for the deceased to 'enjoy' in the afterlife. It's an ancient ritual."

"It's more of a . . . *working*-class custom," Oliver continued. "The families buy paper objects and accessories that represent aspirational things the deceased couldn't afford in this life. Paper mansions, Ferraris, iPads, Gucci bags.* But the paper mansions are usually quite small—like dollhouses. Eddie, of course, has to do everything to the extreme," Oliver noted as Eddie walked around the three-story house excitedly showing off all the objects he had commissioned.

"Check out her closet—I had some little dresses made in

---

* In 2016, Gucci sent out warning letters about trademark infringement to several mom-and-pop shops in Hong Kong that were selling paper Gucci tomb offerings. After a backlash from Chinese shoppers and an avalanche of bad publicity, Gucci issued an apology.

her favorite lotus silk. And I even had them make exact replicas of Hermès Birkin bags, so Ah Ma will have a good selection of handbags to use in heaven!"

The family members stared at the structure in stunned silence. Finally, Eddie's mother said, "Mummy would never use an Hermès handbag. She never carried a handbag—her lady's maids held everything for her."

Eddie glared at his mother angrily. "Ugh! You just don't get it, do you? I know she wouldn't normally carry an Hermès. I'm trying to give Ah Ma the best of everything, that's all."

"It's very impressive, Eddie. Mummy would have been touched," Catherine said, trying to be diplomatic.

Victoria suddenly piped up. "No, no, this is all wrong. It's incredibly tasteless, and what's more, it's extremely un-Christian."

"Auntie Victoria, this is a Chinese tradition—it has nothing to do with religion," Eddie argued.

Victoria shook her head in fury. "I don't want to hear any more of this nonsense! We Christians do not require worldly things in the kingdom of heaven! Remove this monstrosity at once!"

"Do you know how much I spent on this mansion? This cost me over a quarter of a million dollars! We are burning it, and we are burning it now!" Eddie shouted back as he gave Kaspar the signal.

"Wolfgang! Juergen! Helmut! Schatzi! *Entzündet das Feuer!*" Kaspar commanded.

The Aryan minions dashed around the structure, dousing it with kerosene, and Eddie theatrically flicked a long matchstick and held it high for all to see.

"Don't you dare! Don't you dare burn it on this property! It's satanic, I tell you!" Victoria screamed, as she ran up to Eddie and began trying to wrestle the burning matchstick out of his hand. Eddie lobbed the match onto the structure and it ignited instantly, the force of the flames billowing outward suddenly and almost singeing both their heads.

As the enormous replica of Tyersall Park began to be consumed by the fire, all the guests streamed out of the house and surrounded it like a bonfire, taking out their phones and snapping photos. Eddie stared in triumphant silence at the burning house, while Victoria sobbed on the shoulder of the president of China. Cassian, Jake, Augustine, and Kalliste ran around the structure gleefully.

"It's actually rather beautiful, isn't it?" Rachel said as Nick came up behind her, wrapping her in his arms as they stared at the fire together.

"It is. I have to agree with Eddie this time—I think Ah Ma would have enjoyed this. And why shouldn't she have a Birkin bag in heaven?"

Carlton glanced at Scheherazade, marveling at how her hair seemed to glow the most spectacular shades of gold against the rising flames. He took a deep breath, straightened his jacket, and strolled over to where she was standing. "*Je m'appelle Carlton. Je suis le frère de Rachel. Ça va?*"

"*Ça va bien,*" Scheherazade replied, impressed by his perfect French accent.

Breaking into English, Carlton said, "They don't have anything quite like this in Paris, do they?"

"No, they sure don't," she answered with a smile.

As the paper house and all the paper luxury accoutrements smoldered into black ashes, the crowd began to make their way back into the house. Walking through the rose garden, Mrs. Lee Yong Chien shook her head and leaned over to Lillian May Tan's ear. "What did I tell you? Su Yi's body isn't even cold yet, and the family is already up in smoke!"

"This is nothing. Things are going to get far worse when they find out who will get the house," Lillian May said, her eyes flashing in anticipation.

"I think they are in for the shock of their lives," Mrs. Lee whispered back.

A humongous, full-page color notice appeared in the obituary section of *The Straits Times* for five consecutive days:

The Chairman, Board of Directors, and Employees of

the Liechtenburg Group, AG

offer our deepest sympathies to

our esteemed and highly valued partner

Edison Cheng

SENIOR EXECUTIVE VICE CHAIRMAN
PRIVATE BANKING (GLOBAL)

on the passing of his beloved grandmother

Shang Su Yi

"Parting is such sweet sorrow."

—WILLIAM SHAKESPEARE

For inquiries on superlative wealth management,

visit www.liechtenburg.com/myoffshorecapital/edisoncheng

CHAPTER THREE

Oliver T'sien was in the middle of his morning shave in his condo when Kitty rang, so he put her on speaker.

"I'm going to see you today! I'm going to Alistair Cheng's grandmother's funeral this afternoon," Kitty chirped.

"You received an invitation?" Oliver tried to mask the astonishment in his voice.

"I thought since Alistair is my ex-boyfriend, and I *did* meet his grandmother once, it would only be appropriate to convey my condolences in person. It will be so nice to see his family again."

"Where did you even hear about the funeral?" Oliver asked, as he arched his neck toward the mirror and focused his razor on the stray hairs under his chin.

"Everyone was talking about it at Wandi Meggaharto Widjawa's party last night. Apparently, Wandi knows a few of the people from Jakarta flying in for the funeral. She said it was going to be the society funeral of the century."

"I bet she did. But I'm afraid the funeral is really by invitation only."

"Well, you'll be able to get me an invitation, won't you?" Implicit in Kitty's coquettish tone was, *since you're on my payroll.*

Oliver rinsed off his shaving cream. "Kitty, I'm afraid that this is one time where I really don't have the power to help you."

"What if I get dressed up in a very conservative black Roland Mouret dress and wear a nice hat? I'll even use the Bentley instead of the Rolls and bring a few bodyguards along. Surely they won't turn me away?"

"Kitty, you need to trust me on this. This is one funeral you *don't* want to crash. It would be a faux pas of epic proportions. This is a funeral for family and very close friends only. I assure you there will be no one you know, and it really won't matter if you're not there."

"Can you assure me that *Colette* won't be there?"

"Kitty, I can assure you she has probably never even *heard* of my family."

"But that doesn't necessarily mean she won't be there. I heard she got back to Singapore two days ago. It was mentioned in Honey Chai's gossip blog: 'Countess of Palliser is staying at the Raffles Hotel.' Did she leave her orangutans to come to the funeral?"

Oliver rolled his eyes in exasperation. "There is no way Colette or Lady Mary or whatever she calls herself these days will be anywhere near that funeral. I promise."

"I guess I'll go spend the day on Tatiana Saverin's new yacht then. She says it was designed by the same guy that did Giorgio Armani's boat."

"Yes, it is a beautiful day for sailing. Why don't you slip on your sexiest Eres bikini, put on your sailing diamonds, and spend the day sipping Aperol spritzes on a yacht? Stop wasting your precious time thinking about this dreary funeral that I *wish* I didn't have to attend!" (Oliver lied. As much as he adored Su Yi, he had to admit that today was truly going to be the social event of the century.)

"Okay, okay." Kitty laughed and hung up.

Oliver leaned against his bathroom sink, methodically patting some Floris aftershave on his cheeks and throat. The phone rang again.

"Hello, Kitty."

"What are sailing diamonds? Do I need to get some?"

"It's just an expression, Kitty. I made it up."

"But do you think I should wear a diamond necklace with my bikini? I could put on my Chanel Joaillier diamonds, the one in the sunburst floral pattern. Diamonds are waterproof, aren't they?"

"Of course. Go for it. I have to run now, Kitty, or I'm going to be late for the funeral." Two seconds after hanging up, Oliver's mother, Bernadette, walked into the bathroom.

"Mother, I'm not dressed!" Oliver groaned, tightening the towel around his waist.

"Hiyah, what do you have that I haven't already seen? Tell me, is this okay?"

Oliver scrutinized his sixty-nine-year-old mother, slightly annoyed by the graying roots that were showing on the top of her head. Her Beijing hairdresser really wasn't doing a good job maintaining her color. Bernadette, who was born a Ling, came from a family where all the women were renowned for their beauty. Unlike her sisters or her cousins—Jacqueline Ling being the prime example, who appeared preternaturally preserved—Bernadette looked her age. Actually, in the tailored dark blue silk brocade suit with the ribbon tie at the collar, she looked older. *This is what happens when you spend twenty-five years toiling away in China*, Oliver thought to himself.

"Is this the only dark dress you brought with you?"

"No, I brought three dresses, but I already wore the other two during the night visits."

"Then I suppose this one will have to do. Did your tailor in Beijing make this one for you?"

"*Aiyah*, this one was very pricey compared to my Beijing tailor! Mabel Shang's girl in Singapore made this for me more than thirty years ago. It's a copy of some famous Paris designer. Pierre Cardin, I think."

Oliver exploded in laughter. "Mother, no one would copy a Pierre Cardin. It's probably one of those 1980s designers Mabel used to love. Scherrer, Féraud, or Lanvin back when Maryll was in charge. Well, at least you can say it still fits. You didn't bring one of your little cloche hats, did you?"

"No, I didn't. I packed for Singapore weather. But Oliver, what do you think of this?" Bernadette asked, fingering the impressive jade-and-ruby butterfly brooch pinned to her lapel.

"Oh, it's fabulous."

"You sure no one will be able to tell? Heaven forbid I get seated next to your grandmother and she notices," Bernadette fretted.

"With grandma's glaucoma, I don't think she can even see that you have the brooch on. Trust me, I had the best jeweler I know in London replicate it."

"I should never have let the real thing go." Bernadette sighed.

"We didn't really have a choice, did we? Just forget it ever happened. You still have the brooch, right here. The jade looks flawless, the rubies look real, the diamonds are sparkling like they came straight out of Laurence Graff's hands. If I can't tell, no one will be able to tell."

"If you say so. Now, do you have a tie Dad can borrow? The only one he brought got all stained with chocolate cake last night. So sad, once Tyersall Park goes, I'm going to miss that chocolate cake."

"Of course. Go to my closet and pick out anything you'd like for him. One of the Borrellis might be nice. Actually, give me a second and I'll do it." As his mother left the bathroom, Oliver thought to himself, *I've learned my lesson. Next time I'm going to put them up at a hotel, even if they kick and scream.* This flat is just too small for three people.*

---

*   Asian parents visiting their adult children who live in other cities ALWAYS INSIST on staying with them, no matter if the child lives in a studio apartment or the house is already bursting at the seams with too many hormonal teenagers, and even if the parents could afford to buy out a whole floor of the Ritz-Carlton. And of course, even if you're forty-six years old, suffering from sleep apnea and chronic sciatica, you're still expected to give up your master bedroom to your parents and sleep on the inflatable mattress in the living room. Because that's just how it is.

CHAPTER FOUR

Inside the lead Mercedes escorting the funeral cortege from Tyersall Park to the cathedral, Harry Leong was staring out the window, trying to ignore the incessant chatter that came from his wife, Felicity, arguing over last-minute details with her sister Victoria.

"No, we *have* to let the president of Singapore speak first. That follows official protocol," Victoria said.

"But then the Sultan of Borneo will be terribly insulted. Royalty should always come before elected officials," Felicity argued back.

"Rubbish, this is *our* country, and *our* president has precedence. You only care about the sultan because of all the Leong plantations in Borneo."

"I care about him not urinating all over the pulpit at St. Andrew's. His Majesty is an elderly diabetic with a weak bladder. He should get to have the first word. Besides, he knew Mummy even before the president was born."

"Reverend Bo Lor Yong is going to have the first word. He's going to read the blessing."

"WHAT? You invited Bo Lor Yong too? How many pastors are going to be at this funeral?" Felicity asked incredulously.

"Only three. Reverend Bo will deliver the blessing, Bishop

See will give the sermon, and Pastor Tony Chi will say the closing prayer."

"What a pity. Is it too late to ask Tony to deliver the sermon? He's so much better than that See Bei Sien," Felicity scoffed.

Harry Leong groaned. "Can you speak softer? You two are giving me a migraine. If I knew you were going to argue all the way, I would have ridden in Astrid's car."

"You know your security won't let you ride with her. She doesn't have bulletproof windows," Felicity said.

In the Jaguar XJL (which was not bulletproof) following behind them, Eleanor Young sat scrutinizing her son's face intently. "I think next week I should make an appointment for you to see my dermatologist. Those puffy lines under your eyes . . . I'm not happy with them. Dr. Teo can do wonders with his laser."

"Mum, it's fine. I just didn't get much sleep last night," Nick said.

"He was up all night writing his tribute to Ah Ma," Rachel explained.

"Why did it take all night?" Eleanor asked.

"It was the hardest thing I've ever had to write, Mum. You try condensing Ah Ma's entire life into a thousand words."

Rachel squeezed Nick's hand encouragingly. She knew how much he had struggled over his speech, working on it until the wee hours and getting out of bed several times after that to make a change or add another anecdote.

Eleanor kept prodding. "Why should there be a word limit?"

"Auntie Victoria insisted that I only have five minutes for my speech. And that's about a thousand words."

"Five minutes? What nonsense! You were her closest grandson, and the only *Young*. You should be allowed to speak as long as you wish!"

"Apparently there are going to be a lot of speeches, so I'm just toeing the party line," Nick said. "It's fine, Mum. I'm very happy with my speech now."

"Oh my. Who is that woman in the car beside us?" Rachel suddenly asked. Everyone turned to look into the Rolls that was trying to overtake them, where there was a woman wearing a black hat with a dramatic black veil draped over her face.

"Looks like Marlene Dietrich," Philip chuckled as he drove.

"*Aiyah*, Philip! Pay attention to the road!" Eleanor yelled. "Actually, it *does* look like Marlene Dietrich. I wonder which sultan's wife that could be?"

Peering over, Nick laughed. "That's no sultana. That's Fiona Tung behind that getup."

In the backseat of the Rolls-Royce Phantom—the only Rolls in the stately procession of cars—Fiona fidgeted with her hat uncomfortably. "I don't know why you made me wear this ridiculous veil. I can't see out of it, and I can hardly breathe."

Eddie snorted. "I don't know what you're talking about. Kalliste can breathe just fine in hers, can't you?"

Eddie's tween daughter was wearing a hat and veil identical to her mother's, and she stared straight ahead, not answering her father.

"Kalliste, I SAID: CAN YOU BREATHE?"

"She's got headphones on, Dad. She can't see or hear a thing. She's like Helen Keller right now," Augustine said.

"At least Helen Keller could speak!" Eddie said in annoyance.

"Um, actually, she couldn't, Pa. She was mute," Constantine

responded from the front passenger seat. Eddie reached over and tugged his daughter's veil aside. "Get those headphones off! Don't you dare wear them into the church!"

"What difference does it make? No one will be able to see me under this thing. Can't I just listen to Shawn Mendes while I'm in the church? I promise you his songs will make me cry buckets like you want me to."

"No Shawn Mendes! And no Mario Lopez, Rosie Perez, or Lola Montez either! Kids, you are all going to sit in the church with ramrod-straight posture, singing all the hymns and crying pitifully. Cry as if I've cut off your allowance!"

"That's really going to work, Dad. *Boo hoo hoo, what am I going to do without my twenty dollars this week?*" Constantine said sarcastically.

"Okay, you've just lost your allowance for the rest of the year! And if I don't see you crying until your eyes bleed, especially while I'm singing my song—"

"Eddie, ENOUGH! What is the point of trying to force the kids to cry when they don't wish to cry?" Fiona snapped.

"How many times do I have to tell you . . . we need to be the chief mourners at this funeral. We need to show everyone how much we care, because all eyes will be on us! Everyone knows that we are going to be benefiting the most!"

"And how would they know that?"

"Fiona, have you been in dreamland all week? Ah Ma died before she could make any changes to her will! We're going to be the ones getting the lion's share! In a few days, we're going to become bona fide members of the three-comma club!* So we have to really go all out to display our grief!"

---

* Just count the commas and you'll understand what Eddie means: $1,000,000,000.

Fiona shook her head in disgust. At this moment, her husband truly made her feel like crying.

. . .

"Lorena, Lorena, over here! I *choped** this seat for you!" Daisy shouted, waving from her strategically chosen aisle seat.

Lorena made a beeline for Daisy and saw the packet of tissues she had placed next to her on the wooden pew. "Thanks for saving me this seat! I thought I was going to have to sit with my in-laws. Is Q.T. still parking?"

"*Aiyah*, you know my husband doesn't do funerals. Just the sight of a coffin will give him diarrhea." Just then, there was a loud buzzing from Daisy's handbag. "Wait ah, I'm going to take out my iPad. Nadine wanted me to FaceTime her from the funeral. She's beside herself that she didn't get invited."

"What? Ronnie and her didn't get invitations?"

"No, Old Man Shaw got the invitation, and of course he brought the new wife. They are two rows in front of us."

Lorena craned her neck to look at Nadine's father-in-law, the eighty-five-year-old stroke survivor Sir Ronald Shaw and his brand-new twenty-nine-year-old wife from Shenzhen. "I must say she's very pretty, but I'm still surprised that Sir Ronald isn't, you know, *chee cheong fun*."

"*Aiyah*, these days with Viagra, even *chee cheong fun* can become *you char kway*."[†] Daisy giggled as she activated the Face-Time function. Nadine's dramatically made-up face popped up

---

[*]   A Singlish term meaning "to reserve." Singaporeans *chope* seats at concerts, hawker centers, and other public venues by placing a packet of tissue paper on the seat.
[†]   *Chee cheong fun:* a long, limp, rice noodle roll. *You char kway:* a long, stiff, deep-fried breadstick.

on screen. "*Alamak*, Daisy, I've been waiting and waiting! Who's arrived? Who do you see?"

"Well, your father-in-law is here with your new ... er ... mother-in-law."

"Oh, who gives a damn about them! How does Eleanor look? And what's Astrid wearing?" Nadine asked.

"Eleanor of course looks great—I think she's wearing that black Akris suit with notched lapels she bought when we all went to the Harrods sale a couple of years ago. Astrid hasn't arrived yet, or at least I don't see her anywhere. *Oh my goodness!* Who's this? The Bride of Frankenstein just walked in!"

"What? Who? Hold up your iPad, let me see!" Nadine said excitedly.

Daisy covertly pointed her iPad toward the central aisle. "*Alamak*, it's Eddie Cheng's wife, the long-suffering Tung girl. She's dressed up like Queen Victoria in full mourning garb with a big black hat covered by a floor-length black veil. And oh look, their daughter is dressed just like her! And the sons are wearing black brocade Nehru jackets. Good grief, they look like they are in some suicide cult!"

Rachel went along with Nick's parents to the beautifully polished wooden pews reserved for the family, marveling at the beautiful neo-Gothic features of Singapore's oldest cathedral as she walked up the central aisle. Nick meanwhile headed to the chapel behind the altar to confer with his aunt Victoria, who was in the midst of coordinating all the speakers. He shook the president's hand and waited patiently for his marching orders. Victoria finally noticed him. "Oh Nicky, good, you're here. Listen, I hope you don't mind, but we've had to cut your speech from the program. We simply don't have the time, with everyone needing to speak."

Nick stared at her in dismay. "You're not serious?"

"I'm afraid I am. Please understand, we're already running overtime. We have three pastors speaking, the Sultan of Borneo, and the president. And then the Thai ambassador has a special message to deliver, and we also have to fit in Eddie's song—"

"*Eddie's going to sing?*" Nick was incredulous.

"Oh yes. He's been rehearsing a special hymn all week with a very special guest musician who's just flown in."

"So let me understand this: We have six people giving speeches, but *no one* from the family will actually get a chance to speak about Ah Ma?"

"Well, there's also been a last-minute addition. Henry Leong Jr. has decided to give a speech."

"Henry Junior? But he barely knows Ah Ma. He's spent most of his life in Malaysia being doted on by his Leong grandparents!"

Victoria smiled embarrassedly at the president, who was watching the whole exchange with piqued interest. "Nicky, may I remind you that your cousin Henry is the eldest grandson. He has every right to give a speech. And besides," Victoria lowered her voice, "*he's running for a seat in parliament this year. Felicity said we HAVE to let him speak. And of course the president wants him to!*"

Nick stared at his aunt for a moment. Without another word, he turned around and headed back to his pew.

Michael Teo—Astrid's estranged husband—came striding up the central aisle of St. Andrew's Cathedral, dressed in a brand-new Rubinacci suit with shiny black John Lobb wing tips. He looked around for where Leong family members might be seated, and just as he caught sight of Astrid fussing over Cassian's Windsor knot in the second pew from the front, two men in dark suits suddenly appeared, blocking his path.

"I'm sorry, Mr. Teo. *Family only on this side*," the man with the earpiece said.

Michael opened his mouth, about to say something, but as he knew that all eyes were on him, he nodded, smiled politely, and took the nearest empty seat in another pew.

Sitting in the pew opposite from Michael were members of the T'sien family. "Did you just see that? That was *brutal*," Oliver whispered to his aunt Nancy.

"Hnh! Serves him right. I don't know how he even got an invitation," Nancy huffed, as she thought to herself, *That man was wasted on Astrid. The things I could do with that body . . .*

Nancy turned to face Oliver's mother. "Bernadette, how nice you look in that . . . frock." *Ghastly. I can smell the mothballs.*

"Thank you. You look so fashionable, as always," Bernadette replied, eyeing Nancy's Gaultier couture dress. *Wasting my brother-in-law's money. No matter how expensive that dress is, you still look like mutton dressed as lamb.*

"It's always nice to see the T'sien jade come out for an airing." Nancy eyed the brooch Bernadette had on. *This should have been mine. What a travesty to see it pinned on that horrific schmatta she calls a dress.*

The heirloom jewel had been passed down from T'sien Tsai Tay's mother to Bernadette—her favorite granddaughter-in-law—and was said to have belonged to the Empress Dowager Ci'an. Nancy leaned over and said to her mother-in-law, "Do you see Bernadette's brooch . . . doesn't the carved jade butterfly look more translucent and vibrant than ever?"

Rosemary smiled. "It's imperial jade. It always looks better the more it's worn." *I'm so glad we gave it to Bernadette. This is the gift that keeps on giving—just seeing how jealous Nancy still is after all these years.*

Bernadette smiled nervously at the two women and tried desperately to deflect attention from herself. "*Aiyah*, Nancy, this is nothing. I don't have much compared to you. Look at your pearls! My goodness, I've never seen so many worn at the same time." *She looks like a madwoman who just robbed Mikimoto.*

Nancy fingered the enormous Sri Lankan sapphire-and-diamond clasp on her eight-strand pearl necklace. "Oh these? I've had them for ages. I think Dickie bought these for me when we were invited to Prince Abdullah of Jordan's wedding to the beautiful Rania. Of course, this was long before he knew he was going to be king."

Overhearing the exchange, Oliver added, "I don't think Abdullah ever expected it. His uncle was supposed to be the next king, but Hussein bypassed him on his deathbed and anointed his son the successor. It was a shock to everyone."

Nancy sat back in her seat, wondering what shocks lay in store for her Young relatives. What would become of all of Su Yi's jewelry? Her collection was said to be unparalleled in all of Asia, so there was surely going to be a battle royal over her treasures.

Sitting in the middle of her row, Astrid heard an urgent little ping from her cell phone. She got out her phone discreetly and read the text message:

MICHAEL TEO: First u exclude my name from the Straits Times death notice, and now u bar me from sitting next to my own son! Yur gonna pay for this.

Astrid began texting back furiously.

ASTRID LEONG: What are you talking about? My mother and uncle arranged the notice. I didn't even know you were coming.

MT: I'm not a monster. I liked your Ah Ma, ok?

AL: So where are you now? You're going to be late!

MT: Already here. I'm sitting one row behind and across from u.

Astrid swiveled around and saw Michael seated across the aisle.

AL: Why are you over there?

MT: Don't pretend u don't know. Your father's fucking bodyguards wouldn't let me into your row!

AL: I promise you I had nothing to do with that. Come join us now.

Michael stood up, but before he could leave his pew, a cluster of guests walking up the aisle blocked him from moving. Instead, they were being directed into his row, and a lady wearing a chic dark gray silk shantung dress with a silver gray frayed bouclé topper coat and black gloves was ushered into the seat next to him.

Astrid's jaw dropped. She spun around and faced Oliver, who was seated just behind her. "Am I hallucinating, or is that who I think it is over there in head-to-toe Chanel couture?"

Oliver turned and saw the lady who had just taken the seat on the aisle opposite from him. "Holy Anita Sarawak!" he muttered under his breath. It was Colette, sitting with her husband, the Earl of Palliser, and the British ambassador. How stupid of him—of course the earl would attend. His father, the Duke of Glencora, was great friends with Alfred Shang.

Eagle-eyed Nancy T'sien leaned over and whispered to Oliver, "Who is that girl over there?"

"Which girl?" Oliver asked, feigning ignorance.

"The pretty Chinese girl sitting with all those *ang mors*." As the two of them looked at Colette, she suddenly swept her hair aside, revealing an enormous jade butterfly brooch pinned to her left shoulder. Oliver turned white as a sheet.

Nancy almost gasped, but she stopped herself. Instead, she said, "What an exquisite brooch. Mummy, do you see that lady's lovely jade brooch?" She tugged furiously at Rosemary T'sien's elbow.

"Oh. Yes," Rosemary paused for a moment in recognition. "How lovely it is."

Just then, Reverend Bo Lor Yong approached the pulpit and spoke too close to the microphone. His voice came out booming: "Your Majesties, Highnesses, Excellencies, Mr. President, ladies and gentlemen, may I present Shang Su Yi's dearest grandson, Edison Cheng, accompanied by the one and only . . . Lang Lang!"

The crowd murmured excitedly at the announcement of the celebrated pianist, and all eyes were on the main altar as Lang Lang walked to the grand piano and began to play the opening chords of a curiously familiar melody. The doors of the cathedral swung open, and eight Gurkha guards from Tyersall Park stood silhouetted in the dramatic arched entrance, bearing Su Yi's casket on their shoulders. Captain Vikram Ghale was the lead pallbearer, and as they slowly began to enter the nave of the cathedral, Eddie emerged from the shadows of the transept and took his place in front of the piano, a lone spotlight on him. As the guests in the church stood up respectfully, the casket made its way up the central aisle as Eddie began to sing in a quivering tenor:

"It must have been cold there in my shadowwwwww,
to never have sunlight on your faaaaaaace . . ."

"You've got to be fucking kidding me," Nick muttered, burying his face in his hands.

"They cut your speech for *this*?" Rachel was furious and yet trying desperately not to laugh.

"Did I ever tell you you're my heeeeeeeeeeeeero . . ." Eddie belted out, not quite hitting the right pitch.

Victoria turned to Felicity with a frown. "What on earth?"

Felicity whispered to Astrid, "Do you know this hymn?"

"It's not a hymn, Mum. It's 'Wind Beneath My Wings' by Bette Midler."

"Bet who?"

"Exactly. She's a singer Ah Ma would never have heard of either."

As the guards proceeded up the aisle, everyone in the cathedral suddenly went quiet as they caught sight of Su Yi's two devoted Thai lady's maids. Swathed in dark gray silk dresses with a single black orchid pinned above their breasts, they walked five paces behind her casket, tears running down their faces.

CHAPTER FIVE

ST. ANDREW'S CATHEDRAL, SINGAPORE

After the memorial service, guests were invited to a white tent that had been erected next to the cathedral, where everyone could mingle over an elaborate afternoon-tea buffet. The tent was decorated to replicate Su Yi's conservatory at Tyersall Park. Hundreds of pots of orchids in full bloom hung from the ceiling, while towering topiaries composed of roses from Su Yi's rose garden commanded each of the tables covered in Battenberg lace. A battalion of waitstaff rolled around antique silver carts arrayed with steaming cups of Darjeeling tea and ice-cold flutes of Lillet champagne, while chefs in white toques manned the tables filled with afternoon-tea standards like finger sandwiches, scones with clotted cream, and *nyonya* cakes.

Nick, Rachel, and Astrid sat in a quiet corner reminiscing with cousins Alistair, Scheherazade, and Lucia.

"You know, I used to be deathly afraid of Ah Ma when I was little," Alistair confessed. "I think it's maybe because all the adults seemed to fear her, I just picked up on that."

"Really? She always seemed like a fairy godmother to me," Scheherazade said. "I remember one summer hols many years ago, I was wandering around Tyersall Park by myself when I came upon Great-auntie Su Yi. She was standing at the edge of that pond with those enormous lily pads, and when she saw me, she said, 'Zhi Yi, come'—she always called me by my Chinese name. She looked up at the sky and made this clicking sound with her tongue. Out of nowhere these two swans swooped down and landed right on the pond! Su Yi reached into the pocket of that blue gardening coat she always wore and pulled out little sardines. The swans glided up to her and gently ate the sardines out of her hand. I was absolutely mesmerized."

"Yes, those swans were the same pair that were always at the lake in the Botanic Gardens. Ah Ma used to say, 'Everyone thinks these swans live there, but actually this is their pond, and they just visit the Botanic Gardens because they've gotten fat and spoiled by all the tourists that feed them!'" Nick remembered.

"It's not fair, I feel like you got to know Great-auntie Su Yi much better than I did, Scheherazade!" Lucia said with a little pout.

Rachel shot Lucia a smile, and then noticed Carlton strolling nonchalantly toward them. "Carlton! How did you get through Fort Knox?"

"I may or may not have been slipped an invitation by someone," Carlton said with a wink, as Scheherazade blushed.

"Astrid, mind if I have a quick word?" Carlton said.

"Me?" Astrid looked up in surprise.

"Yes."

Astrid got up from her chair and Carlton took her over to a corner. "I have a message from a friend. Go to the chapel behind the north transept of the cathedral right now. Trust me."

"Oh. Okay," Astrid said, her brow furrowed at Carlton's mysterious message. She walked out of the tent and headed into the church through a side door, making her way to the north transept. As she entered the small alcove chapel within the cathedral, her eyes took a moment to adjust to the darkened room. A figure emerged from behind a pillar.

"Charlie! Oh my God! What are you doing here?" Astrid exclaimed as she rushed to embrace him.

"I just couldn't let you be alone today." Charlie hugged her tight, kissing her forehead repeatedly. "How are you?"

"I'm okay, I guess."

"I know this is the last thing on your mind, but you look stunning today," Charlie said, marveling at her knee-length black dress with a white Greek key motif piping on the skirt and collar.

"This was my grandmother's, from the 1930s."

"Was the service beautiful?"

"I wouldn't really call it that. It was grand, and it was strange. The Sultan of Borneo talked about the war and how my great-grandfather helped to save his family. He spoke in Malay, so everything had to be translated by this very perky woman. Then my brother spoke, and he was so weird and stilted he sounded like the Manchurian Candidate. The most emotional moment came when my grandmother's casket first entered the church. When I saw Madri and Patravadee walking behind the casket, I just lost it."

"I know it's been a very sad day. I brought something for you . . . I was debating at first whether or not to show it to you today, but I think it might actually cheer you up." Charlie took a small envelope out of his pocket and handed it to Astrid. She opened it up and unfolded a handwritten note:

Dear Astrid,

I hope you don't mind the intrusion, but I want to express how sorry I am to hear of your grandmother's passing. She was a great lady,

and I know she meant so much to you. I was very close to my Ah
Ma as well, so I can imagine what you must be feeling right now.

I also want to apologize for my actions several months ago
in Singapore. I am so terribly sorry for any pain or embarrass-
ment I might have caused to you and your family. As I'm sure
you're aware, I was not myself that day. I have made a complete
recovery since then, and I can only hope and pray that you will
accept my heartfelt apology now.

In the last few months, I've had the luxury of time. Time
to heal and recover, time to reassess my life. I know now that
I do not ever wish to come between what you and Charlie have
together, and I want to give you my blessing, not that you in any
way need it. Charlie has been so decent to me throughout the
years, and I only want what's best for him now. As we are all
only too painfully aware, life is precious, and much too fleeting,
so I want to wish the both of you everlasting happiness.

Yours truly,
Isabel Wu

"How sweet of her!" Astrid said, looking up from the note.
"I'm glad she's doing so much better."

"I am too. She gave me the note when I went to drop off
the girls last night. She was worried that you wouldn't want to
read it."

"Why wouldn't I? I'm so happy you showed it to me. It's the
best thing that's happened today. It feels like one more burden
has been lifted. You know, all through the service, I was thinking of my grandmother's last conversation with me. She really
wanted me to be happy. She wanted us to ignore all the rules of
mourning and get married as soon as we possibly could."

"We will, Astrid, I promise."

"I never thought Michael would be the one to hold things up," Astrid said with a sigh.

"We'll get through this. I have a plan," Charlie said.

They were suddenly interrupted by voices echoing through the north transept. Astrid peeked out the door for a moment. "It's my mother," she mouthed to Charlie.

Victoria, Felicity, and Alix skulked through the transept and entered the chapel on the opposite side. In the middle of the room was Su Yi's coffin.

"I'm telling you, her dentures were crooked," Felicity said.

"They didn't look crooked to me," Victoria argued.

"You'll see. Whoever the stupid mortician was that worked on her didn't place them properly."

"This is such a bad idea—" Alix began to protest.

"No, we must do this for Mummy. I won't be able to sleep if I let Mummy be cremated with crooked teeth." Felicity began to unfasten the lid of the casket. "Here, help me with this."

The three women lifted the lid of the casket slowly. Looking down at their mother cocooned in her golden robe, the sisters, normally such pillars of discipline and resolve, began to sob quietly. Felicity reached over to embrace Victoria, and the two of them began to cry even harder.

"We must be strong. We're all that's left now." Felicity sniffed as she began to collect herself. "It's funny how lovely she looks. Her complexion is smoother than it's ever been."

"While we're here, do we really want to let this Fabergé spectacle case be cremated? What a waste," Victoria said, sniffing.

"Those were her funerary instructions. We must honor them," Alix insisted.

Victoria scoffed at her little sister. "I don't think Mummy

really considered the implications when she wrote that. Surely she would have wanted us to remove the Fabergé case after the funeral? Just like we removed the gold tiara? You know how she hated waste."

"All right, all right, just take the glasses out and place them beside her pillow. Now, someone help me open her mouth." Felicity leaned into the coffin and tugged at her mother's stiff jaw.

Suddenly she let out a shriek.

"What happened, what happened?" Victoria gasped.

Felicity cried, "The pearl! The Tahitian black pearl! I opened her mouth and it rolled down her throat!"

CHAPTER SIX

EMERALD HILL, SINGAPORE

It was eleven thirty on Sunday night, and Cassian was finally down for the count. Astrid padded back to her bedroom, sinking wearily into bed. It had been a long weekend after a very long week, what with her grandmother's funeral, and she thought that Cassian spending a day with his father would give her a chance to recoup a little. Instead, her son had returned home and had spent the better part of the evening attempting to launch an insurrection. Astrid fired off a text to Michael:

> **ASTRID LEONG:** Simple request—when Cassian spends the day w/ you, could you please refrain from letting him play 7 straight hours of Warcraft? He comes back a total zombie and is just impossible. Thought we were in agreement about the gaming.

A few minutes later, Michael replied:

> **MICHAEL TEO:** Stop exaggerating. He didn't play for 7 hrs.
> **AL:** 7 hours, 6 hours, it was clearly too much. Tomorrow is a school day and he's still up.

MT: Not sure what yr prob is. He always sleeps fine @ my house.

AL: Because you let him go to bed whenever! His schedule is all messed up when he comes back. You have no idea—I have to deal with him all week.

MT: U wanted it this way. He should be at Gordonstoun.

AL: Boarding school in Scotland is not the answer. Not going to argue with you over this again. I just don't understand why you bother having him when you don't even want to spend time with him.

MT: To get him away from your corrupting influence.

Astrid sighed in frustration. She knew Michael was trying to bait her again, and she wasn't going to fall for it. He was just getting back at her for how he perceived he had been treated at her grandmother's funeral. She was about to switch off her phone when his next message popped up:

MT: Anyway, this will be over soon. I'm getting full custody of Cassian.

AL: You're delusional.

MT: No, yur a lying cheating whore.

Astrid's text message app froze for a moment, and then a high-resolution file came through. It was a photograph of Astrid and Charlie lounging together on pillows on the deck of a vintage Chinese junk that had been cruising the South China Sea. Astrid's head was resting intimately against Charlie's chest. Astrid recognized the photo from five years ago, when Charlie had attempted to cheer her up after Michael had dropped a

bombshell on her in Hong Kong, begging to end their marriage.
Michael's follow-up text read:

> **MT:** No judge is going to give u custody now.
>
> **AL:** This photo proves nothing. Charlie was only consoling me
> after you left.
>
> **MT:** "Consoling." Did this include blow jobs?
>
> **AL:** Why do you need to be so crass? You know I never cheated
> on you. You were the one who fake cheated, wanting out of
> our marriage at that time, and I was so destroyed. Charlie
> was just being a good friend.
>
> **MT:** Friends with benefits. I got tons more pics. U have no
> idea.
>
> **AL:** I don't know what else you could possibly have. I've done
> nothing wrong.
>
> **MT:** Yes, jury will really believe you. Wait till they see what
> I've got.

Astrid stared at his words, her face going hot with fury. She
immediately speed-dialed him, but it went straight to voice mail.
*Hi, you've reached Michael Teo. This is my private line, so you must be
damn important. Leave a message and I will get back to you if it's important enough. Heh Heh Heh.*

At the sound of the beep, Astrid spoke: "Michael, this isn't
funny anymore. I don't know what sort of advice that lawyer
of yours has been giving you, but these tactics are only going to
end up harming you. Please just stop, and let's try to come to a
reasonable agreement. For the good of Cassian."

Astrid hung up the phone, placed it on the side table, and
turned off her bedside lamp. She lay in bed in the darkness, furious at Michael, but even more furious with herself because she

knew she'd played right into his trap. She should never have texted him in the first place. Michael just wanted to agitate her. That's all he wanted to do in every interaction they had these days. Her phone beeped again, and she knew it would be another incendiary text from Michael. She was determined not to look at any more of his texts. She needed to get some sleep, because tomorrow was going to be another big day—the reading of her grandmother's will was taking place at 10:00 a.m. sharp.

Her phone buzzed again with another text message notice. And then another. Astrid turned to face away from her phone, clenching her eyes closed. Suddenly it occurred to her . . . *What if it wasn't Michael? What if it was Charlie, who had just returned to Hong Kong?* Sighing, she reached for her phone and turned it on.

There were three text messages, and surprise, surprise, they were from Michael. The first one simply read:

For the good of Cassian.

The second text was a file that was still in the process of downloading, but the third text read:

$5 billion or you lose him forever.

A few seconds later, the download was complete, and Astrid tapped on the icon before she could stop herself. It was a thirty-second video clip, a grainy, night-vision shot, and as Astrid squinted at the glowing screen in the dark, she could make out the figure of a naked girl with her back to the camera, straddling a man lying on a bed. The couple was unmistakably in the midst of sex, and as the woman's body thrust and swayed, her head shifted for a moment, and Astrid could clearly recognize that the man on the bed was Charlie. It was only at that moment that she realized, in absolute horror, that *she* was the girl in the video.

Astrid gasped out loud and dropped her phone as if it had burned her hands. "Ohmygodohmygodohmygod!" she whispered to herself before picking up the phone and attempting to dial Charlie's number. Her trembling fingers somehow couldn't swipe to the correct menu on her phone, and instead made the video play again. Finally, she got to her contacts screen and hit CW1, his private mobile.

After several rings, Charlie picked up. "Baby, I was just thinking about you."

"Oh God Charlie—"

"Are you okay? What is it?"

"Oh God, I don't even know what to say—"

"Just take your time. I'm right here," Charlie said, trying to sound calm. He could hear the terror in her voice.

"Michael just sent me a video. It's of the two of us."

"What kind of video?"

"He texted it to me. It's a video of us . . . having sex."

Charlie almost jumped out of his chair. "What? Where?"

"I don't know. I didn't look too hard. The minute I saw your face, I just freaked out."

"Send it to me right now!"

"Um, is it safe to text it to you?"

"Fuck if I know. Send it via WhatsApp. I think that's supposed to be more secure."

"Okay, hold on." Astrid found the video clip and forwarded it to Charlie. He went silent for a few interminable minutes, and she knew he had to be scrutinizing it. Finally, his voice came back on, sounding preternaturally calm.

"Michael just sent this to you?"

"Yes. We were in the middle of a texting argument. Over Cassian, of course. Charlie, is it really us?"

"It is." Charlie sounded grim.

"Where was it taken? How—"

"It's taken right here in my bedroom in Hong Kong."

"So it must have been taken within the last year. Because I didn't start sleeping over at your place until three months after my formal separation with Michael."

Charlie suddenly groaned. "Fuck, I could still be under surveillance right now! Let me get outta here and call you back."

Astrid paced her bedroom, waiting for Charlie to call her back. She felt herself suddenly becoming paranoid. Michael used to be a high-level security expert for the Ministry of Defense. Had he somehow managed to plant a hidden camera in this bedroom too? Grabbing her phone, she fled her bedroom and went downstairs into her courtyard sitting room. Maybe being in a tranquil space would calm her down. As she sank into the sleek white sofa, it occurred to her that the whole house could be bugged. She didn't feel safe here anymore. She slipped on her sandals and walked out of the house. It was midnight, and a few of the nearby outdoor cafés on Emerald Hill Road were still buzzing with people chatting away and having drinks. She began strolling up the street when Charlie called again.

"Charlie! Are you okay?"

"I'm fine. I'm downstairs now, talking from my car. Sorry it took so long. I just needed to get my security team on the case. They are doing a full sweep of the flat now."

"Did you wake Chloe and Delphine?"

"They are both at a sleepover party tonight."

"Thank God they're out of the house."

"What the fuck is Michael trying to pull? Does he realize how illegal this is?" Charlie fumed.

"He's been in a black mood all weekend, ever since the funeral when my father's bodyguards tried to stop him from sitting in the family row. He wants his full settlement—$5 billion—or he's threatening to leak this video. He's sure I'll lose custody of Cassian, and he knows that's the last thing I want."

"I can't believe the fucker is trying to use his own son as a bargaining chip!"

"What should we do, Charlie? I think my house is bugged now."

"I'll fly my security team down to Singapore tomorrow and they will take care of it. We'll get to the bottom of this. You should go home. You'll be fine. Even if your house is bugged, at least we know who's watching. It's not some gang of thieves trying to rob you or anything."

"It's only one asshole trying to rob me of $5 billion," Astrid sighed.

"You know what? I think we should assign a security detail to you. I'll get the top team in the world."

"You sound like my father now. He's always trying to do this to me. I don't want to live in a cage, Charlie. You know how invisible I try to be. If I can't feel safe in my own house, in my hometown, I don't know what point there is in living here."

"You're right, you're right. I'm just paranoid right now, I guess."

"Well, I'm wandering the streets of Singapore in nothing but a little linen shift and bedroom sandals, and no one's even noticing me."

"I bet you're wrong. I bet every guy on the street is thinking, who is that half-naked babe?"

Astrid laughed. "Oh Charlie, I love you. Even in the midst of all this craziness, you can make me laugh."

"It's important to laugh. Otherwise, we're letting the fucker win."

Astrid had circled back to her terrace house, and now she sat down on the little step that extended just a foot beyond her front gate. "Win, lose, how did this even become a battle? All I ever wanted was for us to be able to find happiness."

Charlie sighed. "Well, it's clear to me that Michael doesn't want to be happy. Ever. He just wants to be in a constant state of war with you. That's why he's been stalking us at every turn and dragging his heels with the divorce negotiations."

"You're right, Charlie. He sent that video tonight because he wanted to scare us and drive us out of our own homes."

"And he damn near succeeded. But you know what? We don't scare so easily. We're both going to go back into our homes now. We're both going to lock our doors, and we're never going to let him in again!"

CHAPTER SEVEN

The OCBC Centre at 65 Chulia Street was nicknamed "the calculator" because of its flat shape and windows that resemble button pads. The architect I. M. Pei had intended for the hulking gray tower to be a symbol of strength and permanence, since it was the headquarters of the Oversea-Chinese Banking Corporation, the island's oldest bank.

Unbeknownst to most people, the thirty-eighth floor of the tower was home to Tan and Tan, a small law firm that kept an exceedingly low profile but was undoubtedly one of the most influential legal powerhouses in the country. The firm almost exclusively represented Singapore's establishment families and did not take on new clients—one had to be specially recommended.

Today, the glowing mahogany-and-glass reception counter had been given an extra polish, fresh-cut roses bloomed in the guest toilets, and every member of the staff had been told to dress in their smartest outfits. At around fifteen minutes to ten, the elevator doors began to work overtime as the descendants of Shang Su Yi started to arrive en masse. The Leongs showed up first—Harry, Felicity, Henry Jr., Peter, and

Astrid* were joined by Victoria Young and the Aakaras. At 9:55 a.m., Philip, Eleanor, and Nick joined the others in the discreet reception room with its imitation Le Corbusier leather couches.

Sitting down next to Astrid, Nick asked, "You okay?" He could always sense whenever things weren't right with his cousin.

Astrid smiled, trying to reassure him. "I'm fine. I just didn't get enough sleep last night, that's all."

"I haven't been sleeping much either. Rachel thinks my body's just catching up to the grief, but it all still feels like some bizarre dream," Nick said. As he made that comment, the grandfather clock in the lobby began to chime ten, and Alix Young Cheng entered with her husband, Malcolm, and Eddie, Cecilia, and Alistair. Eddie cleared his throat as if he were going to make a speech, but he was interrupted by Cathleen Kah,† who came out into the reception area to greet the family.

Cathleen shepherded everyone down the corridor and through the double doors into the main conference room. A massive dark oak table dominated the room, placed in front of the bank of windows framing a panoramic view of the bay. Sitting at one end of the table was Freddie Tan, Su Yi's longtime lawyer, having coffee with Alfred Shang, Leonard Shang, and Oliver T'sien.

I knew Uncle Alfred would be part of this, but what the hell are Leonard and Oliver doing here? Eddie thought to himself.

---

* The Leongs' third son, Alexander, who married a Malay woman and has three children with her, lives in Brentwood, California. He has neither returned to Singapore nor spoken to his father in eleven years.
† None of the grandchildren's spouses were invited to this meeting, with the exception of Henry Leong's wife, Cathleen Kah. The fact that she is a senior partner at Tan and Tan and is descended from the distinguished family that provides the firm with forty percent of its billable hours might have had something to do with it.

"Good morning, everyone," Freddie said jovially. "Please make yourselves comfortable."

Everyone took their seats around the table, clustered more or less in their family units, except for Eddie, who positioned himself at the head of the table.

"That was quite the send-off yesterday, wasn't it? Eddie, I never knew you could sing like that," Freddie remarked.

"Thank you, Freddie. Shall we begin?" Eddie eagerly suggested.

"Relax, kiddo. We're just waiting for one more person," Freddie said.

"Who else is coming?" Eddie asked, suddenly alarmed.

At that moment, the sound of expensive designer heels making soft clicks against marble could be heard in the corridor outside, and the receptionist opened the conference room doors. "This way, ma'am."

Jacqueline Ling breezed into the room in a deep purple wrap dress, her Res Rei sunglasses still on and a Mitford blue Yves Saint Laurent couture overcoat flung across her shoulders. "So sorry to keep you all waiting! Would you believe my driver took me to the wrong place? He thought we were going to the Singapore Land Tower for some reason."

"No need to apologize. It's just a few minutes past ten, so you're fashionably late, haha," Freddie joked.

Jacqueline took a seat next to Nick, who leaned over and gave her a friendly peck on the cheek. Freddie looked around at the anxiously assembled group and decided it was time to put them out of their misery. "Well, we all know why we're here, so let's get on with it."

Eleanor smiled pensively, while Philip leaned back in his chair. Alfred peered down at the sumptuously lacquered wood grain, wondering whether the table had been made by David

Linley. Nick winked at Astrid seated across from him, and Astrid smiled back.

Freddie pressed a button on the telephone next to him. "Tuan, you can bring it in now." An assistant, nattily dressed in a red sweater vest and striped tie, entered the room, ceremoniously holding an oversize parchment envelope folder. The assistant placed the folder on the table next to Freddie, and then handed him a horn-handled letter opener. Everyone could see Su Yi's personal wax seal on the envelope flap. Freddie took the letter opener and dramatically flicked the blade underneath the bloodred wax. Eddie inhaled audibly.

Freddie carefully slid out a legal-size document from the envelope, held it up to the room so everyone could clearly see what it was, and then he began to read:

Last Will and Testament of Shang Su Yi

I, Shang Su Yi of Tyersall Park, Tyersall Avenue, Singapore, revoke all former wills and testamentary dispositions heretofore made by me and declare this to be my last Will.

1. **Appointment of Executors.** I appoint my nephew Sir Leonard SHANG and my great-nephew Oliver T'SIEN to be the Co-Executors of my Will.

(Eddie darted his eyes over at his cousins, a little dismayed. *Why in the world would Ah Ma choose them as the executors? Oliver I can handle but, ugh, now I have to suck up to that pretentious Leonard!*)

2. **Specific Cash Legacies.** I direct my Residuary Estate to
   execute payment on the following legacies:

   a. $3,000,000 to my housekeeper LEE Ah Ling, who has
      served my family with excellence and devotion since she
      was a teenager.

   (Victoria smiled. *Oh good, she deserves it.*)

   b. $2,000,000 to my personal chef LIM Ah Ching, who has
      nourished my family with her fine culinary talents since
      1965.

   (Victoria, shaking her head: *Ah Ching's going to throw a fit
   when she realizes she got less than Ah Ling. Better not eat the soup
   tonight!*)

   c. $1,000,000 to my head gardener Jacob THESEIRA,
      who has maintained the grounds of Tyersall Park with
      such loving care. I further bequeath to him all the
      rights and future royalties related to the orchid
      hybrids we developed together over the course of five
      decades.

   d. $1,000,000 to each of my dear lady's maids Madri
      VISUDHAROMN and Patravadee VAROPRAKORN
      along with the antique Peranakan gold-and-diamond
      bracelets labeled for them in the Tyersall Park vault.

   e. $500,000 to my head of security Captain Vikram
      GHALE, who has diligently protected me since 1983.
      I further bequeath to him the Type 14 Nambu pistol
      given to me by Count Hisaichi Terauchi preceding his
      departure from Singapore in 1944.

(Eleanor: *Wah, so generous! I wonder if Old Lady knew that he made a fortune with his day trading?*)

f. $250,000 to my chauffeur Ahmad BIN YOUSSEF. I further bequeath to him the 1935 Hispano-Suiza Type 68 J12 Cabriolet[*] that was given to me by my father on my sixteenth birthday.

(Alfred: *Damn, I wanted the Hispano! I guess I can buy it off him.*)

g. I bequeath every remaining employee of Tyersall Park not mentioned here the amount of $50,000 each.

3. **Specific Legacies of Personal Property.**
   a. I direct that my jewelry collection be given and distributed according to the detailed list in Appendix A of this my Last Will and Testament, and as labeled in my vault at Tyersall Park.

(Cecilia Cheng Moncur: *I wonder why she bothered. Everyone knows Astrid already got all the good shit.*)

   b. I direct that all artwork, antiques, and other household goods not specifically gifted by my Will be distributed equally among my surviving children by my executors in as nearly equal portions as may be practicable, with the exception of the following:
   i. To my daughter Felicity YOUNG LEONG, I bequeath my collection of Celadon porcelain, which

---

[*] For comparison, a 1936 Hispano-Suiza Type 68 J12 Cabriolet sold at 2010 auction in Scottsdale, Arizona, for $1,400,000.

I know she will cherish and keep immaculately
spotless for all eternity.

(Alix: *Hahaha! Felicity and her OCD. Mummy sure had a sense of
humor when she wrote her will!*)

    ii.   To my daughter Victoria YOUNG, I bequeath a
small painting of a woman by her bedroom window
by Édouard Vuillard. I know she has always
detested this painting, so I trust she will divest of
it immediately and use the proceeds to buy that
dream house in England that she keeps talking
about.

(Victoria: *Criticize me from the grave all you want, but I've already
been town-house shopping on Sothebysrealty.com.*)

    iii.   To my son Philip YOUNG, I bequeath all objects
in Tyersall Park belonging to his father, Sir James
Young.

(Philip: *Did I remember to program the DVR to record the new season
of* Arrow? *Can't wait to get back to Sydney. This is such a colossal waste
of time!*)

    iv.   To my daughter Alexandra YOUNG CHENG, I
bequeath my collection of carved ivory-and-jade
name seals, since she is the only one of my children
who actually knows Mandarin.

    v.   To my daughter-in-law Eleanor SUNG, I bequeath a
box of Santa Maria Novella Almond Soap.

(All the women in the room gasped audibly, while Eleanor simply broke out in laughter. Nick glanced at his mother, not understanding. Jacqueline whispered to Nick, "She's letting everyone know she thinks your mother was a dirty woman.")

vi.   To my cherished granddaughter Astrid LEONG, who in every way takes after my mother's style, I bequeath my collection of cheongsams, ceremonial robes, vintage textiles, hats, and accessories.

vii.   To my dear granddaughter Cecilia CHENG MONCUR, champion equestrienne, I bequeath a Chinese scroll painting of a galloping herd of horses from the Northern Song period by Li Gonglin.

viii. To my loyal and always amusing grand-nephew Oliver T'SIEN, I give and bequeath the pair of Émile-Jacques Ruhlmann table lamps from my dressing room and my signed first edition of W. Somerset Maugham's *Far Eastern Tales*.

(Oliver: *Niiiiiice.*)

ix.   To my devoted grandson Edison CHENG, I bequeath a pair of Asprey sapphire-and-platinum cuff links, gifted to my husband Sir James Young on our golden anniversary by the Sultan of Perawak. James was far too modest to wear the cuff links, but I know Edison will not be so bashful.

(Eddie: *Phwoar! But enough with this piddly shit—can we just get on to the main event?*)

    x.   I have made no specific bequests or provisions for my grandchildren Henry LEONG Jr. and Peter LEONG, for whom I have great affection, because they were left generous legacies in my late-husband Sir James Young's Will, and because I know they have been amply provided for by the Leong Family Trusts.

(Henry Leong Jr.: *What generous legacy? Gong Gong only left me $1 million, and I was just a little kid!*)

4. **Legacy of Historical Archives, Photographs, Documents, Personal Letters, and Ephemera.** I bequeath ownership and all copyrights and intellectual property rights of my personal archive at Tyersall Park, including all family photographs, letters, journals, and documents to my dearest grandson Nicholas YOUNG, the noted historian of our family.

5. **Legacy of Shares.** I bequeath my 1,000,000 Ling Holdings Pte Ltd Preference Shares—which Ling Yin Chao lost to me during an epic mah-jongg battle in 1954—to my beloved goddaughter Jacqueline LING. If she does not survive me, I bequeath the shares to her daughter Amanda LING. It is my hope that this will correct the imbalance of power within the Ling clan.

(Jacqueline's cool, collected visage hid what she was feeling inside: *Dear, dear Su Yi, you've liberated me! My God, I wish I could hug you right now!* Felicity and her sisters frowned a little, not quite understanding what all this meant, but Eleanor, who was on top of the market, immediately started doing the math in her head:

One million shares, and Ling Holdings is around $145 per share today.
Jesus, Jacqueline is getting a huge windfall!)

6. **Residue of My Estate.** The residue of my estate consists
   of: Cash and other financial instruments held at my banks
   (OCBC in Singapore, HSBC in Hong Kong, Bangkok
   Bank in Thailand, C. Hoare & Co. in London, Landolt &
   Cie in Switzerland). I direct all the monies held in these
   institutions to be used toward payment of the legacies
   specified in Clause 2. At the fulfillment of all the specific
   legacies, I ask that any remaining monies be used to fund
   a new charitable foundation to be named THE YOUNG
   FOUNDATION, in memory of my husband Sir James
   Young. I appoint Astrid Leong and Nicholas Young as
   co-executors of the foundation.

7. **Legacies of Real Property.**
   a. I give and bequeath my property in CAMERON
      HIGHLANDS, Malaysia, and all the contents within
      this eighty-acre estate to my dear grandson Alexander
      LEONG. If he does not survive me, I give the property
      to his wife Salimah LEONG and my great-grandchildren
      James, Anwar, and Yasmine LEONG, who I most
      unfortunately have never been able to meet, in equal
      shares.

(Harry Leong was stunned. This was such a slap to his face!
Felicity didn't dare look at her husband, but Astrid couldn't help
but smile: *I can't wait to Skype Alex. I want to see the look on his face*
when he finds out that Ah Ma left the incredible heritage estate in Malay-
sia to HIM—the son who's been disowned by his father for marrying a
native Malay girl.)

b. I give and bequeath my property in CHIANG MAI,
   Thailand, and all the contents within this three-hundred-
   acre estate to my beloved daughter Catherine YOUNG
   AAKARA. If she does not survive me, I give the
   property to her children James, Matthew, and Adam
   AAKARA in equal shares.

(Catherine started to sob, while Felicity, Victoria, and Alix all
bolted up in their seats, staring at her in shock. *What estate in
Chiang Mai?*)

Freddie Tan paused for a moment, and without a hint of fan-
fare, read the final clause of the will.

c. I give and bequeath my house in SINGAPORE to the
   following family members in the portions indicated
   below:
   My only son, PHILIP YOUNG: 30 percent
   My eldest daughter, FELICITY YOUNG: 12.5 percent
   My second daughter, CATHERINE YOUNG
       AAKARA: 12.5 percent
   My third daughter, VICTORIA YOUNG: 12.5 percent
   My youngest daughter, ALEXANDRA YOUNG
       CHENG: 12.5 percent
   My grandson, NICHOLAS YOUNG: 10 percent
   My grandson, ALISTAIR CHENG: 10 percent

SIGNED by SHANG SU YI

Freddie put the document down and looked up at everyone.
Felicity, Victoria, and Alix were still trying to digest the sur-

prising news that their mother had owned a secret estate in Thailand.

"Go on!" Eddie said impatiently.

"I'm finished," Freddie answered.

"What do you mean you're finished? What about Tyersall Park?"

"I just read you that clause."

"What do you mean? You didn't mention Tyersall Park at all!" Eddie insisted.

Freddie sighed and began to recite the final clause again. When he was finally done, the room was completely silent for a moment, and then things erupted as everyone started talking at once.

"We *all* have a share in Tyersall Park?" Felicity asked, utterly confused.

"Yes, you specifically have a 12.5 percent share in the property," Freddie explained.

"Twelve point five percent . . . what does this even mean?" Victoria grumbled.

Eleanor smiled triumphantly at Nick, and then she whispered in Philip's ear, "Your mother can insult me all she wants, but at the end of the day you and Nicky got the majority share and that's what counts!"

Nick glanced across the table at his cousin Alistair, who shook his head in disbelief. "I can't believe Ah Ma actually left me something in her will."

"More than a little something," Nick said with a grin.

Witnessing Nick's exchange with his brother, Eddie grew more livid by the moment. Suddenly he jumped out of his chair, shouting, "THIS IS TOTAL BULLSHIT! Where's my share in Tyersall Park? Let me see that will! Are you sure this is even the latest version?"

Freddie looked at him calmly. "I can assure you this is your grandmother's Last Will and Testament. I was present when she signed it."

Eddie snatched the document from his hands and flipped through to the last page. There, on the bottom of the page, was the notarized seal, accompanied by the following words:

**Signed in the presence of FIONA TUNG CHENG
and ALFRED SHANG
on this the Ninth day of June 2009**

Eddie's eyes almost bulged out of his head. "Fucky fuck, *my wife* was a witness?"

"Indeed she was," Freddie replied.

"That bitch never told me! And the will was signed in *2009*? How is this possible?" Eddie said, almost shrieking.

"Stop asking stupid questions, you *goblok!** She took a pen and signed it!" Alfred scolded him, getting fed up.

Eddie ignored his great-uncle. "But this means she never changed her will? Not even when Nicky married Rachel?"

Nick realized his cousin was right. After all the endless speculation about being disinherited, it turned out his grandmother never once waivered from her original plan. She left a majority stake of Tyersall Park to his father, knowing one day it would be passed down to him. Suddenly he felt an enormous wave of guilt wash over him. Why did he waste so many years being mad at Ah Ma?

But Eddie wasn't done with his tirade. He stormed over to Freddie Tan's chair and looked him in the eye accusingly. "The

---

*   Indonesian slang for someone that is stupid or retarded.

other day when you came to see my grandma, you *told me* I was going to be the main beneficiary!"

Freddie looked startled. "I have no idea what you're talking about. I said no such thing."

"You told me I was the 'man of the hour'!"

Freddie almost began to laugh, but seeing the look on Eddie's face, he tried to soften the blow. "Eddie, I was making a pun about the Patek Philippe you were wearing. You had on the 150th-anniversary Jump Hour Reference 3969 watch. One of my favorite models."

Eddie glared at him incredulously before crumbling into his chair in embarrassment. Alix gave her son a pitiful look, and then turned to the lawyer. "Freddie, I'm not clear about how my mother's financial holdings are going to be divvied up. What about her other stocks and her share of Shang Enterprises?"

Freddie looked very uncomfortable and swiveled his chair in Alfred's direction.

"Your mother had no other stocks, aside from Ling Holdings," Alfred said.

"But Mummy had a huge stock portfolio—she told me she had every blue-chip counter! Wasn't she the biggest private shareholder in Keppel Land, Robinson's, Singapore Press Holdings?" Felicity argued.

Alfred shook his head. "No, I am."

"But doesn't she share all that with you? As co-owner of Shang Enterprises?"

Alfred leaned back in his chair and looked at Felicity. "You need to understand something . . . Shang Enterprises—the shipping company, the trading firm, all our various business interests around the world—are controlled by the Shang Loong Ma Trust. Your mother was a beneficiary of the Trust, but never a co-owner."

"So who owns Shang Enterprises?" Alix asked.

"Once again, the Trust owns Shang Enterprises, and I am the chief custodian of the Trust. Your grandfather's will stipulated that the Trust would be passed down through the male line. Only the Shang men could inherit. He was extremely old-fashioned, as you know."

"So how did my mummy get all her income?" Alix asked.

"She had no income, but the Trust paid for all her expenses. My father's wording in his will was very specific. He stipulated that 'Su Yi's every need, desire, and whim is to be taken care of in her lifetime by the Trust.' So we did."

"The Trust paid for everything?" Felicity was incredulous.

Alfred sighed. "*Everything*. As you well know, your mother did not have any concept of money. She was born to live like a princess, and she continued to live this way for nine decades. Supporting all of you, maintaining her lifestyle at Tyersall Park, in Cameron Highlands, everywhere she traveled. How much do you think it costs to keep a staff of seventy for so many years? To throw grand parties every Friday night? Believe me, your mother blew through a vast amount."

"What will the Trust pay for now?" Victoria asked.

Alfred leaned back in his chair. "Well . . . nothing. The Trust has met all its fiduciary duties to your mother."

Victoria looked at her uncle, almost afraid to ask the next question. "So are you telling us that we are inheriting *nothing* from the Shang Trust?"

Alfred shook his head solemnly. The room went silent for a moment as everyone soaked in this bombshell.

Felicity was silent, the enormity of her uncle's words slowly sinking in. All this time she thought her mother the great heiress had been co-owner of an empire worth hundreds of billions, and now it turns out she had never even been part of the equation. This meant in turn that *she* would inherit nothing from Shang Enterprises. She was not a great heiress to anything. She had only been left 12.5 percent of the house, just like the rest of her sisters. But this wasn't right. She was the eldest child. How could Mummy do this to her? Collecting herself, Felicity steeled herself and looked Alfred in the eye with a question. "How much does Mummy have in her bank accounts?"

"Not much, really. Some of her accounts are absolutely ancient. Hoare's only has about three million pounds—she inherited that account from my mother, and that was Mum's shopping account when she ordered things from Harrods. Landolt & Cie in Switzerland holds her gold bullion, and that was really just in case the world went to absolute hell. I'd say she has about forty-five, fifty million total."

Freddie chimed in, "But that money will automatically go toward paying for all the legacies she left—to Ah Ching, Ah Ling, and so forth."

Victoria frowned at Freddie accusingly. "I don't believe this! I don't believe that all this time Mummy had so little money!"

Freddie sighed. "Well, she did have one major income-producing asset, and that was her Ling Holdings Preference Shares. She had one million shares that paid a considerable dividend, but she reinvested it all in buying more shares. Her shares are valued at about half a billion dollars today, but as you all know, that's spoken for now."

The sisters stared at Jacqueline in absolute horror. Su Yi's beautiful goddaughter had automatically inherited more money from their mother's estate than they did.

"So you're telling me the only thing of any income-generating value we're inheriting from our mother is Tyersall Park?" Felicity said slowly, as if not quite believing her own words.

"Well, that isn't exactly chopped liver. Tyersall Park is worth about a billion dollars today if you sold it," Freddie remarked.

"Two billion," Alfred piped up.

Victoria shook her head vehemently. "But we could never sell Tyersall Park! It has to stay in the family. Where does that leave us? We get nothing! Am I supposed to live off the proceeds of one miserable Vuillard?"

Felicity looked at her husband with tears in her eyes and said in a quivering voice, "If we are forced to sell Tyersall Park I only get a few hundred million. I'm going to be *a nobody* now!"

Harry squeezed her hand encouragingly. "Darling, you're my wife. You're *Puan Sri* Harry Leong and we have our own money. You'll never be a nobody."

Philip got up from the table abruptly and spoke for the first time. "This was obviously Mum's plan all along. If she wanted one of us to get Tyersall Park, she would have left it to that person outright. But the way she divided it up, she knew there would be only one thing we could do. She wanted us to sell the damned house!"

CHAPTER EIGHT

PS.Café was an oasis nestled in the parklands of the former Dempsey Hill barracks, and the moment Nick entered the tranquil space with Astrid he felt like he could breathe easier.

As if echoing his thoughts, Astrid said, "I'm so glad we managed to make our escape."

"Two hours with the family in the lawyers' office . . . I think it's going to take me a year to recover!" Nick laughed, looking around to see if Rachel and Carlton had arrived. "Ah, they're hiding over in the corner."

"So you have a hot date tomorrow night?" Rachel teased her brother as they sat at a table bathed in sunlight filtering through the giant plate-glass windows.

"I'm *hoping* it will be a hot date! You know, sometimes an actual date just screws things up," Carlton said, taking a sip of his lychee-and-lime soda.

"Scheherazade and you have been inseparable for the past week. I don't see how you could possibly screw it up at this point." Rachel looked up and saw Nick and Astrid navigating between the crowded tables toward them. "Here they come. Let's ask Astrid—"

"Noooo!" Carlton said bashfully.

"Ask me what?" Astrid asked as she leaned over to give Rachel a peck on the cheek.

"In your expert opinion, do you think it's a bad idea for Carlton to take your cousin on a date?"

"What, a real date? I figured they were already halfway to Vegas to get married!" Astrid teased.

"Stop it, I'm not sure she's that into me," Carlton said.

"Carlton, if she wasn't into you, you wouldn't even be able to get close."

"Really?" Carlton seemed dubious.

Astrid sat down next to him. "First of all, her parents are pathologically protective of her. You've seen her security detail. I'm told that in Paris, she has undercover agents trailing her everywhere she goes, and even she doesn't know who they are. But aside from that, Scheherazade has left a trail of carnage since she was a teenager. I've never seen so many love-sick puppies get their hearts stomped on. But you, Mr. Dimples, have gotten through the Praetorian Guard."

"So where are you taking her on your hot date?" Nick prodded.

"I thought I'd keep things really casual . . . maybe a walk followed by drinks at LeVeL33?"

Astrid made a little face. "You might want to rethink that."

"You're going to have to up your game, Carlton. Scheherazade Shang does not impress easily," Nick warned.

"Okay, duly noted." Carlton laughed.

Rachel, meanwhile, was on the edge of her seat wanting to know what happened at the reading of the will. "Anyway, enough about Carlton's love life. How are you guys? Did everything . . . um . . . go okay?"

Nick stared out the window. From where he was sitting, it seemed as though the entire café was a glass tree house, and he just wanted to dive out the window and be enveloped by the foliage. "I'm not sure, my brain is totally fried. How do you think it went, Astrid?"

Astrid leaned back in her chair and let out a sigh. "I've never been in a room that was filled with that much tension. There were many surprises, and I think everyone's in shock at the moment. Eddie especially."

"Why Eddie?" Rachel asked.

Nick gave a little laugh. "The poor sod thought he was going to inherit Tyersall Park." Knowing the big question on Rachel's mind, he continued, "It's not going to me either. I have a small share, but Tyersall Park is being divided up like a big wheel of cheese among my father, his sisters . . . and Alistair, as it turns out."

Rachel's jaw dropped. "Alistair? Jeez, no wonder Eddie's in shock!"

"Shock today, fratricide tomorrow," Astrid quipped.

"How about you, Astrid? Are you surprised that you didn't get a share of the house?" Rachel asked.

"I never imagined I would. I'm happy enough that Ah Ma left me a few things she knows I'll cherish." Astrid's phone began to ring, and seeing that it was Charlie, she quickly got up from the table and said, "Back in a moment. If the waitress comes, can I get a peach-and-lychee fizz?"

After Astrid had left the table, Rachel asked, "So if the house is being divided up among so many people, how's that going to work?"

Nick shrugged. "I guess that's what they're trying to figure out now. The rest of the family is back at the house having a big powwow over lunch."

Rachel reached across the table and gave Nick's hand a

squeeze. She could only imagine how difficult it must have been for him, to sit there in that office and find out how his grand-mother's entire life was going to be dismantled and dispersed. Changing the topic, she said cheerily, "Well, let's order. I'm starving, and I hear the Tiger beer-battered fish-and-chips are amazing."

Standing in the patio outside the café, Astrid listened worriedly as Charlie tried to explain the situation. "My security team did a full sweep. They searched every last inch of my apartment but they couldn't find a thing. No hidden cameras, no surveillance devices, nothing. And I just heard back from the Singapore team—they couldn't find anything in your house either."

Astrid frowned. "What does this mean?"

"I'm not sure. It's pretty damn alarming that there's video footage of us in my bed, but no one has any idea how it was recorded."

"Could it have been done from a drone?" Astrid wondered.

"No, it's the wrong angle. We studied every frame of the foot-age, and it had to have been shot from the foot of my bed, not out the window. Whatever device was in my bedroom is now gone."

"Oh that's reassuring," Astrid said mordantly. "So whoever planted the device came back to remove it."

"That would appear to be the case. Listen, I'm flying in more security experts from Israel to do another assessment. I want them to go over everything with an even finer comb. And then I'll send them to Singapore to do another sweep of your house. Until then, I don't think you should go back to your place until we figure this out."

Astrid leaned against a pillar, sighing in frustration. "I can't believe this is happening. I feel so violated, like nowhere I go is safe anymore. I feel like Michael has eyes everywhere in this town."

"Why don't you come to Hong Kong? I'm holed up at the Peninsula now, in their Peninsula Suite. This is where all the heads of state stay. It's really the most secure place you can be at the moment."

"I feel like if I leave now, it's admitting defeat. Michael will know he's managed to intimidate us."

"Astrid, listen to me. What did we say last night? We're not going to let Michael win. We're not going to let him dictate the rules here. You're not fleeing town. You're coming to Hong Kong to see me, to have a good time, to start looking into options for our wedding. Your grandma's funeral is over, and we're getting on with our lives," Charlie said reassuringly.

"You're absolutely right. I have to come to Hong Kong. We have a wedding to plan!" Astrid proclaimed, the fire returning to her voice.

CHAPTER NINE

Even from the service wing downstairs, Eddie's yelling could be heard. Ah Ling, Ah Ching, and a dozen maids craned their necks by the kitchen window, mesmerized by noises wafting down to them from the bedroom where Eddie and Fiona were staying.

"Fucky fuck! You knew all along what was in my grandmother's will, and you didn't tell me a thing!" Eddie shouted.

"I keep telling you I didn't know anything! I was only a witness to the signing, don't you understand? I wasn't going to sit there and read her will!" Fiona argued back.

"Why the hell didn't you?"

"Lower your voice, Eddie! Everyone can hear us!"

"I give precisely zero fucks who can hear us! I want the whole world to know what an idiot you are! You had a chance to read my grandmother's will and you didn't!"

"I have respect for your grandmother's privacy!"

"Respect my ass! What about me? Why don't I get the respect I fucking deserve?" Eddie continued to yell.

"I'm not going to sit here and take this abuse anymore! Take an Effexor and calm the hell down." Fiona got up from the settee and tried to leave, but Eddie grabbed her forcefully.

"Don't you get it? You've ruined your children's lives and

you've ruined my life!" he screamed, taking hold of Fiona by the shoulders and shaking her.

"Let go of me, Eddie!" Fiona shrieked.

"*Aiyoh!* That Eddie is too much," Ah Ching said, shaking her head as she heard his ranting. "It sounds to me like he didn't get the house, did he? Oh thank all the gods!"

"He's an utter fool if he thought Su Yi would leave this place to him!" Ah Ling chimed in.

Just then, the muffled sound of something hitting the marquetry floor could be heard.

Jiayi, the young Chinese scullery maid, flinched in terror. "Oh my God! Did he just hit her? It sounds like she landed on the floor! Someone do something! Ah Ling, what should we do?"

Ah Ling just sighed. "We should stay out of it! Remember, Jiayi, we don't see anything and we don't hear anything. That's what we do. Now, let's get the first five courses out to the dining room. Quickly! The animals are hungry."

As the rest of the kitchen maids sprang into action, Jiayi instead made a dash up to Eddie's bedroom. Fiona had been so sweet to her, she wasn't going to let anyone hurt her. She crept up the stairs to the hallway where the guest bedrooms were, and as she came to their bedroom, she could hear someone moaning in anguish. Jiayi opened the door slowly and whispered, "Ma'am, are you okay?" She looked in and saw Eddie lying on the floor in a fetal position, his head in Fiona's lap. Fiona sat on the floor, calm as a pietà, stroking his hair as he sobbed uncontrollably like a little boy. She looked up at Jiayi, and the maid quickly closed the door.

In the family dining room of Tyersall Park, everyone had gathered around the massive round mahogany dining table designed by the great Shanghai artist Huang Pao Fan. Anticipating that this was going to be a contentious meal, Ah Ling and Ah Ching devised a lunch that consisted of the favorite dishes of the Young siblings when they were children—pumpkin and prawn noodle soup (Catherine's favorite), fried rice with *lap cheong*[*] and extra eggs (Philip's favorite), steamed pomfret in ginger sauce (Felicity's favorite), *lor mai kai*[†] (Alix's favorite), and Yorkshire pudding (Victoria's favorite). If it made for a slightly schizophrenic menu, no one noticed except the in-laws.

Victoria threw out the opening salvo as she savored her first forkful of pudding. "Philip, surely you weren't serious when you said we should sell Tyersall Park?"

"I don't see any other choice," Philip answered.

"Why don't you buy us all out? You have the majority stake, and we'll sell you our shares at a family discount. This way we all can keep our rooms, and Tyersall Park can be like our private family hotel."

Alix looked up from her aromatic chicken rice. What on earth was Victoria suggesting? She had no intention of selling her share at a discount.

Philip shook his head as he swallowed a mouthful of fried rice. "First of all, I can't afford to buy you all out, but that's beside the point. What would I do with this house? I live in Sydney most of the year—I can't be bothered to maintain this white elephant."

"Cat, wouldn't you like to have Tyersall Park? You can afford it, can't you?" Victoria asked her sister hopefully.

---

[*]   Chinese sausage.
[†]   Steamed glutinous rice with chicken in a lotus leaf wrap, my dim sum favorite.

"Everything about this place reminds me of Mummy, and I'd be too sad," Catherine mused, picking at her noodles without much of an appetite.

Alix spoke up. "Cat's right. This house just isn't the same now that Mummy's gone. Look, Mummy clearly wanted us to sell it. She knew none of us would really want to take it on."

Victoria looked distressed. "Then what happens to me? Am I supposed to move in to *a flat*? Goodness gracious, I'd feel like I'm suddenly part of the 'new poor'!"

"Victoria, no one cares anymore," Alix argued. "Look at all our friends, our cousins—the T'siens, the Tans, the Shangs. No one we know still lives in their original houses. Buitenzorg, Eu Villa, 38 Newton Road, the House of Jade. All the great estates are long gone. Even Command House is now part of bloody UBS. I've lived in a three-bedroom condo for decades and I love it."

Harry nodded in agreement. "I *dream* of the luxury of living someplace small, like one of those HDB flats! Why, I hear that most of them even have elevators these days!"*

Alix looked around the table at each of her siblings. "A property of this size has not come on the market in almost a century—this is like Central Park going up for sale in New York. In this neighborhood, the going rate is $1,000 per square foot. We have more than 2.8 *million* square feet here, and that adds up to $2.8 billion. But I think developers would pay even more, and there's going to be a bidding war. Trust me, I've been flipping properties in Hong Kong for years. We have to orchestrate this very methodically, because this is our one chance to make an absolute killing."

---

* Harry Leong has obviously never set foot in a Housing and Development Board flat in his entire life, but like so many oblivious one-percenters is always fantasizing about downsizing and moving in to an HDB flat "since I am entitled to one."

Victoria gave a dramatic sigh, although secretly she was already thinking of the cute topiaries she would put on the doorstep of her town house in London. "Okay, so let's sell the house. But we can't appear to want to sell it anytime soon. That would be unseemly."

"I think we should wait at least six months. We wouldn't want to look like greedy pigs," Felicity stated as she sucked on a fish bone.

Philip took a sip of his coffee and winced. "All right then, I'm heading back to Sydney tonight—I can't stand another day without a proper flat white. I'll be back in six months and we can officially put the house on the market."

Just then, Ah Ling entered the dining room with an announcement: "Something just arrived that I think you all should see."

Two Gurkha guards wheeled a large flatbed dolly into the room. Piled on it was a mountain of colorful ribboned boxes, all from Ladurée in Paris. There were boxes upon boxes of chocolates and truffles, macaroons and cakes—all manner of delicious confections from the legendary dessert maker. Crowning this elaborate display was a *croquembouche*, with a large embossed gold card affixed to the front. Ah Ling took the card and handed it to Philip. He tore it open and began to laugh.

"What is it?" Eleanor asked excitedly.

Philip read the card aloud. "Bright Star Properties wishes the Young family prosperity and good tidings in the coming Year of the Goat. May we respectfully extend an all-cash tender offer of $1.88 billion for the purchase of Tyersall Park."

Felicity gasped, while Alix turned to Victoria with a smirk. "I don't think we have to worry about looking like greedy pigs."

CHAPTER TEN

Kitty was floating on an inflatable lounger in the middle of her pool in an alluring one-shoulder cutout Araks swimsuit when she heard the car returning to the house. She had been waiting impatiently for the past hour, after sending a maid to the bookstore to buy a whole stack of the new issue of *Tattle*, which had just been released this morning.

Kitty paddled her lounger over to the edge of the pool as the maid came rushing down the stone steps with a stack of magazines in her arms, followed by the driver, who was also carrying a big stack. "What took you so long?" Kitty asked.

"I'm sorry, ma'am. We got there before the bookstore opened, but they had to unpack the magazines from the boxes and scan them into the computer first. But here, we bought all forty copies," she said, handing Kitty the top copy from her stack.

It was wrapped in plastic, with a big gold panel over the cover and words that screamed: "OUR WILDEST ISSUE EVER!" Kitty felt her heart race as she tried to tear into the plastic, desperate to get to the magazine. She couldn't wait to see her photo on the cover under the headline "Princess Kitty." The lounger wobbled, and her wet fingers kept slipping against the plastic.

"Here, let me help you!" the maid said, sensing her mistress's excitement. She ripped through the plastic, slipped the glossy magazine out of its sleeve, and handed it to Kitty.

Kitty stared at the cover, her face changing from anticipation to absolute horror. Staring back at her on the cover of *Tattle* was a photograph of Colette and her husband, Lucien, seated at a breakfast table with a huge orangutan.

"Aaaahhh! What is this? This is the wrong issue!" Kitty screamed from her reclining position.

"No ma'am, this is the new issue. Brand-new. I saw them take it out of the boxes."

Kitty scrutinized the cover, where the headline read: LORDS OF THE JUNGLE: THE EARL AND COUNTESS OF PALLISER.

"No! No! No! This can't be real," Kitty sat up on the lounger, tearing through the magazine maniacally and getting the pages wet as she searched for her story. What happened to her beautiful photo shoot with Nigel Barker? The photos of Harvard kissing her? They were nowhere to be found. Instead, the feature article was a ten-page spread dedicated to pictures of Colette and Lucien's visit to a conservation center in Indonesia. There were photos of Colette hosting a tea party for a family of orangutans at a wrought-iron table by the edge of a river, Colette trekking through the rain forest with a group of primatologists, and Colette cradling a baby orangutan.

By this point, Kitty's lounger had drifted to the middle of the pool, and she screeched at the maid, "Get me my phone!"

Kitty jabbed at her phone angrily, calling Oliver T'sien. It rang a few times before he picked up.

"Ollie's Psychic Hotline," he answered jokingly.

"Have you seen the latest *Tattle* yet?" Kitty said, her voice shaking with fury.

"No. Did it come out today? I'm in Hong Kong this week, so I haven't seen it yet. Congratulations! How does it look?"

"Congratulations? Go look at the magazine and tell me how I fucking look on the cover!" Kitty screamed, before hanging up.

God, what now? Oliver thought to himself. Did they end up going with a photo that was slightly less flattering to her surgically sculpted nose? There was no way he would find a copy of the magazine in Hong Kong, but maybe the issue was already online. He went to his browser and logged on to Tattle.com.sg. Within seconds, the page loaded, and the cover of *Tattle* popped up.

"Oh for fuck's sake!" Oliver cursed, as he began to scan through the story.

ECO WARRIOR PRINCESS: AN EXCLUSIVE INTERVIEW WITH COLETTE, THE COUNTESS OF PALLISER

The Countess of Palliser enters the garden of the British embassy in Singapore with no pomp or circumstance, no personal assistant or PR handler in sight. She shakes my hand and immediately starts fretting that I'm seated in the sun. Am I too hot? Would I like to swap seats? Has no one brought me a drink?

This was not the woman I was expecting to meet. The former Colette Bing, once China's most influential fashion blogger—with over 55 million followers—is today sitting before me in a simple yet lovely floral dress with not a dab of makeup on her face or any jewelry except for a simple wedding band of Welsh gold. I ask her who designed her dress and she laughs. "This is a Laura Ashley dress that I got out of a bin at an Oxfam thrift shop in the village near where I live."

It's the first hint that as ordinary as the Countess's life seems to be, things are not all that ordinary. The village she is referring to is Barchester, perhaps one of the most charming in all of England, and home for the Countess and her husband, Lucien Montagu-Scott, the Earl of Palliser, is a charming old vicarage with 10 bedrooms tucked away at Gatherum Castle, the 35,000-acre Barsetshire estate of her father-in-law, the Duke of Glencora.

I've heard rumors that the interior designer Henrietta Spencer-Churchill, of the Blenheim Palace Spencer-Churchills, has been busy transforming the cottage into an elysian paradise, but when I try to ask the Countess about it, she simply says that the house is being refurbished and redirects me to the matter at hand. "My life is not that interesting. Let's talk about Indonesia," she says with an effervescent smile.

Indonesia is the reason the Earl and Countess have been spending so much time in these parts of late. The Earl, a renowned environmental activist, and the Countess actually met there. "I was a bit adrift, traveling to various spa resorts on my own for a few months," the Countess admits. "By chance I met Lucien in Bali, and he told me that he was on the way to a remote part of North Sumatra. I decided on a whim to follow him."

It was a decision that changed her life forever. "Lucien brought me to an orangutan rescue center, and it was my first exposure to the terrible environmental tragedy that's been unfolding here. Sumatran orangutans are classified as 'critically endangered,' and the population is being decimated, along with scores of other species, because of deforestation and illegal poaching. Infant orangutans are being sold to the pet trade, and the way they do this is by killing the mother first. For every baby orangutan sold, it's estimated that six to eight adult orangutans die in the process of capturing them. Can you imagine?" the Countess says, her normally pearl-white complexion flushed with fury.

What she witnessed those first weeks in Sumatra has given the Countess a singular mission in life: to spread awareness of this environmental tragedy and to advocate for change. "People talk about the Amazon, but it's horrific what's being done in this part of Southeast Asia. The main culprit is the palm oil industry. *Everyone* should stop consuming products that contain palm oil! In the quest for more land to create more palm oil plantations, ancient forests are being burned down, destroyed completely, and we are losing so many species that will never be seen again. Orangutans, one of our planet's most precious animals, could be extinct in the wild within 25 years," the Countess says with tears in her eyes.

"And beyond this, look at what the massive bushfires and deforestation have done environmentally to the region— look what it's doing to the air quality right here in Singapore. You can feel the effects of these forest fires right now if you just take a deep breath!"

At this point in the interview, the Countess's husband walks out onto the terrace to join us. He is a tall, blindingly handsome blond fellow who immediately reminds me of Westley from *The Princess Bride*. I'm surprised by how down-to-earth the Earl is, and when he talks about his new wife, his face lights up like a love-struck teen. "Colette's dedication to the orangutan babies—how she handled them, how she wasn't afraid to get her hands dirty and really just give her all to the cause—really surprised me. It one hundred percent made me fall in love with her. I knew I had found my eco-

warrior princess, and after our time together at the camp, I
never wanted to let her go."

"Our mission is just beginning. There's just so much to do,
and that's why we've decided to move to Singapore for the
next few years," the Countess reveals. "This will be an excellent base for our work all over the region," the Earl chimes in.

Are the Earl and Countess going to commandeer one of
Singapore's toniest properties? "I don't know if we'll actually be here all that much, so I think we'll just lease a little
flat someplace very central," the Countess says. In case you
are misled into thinking that the Pallisers have completely
hidden away their ermine robes and tiaras in favor of cargo
pants and Tevas, Colette reveals that she is in the midst of
organizing an event that will no doubt send every reader
of this article scrambling for their best jewels.

"I'm going to host a fund-raising ball in aid of orangutan
rescue with my friends the Duchess of Oxbridge and Cornelia Guest. Both of them are dedicated conservationists doing
such amazing rescue work with animals—Alice with endangered sea turtles, and Cornelia with miniature horses. Hopefully we'll have friends from all over the world jetting in for
a ball that will be inspired by Marie-Hélène de Rothschild's
legendary Proust Ball at Château Ferrières."

If history is to be repeated again, the enchanted evening promises to be the most highly anticipated gala of the
spring charity season, and hopefully, it's the start of many
good things to come from this gorgeous, aristocratic, and
conscious couple.

When he was done reading, Oliver immediately called Violet Poon at *Tattle*. "Can you please explain why there's a fucking

monkey on the cover of your magazine this month instead of Kitty Bing?"

"Oh Oliver, I was going to call you! It was a last-minute mandate that came from my boss. They're running this cover story on every edition of *Tattle* around the world this month. It's such an important story."

"So what happens to Kitty's important story?"

"Well, since Colette was on the cover this month, we felt like a little, ahem, diplomacy was in order. Of course we couldn't put Kitty's story in the same issue. I mean, she *is* her stepmother. We wouldn't want to offend either of them. But you know I adore Kitty's cover! Those Nigel pictures are just beyond! We're going to save it for later in the year. It'll actually be much better in the fall, don't you think? Wouldn't it be a fabulous cover for the September issue?"

Oliver went silent for a moment, trying to figure out how he was going to explain all this to Kitty.

"I hope Kitty won't be upset about this? We will give her the star treatment, I promise. We'll throw a cover launch party at some boutique."

"Upset? Violet, I don't think you have any clue what you've done. You've just started World War III."

"Oh dear . . ."

"I have to go. I need to see if I can disarm the nuclear warhead now."

Oliver hung up with Violet, took a deep breath, and called Kitty's number. He found her eerily composed when he explained the whole situation to her. "I actually think this is going to be much better for you, Kitty. Landing a fall cover is more prestigious. Think of the September issue of *Vogue*. That's always the biggest issue of the year. You'll get so much more exposure. Far less people will see the March issue of *Tattle*, and to be honest, it's a ghastly cover. Look at that mother orangutan and her saggy brown nipples."

"Did you read the article?" Kitty said quietly.

"I did."

"So you know that Colette is moving to Singapore with her husband. The royal couple!"

"Kitty, they aren't royal."

"Oh yeah? So tell me why they were getting the royal treatment at your great-aunt's funeral? Don't try to deny it, I saw the pictures of Colette with the Dowager Sultana of Perawak on the official royal Instagram! You lied to me! You *promised* me she wouldn't be there!"

"Kitty, I had no clue that her husband's family knew my great-uncle Alfred's family. This isn't some conspiracy."

"It's not? Then why does it feel like she's doing everything she can to outshine me? She gets invited to the funeral of the century, she steals my *Tattle* cover, and now she's throwing this big charity ball in Singapore to raise money for her damn monkeys!"

"Those orangutans need all the help they can get, Kitty."

"That's not the point. Colette is hosting this huge ball so that all of Singapore society can come out and curtsy at her feet, like she's the Queen of fucking Sheba! You know she's doing all this as revenge, don't you? She's just trying to insult me over and over again!"

Oliver sighed in exasperation. "Kitty, don't you think you're blowing this out of proportion? You haven't even met Colette. You have no idea what's going through her mind! I really don't think this girl has any interest in insulting you."

"Of course she's insulted me, and she's insulted my husband.

Did you notice that she didn't mention Jack once? Who do you think is funding all her monkey business?"

"Kitty, you're just building all this up in your head and sending yourself into a tailspin."

"No, I'm sending *you* into a tailspin. I want you to get me a title. I want a proper royal title that's higher-ranking than Colette's."

Oliver sighed. "Kitty, getting you any sort of title is going to take time. Living in Singapore, you could aim for an honorific from one of the Malay royal families. But you'd have to do an obscene amount of sucking up. Best-case scenario if you play your cards right, you may be able to receive a title within a few years."

"No, I'm not waiting that long. I don't care what you have to do, how much you have to spend. I want a title and I want it before Colette's stupid monkey ball."

"That's just not realistic, Kitty. I mean, I do know a few bisexual Italian princes that might be willing—in exchange for certain financial incentives—to marry you, but you'll have to divorce Jack."

Kitty scoffed. "What are you talking about? I'm not divorcing my husband!"

"Then I'm afraid there's really no way to get you a royal title within a month."

"Well then, you're out of a job! I'm not going to pay your retainer anymore. In fact, I'm stopping payment on everything right now. The Nigel Barker photo-shoot fees, all the money you've spent decorating my house, *everything.*"

"Kitty, stop being unreasonable. That's close to a hundred million dollars. You know I'll be on the hook for all those bills if you don't pay them," Oliver sputtered in alarm.

"Exactly. So get me that title! What's higher-ranking than a countess? A duchess? A princess? An empress? I don't care if you need to bribe Prince Bibimbap of Korea, I just want Colette to have to curtsy to me the next time I encounter her. I want to wipe the floor with her face!" Kitty screamed.

"Kitty, please calm down. Kitty?" Oliver realized she had hung up on him. A wave of fear suddenly passed through his body. Kitty was one client he could not risk losing. His monthly retainer from her was the one thing that kept the wolves at bay.

Unbeknownst to the Youngs, the Shangs, or the rest of the world, Oliver's family had fallen on hard times, ever since Barings went bust in 1995. Most of the T'sien portfolio had been invested with the storied investment firm in London that were bankers to Britain's most aristocratic families, including the queen. But after the firm went bankrupt—ironically due to a rogue trader based in Singapore—the T'siens along with every Barings investor had been wiped out.

What remained in the other T'sien accounts was a pittance, about ten million, and all that went into maintaining his grandmother Rosemary's lifestyle. It was her money rightfully, and she was entitled to live out her last years in comfort, but it meant that there would be barely anything left for her five children. The T'siens had been one of Singapore's largest landowners in the 1900s, but there was only one property left now— his grandmother's sprawling bungalow on Dalvey Road that was maybe worth thirty-five million, forty if the market ever recovered. Split five ways between her children, that meant his father would only inherit six or seven million at the most if the house was ever sold. Far, far less than what his parents were now in debt for.

For years, they had taken out loan after loan, and Oliver had spent his youth living the life of a rich man's son, sent abroad to the best schools money could buy—from Le Rosey to Oxford. But after the Barings crash, he found himself in the unthinkable position of having to work for a living. Oliver had always existed among the world's point-one percent crowd, and very few people understood the special hell of having to live in a world where every single person around you was staggeringly rich but you were not.

No one knew the degrees of subterfuge he took to keep up appearances for the sake of his family and career. There were the ballooning interest payments on all their bank loans. There were ten credit cards that he had to play Russian roulette with month after month. There were the mortgages on his parents' *hutong* in Beijing, his flat in London, and the condo in Singapore. Last year had been the worst, when his mother had been forced to sell off the legendary T'sien jade brooch along with other family heirlooms in order to pay for unexpected medical expenses. The bills kept coming, and they were endless. And now Kitty was threatening to renege on her gargantuan decorating bills— bills he had signed off on. If he couldn't work a miracle and get Kitty her title, he knew his whole life, his family, his career, his reputation—all would come crashing down.

CHAPTER ELEVEN

TYERSALL PARK, SINGAPORE

Walking in to lunch the next day, Nick and Rachel found that the dining room had been transformed into a makeshift situation room. Rolling bulletin boards had been placed around the room, and the dining table was lined with stacks of documents and various brochures, and seven or eight young staffers huddled over spreadsheets on their laptops.

Ah Ling entered with another package that had just arrived and noticed the baffled couple. "Oh, Nicky, lunch is being served on the terrace today."

"Um . . . who are these people?" Nick whispered.

"They're from Uncle Harry's office. They're helping out with all the house offers," Ah Ling responded, giving Nick a look that clearly registered her disapproval.

Nick and Rachel went out to the terrace to find a much smaller gathering of relatives. The Aakaras had flown back to Bangkok earlier in the morning, while most of the Chengs had left the day before. The only out-of-town guests that remained were Alix and Alistair, since they were both shareholders in the property.

While Nick and Rachel stood by the buffet table arrayed with different dishes, Victoria spoke up as she looked over a prospectus. "This offer from the Far East people is an insult! Two point five billion, paid out over five years. Do they think we fell off the turnip truck yesterday?"

"Let's not even bother responding," Alix declared. She looked up as Nick and Rachel sat down at the wrought-iron table with their lunch plates. "Nicky, do you have any idea what time your father will be here? We have so much to go over with him."

"Dad's back in Sydney."

"What? When did he leave?"

"Last night. Didn't he tell you he was heading home?"

"Yes, but we assumed he would have changed his plans now that the offers are flooding in. Ugggh! That irresponsible boy! We're in the midst of a bidding war, and he *knows* we can't make any moves without him," Felicity huffed.

"Dad's become quite set in his ways, and he really missed the coffee from this café he goes to every morning in Rose Bay," Nick tried explaining.

"There are billions of dollars at stake here and he's complaining about the coffee? As if Folgers Crystals here aren't good enough for him!" Victoria scoffed.

Rachel jumped into the conversation. "Some people really can't function without their coffee. In New York, I have to grab my usual cup at Joe Coffee on the way to work or I won't be able to get through the morning."

"I'll never understand you coffee people." Victoria tut-tutted as she carefully stirred her cup of tea made from GFBOP* Orthodox leaves she had flown in every month from a special reserve estate in Tanzania.

"Call your father. Tell him we're in the middle of a heated

---

* Any good tea sommelier will tell you that GFBOP stands for Golden Flowery Broken Orange Pekoe tea leaves, but of course.

bidding war and the house could be sold before the end of the week," Felicity ordered.

Nick looked at his aunts in surprise. "Are you all really intending on selling Tyersall Park that quickly?"

"We need to close the deal while the wok is sizzling! It's almost Chinese New Year, and everyone is feeling particularly prosperous and bold right now. Do you know that our top bid now exceeds three billion?" Alix excitedly reported.

Nick raised his eyebrows. "Who is it from, and how will they ensure that they will preserve the house?"

Felicity laughed. "Come on, Nicky, no one is going to preserve this house. The developers are only interested in the land—they are going to tear it all down."

Nick looked at Felicity in horror. "Wait a minute—how can they tear down the house? Isn't this a protected heritage property?"

Victoria shook her head. "If this was a Peranakan-style house, or a colonial Black and White, maybe it would have heritage protection, but this house is such a mishmash of styles. It was built by some Dutch architect that the sultan who originally owned the place brought in from Malaysia. It's an architectural folly."

"But of course, this is also what makes it so valuable. This is a freehold property with absolutely no heritage or zoning regulations. It's every developer's dream! Here, look at the leading proposal," Alix said, handing Nick a glossy brochure.

Zion Estates

A LUXURY CHRISTIAN COMMUNITY

Imagine an exclusive gated community for high-net-worth families who share in the blessings of the Holy Spirit.

Ninety-nine splendid villas, inspired by the Hanging Gardens of Babylon, ranging from 5,000 to 15,000 square feet on half-acre lots will surround Galilee, a glorious artificial lagoon complete with the world's tallest man-made waterfall supplied only with water imported from the River Jordan. At the heart of the community lies the Twelve Apostles, a unique twelve-hole golf course designed by our faithful brother Tiger Woods, and an exquisite clubhouse—the King David—which will boast a trinity of world-class restaurants operated by Michelin-starred chefs, along with Jericho, sure to become Singapore's most decadent spa and state-of-the-art health club.

Come to Zion—live abundantly and be saved.

Nick looked up from the brochure in disbelief. "Are you seriously telling me that these people are the front-runners? *A luxury Christian community?*"

"Isn't it inspired? It's Rosalind Fung's company—your mother goes to her Christian Fellowship Banquets at the Fullerton. They've offered us $3.3 billion, and they will throw in a villa for each of us!" Victoria said breathlessly.

Nick was barely able to hide his disgust. "Auntie Victoria, in case you've forgotten, Jesus served the poor."

"Of course he did. What's your point?"

Felicity chimed in. "Jesus said, 'To grow rich is glorious.'"

"Actually, Deng Xiaoping, the late Communist leader of China, said that!" Nick shot back. He got up from the table abruptly and said to Rachel, "Let's get out of here."

As they got into Nick's father's vintage Jaguar XKE convertible and sped down the driveway, Nick turned to Rachel. "Sorry, I lost my appetite sitting there with my aunts. I just couldn't stand listening to them one minute longer."

"Trust me, I get it. Where are we going?"

"I thought I'd take you to my favorite restaurant for a proper lunch—Sun Yik Noodles. It's a little café that's been around since the 1930s."

"Fantastic! I was just starting to get hungry."

Within fifteen minutes they had arrived in the Chinatown neighborhood, and after parking the car, they strolled down Club Street with its picturesque old shop houses toward Ann Siang Road as Nick began to fill Rachel in on the place.

"It's a total hole-in-the-wall, and they haven't even changed the Formica tables since the fifties, I bet. But they have the best noodles in Singapore, and so everyone comes here. The former chief justice of the Supreme Court used to eat lunch here every day, because the noodles were so addictive. You're gonna die when you taste these noodles. They are hand-pulled egg noodles, and they have this incredible, perfectly chewy texture to them. And they serve it with braised chicken that's been simmering for hours in this garlicky gravy. Oh man, the gravy! I wanna see if you think you can possibly replicate it. We're here after lunch rush, so we probably won't have to wait too long for a ta—"

Nick stopped dead in his tracks, staring at a façade across the road that had been covered by a metal construction fence.

"What's wrong?"

"This is it! Sun Yik Noodles! But where is it?"

They crossed the street and came to a small sign that was glued to the metal sheeting. It read:

TORY BURCH

Opening Summer 2015

Nick ran in to the shop next door, and Rachel could see him gesturing frantically to the baffled salesman inside. A few moments later, he came outside, his face registering nothing but shock.

"It's gone, Rachel. No more Sun Yik. This area has become so trendy, the original owner's son apparently sold the building for an insane amount of money and decided to retire. And now it's going to be a friggin' Tory Burch boutique."

"I'm so sorry, Nick."

"What the fuck!" Nick yelled, kicking the metal sheeting angrily. He sank down onto the pavement and covered his face with his hands despondently. Rachel had never seen him look quite so upset before. She sat down next to him on the pavement and put her arm around his shoulder. Nick sat there for a few minutes, staring off into space. After a while, he finally spoke.

"Everything I love about Singapore is gone. Or it's disappearing fast. Every time I'm back, more and more of my favorite haunts have closed or been torn down. Restaurants, shops, buildings, cemeteries, nothing is sacred anymore. The whole character of the island I knew growing up is almost completely obliterated."

Rachel simply nodded.

"Sun Yik was such an institution, I thought it would always be safe. I mean, I swear to God, *they had the best noodles in the whole world.* Everyone loved it. But now it's gone forever, and we can never ever get that back."

"I don't think people ever realize what they've lost until it's too late," Rachel said.

Nick looked into her eyes with a sudden intensity. "Rachel, I have to save Tyersall Park. I can't let it be torn down and turned into some grotesque gated community that only allows in millionaire Christians."

"I've been thinking the same thing."

"I thought for a while that I would be okay with everything. I thought I wouldn't care if I didn't inherit the estate as long as someone in the family got it and maintained it properly. But now I know I'm not."

"You know, I've been wondering all along if you were really okay with losing the house," Rachel observed.

Nick considered what she'd said for a moment. "I think part of me always resented Tyersall Park in a subconscious way, because everyone always associated me with the house, and I could never detach from it when I was younger. I think that's why Colin and I became such good friends . . . I was always 'the Tyersall Park Boy' and he was always 'that Khoo Enterprises Boy.' But we were just *boys*."

"It was like a curse in a way, wasn't it? It's amazing how you both managed not to let it define you," Rachel remarked.

"Well, at some point I made my peace with it, and getting away also helped me appreciate it in a new light. I realized how much the place nurtured me, how I found my adventurous side climbing trees and building forts, and how spending all those hours in the library reading all my grandfather's old books—Winston Churchill's memoirs, Sun Yat-sen's letters—got me fascinated with history. But now it feels like I'm seeing my entire childhood sold off to the highest bidder."

"I know, Nick. It's been so painful even for me to watch on the sidelines. I just can't believe how it's happening so quick, and how your aunts who also grew up in the house don't seem to care about letting it go."

"Even though my grandmother's will clearly states what it

does, I don't think she would have wanted Tyersall Park to be demolished and forgotten like this. To me, there are so many things that just don't add up with my grandmother's will and everything."

"That's been my suspicion all along too, but I didn't feel like it was my place to say anything," Rachel said with a frown.

"I wish I had more time to dig deeper, and figure out why my grandmother wanted the house sold off like this. But things are moving so fast with my aunties."

"Wait a minute—your aunties can move as fast as they want, but you heard them yourself, nothing is going to happen without your father. And as far as I know, he's somewhere in Sydney sipping a well-made cappuccino. And how about Alistair? He's got a stake in all this too."

"Hmm . . . come to think of it, Alistair hasn't been around the house much over the past few days, has he?" Nick said.

"If your father, Alistair, and you join forces, the three of you have enough votes to block any sale."

Nick kissed Rachel excitedly and leapt up from the pavement. "You're brilliant, you know that?"

"I'm not sure that required much brilliance."

"No, you're a genius, and you just gave me the best idea! Let's go call my dad!"

CHAPTER TWELVE

Astrid walked into the dining room at the Helena May, Hong Kong's historic private ladies' club, and Isabel Wu waved to her from her table by the window. She strolled toward Charlie's ex-wife a little trepidatiously. It was only the third time they were meeting, and the last time in Singapore hadn't gone so well.

"Astrid. Thank you so much for agreeing to meet with me for lunch. I know it's your last day in Hong Kong, and you must be so busy," Isabel said, getting up from her chair and giving Astrid a peck on the cheek.

"Thank you for inviting me. I love coming here."

"Yes, it's such a special place, isn't it? There are very few places like this anymore."

Astrid took a moment to look around at the other smartly dressed ladies having lunch together. The dining room with its Queen Anne furniture and botanical prints covering the walls was a throwback to another era, when Hong Kong was a British Crown Colony and this was the exclusive bastion for all the wives of high-ranking officials and expatriates. It was all so civilized.

Astrid was relieved by such a warm welcome from Charlie's ex-wife, and glad to see Isabel looking so well, and so chic in white jeans, a rose-colored cashmere sweater with a quilted vest thrown over it. She looked the epitome of Hong Kong old money.

"What have you been doing since you got here?"

Astrid hesitated for a moment. She didn't think it would be a good idea to tell Isabel that she'd spent most of the week planning her upcoming Hong Kong wedding, and yesterday, Charlie had taken her to see the breathtaking new house he had built for them in Shek O. "Not much really, I've just been decompressing. It's good to be away from Singapore, you know?"

"Yes, the past few weeks must have been very hard on you. I'm so sorry about your grandmother's passing. She was a great lady, from everything I know."

"Thank you."

"As I told you in my note, I was very close to my Ah Ma. In fact, she used to bring me here for afternoon tea once a month. So this place holds many memories for me."

"My grandmother used to take me to afternoon tea as well. One of my earliest memories, I think, is of having tea with her at the Raffles in Singapore. But soon after that, she stopped going out."

"So she became a recluse?" Isabel asked.

"Yes, and no. She didn't go out much, but that's because she felt that the standards had slipped everywhere. She had very exacting standards, and she didn't much care for restaurant food. So she only went to friends' houses—the ones that she knew had good chefs—or she entertained at home. She liked to have people over all the time, and she was very social up until the end of her life."

"Sounds like quite a character. All the women of her generation, like my grandmother, were characters. My grandmother was known as the hat lady. She had the most incredible collection of hats, and she never left the house without one."

The waitress came over and took their orders. After Astrid ordered the cream of asparagus soup, Isabel looked across the table at her with an almost embarrassed look. "You know, I have to confess I've been so nervous all morning about this lunch. I am still so mortified over what I did when I was in Singapore."

"It's fine, really. I'm just happy to see you so well again."

"Those women whom I scalded. Was one of them a nun or something? Is she okay? I have such a strange memory of that day. Because I remember everything, you know, but I just had no control over my actions."

"A nun?" Astrid didn't know what she was referring to.

"I remember the look on her face when I threw that soup. Her eyes got so huge, and she had Tammy Faye levels of mascara on. She was wearing a nun's habit."

"Oh! You're talking about the Dowager Sultana of Perawak— she was wearing a hijab. She was fine, the soup hardly touched her. Don't worry, it was probably the most thrilling thing that's happened to her in decades."

"Well, I appreciate your understanding, and I really must thank you for taking such good care of my daughters during that difficult time."

"Don't mention it. Chloe and Delphine are lovely girls."

Isabel paused for a moment and looked out the window at the view of the hillside park. It was apparent to Astrid that she was going through a spectrum of emotions. "Soon, you will be their stepmother. You'll be spending much more time with them, and I'm . . . I'm actually glad they will have you in their lives. Not just their crazy mother."

Astrid reached out and put her hand over Isabel's. "Don't

say that. You've done such a great job raising them. You're their mother, and I'm not going to try to be any sort of substitute mother. I only hope that in time they will come to see me as a friend."

Isabel smiled. "Astrid, I'm so glad we are having lunch together. I feel like I finally know who you are now."

After lunch, as the two of them stood at the entrance of the Helena May on Garden Road bidding farewell to each other, Isabel asked, "What are you going to do now? Some shopping in Central? Can my driver drop you off anywhere?"

"Well, I'm leaving for Singapore in a few hours, but I'm going to meet with Charlie first. I think he's at the house, waiting for me to make some decisions about the decor."

"The new house in Shek O? I'd love to see it sometime. After all, Chloe and Delphine are going to be spending half their lives there."

"Of course. Actually, if you're free, why don't you come with me right now?"

"Oh . . . well . . . I wouldn't want to intrude . . ." Isabel said hesitantly.

"No, no, I'm sure it will be fine. Let me just text Charlie."

Astrid quickly shot off a text:

ASTRID LEONG: Hey! Just finishing up with Isabel. It went GREAT.

CHARLIE WU: I'm so glad.

AL: Isabel would like to see the house. Ok if I bring her?

CW: Sure, if you don't mind.

AL: Of course not. See you soon.

"Let's go!" Astrid said, looking up from her phone. The two of them jumped into the back of Isabel's chauffeured Range Rover and sped off. As they made their way around the south side of Hong Kong Island, the landscape began to change dramatically as the dense skyscrapers that cascaded down the mountainside gave way to picturesque bays and ocean vistas.

The winding highway took them through Repulse Bay and its crescent-shaped beaches, hugging the coastline as they passed Deep Water Bay and the village of Stanley. Finally, they arrived in Shek O, a historic fishing village on the southeast corner of Hong Kong Island, which was also home to one of the world's most exclusive neighborhoods.

"Charlie's always longed to live here, but I would never let him. I prefer being closer to town. I could never live way out here in the middle of nowhere—I'm too much of a city girl," Isabel remarked as they pulled up in front of an imposing metal gate with an attached gatehouse.

"There's no one there," the chauffeur said.

"Oh, we don't have it staffed yet. Just enter 110011 into the keypad," Astrid said, glancing at the instructions Charlie had texted her. The gate slid open silently, and they proceeded down the long driveway to the house. Rounding the corner, the ocean-front villa cantilevered on a rocky cliff came into view.

"This place is so Charlie." Isabel laughed as they drove up to the imposing series of contemporary structures designed by Tom Kundig clad in steel, limestone, and glass.

"Your house on The Peak is more traditional, isn't it?" Astrid inquired.

"I'm not sure where you heard that, but it's classical Palladian, built in the twenties. I have it done in a French provincial style. I wanted it to feel like a manor in Provence. You must come over the next time you're back."

"I've heard that it's one of the most elegant houses in Hong Kong," Astrid said.

They stepped out of the car and entered a large courtyard dominated by a reflecting pool. Here the walls of the main villa were made entirely of glass, allowing for a seamless transition between the inside and outdoors. Entering the house, Astrid was once again taken aback by the spectacular ocean views from every vantage point in the house.

In the great hall, an immense window perfectly framed a tiny island just beyond the coastline, and stepping into the living room, a wall of windows opened onto the terrace, where an infinity pool ran along the entire side of the house, its horizon line melding into the South China Sea.

As Charlie came around the corner to greet them, Isabel graciously offered, "Charlie, you've outdone yourself. You finally have your dream house by the sea."

"I'm glad you approve, Izzie. We're still quite a way from being done and we've just received the first big pieces of furniture, but here, let me show you Chloe and Delphine's private wing."

After giving Isabel a tour of her daughters' rooms, the three of them entered the dining room, where an immense vintage George Nakashima dining table had just been delivered. Standing around the free-form structure that resembled an immense piece of driftwood, Charlie looked at Astrid. "What do you think? Is it too Pacific Northwest?"

Astrid considered the piece for several moments. "I love it— it goes great under the Lindsey Adelman chandelier."

"Phew, I'm so relieved!" Charlie said with a chuckle.

Isabel stared up at the bronze light fixture that resembled blown-glass bubbles budding from the stems of an intricate tree branch, saying nothing. In her former life as Mrs. Charles Wu, she would have vetoed all of this, but now as the three of them headed for the front door, she simply said, "I do think Chloe and Delphine will love it here."

"Well, you will always be welcome," Astrid said, her heart soaring that Isabel was being so agreeable about everything. It had been such an unexpectedly lovely day. As they stepped outside into the courtyard, Astrid's phone pinged, and she saw four text messages suddenly pop up:

LUDIVINE DOLAN: I went to pick up Cassian after school but found out that his father already got him.

· · · ·

FELICITY LEONG: WHERE ARE YOU? WHAT TIME YOU GETTING BACK TONIGHT? COME STRAIGHT TO TYERSALL PK! SO MUCH HAPPENING WITH THE HOUSE! WE NEED YOU!

· · · ·

OLIVER T'SIEN: Aren't you friends with Prince Alois of Liechtenstein? And that Poet Prince Fazza of Dubai? Can you connect us? Call me, will explain.

· · · ·

LUDIVINE DOLAN: Just spoke to Mr. Teo and asked if he needed me to help with Cassian but he wants me to take the rest of the day off. No idea what's happening.

Astrid put her phone back into her purse, suddenly feeling a bit sick to her stomach. Why the hell did she have to go back to Singapore?

CHAPTER THIRTEEN

BONDI BEACH, SYDNEY

"Are you fishing on your dock?" Nick asked when his father picked up the phone. He could hear the crashing waves along the seashore.

"No, I'm doing the cliff walk from Bondi to Coogee right now."

"I love that hike."

"Yeah, it's a good day for it. You know your mother invited Daisy, Nadine, Lorena, and Carol to Sydney? The whole gin gang's here, and it's such a toilet-seat-down invasion, I needed to get out of the house. The ladies are busy hatching some kind of plot . . . I think involving Tyersall Park."

"That's the reason I was calling, Dad. It looks like things are moving far too quickly with the house. Your sisters seem really primed to sell it to the highest bidder, and I don't even want to tell you what those developers have planned."

"Does it even matter? Once we sell it, the new owners can do whatever they want."

"But I feel like everyone's losing sight of the big picture," Nick argued. "Tyersall Park is a unique property, and we need to make sure that it's preserved. I mean, I'm at the house right now, and even just looking out the window onto the gardens—

the rambutan trees are bearing fruit, and they are flaming red. There's nothing quite like it."

"I think you're being too sentimental," Philip said.

"Maybe I am, but I'm just surprised that no one else cares about this house in the way that I do. Everyone's just seeing dollar signs while I see something so rare that needs to be protected."

Philip sighed. "Nicky, I know for you this house was like some never-never land, but for the rest of us, it was a bit of a prison. Living in a palace was no fun as a kid. I grew up with nothing but rules. There were so many rooms I wasn't even allowed to enter, chairs I couldn't sit in because they were too valuable. You have no idea, because by the time you came along, my mother was a very different person."

"Yes, I've heard the stories. But surely you must have some good memories?"

"To me, it's just one gigantic headache. Don't forget, I was shipped off to boarding school practically as soon as I could walk, so it never truly felt like home to me. Now, even the thought of having to come back to Singapore to deal with all these property folks fills me with dread. Do you know how many ACS old boys have called me up out of the blue to invite me to lunch, to golf, all that nonsense? People I haven't seen in eons are suddenly behaving like my best friend because they can smell the money."

"I'm sorry that's happening, Dad. But let me ask you something." Nick took a deep breath as he prepared to make his pitch. "If I can somehow raise the money, would you consider leveraging your thirty percent stake and joining me and possibly Alistair to buy everyone else out? If you give me a little time, I know I can find a way to make it financially worthwhile for us to own the estate."

The line went silent for a moment, and Nick wasn't sure if his father was upset or if he was just on a particularly arduous stretch of the hike. Suddenly he spoke up again. "If you care that much about Tyersall Park, why don't you handle this whole house sale? Do what you think is best. I'll give you permission to act as my proxy, power of attorney, whatever they call it. In fact, I'll sign over my thirty percent stake to you right now."

"Really?" Nick said, not quite believing what he was hearing.

"Sure. I mean, it's all going to be yours one day anyway."

"I don't even know what to say."

"Do whatever you want with the house, just keep me out of it," Philip said, climbing along the edge of a beautiful cliff-side cemetery overlooking the South Pacific. "Nicky, I'm up at that cemetery by Bronte now. Will you make sure—"

"Yes, Dad, you've told me many times before. You want to be buried there. You want to have a view of the humpback whales doing backflips for all of eternity."

"And if they run out of lots, you'll find another ocean-side spot? New Zealand, Tasmania, anyplace but Singapore."

"Of course." Nick laughed. He hung up the phone and found Rachel staring at him curiously. "That sounded weird, from what I heard."

"Yeah, it was one of the weirdest calls I've ever made. I think my father just gave me his share of Tyersall Park."

"WHAAT?" Rachel's eyes got huge.

"He told me he'd sign over his stake, and I can do whatever I want as long as I leave him out of it."

"What's the catch?"

"There's no catch. My dad has never been interested in financial matters at all. He really would rather not be bothered with it."

"I guess when you've been born with it . . ." Rachel shrugged.

"Precisely! I still can't believe how easy it was to convince him, though. I thought I was going to have to fly down to Sydney and grovel on my knees."

"With your father's share in your hands, you're the biggest stakeholder now!" Rachel said excitedly.

"No, *we are*. And this gives us the leverage to stall the bidding war and buy some time."

"Do you want to go downstairs and break the news to your aunties?"

Nick grinned. "No time like the present."

They left their bedroom and walked over to the drawing room where Felicity, Victoria, and Alix were all sitting, unusually silent.

"I have an announcement to make," Nick said boldly.

Felicity had a peculiar look on her face. "Nicky, we just got off the phone. It seems we have a new offer on the table."

"I have an offer to propose as well."

"Well, this is a very unusual offer . . . it comes from someone who wants to preserve the house entirely and not build a single new structure on the estate," Alix said.

Nick and Rachel exchanged looks of surprise. "Really? And they are offering more than those Zion people?" Rachel asked dubiously.

"A great deal more. The offer is for ten billion dollars."

Nick was incredulous. "Ten BILLION? Who on earth would want to pay so much money and *not* develop the property?"

"It's some fellow from China. He wants to come and see the house tomorrow."

"China? What's his name?" Rachel asked.

Felicity frowned. "If I recall correctly, I think Oliver said his name was Jack something. Jack Ting? Jack Ping?"

Nick put his hand on his forehead in dismay. "Oh God—Jack Bing."

TWENTY-FOUR HOURS EARLIER . . .

KUALA LUMPUR, MALAYSIA

"So, she is the queen?"

"No, Kitty, she is the mother of the current Sultan of Perawak, so she's the Queen Mother but she's called the Dowager Sultana," Oliver explained through his headset microphone as they rode together in the helicopter.

"Ah. So I have to curtsy to her?"

"You certainly do. She's as royal as it gets. And remember, only speak when you are spoken to."

"What do you mean?"

"I mean, you're not allowed to speak to her. The sultana initiates the conversation and gets to do all the talking—you simply keep your pretty mouth shut until she asks you a question. And if you have to leave the room for any reason—which you really shouldn't before she does—but if you feel the sudden urge to vomit, make sure to walk out of the room *facing* her. The sultana must never see your ass, so you are never to turn your back on her, understood?"

Kitty nodded diligently. "I understand—no talking, no vomiting, no ass-backing."

"Now, as I said, I don't want you to expect too much today. This is just an introduction, and a chance for Her Majesty to become acquainted with you."

"So you're saying she isn't going to give me a knighthood today?"

"Kitty, women don't get knighted in Malaysia. There is a whole different system of honors here. The sultana can bestow a title whenever she pleases, but don't get your hopes up that it's going to happen today."

"You sound angry at me," Kitty said with a little pout.

"I am not angry, Kitty. I'm just speaking over the chopper noise." Truth be told, Oliver had been on the verge of a nervous breakdown ever since Kitty had delivered her ultimatum, and he was anxious for everything to go as planned today. He had way too much to lose if it didn't. Trying to placate her a bit, he continued, "I'm just trying to make you understand that these titles given by royals like the sultana are *real* honors. They honor truly deserving people who have done a tremendous amount of good for Malaysia over a lifetime. People who build hospitals and schools, who start companies that support entire towns and provide work to thousands of locals. These honors mean a great deal more than Colette's title. All she ever did was spread her legs for some posh dimwit."

The helicopter swooped over the Kuala Lumpur skyline, passing the iconic Petronas Towers as it started to descend. "So this is where the sultana lives?" Kitty asked as she peered out at the exclusive leafy neighborhood of Bukit Tunku.

"This is just her little crash pad in KL for when she comes to the capital. She has residences all over the world—a house on Kensington Palace Gardens, a villa overlooking Lake Geneva, and of course, the gigantic palace in Perawak," Oliver informed her as the chopper touched down on the great lawn.

The two of them jumped out of the chopper, and a uniformed

officer awaited them on the lawn. "Welcome to the Istana al Noor," he said as he led them toward a humongous white palace that resembled a wedding cake. Entering through the front doors, Oliver and Kitty found themselves in a vast reception hall with nine gigantic pyramidal chandeliers that descended from the coffered gold-leafed ceiling like upside-down versions of the Rockefeller Center Christmas tree.

"This is her *little* crash pad?" Kitty remarked.

"Oh, you have no idea, Kitty. Her home in Perawak is twice the size of Buckingham Palace."

They were shown into the drawing room, which had dramatic black marble floors and walls painted in a shimmering crimson hue. The space was filled with priceless Peranakan gilded wood antiques mixed with fantastical Claude Lalanne bronze furniture. Facing them was a vibrant pink-and-yellow triptych of Andy Warhol paintings depicting the Dowager Sultana in her younger days. "Wow, this was not what I was expecting," Kitty said, clearly in awe of her surroundings.

"Yes, the Dowager Sultana was definitely a hell-raiser back in the seventies," Oliver noted as they both sat down on a backless velvet settee. Next to the settee was a round Lalanne table laden with gold-framed photographs of the sultana posing with famous personages. Kitty peered at the pictures, recognizing the Queen of England, Pope John Paul II, Barack and Michelle Obama, Indira Gandhi, and a woman with an enormous pile of blond hair.

"Who is that blond woman? She looks so familiar. Is she some queen?" Kitty asked.

Oliver squinted at the picture and then let out a quick laugh. "No, but she is adored by many queens. That's Dolly Parton."

"Ah," Kitty said. Suddenly the double doors opened, and two honor guards in full-dress uniform entered. Flanking the doorway, they clicked their heels at attention and tapped the base of their long bayonets on the marble floor twice in unison. "We need to stand, Kitty," Oliver suggested. Kitty quickly stood up, smoothing out the wrinkles on the front of her ankle-length Roksanda skirt and then adjusting her posture.

The guard on the right side shouted sternly, "*Sama-sama, maju kehadapan! Pandai cari pelajaran!*" They tapped their bayonets on the floor again, as the sultana swept into the room in a flaming violet silk kebaya, followed by four attendants. Her head was covered in a matching violet, blue, and white headscarf, and she resembled Queen Mary, covered in precious jewels from the waist up. Pinned in the middle of her hijab right above her forehead was an enormous sunburst diamond brooch with a forty-five-carat pink diamond in the center. On her ears were a pair of diamond-and-pearl girandole earrings, and around her neck were what appeared to be ten or twelve heaping necklaces of nothing but diamonds, diamonds, and more diamonds.

Kitty's jaw hung open at the sight of this Queen Mother ablaze in diamonds and she dropped to a curtsy so deep, Oliver thought she was doing the limbo. Oliver bowed smartly.

"Oliver T'sien, what a pleasure!"

"The pleasure is all mine, ma'am. May I humbly present Mrs. Kitty Bing of Shanghai, Los Angeles, and Singapore."

"It's an honor to be in your beautiful country, Your Majesty," Kitty blurted out nervously, before remembering that she wasn't supposed to speak first.

The Dowager Sultana pursed her lips and stared at Kitty for a brief moment, saying nothing. She sat down on a throne-like

Bergère chair, and Oliver and Kitty took their seats again. An army of maids entered the room bearing gold-lacquered platters filled with Malay desserts and steaming pots of tea.

As the maids began serving tea to everyone, the Dowager Sultana smiled at Oliver. "Come, don't be shy! I know how much you love *ondeh ondeh*."

"You know me too well," Oliver said, helping himself to one of the bright green rice-cake balls stuffed with palm sugar and rolled in grated coconut.

"Now, what brings you to this neck of the woods today?"

"Well, Kitty has recently become enchanted with Malaysia, so since we were in town, I thought it only fitting that she meet this country's greatest living legend."

The Dowager Sultana beamed. "Oh Oliver, you make me sound like a fossil! Tell me, child, what do you like about my country?"

Kitty stared at the sultana blankly. Until today, she had never set foot on Malay soil and didn't know a thing about the country. "Er . . . well . . . I love the people most of all, Your Majesty. So warm and . . . hardworking," Kitty said, thinking of the half a dozen or so Malay maids that worked at Cluny Park Road.

The Dowager Sultana pursed her lips again. "Really? I was not expecting to hear that at all. Most people tell me how much they love our beaches and our satay. So do you intend to put down some roots here?"

"Well, if I can find a palace as beautiful as yours, I'd be very tempted."

"Why thank you, but this is no palace. This is just a house."

"Kitty's husband, Jack Bing, is one of China's premier industrialists. So they are highly interested in investing in Malaysia."

"Well we do have such a wonderful relationship with China. And I do adore that First Lady of yours," the Dowager Sultana said, picking up a piece of *ondeh ondeh* with her fingers and chewing on it slowly.

"Oh, you've met her?" Kitty said excitedly, forgetting royal protocol again.

"Why yes. I gave her an audience at my palace in Perawak. What an accomplished woman, and what a voice! Now, tell me, Oliver, how has your dear grandmama been since I last saw her?"

"Her health is excellent, ma'am. But I must confess her spirits have been rather low lately. As you know, my great-aunt Su Yi's passing has affected her greatly."

Kitty, feeling bored, began to zone out on the photo of the sultana with Michelle Obama. She was trying to identify the designer of Michelle's red dress. Was it Isabel Toledo or Jason Wu? She felt sorry for the First Lady—that poor woman was obligated to only wear American designers.

The sultana continued to speak. "Ah yes, it was such a beautiful funeral. Did you not enjoy my son's eulogy to Su Yi?"

"It was remarkable. I did not know that the sultan spent a year living at Tyersall Park."

"Yes, when he was doing a special course at the National University of Singapore, Su Yi was kind enough to host him. I'm afraid he found the Malay embassy accommodations to be lacking, and he was much more at home at Tyersall. You do know his great-grandfather was the sultan who originally built it?"

"Forgive me, ma'am, I had forgotten. No wonder he would feel a kinship to the place. If I might venture to ask, was Su Yi ever conferred with a title?"

Kitty's ears suddenly pricked up.

"To my knowledge, she wasn't. I believe in the 1970s the

Agong[*]—whoever it was back then, I've lost track—tried to honor her, but she graciously turned it down. She was already Lady Young, and never even used that title. *Alamak*, what would Su Yi need a title for? There was never any doubt of her position. I mean, she already had Tyersall Park. What more do you need?"

"That's quite true." Oliver nodded, stirring his tea.

"Tell me, Oliver, what is going to happen to that spectacular palace now?" the sultana asked, her brow furrowing.

"Oh it's anyone's guess. My cousins are entertaining an avalanche of offers. Every day I hear there's someone new coming in with an even higher bid. We're in the billions now."

"I'm not surprised at all. If I was younger, I might have considered it as a home in Singapore myself. Of course, it will never be the same without Su Yi, but whoever ends up living there will be tremendously fortunate."

Oliver sighed dramatically. "Sadly, though, I don't think that will happen. The house will surely be torn down."

"Oh my goodness, how can that be?" The sultana placed her hand to her chest in shock, showing off her fifty-eight-carat blue diamond ring. Kitty's eyes followed the solitaire like a cat distracted by a shiny toy.

"The land is far too valuable. All the developers that have put in bids have ambitious plans for Tyersall Park, and I don't believe that would include the old house."

"But what a travesty that would be! Tyersall Park is one of the most elegant estates in Southeast Asia. That rose garden, and

---

[*] The Yang di-Pertuan Agong, or Agong for short, is the monarch of Malaysia. The nine Malay states each have their own hereditary rulers and royal families, and the Agong is elected from among these rulers every five years.

the grand salon—such sophistication! Someone needs to rescue it from the greedy developers!"

"I couldn't agree more," Oliver said.

Kitty listened to them with fascination. This was the first time she had heard anything about this old house.

"Well, Oliver, surely you know someone who will want to buy the estate and maintain it to the same standards as Su Yi did? What about that new Chinese duchess whatshername who's moving to Singapore to save the chimpanzees? I met her at the funeral."

Kitty looked up from her tea in alarm.

"Um, you're referring to the Countess of Palliser?" Oliver said, glancing at Kitty uncomfortably.

"Yes, that one. Do you know her? She should buy the house. Then she would become the undisputed queen of Singapore!" the Dowager Sultana declared, popping another sweet coconut ball in her mouth.

After their audience with the sultana, Kitty remained silent during the helicopter ride back to Singapore. As she alighted from the chopper, she turned to Oliver and said, "This house the sultana was referring to, how much are we talking about?"

"Kitty, I know you heard what you heard, but the Dowager Sultana lives in a bit of a fantasy land. Colette would never buy Tyersall Park."

"And why not?"

"I know my cousins—they would never sell the house to her."

"Oh really? You said Colette would never be at your auntie's funeral, and yet there she was. You said Colette wasn't a threat, but then she bumped me off the cover of *Tattle*. I don't think I can believe anything you say anymore."

"All right, I'll admit, I'm not the Oracle of Delphi. But there are some things that even Colette could not make happen. For one thing, there is no way she can afford that house."

"Really? How much is it?"

"Well, I'm told the highest bid right now is four billion. And I know Colette doesn't have that kind of money on her own."

Kitty frowned. "She doesn't, but she has a trust fund worth five billion. She can borrow against that trust if she really wants this house. And something tells me she does. She wants so desperately to be the queen of Singapore, queen of the fucking universe!"

"Look, Kitty, if it will stop you from losing your mind from this ridiculous rivalry, go ahead, try to buy the house. I'll even go to my cousins with your offer for you. But just so you know, in order for the Youngs to regard your offer as serious, you've got to come in with a bid that wipes everything else off the table clean."

"So we offer them five billion."

"That's not going to work. You have to realize something, Kitty: You are a *Mainlander* who's married to a mogul with a very big but very new fortune. You haven't yet gained the degree of respectability that these people value. If you want to steal Singapore's most prized estate away from its snottiest family, you've got to do it in a big way. You need to shock and awe them with your money."

"How much will that take?"

"Ten billion."

Kitty inhaled deeply. "Okay then, offer them ten billion."

Oliver was taken aback by how quickly she responded. "Are you serious? Don't you need to talk to Jack first?"

"I'll worry about my husband. You worry about getting me

that house and you better get it before that little snake Colette comes around with her tongue out. If she steals this house from under my nose, I will never ever forgive you. And you know what that means," Kitty warned, as she got in to her waiting car.

After waving her off, Oliver took out his cell phone and punched a number on his speed dial.

"Hallooooo?" a voice answered.

"It worked. It bloody worked." Oliver sighed in relief.

"That Kitty girl is going to buy the house?"

"You better believe it. Auntie Zarah, I could kiss your feet."

"I can't believe it was that easy," the Dowager Sultana of Perawak said.

"The minute you started talking about Tyersall Park, she forgot all about the stupid title. You were absolutely brilliant!"

"Was I?"

"I had no idea you could act like that!"

The Dowager Sultana giggled like a schoolgirl. "Oh my goodness, I haven't had this much fun in a long time! That ridiculously formal way you were speaking to me—'*If I might venture to ask*'—hahahaha, you sounded like you were in a Jane Austen novel! I was biting my lip to stop from laughing. And oh, I have a horrible neck ache now from wearing all those damn necklaces! I thought I was going to be strangled by diamonds, heeheeheeheehee!"

"If you hadn't been dressed like that, Kitty would not have been in such awe of you. She's been spoiled with jewels herself, so we really had to lay on the shock and awe."

"Shock and awe indeed! Did you like what I had my guards chant before I made my grand entrance into the room?"

"Oh my God, I almost peed in my pants! I was thinking, why are they chanting the Singapore Children's Day song?"

"Heeheehee! Remember when your mummy made you sing it to me one day when you came home from school? You were so proud to sing a song in Malay. Now, did you like my mention of China's First Lady?"

"I did, I did. Very appropriate, Auntie Zarah."

"I've never even met her, heeheeheehee!"

"You deserve an Oscar, Auntie Zarah. I owe you big-time."

"Just send me a jar of those pineapple tarts that your cook makes, and we'll call it even."

"Auntie Zarah, you're going to get a whole crate of those pineapple tarts."

"*Alamak*, no! Please don't! I'm on a diet! I was so nervous during my performance, I ate too many of those coconut puffs today, heeheeheehee. I have to force myself to go to my granddaughter's zoomba class in the ballroom now!"

CHAPTER FOURTEEN

It had been a long, hot, mosquito-ridden hike, and as Carlton pounded his way up another sloping hill, he wondered what the hell he had been thinking when he suggested this plan to Scheherazade. His shirt was drenched in sweat, and he was certain that no amount of Serge Lutens cologne could mask how he smelled at this point. He turned around to check on Scheherazade and saw that she was crouched on the ground, staring at something. At a discreet distance, three of her bodyguards in jogging clothes stood watching them.

"Look! It's a monitor lizard!" She pointed.

"He's a pretty big fella," Carlton said as he caught sight of the three-foot-long reptile resting under a clump of bushes.

"It's a she, I believe," Scheherazade corrected. "We had quite a big menagerie of pets when I was growing up. Reptiles were my thing."

"This was in Surrey?"

"Actually, this was when we were in Bali. My family lived there for about three years when I was a little girl. I was a bit of a wild child then, going barefoot everywhere around the island."

"That explains why you're not even breaking a sweat right

now," Carlton said, trying his best not to stare too hard at her goddess-like physique shown off to perfection in her mesh paneled leggings and stretch knit sports bra.

"You know it's funny—I never sweat. Ever. I'm told that Queen Elizabeth doesn't either."

"Well, you're in good company," Carlton remarked, as they finally arrived at the TreeTop Walk, a 250-meter suspension bridge that stretches from Bukit Peirce to Bukit Kalang, the two highest points of the preserve. As they traversed the narrow bridge, it began to sway slightly, but then the view opened up and suddenly it felt as though they were floating above the trees.

They reached the middle of the bridge and stood in silence for a while, taking in the remarkable view. The tropical-forest canopy stretched all around them as far as the eye could see, and the sounds of cackling birds echoed through the breeze.

"Unbelievable! Thanks for bringing me here," Scheherazade said.

"It doesn't feel like we're in Singapore anymore, does it?"

"Sure doesn't. This is the first place I've been to in a long while that's reminded me of my childhood. I mean, it's quite a relief to see that all this nature still exists here." Scheherazade stared at the calm reservoir in the distance, the water glinting in the late-afternoon sun.

"Has the island changed that much? I only started coming here about five years ago."

"Carlton, you can't even imagine. Every time I'm back I hardly recognize it anymore. So much of the old atmosphere has just been wiped clean."

"I guess that's why you like living in Paris?"

"Partly. Paris is great because every street you walk down is like an unfolding novel. I actually love it because even though there's history everywhere, it's not *my* history. Does that make any sense?"

"Sure. Shanghai is my hometown, but it doesn't feel like home anymore. Whenever I'm back it feels I can never escape my past. Everyone remembers everything about you—your family history, your mistakes," Carlton said, his face clouding for a moment before he turned back to her. "But that's not what you meant, was it?"

"Not really. For me, Paris is like neutral territory because it's neither Singapore nor England. You know, even though I was born in Singapore and lived here until I was ten, I never felt like I truly belonged. Maybe it was because of how I looked—my hair was almost blond back then—it seemed like most people just assumed I was *ang mor*. And my mum inadvertently reinforced this by pretty much raising me as though I was British. Aside from my Chinese cousins, everyone else we knew was part of the British set. I don't blame her at all—she felt awfully homesick and was overwhelmed at first by my father's family. So we sort of existed in this English expat bubble, and for the first ten years of my life I went along thinking of myself as completely English."

Carlton gave her a knowing smile. "Bit of a shock when you actually got to England, wasn't it?"

"Uh-huh. When we finally moved to Surrey, I realized that the English didn't really see me as I saw myself. I was this exotic, half-Chinese girl to them. So I felt like I was just absolutely screwed on both ends—I wasn't Singaporean enough, but neither was I English enough."

Carlton nodded in agreement. "I was sent away to school in England for most of my life, and now I can't really relate to the Chinese back home. In Shanghai, I'm seen as too Westernized. Here in Singapore, I'm seen as an uncivilized Mainlander. But in London, even though I'm clearly an outsider, I feel like I can just be myself and no one's judging my every move. I guess that's what Paris does for you. You feel liberated."

"Exactly!" Scheherazade said, flashing Carlton a smile so alluring, he had to stop himself from staring.

A group of men entered the bridge from the other end, and as they came closer Scheherazade couldn't help but notice that they all looked Italian and were impeccably dressed in white jackets and bow ties.

"Looks like we're being joined by extras from a Fellini movie," Scheherazade joked.

"Yes, *La Dolce Vita*. And right on time," Carlton said. The men began setting up an elaborate bar right in front of them, taking out a mixture of spirits, cocktail implements, and glassware.

"Did you arrange this?" Scheherazade asked wide-eyed.

"Well, I couldn't take you on a sweltering sunset hike and not provide you with sunset drinks."

Three of the men whipped out a bass, a saxophone, and a small drum set and began to play a Miles Davis tune.

"Can I offer you a Negroni, signora?" the bartender said, handing Scheherazade a highball glass filled with Campari, gin, and red vermouth over ice with an orange peel elaborately curled over the rim.

"*Grazie mille,*" Scheherazade replied.

"*Salute!*" Carlton said, clinking her glass with his Negroni.

"How in the world did you know this was my favorite drink?" Scheherazade asked as she sipped her aperitif.

"Um . . . I might have done some Instagram stalking."

"But my Instagram account is locked."

"Um . . . I might have been on Nick's Instagram," Carlton confessed.

Scheherazade laughed, utterly charmed.

Carlton looked into her eyes, and then glanced over her shoulder at her security guards loitering at the end of the bridge. "Would it be crazy if I kissed you? I mean, would your guards have me on the ground in under two seconds?"

"It would be crazy if you didn't," Scheherazade said, leaning in to kiss him.

After a long, lingering kiss, the two of them stood wrapped in each other's arms in the middle of the bridge, watching as the setting sun glimmered over the treetops, casting a glow of flaming amber over the horizon.

It was almost seven thirty by the time Carlton pulled up to the driveway of Scheherazade's home. He didn't want to drop her off just yet, and wished he could whisk her off to dinner and spend the whole evening with her. But his sense of decorum took over, and he wanted her to set the pace of how things should go.

Scheherazade smiled at him, and it was obvious that she didn't want their date to end just yet either. "Why don't you come up? My parents usually have drinks around this time."

"Are you sure? I wouldn't want to intrude."

"Not at all. I think they'd like to meet you properly. They've been rather curious about you."

"Well, if you don't think I'm unpresentable right now in my soiled hiking gear."

"Oh, you're fine. It's all very casual."

Carlton handed off the keys to his vintage 1975 Toyota Land Cruiser to the valet in the driveway and they strolled through the elegant lobby of the sleek glass tower. For a family that arguably controlled the majority of the country's GDP, the Shangs lived modestly when they were in Singapore. Alfred had long ago divested all of his landed properties on the island, but he had built this exceedingly discreet private apartment tower on Grange Road, where each of his children had been given several floors.

"Good evening, Miss Shang," the guards at the reception desk said in unison. One of them escorted them to the elevators, reaching inside to enter a security code into a keypad. They zoomed up to the penthouse, and when the doors opened, Carlton could hear the murmur of voices just off the entrance foyer.

The two of them strolled into a circular, atrium-like sunken living room, and then Carlton stopped dead in his tracks. Standing in the middle of the room in a shimmering peacock blue cocktail dress was his ex-girlfriend Colette. He had not spoken to or seen her in almost two years, not since he discovered that she was responsible for poisoning Rachel.

"Oh hello. Looks like we have more guests than I thought," Scheherazade said.

Her father turned to them and said, "Ah, at last, the prodigal daughter returns! Scheherazade, come meet Lucien and Colette, the Earl and Countess of Palliser."

Scheherazade strolled over to greet them and then she proceeded to introduce Carlton to everyone. Still in shock, Carlton shook hands numbly with Leonard and India Shang, who were dressed to the nines and gave Carlton's hiking attire a rather disapproving once-over. Then the unavoidable moment came when he was face-to-face with Lucien and Colette. She looked different. Her hair was pulled into an elegant ballerina's knot at the nape of her neck and she wore far less makeup than he remembered, but he was surprised at how all his anger toward her suddenly came flooding back. The last time they had seen each other, he had accused her of trying to poison his sister.

"Hello, Carlton," Colette said, perfectly composed.

"Colette," Carlton murmured back, trying valiantly to stay calm.

"Oh, you two know each other?" India Shang said in surprise. "But of course, you lived in Shanghai for a period."

"For a period," Colette said.

"Well then, you must stay for dinner," India insisted.

"Yes, do stay," Colette said sweetly.

Carlton forced a smile at his hostess. "It would be a pleasure to join you for dinner, Mrs. Shang."

Soon they were all seated around the table in a dining room enjoying a twelve-course tasting menu prepared by Marcus Sim, the Shangs' personal chef. Carlton looked around at the exquisite minimalist paintings surrounding them and commented, "Are these works by Agnes Martin?"

"Indeed they are," Leonard Shang replied, impressed that Carlton recognized the artist.

"Do you collect?" India asked.

"Not really, no," Carlton replied.

"Carlton collects cars," Colette said, with a gleam in her eye.

"Oh really? What sort? I'm restoring an MG Midget at the moment," Lucien said.

"I do love MGs, but I actually have a car import business in China. We specialize in exotics like McLarens, Bugattis, and Koenigseggs."

"My goodness, those are awfully fast cars, aren't they?" India commented.

"They are incredibly engineered automobiles—works of art, really—and yes, they are built for speed," Carlton answered calmly.

"Carlton likes to go *very* fast. He used to race." Colette took a bite of her grilled octopus and gave him an innocent look across the table.

Scheherazade glanced at Carlton, noticing the tension on his face.

"Oh dear. Have you ever been in an accident?" India asked, making up her mind right then that Scheherazade should never ride in this young man's car again.

"Actually, I have," Carlton replied.

"What happened? Hope you didn't wreck one of those million-dollar sports cars." Lucien laughed.

"It was a very unfortunate accident. But it taught me to be extremely careful. I don't race anymore," Carlton said.

"I'm glad you're okay," Scheherazade said with a little smile.

"Well," Colette interjected with a glint in her eye, "when you kill one girl and paralyze another from the waist down, it's probably best not to, isn't it?"

While Leonard Shang choked on his chardonnay and his wife froze as if she had just been turned into a pillar of salt, Colette flashed a smile at Carlton. It was a smile he knew only too well, and at that moment he realized that Colette Bing might call herself the Countess of Palliser these days, but she hadn't changed one fucking bit.

CHAPTER FIFTEEN

Chloe made the call from her bathroom, with the shower turned on full blast. "Dad, you said to call . . . you know . . . if Mum was ever acting weird again."

Charlie felt his gut tighten. "What happened? Are you and Delphine okay?"

"Um, we're fine. But maybe you should come over."

Charlie looked at his watch. It was just past eleven at night. "I'm leaving my office right this second. Be there in fifteen minutes! Do me a favor, honey. Stay with your mother?"

"Um, okay."

Charlie could hear the fear in her voice. He raced to the house in his Porsche 911, the sports car careening dangerously along the hairpin curves and steep hills all the way up to The Peak. He speed-dialed Isabel's lead security officer, Jonny Fung, from his Bluetooth but it went straight to voice mail. All the while, his heart was beating a mile a minute as he dreaded what he would find when he arrived at the house. Isabel had been doing so well. Was this really another breakdown, or did she stop taking her meds again?

A few blocks from the house, Charlie got caught in a traffic jam as cars waited bumper to bumper. He leaned on his horn anxiously, and then decided, fuck it, he would cut onto the oncoming traffic lane. He raced past the line of cars and discovered that they were all trying to go to the same place—Isabel's house. There was a cluster of people in front of the gates as Charlie pulled up. He jumped out of the car and approached the security guards stationed by the gate. "What the hell is happening?"

"Private party," one of the guards said in Cantonese.

"Party? *Tonight?* I'm going in."

"Wait a second, are you on the list? What's your name?" the baby-faced guard asked, holding an iPad with a list of names glowing on the screen.

"My name? Jesus, get out of my face!" Charlie seethed, pushing past him and running down the driveway. Just as he reached the porte cochere of the house, three bodyguards in black suits suddenly appeared out of nowhere and jumped on top of him. "Got the crasher!" one of the guards said into his earpiece as he pinned Charlie's face to the ground.

"Get off me! This is my house!" Charlie grunted as one of the guards held him in a knee-lock.

"Yeah right," the guards laughed mockingly.

"Get Mr. Fung out here now! I'm Charlie Wu and this is my house! I sign all your paychecks!"

At the mention of their boss's name, one of the guards started talking urgently into his earpiece. Moments later, the head of security came out of the house and began shouting, "That's Mr. Wu! Get off him, you fucking morons!"

Charlie got up from the ground and brushed the dirt off his face. "Jonny, what the fuck is going on here? Why aren't you picking up your phone?"

"Sorry, I was inside, and it's very loud in there," Jonny apologized. "Mrs. Wu decided to have the party just this afternoon. It's a benefit for the earthquake victims in Yunnan Province."

"You've got to be fucking kidding me," Charlie muttered as he entered the house. There were at least fifty people crowded in the foyer, and a man suddenly grabbed him from behind and gave him a full-on bear hug. "Charlie! You're here!" It was Pascal Pang, his face inexplicably powdered white, with rouge on his cheeks. "I was just telling Tilda that I've never seen *such* a pleasant divorce as you and Isabel had. Look, he even comes to her parties! My ex-wives won't even take my calls, hahaha."

Charlie was bewildered as a pale, thin woman with uniquely androgynous features dressed in a silver jumpsuit smiled at him sweetly. "So you're Charlie! Astrid's told me so much about you," she said in a lilting British accent.

"Has she? Excuse me, I just need to find someone." Charlie squeezed through the crowded foyer and into the sprawling formal room, which had been utterly transformed into a dark, funereal space. All of Isabel's pretty French furniture had been covered in black fabric, and even the walls were draped in black. Guests sat at little black bistro tables lit with red votive candles, and a woman dressed in a long dark red velvet dress lay on top of the grand piano with a microphone in her hand. As the pianist tickled the keys, she sang in a deep, throaty voice,

"Fawwwwwwl-ling in love again, never wanted to,
what am I to do, I can't help it . . ."

Charlie spotted Isabel at one of the front tables, dressed in a man's tuxedo with her hair slicked back, sitting on the lap of a male model who looked to be no older than twenty-five. Chloe and Delphine stood behind her, dressed in matching outfits of black vests, black shorts with garter belts, and black bowler hats, looking extremely uncomfortable. Chloe's face lit up in relief the moment she saw her father.

Charlie marched up to Isabel's table and demanded, "Can we talk?"

"Shh! Ute Lemper's singing!" Isabel said, waving him off.

"We really need to talk *now*," Charlie said as calmly as possible, grabbing her arm and leading her to the back of the room.

"What is your problem? We have one of the greatest chanteuses in the world right here, and you're interrupting!" Isabel's breath reeked of vodka, and Charlie looked into her eyes, trying to figure out if she was just drunk or having a manic episode.

"Isabel, it's Thursday night. Why are you hosting a party for two hundred people right now, and what on earth did you make the girls put on?"

"Don't you get it? This is the Weimar Republic. It's 1931 Berlin and we're at the Kit Kat Club. Chloe and Delphine are both dressed like Sally Bowles!"

Sighing deeply, he said, "I'm going to take them home with me right now. It's past midnight on a school night and they can hardly keep their eyes open."

"What are you talking about? The girls are having the time of their lives! I especially invited Hao Yun Xiang to the party because Chloe's got a crush on him!" Isabel gestured to the strapping male model whose lap she had been keeping warm. "You're just jealous, aren't you? Don't worry, I think you've got a bigger cock."

At that moment, Charlie knew she was out of her mind. Isabel could do some outrageous things, but she was never profane. "I'm not jealous—" he began calmly.

"Well then, stop spoiling all the fun for the rest of us!" Isabel declared, going back to her chair. She straddled her male model this time and began swaying to the music.

It was obvious to Charlie that Isabel was in the midst of a manic high, and sooner or later she was going to come crashing down, and who knows what she would do. It was useless to argue with her like this. He grabbed Chloe and Delphine by their hands and marched them toward the exit. At the front door, he whispered to Jonny Fung, "You don't let Isabel out of your sight, you hear me? And don't let her leave the house until I come back tomorrow morning with her doctors."

"Of course," the head of security nodded.

At 3:00 a.m., Charlie was woken up by a phone call. Seeing it was Isabel, he rolled over onto his back with a sigh and answered.

"Where are my girls?" Isabel said, sounding preternaturally calm.

"They're here with me. Fast asleep."

"Why did you drag them off like that?"

"I didn't drag them off. They were only too happy to leave the freak show and come home with me."

"You know, you deprived them of seeing Ute's full performance. She sang three encores. She sang 'Non, Je Ne Regrette Rien.' And I wanted Chloe to meet Tilda Swinton. When will she ever get a chance like this again?"

"I'm sorry, Isabel. I'm sorry Chloe didn't get a chance to meet Tilda. But apparently she's friends with Astrid, so maybe she'll have another chance—"

"I don't give a flying fuck about Astrid! Don't you see that there are people suffering in the world? Do you know we raised two million dollars tonight for the earthquake victims? Think of all the children we are helping!"

Charlie gave an exasperated laugh. He knew it was pointless

to argue with her when she was having one of these episodes, but he couldn't help himself. "You could start with your own children."

"So you think I'm a bad mother," Isabel said, suddenly sounding very sad.

"I don't think that. I think you're a wonderful mother, but you're just having a bad night."

"I am NOT having a bad night! I am having a *fantabulous* evening! I am a charity fund-raiser par extraordinaire, and I am trying to help our children." Isabel began to sing in a slow, soulful voice: "*I believe the children are our future. Teach them well and leeeeet them lead the way . . .*"

"Izzie, it's three in the morning. Can we stop with the Whitney Houston?" Charlie said wearily.

"I'll never stop! Those bastards crushed Whitney's spirit, but they will never crush mine, do you hear me?"

"Izzie, I'm going to sleep now. I will see you tomorrow morning first thing. I'll bring the girls home before school so they can change into their uniforms."

"Don't you dare hang up on me, Charlie Wu!" Isabel demanded. But it was too late. Charlie had hung up. He had hung up on her in the way that he never used to. Isabel's mind went into a roller-coaster dip as she stared out the window onto the crashing waves of the ocean. Unbeknownst to Charlie, she had been sitting in the bedroom of his new house in Shek O during the entire call. Foiling her security crew, she had swapped outfits with Ute Lemper after her second encore and slipped unnoticed out of her own party in a deep red velvet dress. She had taken the first car in the valet line and driven in a manic rage all the way to Charlie's house. She had punched in the code she remembered: 110011. And now she was wandering through the empty Tom Kundig–designed house, spiraling into greater and greater rage.

So this is what it's going to be like now. This is how it is now that you have your new life in this perfect glass house by the sea. This boring bourgeois Architectural Digest *fantasy, with all your boring mid-century furniture and that boring little decorative object you wake up next to every morning. Because that's what she is. That Astrid Leong and her sham aesthetics. Just because she wears Alexis Mabille to lunch she thinks she's hot shit, she thinks she's an original. She's nothing but a perfectly bred decorative doll with no substance and no grit. Everyone thinks she's soooo exquisite and soooo elegant, but I know the truth. I know what kind of woman she really is.*

Isabel leaned against the dining table, took out her cell phone, and swiped around the screen furiously until she found what she was looking for. It was a video clip she had saved in a locked folder. It was the video of Charlie and Astrid making love, and as she played the video, the sound of their moans echoed through the vast, empty house. *Look at her. She's no better than a whore. Look at the way she straddles him, commanding his invading prick like she's riding one of her Thoroughbreds. This isn't a woman who will just settle for being "friends" with Chloe and Delphine. This is a woman who wants it all. And because of all her money she thinks she can buy whatever she wants. She bought Charlie and now she wants to buy my children and buy their love and turn them into little carbon copies of herself, with long ballerina necks and perfect couture outfits. She wants to sit in this perfect house and look out at the perfect view of the sea with my daughters and stroke their hair in the golden sunlight and twirl them around the garden like they are all in some goddamn Terrence Malick movie and convince them that this is the only life they should ever want. "You'll always be welcome here," she says. Like hell I will. The day after her wedding she's going to shut me out forever. I just know it. She thinks she's going to erase me from their lives, but I will never let this happen. Never never never!* With trembling fingers, Isabel jammed out a message on the gossip columnist Honey Chai's WeChat message board:

> Astrid Leong has stolen my life. She is a cheating, husband-stealing whore. Just look at her whoring herself in this video. She is nothing but a vapid rich girl, an heiress to an evil fortune that destroys our planet. I curse her! I curse Charlie Wu! I curse this house built on deceit and sin! For the rest of eternity, there will never ever be any peace in this house!

Isabel attached the video clip and hit "post," as the video streamed out to millions of WeChat users all over the world. Then she climbed up on the wooden Nakashima dining table as if it was a giant surfboard, took off her long velvet gown, rolled it into a tight long rope and threw one end around the Lindsey Adelman chandelier. She fastened the other end taut over the white, tender part of her neck and inched to the edge of the table slowly, step by step, gazing out the window at the moonlit sea. And then she jumped.

CHAPTER SIXTEEN

"It was an epic fail, a disaster of titanic proportions," Carlton sighed over the phone to his sister as he recounted his date with Scheherazade.

"I'm so sorry, Carlton—it sounds traumatic," Rachel said. "So what happened after Colette dropped her bombshell?"

"Well, it basically killed the dinner for everyone. Scheherazade didn't eat a thing after that, and I bolted right after dessert was served. It became apparent to me that Scheherazade's parents were going to file a restraining order against me if I stuck around one minute longer."

"I'm sure it wasn't that bad."

"No, actually, it probably got worse. Everyone went into the drawing room for drinks and coffee, and I *just know* Colette was itching to get into all the details of exactly what happened in London. I'm sure she went on a no-holds-barred campaign to tell the Shangs what a murderous monster I am. Scheherazade walked me down to my car, and I tried to tell her the whole story but it just all came out wrong. I was rushing and nervous, and I think she was too in shock to process anything."

"It's a lot of story for a first date, Carlton. Give her a little time to recover," Rachel said gently.

"She'll have all the time in the world—I heard she left for Paris first thing this morning. Game over."

"It's not game over. Maybe her leaving had nothing to do with you."

"Uh-uh, I don't think so. She hasn't responded to any of my texts in the past twenty-four hours."

Rachel rolled her eyes. "Jesus, you millennials! If you really want to win her back, fly to Paris, send her a thousand roses, take her to dinner at some romantic rooftop in the Marais, *just do something other than text her!*"

"It's not so simple. She's surrounded by bodyguards 24/7. If she's not going to respond to my texts, I don't want to be some creepy stalker who shows up at her doorstep."

"Carlton, even if you tried, you would never come across as a creepy stalker. Scheherazade's obviously freaked out because she's been fed a line of bullshit from Colette. So you need to show her who you really are. She's waiting for you to do that, don't you see?"

"I think she's back in Paris living her life, probably dating some French count with three-week-old stubble by now."

Rachel sighed. "You know what it is, Carlton? You're just spoiled. You had the fortune, or maybe the misfortune, of being born good-looking, and girls have been throwing themselves at you all your life. You've never had to lift a finger. Scheherazade is the first girl who's challenging you, who's making you work for it. You've met your match. So are you gonna step up?"

Carlton was quiet for a moment. "So what's my next move, Rachel?"

"You need to figure that out. I'm not going to give you a cheat sheet! You need to win her back with a wildly romantic gesture. Look, I need to go. There's a potential buyer coming to tour Tyersall Park this morning, and you *don't* want to know who it is."

"Why not?" Carlton asked.

"Because it's Jack Bing."

"Bollocks! You're pulling my leg!"

"I wish I was. He's offering an insane amount of money for the house."

"Bloody hell, between Colette and her father, the Bings are clearly out for blood in Singapore. Don't sell it to him."

Rachel sighed. "I wish it were up to me. Nick and I are actually trying to avoid him, and I think I hear people arriving."

"Okay, call me later."

. . .

Jack Bing stood in the middle of the Andalusian Cloister, puffing away on his cigar as he stared at the ornately carved columns. "This is incredible. I've never seen a house like this in my whole life," he said in Mandarin.

"I love this inner courtyard! We can take out this reflecting pool and put in a *real* swimming pool," Kitty suggested in English.

Felicity, Victoria, and Alix winced but said nothing.

Oliver stepped in diplomatically. "Kitty, this reflecting pool was brought over tile by tile from Córdoba, Spain. Do you see these blue-and-coral Moorish tiles lining the pool? They're extraordinarily rare, from the thirteenth century."

"Oh, I had no idea. Of course we must keep them, then," Kitty said.

Jack stared at the lotus-shaped rose quartz in the middle of the fountain that was bubbling a slow, hypnotic trickle of water. "No, we mustn't change a thing. This house may not be as grand as our place in Shanghai, but it has amazing feng shui. I can feel the chi flowing through everywhere. No wonder your family prospered here," Jack told the assembled ladies.

The Young sisters nodded politely, as none of them spoke Mandarin and only understood about thirty percent of what he said. Jack looked at the three frumpily dressed sisters, thinking to himself, *Only women who grew up in a place like this can get away with looking like that. And they can't even speak a word of Mandarin. They are like dodo birds, a useless species. No wonder they are losing their house.*

The group proceeded through the arcade into the library.

Jack looked around at all the old books lining the double-height bookcases and the sleek Indian rosewood desk. "I love this kind of furniture. Art deco, isn't it?"

"Actually, this was Sir James's library, and he had all the furniture custom designed by Pierre Jeanneret in the late 1940s," Oliver informed him.

"Well, it reminds me a bit of the old Shanghai clubs where my grandfather used to play," Jack remarked. Turning to the ladies, he said, "My grandfather worked in a water-boiler factory, but he was also a trumpet player. Every night for extra money, he would play in a jazz band that performed in all of the clubs frequented by Westerners. When I was a little boy, it was my duty to shine his trumpet for him every night. I would spit and spit at the trumpet to clean it, in order to make the polish go farther."

Felicity backed away nervously, afraid that he might actually perform one of his spitting demonstrations near her.

"How much for the furniture?" Jack asked.

"Er ... which pieces did you have in mind? Some of them are ... things ... that we could never part with," Victoria said in the rudimentary Mandarin she used with her servants. "Oliver, how do you say 'heirloom' in Mandarin?"

"Ah, that's '*chuan jia bao*,'" Oliver told her.

"Oh, I love the tables, the chairs, this purple-and-blue rug, especially." Jack pointed at the floor. Felicity stared down at the purple silk rug and a story her aunt Rosemary T'sien had once told her suddenly came flooding back . . .

You know your mother once stared a Japanese general in the eye and dared him to shoot her? It happened right here in this library, where Su Yi was hosting a card party for some high-ranking officers. They were always forcing her to do things like this during the occupation, host these horrible debauched parties for them. My husband—your uncle Tsai Tay—had just been arrested for some ridiculous offense, and when the general lost a game of gin rummy to your mother, she demanded that in return he free Tsai Tay. Of course the general was outraged by her boldness, and immediately took out his pistol and held it to her temple. I was sitting right next to her, and I thought she was a gone case.

Su Yi remained completely calm and said in that imperious way of hers, "General, you are going to ruin Rosemary's beautiful cheongsam if you shoot me right now. My brains will be all over it, not to mention this beautiful art deco carpet from Paris. Do you know how much this carpet is worth? It's designed by a very famous French artist named Christian Bérard, and would make such a beautiful present for your wife, if only it wasn't stained with my blood. Now, you wouldn't want to disappoint your wife, would you?" The general was silent for a moment, but then he burst into laughter. And then he put down his gun, took the rug with him, and the next day, they released my husband from prison. Tsai Tay would never forget what Su Yi did for him.

Hiyah, there are so many stories I can tell you about the war years, but Su Yi wouldn't want me to. But you know, she saved the lives of so many people, and most of them didn't even realize she was the one responsible. She wanted it that way. After the war was over, we heard that the general was executed for war crimes during the war tribunals in Manila. One day, your mother called me up and said, "You'll never guess what just arrived in a long box. That purple art deco rug that the general took back to Japan. I suppose his wife never approved of it."

Felicity snapped out of her reverie and said decisively, "Mr. Bing, this rug isn't for sale. But there are some items that we could offer with the house."

"All right then. Oliver, could you make an assessment of how much everything is worth? I'll take whatever *chuan jia biao* these nice ladies will let me have," Jack said, turning to the Young sisters with a little smile.

"Of course," Oliver said.

"Ladies, I approve of this house, and I think my family will be very happy using it whenever we visit Singapore. Thank you for showing us around this morning, and please, this is a standing offer, so take your time to decide. I know this must not be an easy decision for all of you," Jack said. He then strolled out the front doors, flicked his cigar onto the gravel driveway, and got into the back of the first black Audi SUV. Kitty climbed in after him, the bodyguards got into their SUVs, and the convoy of cars zoomed off.

"Well *that* was excruciating," Victoria said as they sank into the sofas in the drawing room.

"Oliver, where on earth did you ever dig up these people?" Felicity asked contemptuously.

"Believe it or not, they're far from the worst. Jack has become quite an astute art collector—they have one of the top private museums in Shanghai—and Kitty's taste has actually matured. Plus, she's willing to learn. Don't worry, they won't do anything to the house without my approval."

Victoria looked up in surprise to see Nick and Rachel entering the drawing room. "I didn't realize you two were home! Why didn't you come out and meet these people? Rachel, we could have used another Chinese translator!"

Nick plopped down on one of the art deco club chairs. "Oh I've met them before—I met Jack in Shanghai a couple of years ago and had hoped never to meet him again, and his wife we all met when she came for Colin's wedding."

"Wait a minute . . . that woman was at Colin Khoo's wedding?" Felicity looked taken aback.

"Auntie Felicity, *she was at your house.* She used to be Alistair's girlfriend," Nick said irritatedly.

"Good grief, *that was her*? The one with the big brown cow nipples? Pussy Ping or whatever her name was?" Alix blurted out.

"Her name is Kitty Pong," Rachel said.

"Dear me, I didn't recognize her at all. She has a completely new face! No wonder Alistair suddenly flew back to Hong Kong first thing this morning! But I thought she was married to that ghastly boy, Carol Tai's good-for-nothing son? The one that butchered his face with plastic surgery too?" Alix said.

"That was ages ago, Auntie Alix. Kitty's traded up."

"She most certainly has. I actually quite liked her pretty floral dress today. Why, she didn't look very vulgar at all," Victoria noted.

"It's *impossible* to look vulgar in Dries Van Noten," Oliver declared.

"So you really want to sell the house to them?" Nick asked gruffly.

"Nicky, you tell me how we can say no to *ten billion dollars*?

That's three times more than our top offer. It would be pure stupidity to refuse this kind of money!" Felicity reasoned.

Oliver nodded. "It would be looking a gift horse in the mouth."

Nick glanced over at Oliver in annoyance. "That's easy for you to say. You didn't grow up in this house. For some of us, it's not just about the money."

Oliver sighed. "Look, Nicky, I know you're upset with me, but I really didn't mean for any of this to hurt you. I loved your grandmother and I love this house more than you can possibly imagine. I thought you *wanted* to preserve Tyersall Park, and when I heard that the Bings were on the lookout for a new place in Singapore, I just put two and two together. These people love the house, and they're committed to maintaining its architectural integrity. And they actually have the kind of money it takes to restore the house and keep the estate in tip-top condition for generations to come."

Rachel spoke up. "Do those generations include Colette Bing?"

Oliver's face flushed red, while Felicity asked, "Who's Colette Bing?"

"Colette Bing is Jack's daughter. Two years ago, her personal assistant, Roxanne, tried to poison Rachel, on Colette's behalf," Nick answered sharply.

"WHAAAT?" Felicity and Victoria shrieked in horror.

"Oh my goodness, I had completely forgotten that this was *that family*." Alix moaned, putting her hands to her face.

"Rachel, that was such an unfortunate incident, but you should know that Jack and Kitty have absolutely *nothing* to do with Colette anymore," Oliver said.

Nick's face flashed with anger. "It wasn't an unfortunate incident. My wife almost died! Just how much do you stand to make on this deal, Oliver? Aside from your commission on the sale, which will be in the millions, how much will you and that auction house of yours be making selling new stuff to these eager Bings?"

Oliver got up from the divan and smiled apologetically. "You know, I think I will leave you all now. I can see that I've frayed a few nerves. The offer's on the table, and I look forward to hearing your response."

As soon as Oliver had left the room, Victoria spoke up. "You know, I've been thinking . . . there is something to all this that's just been so serendipitous, so impossible to believe, this has to be a sign. Nicky, this incredible offer from the Bings, I think part of it is because they are atoning for what happened to Rachel. I think this is all Mummy's work. She is looking out for us from heaven."

Nick rolled his eyes in frustration.

"It is hard to believe that anyone would pay this much over the market value for Tyersall Park—" Alix began.

"Mummy had it planned all along. She knew we wouldn't be getting any money from the Shang Trust, and so she wanted us all to get the most money possible out of Tyersall Park. That's why she split it up like she did, and now she's working a miracle for us." Victoria's voice brimmed with conviction.

Nick suddenly stood up and looked at his aunties. "Look, you can tell yourself any story you want if it helps you to sleep at night. Personally, I can't stand the idea of this house going to the family that almost killed my wife! I don't think we can trust them to keep their word about preserving the house—I can tell that Kitty's just waiting to get her claws into redesigning it from top to bottom. But if I can match Jack's offer, will you sell it to me?"

Rachel looked at him in surprise, while Alix answered, "Nicky, don't be silly. It would be absurd for you to buy this house at that price! We couldn't let you do that!"

"You didn't answer my question. If I can get us ten billion, do we have a deal?"

The aunties looked at one another.

"Okay, we will give you one month," Felicity finally relented.

CHAPTER SEVENTEEN

Twice a year, the acquisitions board of the Singapore Museum of Modern Art convened to go over potential new purchases for the permanent collection. The exclusive board was composed of the city's young elite collectors, mostly descended from the country's most powerful families. As with most entitled scions, it simply wouldn't do for them to actually have to perform their duties at the museum's perfectly nice but rather ordinary offices, so some new fabulous location with celebrity-chef-prepared cuisine was always selected for the acquisitions board meetings.

Today, the meeting took place over breakfast at the Capella on Sentosa, the island playground off Singapore's southern coast. When the museum's curator Felipe Hsu arrived at the gorgeous reception room overlooking a beautiful tiered infinity pool, he found the atmosphere positively buzzing among the dozen or so members that had already assembled.

"I couldn't believe it! Absolutely couldn't believe it!" Lauren Lee Liang (the wife of Roderick Liang of the Liang Finance Liangs, and a granddaughter of Mrs. Lee Yong Chien) whispered in a corner to Sarita Singh (former Bollywood actress and daughter-in-law of Gayatri Singh).

"How can you possibly recover from something like that?" Sarita shook her head as she fingered the mother-of-pearl medallions on her Van Cleef and Arpels necklace as if they were rosary beads.

"Well, the one consolation is that her tits did look great. I wonder if she's had them lifted?" Lauren said as she shielded her mouth with her VBH clutch.

Felipe strolled over to the buffet to help himself to two soft-boiled eggs and some toast points. Patricia Lim (of the Lim Rubber Lims), who was standing next to him trying to decide between eggs Benedict or eggs Norwegian, gave him a look. "What a morning, huh?"

"Yes, it seems like everyone's caffeinated and ready to go! Good, good, we have quite a long agenda today."

"Are you thinking of making any sort of announcement, or do you plan to maintain a dignified silence?"

"I'm not sure what you're referring to, Pat." The curator frowned.

"Don't play dumb with me, Felipe! Oh dear lord . . . SHE'S ACTUALLY HERE!"

The room went dead silent as Astrid entered. She said hi to her cousin Sophie Khoo (of the Khoo Enterprises Khoos),[*] grabbed a pain au chocolat from the buffet and sat down at the head of the long marble table as everyone took their places. Then she stood up abruptly. "Good morning, everyone. Before we dive headlong into our agenda, I have a confession to make."

Most of the board members gasped audibly as they stared wide-eyed at Astrid.

"When it comes to Anish Kapoor, I am totally biased. I have loved his work for many years now, and as you probably know I

---

[*] Sophie is the sister of Colin Khoo, and they are cousins to Astrid through their late mother, who was Harry Leong's sister. Yes, Singapore is a very small world, and even smaller within the high-net-worth crowd.

own several of his pieces and yes, I was the anonymous donor who helped to fund the new installation in Antwerp. So we will be examining two new artworks from him for possible acquisition, and I will recuse myself from that vote." Astrid smiled at everyone and sat down again.

"Un-fucking-believable . . ." Lauren Lee muttered under her breath.

Sarita Singh tapped on her coffee mug with her spoon, and everyone looked at her as she spoke up in a righteous tone. "I was expecting our chairwoman to humbly announce her resignation, but since she has shown no intention of doing that, I'd like to start a motion for Astrid Leong's immediate removal from the acquisitions board."

Astrid stared at Sarita in shock.

"I second that motion," Lauren Lee immediately said.

"What the hell?" Felipe blurted out, his mouth still full of soft-boiled egg as the room erupted in commotion.

"Sarita, why are you suddenly suggesting this motion?" Astrid asked.

"Astrid, let's be perfectly honest here. We're going to lose funding now because of your actions. The entire museum's reputation is going to be affected because of you. I can't even believe you dared to show up here this morning."

"I'm really not following . . . is this because of my divorce?" Astrid asked, trying to remain gracious and calm.

From the other end of the table, Sophie Khoo stood up and ran over to Astrid's side. "Come with me now," she whispered, taking hold of her arm.

Astrid stood up and followed Sophie out of the room. "What is going on in there?" she asked, absolutely bewildered.

"Astrid, it just became apparent to me that you don't even know yet."

"Know what?"

Sophie closed her eyes for a moment and inhaled. "There is a video of you that leaked late last night. It's gone viral."

"A video?" Astrid still didn't catch on.

"Yes, of you . . . with Charlie Wu."

All the color drained from Astrid's face. "Oh my God."

"I'm so sorry . . ." Sophie began.

Astrid stood stock-still for a moment, and then she snapped into crisis-management mode. "I need to go. I need to get Cassian out of school. Please tell them I needed to go," Astrid said, as she made a run for her car.

As Astrid sped along the Sentosa Gateway heading back to Singapore, she found herself unusually calm and collected. She tried ringing Charlie from her Bluetooth but his cell kept going straight to voice mail. Finally, she left a message: "Charlie, I suspect you've already heard about the video leak since you're not answering. I just found out minutes ago. I'm fine, don't worry, I'm on my way to ACS now to get Cassian. I would suggest doing the same for Chloe and Delphine. If they haven't found out already, it's better coming from us than from some classmate. You know how kids can be. I'll talk to you soon."

The minute Astrid ended the call, her phone started ringing again. "Charlie?"

There was a brief silence on the other end, and then a screeching voice filled her car. "Oh my God, you are still talking to that horrible pervert! I can't believe you!" It was her mother.

"Mum, please calm down."

"A sex tape! Ohmygod, in my worst nightmare I never imagined I would ever hear those words uttered about one of my children! I just got home from showing Tyersall Park to some dreadful Chinese people, and now I hear this news from Cassandra Shang? Your father is so angry, I'm worried he's going to drop dead of a heart attack!" Felicity cried.

Astrid couldn't help but notice how her mother always managed to sob hysterically, scold, and guilt-trip her simultaneously. "Mother, we did nothing wrong! Michael secretly videotaped us in the privacy of Charlie's home, and now he's leaked the video everywhere. This is a crime, Mum."

"The crime is you sleeping with Charlie in the first place!"

"How is that a crime?"

"You're a harlot! Your reputation has gone down the toilet, and you're branded for life now!"

"Did you even see the video? It's ten seconds of grainy footage—"

"Ohmygod, if I were to actually see the video I think I would instantly go blind! How could you have slept with that man when you're not even married to him? This is God punishing you!"

"I'm sorry, I've had sex before marriage, okay, and I've had sex with Charlie, who, by the way, I was having sex with the first time he was my fiancé over a decade ago!"

"The two of you have brought nothing but disgrace onto us. You have disgraced your father and me and you have disgraced your family for generations! And you have ruined poor Cassian's life! How will he ever show his face at ACS again?"

"I'm on my way to get Cassian now."

"We already got him. Ludivine just collected him from school and is bringing him over here."

"Oh good, I'll be there in ten minutes."

"Absolutely not! What are you thinking? We don't want you anywhere near this house!"

"Stop being ridiculous, Mum—"

"Ridiculous? I don't know how I'm ever going to recover from this! You need to leave Singapore and not come back until things blow over! Don't you realize what this scandal has done to your father's reputation? Good grief, this might affect the next election! This might throw the sale of Tyersall Park into jeopardy! My God, the price might come tumbling down! I can feel my blood pressure skyrocketing now. Oh my goodness I need my pills. Sunali, where are my pills?" Felicity shrieked to one of her maids.

"Calm down, Mum, I don't see how this has anything to do with Tyersall Park!"

"How can you not see it? You have tainted the family legacy! Do not come over to Nassim Road, do you understand? Your father does not want to see your face! He says you are dead to him!"

Astrid felt winded for a few moments, overwhelmed by her mother's attack. Thankfully, her phone beeped and Charlie's number flashed on the screen.

"Okay, Mum, don't worry, I'm not coming over. I'm not going to shame you for one moment longer," she said, switching over to Charlie.

There was a short pause, and then Charlie's voice came through. "Astrid, are you okay?"

"Yes, thank God it's you!" Astrid said with a heavy sigh.

"Are you driving?"

"Yes, I was on the way to get Cassian out of school, but—"

"Can you find someplace to pull over?" Charlie's voice sounded strange.

"Sure, I just got to Tanglin Road. Let me pull over into this Esso right here."

Astrid parked in the gas station and relaxed into her seat. "Okay, I'm parked."

"Good, good. First of all, are you okay?" Charlie asked.

"Well, my mum just screamed at me in a way I've never heard before and ordered me to leave the country. Otherwise, life is peachy. How has your day been so far?"

"I'm not sure how to tell you this, Astrid," Charlie said in a shaky voice.

"Let me guess, you found out why Michael leaked the video?"

"Actually, Michael didn't leak it."

"He didn't?"

"No. It was Isabel."

"ISABEL? How did she even get the video?"

"We're not sure . . . we're still trying to piece it all together, but the video came from her phone. She posted it to the gossip blog."

"Why on earth would she do that?"

"She had another psychotic episode, Astrid. And this time, she tried to hang herself."

"She *what*?" Astrid found herself going numb.

"She tried hanging herself in our new house, on the dining-room chandelier. She wanted to curse the house and curse our marriage forever."

"So what happened?" Astrid barely got the words out.

"The chandelier broke, and that saved her. But now she's on life support. She's in a coma, and they don't know if she'll ever come out of it," Charlie said, his voice cracking in grief.

"No. No, no, no, no, no," Astrid cried, breaking down into uncontrollable sobs.

PART FOUR

I often think how unfairly life's good fortune is sometimes distributed.

—LEO TOLSTOY, *WAR AND PEACE*

What's a soup kitchen?

—PARIS HILTON

Four days after Isabel's suicide attempt, an exclusive story broke in *The Daily Post*:

HEIRESS DRIVES RIVAL TO SUICIDE ATTEMPT
AFTER SEX VIDEO LEAK!

The gorgeous Singaporean heiress **Astrid Leong's** sensational $5 billion divorce from venture capitalist **Michael Teo** continues to pile up collateral damage. The latest victim is **Isabel Wu**, the ex-wife of Astrid's current boyfriend, tech billionaire **Charles Wu.**

Apparently, an explicit video of Ms. Leong in bed with Mr. Wu sent Mrs. Wu into an emotional tailspin, and after leaking the video to a popular Chinese gossip blog, Mrs. Wu tried to hang herself at the spectacular new Tom Kundig–designed mansion that her ex-husband has been building in Shek O.

Isabel has been in a coma at Hong Kong Sanatorium, where sources say there had been a concerted attempt by Mr. Wu to keep the tragedy under wraps. But Isabel's mother, **The Hon. Madam Justice Deirdre Lai,** demands a further investigation into her daughter's suicide attempt. "Charlie and Astrid are responsible, and I want the world to know what they have done to my daughter!" sobbed the Hong Kong High Court Judge.

The scandal has become the talk of Asia, splitting Hong Kong society as friends and family take opposing sides. An insider on Team Charlie says, "Isabel has been suffering from mental health issues for over two decades. The footage in question was secretly recorded long after Isabel and Charlie's marriage fell apart, and Isabel leaked it while she was suffering from a manic episode. Charlie and Astrid are the real victims here."

"Nonsense!" counters an insider from Team Isabel. "Izzie was devastated by this video. It was recorded while Isabel and Charlie were happily married, and it really put her over the edge to learn just how long their affair had been going on."

Deirdre Lai says, "My poor granddaughters Chloe and Delphine! First they have a porn star for a father, and now they might lose their mother! Can you believe that after all this, that dirty woman dared to show up at the hospital where my poor daughter lies in a coma?"

The Daily Post tried to contact Ms. Leong for a comment, but since her appearance at Hong Kong Sanatorium, Ms. Leong has seemingly vanished. When we contacted her family's company, Leong Holdings, for comment, spokeswoman **Zoe Quan** said, "Astrid Leong has no functioning role in this company, and we have no comment." When we inquired as to Astrid's whereabouts, Ms. Quan hurriedly barked, "No idea, *lah*! She is out of the country for an indefinite period."

CHAPTER ONE

PLACE DE FURSTENBERG, PARIS

Scheherazade padded into the gleaming, state-of-the-art kitchen of her apartment in Saint-Germain, lifted the lid from her frying pan, and put a finger on the crust. Not ready yet. She put the lid over the pan again, went back into her dressing room, and took off her sheer ruffled Delpozo blouse. She had just returned from a party at the loft of a fashion photography couple, where the former pastry chef at Noma had cooked up the most elaborate feast ever, but all through the dinner, Scheherazade only dreamed of getting back to her place, heating up some two-day-old pizza in her frying pan,* opening a bottle of red wine, and catching up on *The Walking Dead*.

Changing into her pajamas, she brought the plate of pizza into her living room, sank down into her gray suede sofa, turned on her television, and selected the latest episode. As her favorite show began to play, the dialogue was suddenly drowned out by the sound of muffled music outside her window. Scheherazade turned up the volume on her TV, hoping to drown out the noise,

---

*   Truly the best way to heat up two-day-old pizza. The crust gets crispy and the cheese gets cheesy if you leave a lid on for a minute at the end.

but it only got louder. Cars started honking on the street and a neighbor could be heard screaming out his window.

Getting annoyed, Scheherazade paused the show, walked over to her balcony, and opened the glass-paned doors. Suddenly the full force of the music flooded her ears, and as Scheherazade peered over her railing, she saw the most curious sight. Carlton Bao was standing on the roof of a Range Rover parked outside her building, holding up a boom box that was blasting Peter Gabriel's "In Your Eyes."

"Carlton! What the hell are you doing?" Scheherazade shouted down at him, absolutely mortified.

"I'm trying to get your attention!" Carlton shouted back.

"What do you want?"

"I want you to listen to me. I want you to know that I'm not some reckless killer! The only thing I'm guilty of is falling—"

"What? Turn down the music! I can't hear you!"

Carlton refused to turn down the music, but yelled louder, "I said the only thing I'm guilty of is falling in love with yo—"

At that moment, four bodyguards dressed in civilian clothes suddenly grabbed him by the legs, yanked him off the car, and body tackled him onto the ground.

"Oh fuck!" Scheherazade started giggling. She ran out the door, down four flights of stairs, and out the front door. "Get off him!" she told the security guards that were now standing over Carlton.

"Miss Shang, are you sure?"

"Yes, I'm sure! He's fine. He's with me," Scheherazade insisted.

The beefiest guard reluctantly released his knee from Carlton's back, and when Carlton got off the ground, Scheherazade saw that the left side of his face was all cut up from the asphalt.

"Oh no. Come upstairs—let's get some disinfectant on that,"

Scheherazade said. As they entered her building and rode up in the ornate wrought-iron elevator, she looked him over again.

"What did you think you were doing?"

"That was my wildly romantic gesture!"

Scheherazade frowned. "That was supposed to be romantic?"

"I was doing my best John Cusack impersonation."

"Who?"

"You know, *Say Anything.*"

"Say what?"

"You haven't seen the movie, have you?" Carlton said, suddenly crestfallen.

"No, but you did look cute standing on top of that car," Scheherazade said, pulling him in for a kiss.

. . .

At the other end of Paris, Charlie was walking back to the Hotel George V after a very frustrating dinner with Astrid's old friend Grégoire L'Herme-Pierre. Grégoire had been more charming than usual, and Charlie suspected that he knew far more about Astrid's whereabouts than he let on. She had been in Paris for probably three days, Grégoire surmised, and then she was gone. *No, she hadn't seemed distraught—I just assumed she was making her usual semiannual trip to the city for her couture fittings.*

Over the past two weeks, Charlie had crisscrossed the globe frantically searching for Astrid. Mad with worry, he had started in Singapore, then Paris and London, going to all their familiar haunts and speaking with all her friends. He then headed down to Venice to see if she was hiding out in her friend Domiella Finzi-Contini's palazzo, but Domi, like so many of Astrid's friends, remained as silent as the Sphinx. *I haven't heard a peep from Astrid, but then I've been in Ferrara for the past month. We*

*always spend the winter in Ferrara. No, I didn't hear about the scandal
at all.*

Now he was back in Paris, trying to retrace her steps, trying to
understand how she could have abandoned her entire life, and
how her family didn't seem to care that she had been missing
for the past month. Entering the hotel, he went to the reception
desk to see if there had been any messages. *No, monsieur, nothing
for you tonight.*

Charlie went up to his suite and opened the doors to the balcony, letting in some fresh cold air. The cold air kept him on his
toes, helped him to think clearly. Paris had been a dud. She had
been here, but she clearly wasn't coming back. He should try Los
Angeles next. Even though her brother Alex had assured him
she wasn't there, he was still suspicious. His entire security team
and all the private investigators he had hired had been poring
over everything since day one. Astrid had been meticulous. She
hadn't left any sort of paper trail, no bank transfers, no credit
card charges in more than five weeks. Someone had to be helping her. Someone close.

He stepped out onto the balcony and leaned against the railing, gazing at the soft golden glow that always seemed to hover
over Paris at night. The city, breathtakingly lovely as always, suddenly seemed so lonely. He should never have let her come to
Hong Kong. She had insisted on coming, wanting to help him
through his crisis, but when she saw Isabel in the ICU, hooked
up to all those machines . . . he knew she was trying to be strong
for him, for the girls, but he could see that it just devastated her.
And then when Isabel's mother saw Astrid at the hospital, she
went berserk, and that's when she gave the whole story to *The
Daily Post*, breaking the scandal wide open. It was all his fault.
His stupid damn fault.

Charlie went back into the suite and sat down on the bed. He opened the drawer beside the bed and took out a small brown padded envelope. It was an envelope that had been mailed to him in Hong Kong from this very hotel a few weeks ago, and inside was a box containing the engagement ring he had given Astrid, along with a handwritten note that he had now read hundreds of times:

Dear Charlie,

I've been doing a great deal of thinking over the past days. Ever since I came back into your life five years ago, I've only caused you heartache. I dragged you into my problems with Michael, I dragged you into my horrendous divorce, and now I have dragged you and your daughters into an unthinkable tragedy. Chloe and Delphine almost lost their mother, and I am the only one to blame. I feel like no matter how hard I try, nothing I do ever leads to anything good, and so the best I can think to do is to simply go away so that no more damage can be done. I don't think I will ever be fit to be your wife, and I can only hope and pray that you and your family will in time be able to find happiness and peace again.

Yours truly,
Astrid

P.S. Please give this ring to my cousin Nicky when you next have the chance. He should have it for Rachel.

Charlie put down the note and reclined on the bed, staring up at the ceiling. Astrid had been lying on this very bed, probably staring at the same view. It was her favorite suite at the George

V and he had been the one to introduce her to it the first time he brought her to Paris back in their university days. It seemed like a lifetime ago, and he wished he could just go back to that time and do everything differently. Charlie rolled over and buried his face in the pillow, inhaling deeply. He thought that if he breathed deep enough, maybe her scent would return.

CHAPTER TWO

Rachel was walking through the rose garden, looking at the fresh new blooms and inhaling their deep, intoxicating scent when Nick returned. He had been to see Alfred Shang in the hope of raising enough money to buy Tyersall Park from his aunts.

"How did it go?" she asked as he entered the garden, although from the look on his face she already knew the answer.

"I walked him through the entire proposal, thinking he would at least throw me some kind of bone since Tyersall Park had been his father's estate. Do you know what he told me? He thinks that we are in the midst of another financial bubble waiting to burst, and when that implodes all of the property markets in Asia will collapse. He said, 'If this idiot really wants to give you ten billion for Tyersall Park, you would be an even bigger idiot not to take it. Take his money and go buy some gold. It's the only asset worth keeping in the long run.'"

Nick leaned into one of the rosebushes and said, "This is maybe the third time I've actually stood here and smelled the roses. It's funny how one takes things for granted when they've always been around."

"We'll plant our own rose garden," Rachel said encouragingly. "I think we can afford a little country house now, don't you think? Maybe in Vermont, or even in Maine. I hear North Haven is beautiful."

"I dunno, Rachel. With four billion dollars, it's going to be tough finding something out there," Nick deadpanned.

Rachel smiled. It was still impossible for her to fathom that kind of money coming into her life, especially since Nick had just spent the past month desperately trying to raise funds and not getting anywhere close to what he needed. Now that the deadline was up, and his last-ditch effort with Uncle Alfred had failed, Nick had no choice but to give in to his aunts' demands.

Picking a beautiful blossom that was dangling from a half-broken stem, Rachel looked up at Nick. "Shall we go in?"

"Yes, let's do this." Nick took her hand and they walked up the stone steps into the house, where Nick's aunts sat pensively around a table in the library.

Alix looked up at him. "Are we ready to make the call?"

Nick nodded, and Felicity picked up the telephone in the middle of the table and dialed Oliver's number. "Hiyah! It's his international cell phone. Now we'll have to pay the long-distance rates," Felicity grumbled.

The phone rang a number of times before Oliver picked up.

"Oliver, can you hear us? We have you on speakerphone here," Alix shouted into the phone.

"Yes, yes, you can lower your voice. I can hear you just fine."

"Where are you right now, Oliver?"

"I'm back in London at the moment."

"Ah, how lovely. How's the weather today?"

"Hiyah, gum cheong hay![*] Let's just get on with it, Alix!" Victoria scolded.

---

[*]   Cantonese for "so long-winded."

"Oh, okay . . . um, I'll let Nicky speak, since he is technically the majority shareholder," Alix said.

"Hi Oliver. Yes, I just wanted to inform you that we've reached a consensus." Nick paused for a moment, took a breath, and then continued. "We're ready to take Jack Bing's offer of ten billion dollars for Tyersall Park."

"Okay. And I am accepting on their behalf. We have a deal!" Oliver replied.

Felicity leaned in. "And Oliver, we'd like your expertise on valuing the furniture. We'll sell him most of the furniture and objects in the house, with the exception of a few things that we wish to keep."

"He's not getting Mummy's Battenberg lace doilies, that's for sure," Victoria muttered under her breath.

"Super. The Bings will be thrilled, and I know it hasn't been easy for all of you to reach this decision, but I can tell you that you have made a superb deal. This is a record-breaking amount for real estate, and I don't think you would have realized a price like this from anyone else on the planet. Great-aunt Su Yi would have been pleased."

Nick rolled his eyes, while Victoria and Alix nodded.

"You'll let them know, Oliver?" Felicity asked.

"Of course. I will call Jack right after we get off the phone, and then I'll e-mail Freddie Tan to begin drawing up the contract."

"Okay then, goodbye." Nick turned off the speakerphone.

The ladies sighed collectively. "It's done," Felicity muttered, as though she had just drowned a litter of puppies.

"It was the right thing to do. Ten billion dollars! Mummy would be so proud of us," Alix said, dabbing her eyes with a rolled-up tissue. Felicity looked at her sister, wondering if what she said was true. Would her mother ever be proud of her?

Nick got up from the table and walked out the French doors into the garden again. Rachel was about to go after him when Alix placed a hand on her arm. "He'll be fine," she said to Rachel.

"I know he will," Rachel said softly.

. . .

I just put four billion dollars into his pocket and that fucker didn't even thank me, Oliver thought after Nick had abruptly hung up. Then he picked up his phone again and called Kitty's cell phone.

"Kitty? It's done. The Youngs have accepted the offer . . . Yes, really . . . No, no, you can't move in next week, it's going to take a few months at the very least to get the deal done . . . Yes, they will sell some of the furnishings . . . Of course I will tell you what's worth acquiring, don't worry . . . I don't think we can pay them more to move out tomorrow. This has been a home to the family for more than a century, Kitty. They need some time to get things sorted and dismantle the estate. The silver lining is that you'll have time to plan the new interiors . . . Henrietta Spencer-Churchill? Yes, I do know her, but Kitty, why would you want the same designer who's already doing Colette's new house? . . . I know she's related to Princess Diana, but I have an even better idea . . . I can think of only one person in the whole world I would trust with a redo of Tyersall Park. Can you meet me in Europe next week? . . . No, not Paris. We're going to Antwerp, Kitty . . . No, it's not in Austria. Antwerp is a city in Belgium . . . Oh, you'll swing by London to pick me up? How awfully kind of you . . . Perfect. Look forward to it."

Oliver hung up the phone and stared into his computer screen for a few minutes. Then he clicked on iTunes and scrolled through his albums until he found a song. He clicked play, and

Puccini's "Nessun Dorma" came blasting on.[*] Oliver sat in his chair and listened to the first few verses of the aria. As it reached the crescendo, Oliver suddenly leapt out of his chair and started dancing madly around his flat. It was a wild, Dionysian release, and then he collapsed on the floor and started sobbing.

He was safe. Safe at last. With the commission earned on the sale of Tyersall Park, the long nightmare of the past two decades was finally over. His 1.5 percent commission on the Tyersall Park sale would garner $150 million, enough to pay off all his student loans and his parents' crushing debts. They wouldn't be rich, but at least they would have enough to survive. His family could be restored to a proper level of respectability again. He would never, ever have to fly economy again. As Oliver lay on the carpet of his London flat, staring up at the cracked plasterwork on the ceiling that had needed fixing ten years ago, he cried out in joy, *"All'alba vincerò! Vincerò, vinceròòòòòòò!"*

---

[*] The Pavarotti version, of course.

CHAPTER THREE

THE PENINSULA HOTEL, LOS ANGELES

"It's as baffling to me as it is to you," Alex Leong said, stirring the ice cubes in his scotch glass with his finger. "Astrid's never left Cassian for this long a period before. I can't imagine what's going through her mind."

From his chair on the rooftop bar, Charlie gazed out at the palm trees that seemed to line every street in Beverly Hills. He didn't know if Astrid's brother was truly sincere or putting on a performance, especially since he knew that Alex—long estranged from his parents—was especially close to Astrid. Trying a different tactic, Charlie said, "I'm worried Astrid's had some sort of breakdown and she's unable to get help. She's been MIA for *five weeks* now. You'd think your parents would be the least bit concerned."

Alex jerked his head indignantly, his Persol sunglasses reflecting against the setting sun. "I am the last person to answer this question, since I haven't spoken to my father in years."

"But surely you know them well enough to know how they might react?" Charlie pressed on.

"I was always the black sheep of the family, so I suppose I was more prepared when my parents took out the knives. But

Astrid has always been the darling princess. She's been raised her whole life to be absolutely perfect, to never put a wrong foot forward, so it must have really hit her hard when things didn't go so perfectly. Astrid's scandal makes me look like a saint at this point—I can't begin to imagine how they must have reacted, the things they must have said."

"She did tell me that her parents ordered her to go into hiding. But if they adore Astrid as much as I know they do, I don't understand how they could be so coldhearted. I mean, she's done absolutely nothing wrong! None of this was her fault," Charlie tried to reason.

Alex leaned back in his chair and grabbed a fistful of wasabi peas from the little bowl on the table. "The thing you have to understand about my parents is that the only thing that matters to them is their reputation. They care about appearances more than anything else in life. My father has spent his whole life crafting his legacy—being the elder statesman and all that shit, and my mum just cares that she's the queen bee of the establishment crowd. So everything in their world has to be according to their exacting standards. They excommunicated me for defying their wishes and marrying a girl whose skin tone was just one shade too dark for them."

"I still can't believe they disowned you for marrying Salimah. She's a Cambridge-educated pediatrician, for God's sake!" Charlie exclaimed.

"How accomplished she was didn't matter to them one bit. I'll never forget what my father said to me when I told him I was marrying her with or without his blessing. He said, 'If you don't care about your own future, think of the children you will have with that woman. For eleven generations, the blood will never be pure.' And that's the last conversation I ever had with my father."

"Unbelievable!" Charlie shook his head. "Were you surprised that he harbored those feelings?"

"Not really. My parents have always been racist and elitist to the extreme, like so many in their crowd. Peel away the veneer of wealth and sophistication and you'll find extremely provincial, narrow-minded people. The problem is that they all have too much money, and it's come so easily to them that they think they're bloody geniuses and so they are always right."

Charlie laughed as he took a swig of his beer. "I'm lucky, I guess—my father always told me I was an idiot who was wrong about everything."

"By sheer dumb luck, my father was born in the right place at the right moment in time—when the whole region was going through enormous, unprecedented growth. And oh yeah, he also inherited an empire that had already been set up four generations before him. I think he looks down on people like your father—people who are self-made—because at the heart of it he is a deeply insecure individual. He knows he did absolutely nothing to deserve his fortune, and so the only thing he can do is disparage others who have the audacity to *make their own money*. His friends are all the same—they are frightened of the new money that's rolling in, and that's why they cluster in their little enclaves. I'm so glad I got away from all those people."

"If Astrid ever comes back to me, she'll never have to put up with her parents if she doesn't wish to. I want to build a whole new life for us, and I want her to live anywhere in the world she wants to live," Charlie said, his voice thick with emotion.

Alex raised his glass to Charlie. "You know, I always thought it was a pity the two of you didn't get married the first time around. You and Astrid let my parents scare you off too easily then. I swear to you, if I knew where Astrid was, you'd be the first person to know. But my sister is a smart girl. She knows how to disappear, and she knows where everyone's likely to be looking for her. If I were you, I'd be looking in all the unlikeliest places, rather than all her old haunts or cities where her best friends are."

After seeing Alex off, Charlie went back to his suite and found that the butler had already performed the turndown service. The shades were drawn, and the television was set on the channel with New Age music playing softly. He threw off his shoes, unbuttoned his shirt, and sank into the bed. After dialing room service to order a hamburger, he reached into his pocket and took out the letter that Astrid wrote to him from Paris, reading it yet again.

As Charlie stared at the words, the glow coming from the flat-screen TV at the foot of the bed shined through the piece of paper, and Charlie saw for the first time something on the heavy stationery that he'd never noticed before. Near the bottom-right corner was a faint watermark with a distinctive, ornate monogram pattern:

DSA

It suddenly occurred to Charlie that while the envelope had been from the Hotel George V in Paris, the letter itself was written on someone else's expensive custom stationery. Who in the world was DSA? On a lark, Charlie decided to call his friend Janice in Hong Kong, who was one of those people who seemed to know everybody on the planet.

"Charlie, I can't believe it's you. It's been ages!" Janice purred into the phone.

"Yes, it's been much too long. Listen, I'm trying to solve a little mystery here."

"Ooh, I love a good mystery!"

"I have a piece of monogrammed stationery, and I'm trying to figure out who it belongs to. I was wondering if you might be able to help."

"Can you send me a snapshot? I'll circulate it to everyone I know."

"Well, this needs to be kept private, if you don't mind."

"Okay, not everyone then. Just a few key people." Janice laughed.

"I'll take a picture and send it to you right now," Charlie said. He hung up his phone, got out of bed, and threw open the window shades. The setting sun streamed into the room, almost blinding him for a moment as he held the letter against the windowpane. He took a few pictures and sent the sharpest image to Janice.

Just then, the doorbell rang. Charlie went to the door and looked out the peephole. It was room service with his burger. As he opened the door to let the uniformed waiter in with his trolley, his phone began to ring again. He saw that it was Janice calling and rushed to pick it up.

"Charlie? This is your lucky day. I thought I would have to send your picture around, but I recognized that monogram from a mile away. I know those initials well."

"Really? Who is it?"

"There is only one DSA in the whole world that matters, and that's Diego San Antonio."

"Who is Diego San Antonio?"

"He's one of the leading social figures in the Philippines. He's the host with the most in Manila."

Charlie turned to the waiter just as he was lifting the silver dome to reveal a delicious, juicy burger. "Actually, I'm going to need that to go."

CHAPTER FOUR

Rachel and her best friend Peik Lin stood on the veranda, look-ing at the figure of Nick in the distance as he disappeared into a wooded part of the garden.

"He's been like this for the past week. Going off for walks on his own in the afternoons. I think he's saying goodbye to the place, in his own way," Rachel said.

"Is there nothing more that can be done?" Peik Lin asked.

Rachel shook her head sadly. "No, we already agreed to sell yesterday. I know it makes no sense, since we've just come into a huge windfall, but my heart still hurts for Nick. It's like I'm in sync with his every emotion."

"I wish I could find someone I could be in sync with like that," Peik Lin sighed.

"I thought there was some secret new Mr. Perfect you prom-ised to tell me about 'when the time was right'?"

"Yeah, I thought so too. I thought I'd finally met a guy who wasn't intimidated by me, but like all the other losers, he disap-peared with no explanation."

"I'm sorry."

Peik Lin leaned on the veranda railing and squinted into the afternoon sun. "Sometimes I feel like it would be far easier not to tell guys that I went to Stanford, that I run a huge property development company, that I actually love what I do."

"Peik Lin, that's total bullshit and you know it. If a guy can't handle exactly who you are, then he clearly doesn't deserve you!" Rachel scoffed.

"Damn right he doesn't! Now, let's go get smashed. Where do they keep the vodka around here?" Peik Lin asked.

Rachel led Peik Lin back into her bedroom and showed her a small button by the bedside wall. "Now, here's one thing I'm really going to miss about Tyersall Park. You press this button and a bell rings downstairs somewhere. And before you can even count to ten—"

Suddenly there was a soft knock on the door, and a young maid entered the room with a curtsy. "Yes, Mrs. Young?"

"Hi, Jiayi. We'd like some drinks. Can we have two vodka martinis on the rocks?"

"Extra olives, please," Peik Lin added.

Nick walked down the pathway past the lily pond, entering the deepest part of the woods in the northwest section of the property. When he was a boy, this was the area of the estate he never dared to venture into, probably because one of the old Malay servants from ages past had told him this was where all the tree spirits lived, and they should be left undisturbed.

A bird high in one of the trees made a strange, piercing call that Nick had never heard before, and he looked up into the thick foliage, trying to spot what it was. Suddenly a blur of white flickered past his eyes, startling him for a second. Collecting himself, he saw it again, something white and shiny on the other side of a grove of trees. He crept slowly toward the trees, and as the

bushes cleared, he saw the figure of Ah Ling facing a large tem-
busu tree, clutching a few joss sticks. As she prayed and bowed
from the waist repeatedly, the smoke from the joss sticks wafted
around her, and her white blouse would shimmer as it caught
the rays of sunlight filtering through the low-hanging branches.

When Ah Ling was finished with her prayers, she took the
joss sticks and stuck them inside an old Milo can that had been
placed in the hollow of the bark. She turned around and smiled
when she caught sight of Nick.

"I didn't know you came out here to pray. I always thought
you did your prayers in the garden behind the service wing,"
Nick said.

"I go to different places to pray. This is my special tree,
when I really want my prayers to be answered," Ah Ling said in
Cantonese.

"If you don't mind me asking, who do you pray to here?"

"Sometimes to ancestors, sometimes to the Monkey God,
and sometimes to my mother."

It occurred to Nick that Ah Ling had seen her mother fewer
than a dozen times since she had moved to Singapore as a teenager. Suddenly the memory of one day from his childhood came
rushing back. He remembered going into Ah Ling's bedroom
and seeing her stuff a suitcase full of things—McVitie's Diges-
tive Biscuits, Rowntree's sweets, packs of Lux soap, a few cheap
plastic toys—and when he asked her what these were for, Ah
Ling told him they were gifts for her family. She was going back
to China for a month to visit them. Nick had thrown a tantrum,
not wanting her to go.

Decades had passed since that day, but now Nick stood in the
middle of a forest with his nanny overwhelmed with guilt. This
was a woman who had dedicated nearly her entire life to serving

his family, leaving her own parents and siblings behind in China and only seeing them once every few years when she had saved up enough to go back. Ah Ling, Ah Ching the head chef, Jacob the gardener, Ahmad the chauffeur, all these people had served his family for most of their lives. This was their home, and now they were about to lose it too. Now he was letting them all down.

As if reading his mind, Ah Ling came over and put her hand on his face. "Don't look so sad, Nicky. It's not the end of the world."

Suddenly, tears began to spring from his eyes uncontrollably. Ah Ling embraced him, in the way she had so many times when he cried as a child, stroking the back of his head as he wept quietly against her shoulder. Nick hadn't shed a single tear during the entire week of his grandmother's funeral, and now he was letting it all out.

After he had recovered himself, Nick walked quietly next to Ah Ling along the wooded pathway. When they reached the lily pond, they sat on the stone bench at the water's edge, watching a lone egret as it stepped gingerly among the shallow marshes looking for little minnows. Nick asked, "Do you think you'll stay in Singapore?"

"I think I will go back to China, for a year at least. I want to build a house in my old village, and spend a little time with my family. My brothers are getting older, I have so many new grandnephews and grandnieces who I have never met. Now I can finally be the rich old auntie who spoils them."

Nick chuckled at the thought. "I'm so glad Ah Ma provided for you in her will."

"Your Ah Ma was very generous to me, and I will always be grateful to her. For the first few decades I worked here, she frightened me to death. She was not the easiest woman to please, but I think in the last twenty years or so, she came to see me as a friend and not just a servant. Did I ever tell you that a few years ago she invited me to take a room in the big house? She thought I was getting a bit old to be trudging back and forth from the servants' wing to the house. But I turned her down. I wouldn't feel comfortable in one of those grand bedrooms."

Nick smiled, remaining silent.

"You know, Nicky, I really don't think your grandmother wanted this house to go on after she was gone. That's why she prepared things the way she did. She wouldn't have taken care of me and Ah Ching and everyone else like she did. She thought of every detail."

"She may have thought of every detail, but for me, so many questions remain unanswered. I keep beating myself up about how stubborn I was, refusing to come back to make peace with her until the very end. I wasted so much time," Nick lamented.

"We never know how much time any of us have. Your Ah Ma could have gone on living for many more months, or even years, you never know. Don't regret anything. You are lucky you were back in time to say goodbye," Ah Ling said soothingly.

"I know. I just wish I could talk to her again, to understand what she truly wanted," Nick said.

Ah Ling suddenly sat up on the bench. "*Alamak!* I'm getting so absentminded, I almost forgot that I have a few things for you from your Ah Ma. Come, come to my room with me."

Nick followed Ah Ling to her quarters, where she produced an old imitation Samsonite suitcase from the back of her closet. He recognized it as the suitcase she used when she had gone back to China all those decades ago. Ah Ling opened the suitcase on the floor, and Nick saw that it contained stacks and stacks of different-colored fabrics, the kind she used to make the beautiful silk patchwork quilts that hung at the foot of the bed in every guest room. At the bottom of the suitcase was a bundle tied in dark blue satin fabric.

"When your Ah Ma was in the hospital, she asked Astrid to gather a few things from the vault and various hiding places she had. Astrid brought these down to me, to be kept for you. I don't think your Ah Ma wanted any of your aunties getting their hands on these," Ah Ling said, handing Nick the bundle. He undid the knotted satin and found a small rectangular leather box. Inside was a vintage pocket watch on a gold chain signed Patek, Philippe & Cie, a silk coin purse full of gold sovereigns, and a small stack of old letters tied in yellowed ribbon. At the bottom of the box lay a newer, crisper envelope with "Nicky" on the front in his grandmother's elegant handwriting. Nick tore open the letter and began reading it immediately:

Dear Nicky,

I feel that time is running short and I don't know whether I will see you again. There are so many things I had wished to tell you, but never found the chance or the courage. Here are some things I am entrusting to you. They do not belong to me, but to a gentleman named Jirasit Sirisindhu. Please return these things to him on my behalf. He lives in Thailand, and your auntie Cat will know how to find him. I am also entrusting you with this mission because you will want to meet Jirasit in person. When I am no longer here, he will be able to provide you with the resources that you will need. I know I can count on him to be of great help to you.

Love,
Your Ah Ma

"Thank you for safeguarding these things for me!" Nick said, kissing Ah Ling on the cheek as he left her room. He walked across the courtyard to the main house and went up the stairs to his bedroom, where he found Rachel working on her laptop.

"Good walk?" Rachel looked up.

"You'll never believe this, but something rather remarkable just landed in my hands!" Nick waved the letter at her excitedly.

Nick sat on the edge of the bed and quickly read the letter to her.

Rachel's brow furrowed as she listened to the cryptic letter. "I wonder what it all means? Do you know this guy? Jirasit?"

"I've never once heard my grandmother utter his name."

"Let's google him quickly," Rachel said. She typed in the name and it popped up immediately.

"M.C. Jirasit Sirisindhu is a grandson of King Chulalongkorn of Thailand. He is an exceedingly reclusive figure but is said to be one of the wealthiest individuals in the world, with interests in banking, real estate, agriculture, fisheries, and—"

Nick's eyes suddenly lit up. "Oh my God, don't you see? 'He will be able to provide you with the resources you need.' He's one of the richest men in the world—I think this man holds the key in helping us get Tyersall Park!"

"I'm not sure if I would read so much into this letter," Rachel cautioned.

"No, no, you don't know my grandmother like I do. She doesn't do anything without precision. She wants me to go to Thailand and meet this man—it says right here that Auntie Cat in Bangkok will know how to find him. Rachel, this is the plan she had all along!"

"But what about the deal we've made with the Bings?"

"It's only been a day, and we haven't signed any contracts yet.

It's still not too late to rescind the deal, especially if this man can help us! We should catch the next flight to Thailand!"

"Actually, maybe *you* should catch the next flight out, and I should stay here to put the brakes on anything that comes up. We wouldn't want your aunts signing anything until you're back," Rachel suggested.

"You're absolutely right! Honey, you're an angel—I'm not sure what I'd do without you!" Nick said breathlessly, grabbing his travel duffel from the cupboard.

CHAPTER FIVE

CHIANG MAI, THAILAND

After landing in Chiang Mai, the ancient Thai city known as the "rose of the north," Nick was driven by Jeep to an estate nestled in the foothills of Doi Inthanon. Like so many of the great houses hidden in these parts, the walled compound was tucked away up a long, steep road and virtually invisible from the outside. But past the tall, fortresslike gate, Nick found himself in a sybaritic paradise that defied description.

The residence was comprised of eight wood-and-stone pavilions built in the traditional Royal Lanna Thai style around an artificial lake, all interconnected by a series of bridges and walkways. As Nick was led through the lush gardens and onto a wooden walkway that floated on the lake, a thin layer of mist hovered over the still waters, adding to the feeling that he had stepped back in time.

At an open pavilion overlooking the center of a lake, an elderly man nattily dressed in tweed trousers, a maroon cardigan, and a peak cap was sitting at a beautiful wooden table, cleaning the inside of an old Leica camera with a tiny brush. On the table rested three or four other old cameras in various states of repair.

The man looked up as Nick approached and grinned widely.

Nick could see that the hair under his cap was snow-white, and though he must have been in his early nineties, his face still retained its handsome features. He put down the camera and got up with an agility that surprised Nick.

"Nicholas Young, what a pleasure! Did you have a good journey?" the man said in English tinged with the slightest British accent.

"Yes, Your Highness, thank you."

"Please call me Jirasit. I hope I didn't rouse you too early?"

"Not at all—it was great to get an early start, and your plane landed just as the sun was rising."

"I had your aunt Catherine arrange it for you this way. I think the mountains are at their most beautiful right at dawn, and I must confess, I am a very early bird. At my age, I'm up by five and quite useless by midafternoon."

Nick simply smiled, and Jirasit clasped Nick's hands in his own. "I am glad we are meeting. I've heard so much about you over the years!"

"Really?"

"Yes, your grandmother was inordinately proud of you. She talked about you all the time. Come, sit, sit. Do you take tea or coffee?" Jirasit asked as a flurry of servants appeared with trays of refreshments and food.

"Coffee would be great."

Jirasit uttered a few words in Thai as the servants began setting up an elaborate breakfast on the wide stone ledge of the pavilion. "You'll have to excuse the mess, I have been indulging in my favorite pastime," Jirasit said, as he moved his cameras to one side of the table to make room for the coffee service.

"That's quite a collection you have there," Nick said.

"Oh, they're all rather obsolete at this point. I prefer shooting with my digital Canon EOS these days, but I do enjoy cleaning these old cameras. It's very meditative."

"So you were in quite frequent contact with my grandmother, then?" Nick asked.

"Off and on, over the years. You know how old friends are . . . we would skip a year here and there, but we did try to stay in touch." Jirasit paused for a moment, staring at an old Rolleiflex twin lens on the table. "That Su Yi . . . I shall miss her."

Nick took a sip of his coffee. "How did you two become acquainted?"

"We met in Bombay in 1941, when we both worked at the British India Office."

Nick sat forward in his chair, surprised. "Wait a minute, is this the Indian branch of the War Office? My grandmother worked there?"

"Oh yes. She never told you? Your grandmother started out in the code-breaking office, and I was in the cartography department, helping to create a detailed map of Thailand. The cartographers didn't really know Thailand well, especially in these remote northern parts near the border, and we needed accurate maps in the event of an invasion."

"How fascinating. I always pictured her luxuriating away in some maharaja's palace during the Japanese occupation."

"Well, she did that too, but the British, you see, enlisted her to do some . . . sensitive diplomatic work as soon as they realized what she was capable of."

"I had no idea . . ."

"Your grandmother had a certain allure that's hard to put your finger on. She was never one of those typical beauties, but men just fell at her feet. It came in very useful during the war. She was good at influencing those rajahs in certain directions."

Nick reached into his satchel and took out the leather box that Su Yi had entrusted to him, placing it on the table. "Well, the reason I'm here is because my grandmother wanted me to return these to you."

"Ah, my old Dunhill case! I never thought I'd be reunited with it after all these years," Jirasit said like an excited child. "You know, your grandmother was a very stubborn woman. When she insisted on returning to Singapore during the height of the war—complete madness, I tell you—I gave her a few of my most valuable possessions. My father's Patek and these gold sovereigns, and a few other things, I can't remember what. I thought she would need them to bribe her way into Singapore. But see, she hardly needed them after all." Jirasit began winding the pocket watch, and then he held it up to his ear. "Listen? Still ticking perfectly after all these years! I'm going to have to tell my friend Philippe Stern about this!" Jirasit picked up the packet of old envelopes tied in ribbon and studied them for a moment. "What's this?"

"I have no idea. I assumed they were yours, so I didn't open them," Nick said.

Jirasit untied the ribbon and began sifting through the letters. "My goodness! These were my letters to her after the war. She saved every last one of them!" His pale gray eyes clouded over with tears, which he flicked away quickly.

Nick had brought with him a prospectus of his Tyersall Park buyback scheme, and he was about to take it out of his satchel to show Jirasit when the man abruptly stood up and announced, "Come, let us attend to the matter at hand!"

Nick had no idea what he was talking about, but he followed Jirasit as he strolled swiftly toward a pavilion on the other side of the lake, marveling at his pace. "Jirasit, I hope I'll be as agile as you are when I'm your age!"

"Yes, I hope so too. You seem quite slow for your age. Do keep up! I picked up yoga when I lived in India, and I've never stopped my daily practice. Also, it's important to keep your body alkaline, young man. Do you eat chicken?"

"I love chicken."

"Well, stop loving it. Chickens reabsorb their own urine—and so their meat is extremely acidic," the man said as he quickened his pace. When they reached the glass-walled pavilion, Nick noticed two guards flanking the entrance.

"This is my private office," Jirasit explained. They entered the room, which contained nothing but an ancient gold statue of Buddha inset into a niche on one wall and a beautiful black-and-gilt desk facing a window onto the lake. Jirasit went to a door against the back wall, and placed his hand on the security scanning pad. A few seconds later, the deadbolt unlocked automatically and he gestured for Nick to follow him into the room.

Inside, Nick found a space that resembled a walk-in vault with built-in cabinets along every wall. At the corner was an old antique Wells Fargo safe that had been bolted into the floor. Jirasit turned to Nick and said, "Here we are. The combination please?"

"I'm sorry, you want *me* to give you the combination?"

"Of course. This is your grandmother's safe from Singapore."

"Um, I have no idea what it is," Nick said, surprised by this turn of events.

"Well, unless you're good at safe-cracking, you're going to need the combination. Let's see, why don't we call Catherine in

Bangkok and see if she knows what it is?" Jirasit took out his phone and moments later had Catherine on the line. The two of them spoke animatedly in Thai for a few moments, and then Jirasit glanced up at Nick. "Did you bring the earrings?"

"What earrings?"

"Your grandmother's pearl earrings. The combination is on them."

"Oh my God! The earrings! Let me call my wife!" Nick said in astonishment. He quickly called Rachel's cell phone, and moments later she answered in a sleepy voice.

"Honey, sorry to wake you. Yes, I'm in Chiang Mai now. Remember those earrings I gave you? The pearl earrings from my grandmother?"

Rachel crawled out of bed, went over to the dressing table and opened the drawer where she kept her jewelry.

"What am I looking for exactly?" she asked, still half asleep.

"Do you see any numbers carved on the pearls?"

Rachel held a pearl stud up to the window light. "Nothing, Nick. It's totally smooth and luminous."

"Really? Can you look again?"

Rachel closed one eye and squinted at each pearl as closely as she could. "I'm sorry, Nick, I see nothing. Are you sure we're talking about these earrings? They are so tiny, I can't imagine where someone would hide any information, unless it's *inside* the pearl."

Nick thought back to what his Ah Ma told him when she had handed them over. *My father gave these to me when I escaped Singapore before the war, when the Japanese soldiers had finally reached Johor and we knew all was lost. They are very special. Please look after them carefully.* The words took on a whole new significance now. He stared at the safe, wondering what it could possibly hold. Would there be gold bullion bars, stacks of old bonds or some other type of financial documents that would help him secure Tyersall Park? What was in there that was so valuable to his grandmother that she would go to such great lengths to protect it?

"Rachel, I'm sure those are the earrings. Maybe we do need to crack them open. Or maybe the numbers appear if you put them in water? I dunno, try anything," Nick said in frustration.

"Well, before we destroy these lovely pearls, let me try the water thing." Rachel went into the bathroom and turned on the tap to fill the sink. She looked at the earrings again—they were simple pearl studs on gold posts, each with a little gold disk as backing. Before dipping one of the earrings into the water, she decided to pry the backing off the stud. Suddenly she gasped. There, on the underside of the backing were tiny Chinese characters carved into the gold. "Nick, I never thought I'd ever get to say these words, but . . . EUREKA, I'VE FOUND IT! There are Chinese characters carved into the backing of the earrings!"

Rachel quickly deciphered the numbers: "9, 32, 11, 17, 8." Nick turned the dial to the corresponding numbers, his heart pounding as each of the locks seemed to click into place one by one. When he finally turned the lever to open the safe, he held his breath, wondering what he would find inside.

The safe door creaked open, and when Nick peered inside, all he saw were small red leather-bound books, neatly arranged in stacks. He took one of them out and began flipping through its pages. Every page was written in Chinese, and Nick realized he was looking at his grandmother's private diaries, beginning from the time she was a child to her adulthood.

"Why are these here?" Nick was completely mystified.

Jirasit gave Nick a serene smile. "Your grandmother was a very private person, and I think she felt that this was the only place she could leave them for safekeeping, without the risk of anyone seeing them or censoring them after she was gone. She never wanted them kept in Singapore, and she never wanted them to leave this compound. You are the historian, from what I'm told, so she wanted you to have access to them. She told me you would one day come."

"Is this all there is? These diaries?" Nick asked, bending down to peer more closely into the dark safe.

"I believe so. Was there something else you were looking for?"

"I don't know. I guess I had imagined that she would have some other valuable treasures stored away in here," Nick said a little disappointedly.

Jirasit frowned. "Well you should read them, Nicholas. You may find a great many unexpected treasures within those pages. I'll leave you be, and perhaps we can meet up again for lunch at noon?"

Nick nodded, as he took a stack of journals out to the desk. Deciding that the best thing to do was read the journals chronologically, he reached to the bottom of the pile for the oldest journal. As he opened the cover gently, the leather binding cracking after decades of stillness, he began to hear his grandmother's young voice in her handwritten words.

March 1, 1943

It feels like we have been riding for a week, but Keng tells me it has only been three days. Whenever we reach a new outpost I ask him if we are still on the estate and he sighs frustratedly. Yes, we are. Apparently, my mother's family is the largest landowner in West Sumatra, and it would take a full week on horseback to traverse the estate. The highlands are glorious—rugged with a strange wildness to everything. On another trip, it might have even seemed romantic. If I had only known we would be spending so many days riding just to get to my brother's house, I would have brought my own saddle!

March 2, 1943

Finally arrived. They take me upstairs to see Ah Jit, and at first I don't understand what is going on. My brother lies unconscious, his handsome face so swollen and purple I can hardly recognize him. There is a deep, bloody gash on his right jaw that they are trying to keep from being infected. I asked what was going on? I thought the cholera was under control? "We didn't want to tell you till you got here. It's not cholera. He's bleeding internally. He was tortured by Japanese agents. They were trying to get him to give up the locations of some key people. They broke his body, but they couldn't break him."

March 5, 1943

Ah Jit died yesterday. He was awake for a while, and I know he was happy to see me. He tried to talk, but I stopped him. I held him in my arms and kept whispering into his ear, "I know, I know. Don't worry. All is well." But all is not well. My darling brother is gone now and I have no idea what is to be done. This morning I walked outside into the garden and saw that all the rhododendron trees have bloomed overnight. Suddenly they are bursting with flowers, in shades of pink I never knew could exist. Blooms so thick, they brushed against my face as I walked through the garden weeping uncontrollably. Ah Jit knew how much I loved these flowers. He did this for me. I know he did.

Nick stared at the journal, feeling utterly confused. None of this made any sense. His great-uncle Ah Jit was tortured by the Japanese, and his grandmother was there? But wasn't she supposed to be in India during the war? He leafed through a few more pages, and a loose letter fell out. As Nick glanced over the crisp but yellowing letter, a chill ran down his spine. He couldn't believe his eyes.

CHAPTER SIX

THE STAR TREK HOUSE, SINGAPORE

Eleanor paced around the room restlessly. "She's late. Maybe she changed her mind."

"*Aiyah*, Eleanor, don't be so *kan jyeong*. She's not late. It's only two minutes past one. Don't worry, I'm sure she'll turn up," Lorena tried to assure her as she lounged on one of the plush white sofas in Carol's enormous poolside bedroom.

"Traffic was hideous today! My driver had to take two detours just to get here! I don't know what is wrong. It seems like traffic is getting worse and worse these days. What is the whole point of all these ERPs* when everywhere is so damn congested? I'm going to have Ronnie call our local MP and complain!" Nadine tut-tutted.

Daisy went over the plan again like a battalion leader. "When she does come, everyone knows the plan, right? We'll serve the champagne first, and then I'll just speed through a very short Bible verse, something from Proverbs. Then we get interrupted for lunch. I had my cook put *extra* chicken fat into the rice today, so hopefully between the champagne, the chicken rice, and all the *nyonya*

---

* Singapore's impressive Electronic Road Pricing system (ERP), used to manage road congestion, has also led to impressive levels of bitching from citizens.

kuehs, she'll get very full, tipsy, and drowsy. The perfect combination! Then while we're all eating, Nadine, you know what to do."

Nadine gave a conspiring grin. "Yes, yes, I just sent the nanny very specific instructions."

"Ladies, I'm going to say it again. I think this is a very bad idea," Carol warned, grasping her hands nervously.

"No, *lah*! This is serendipity! How lucky are we that my niece Jackie just happened to be visiting from Brisbane this week? We might never have an opportunity like this again!" Eleanor rubbed her hands together excitedly as her niece reentered the bedroom. "Is it okay? They promised me that everything would be state of the art."

"Don't worry, Auntie Elle, everything is all set up and ready to go," Jackie said.

"Jackie, this won't be breaking the Hypocritical code, will it?" Lorena asked delicately.

"You mean the Hippocratic oath? No, not at all. As long as the person doesn't object, there is no issue," Jackie replied.

Nadine flipped through the latest issue of *Tattle* idly. "Hey, are you all going to go to this costume ball being thrown by this Countess Colette? It seems like *everyone* from *everywhere* is coming to town for the big event."

"Who is everyone?" Lorena asked.

"All these socialites from Europe and America, Hollywood celebrities, and the environmentalists. It says here that all the world's top designers are going insane trying to keep up with all the orders for costumes for the ball. Apparently everyone is going to dress up like Prowst."

"Hahaha, I highly doubt everyone's going to dress up like Proust—he was a small, pasty little man. They are dressing up like characters from his books!" Lorena corrected.

"I've never read any of his books. Did he write that *Da Vinci Code* one? I saw the movie and didn't understand a thing!" Nadine said. "Anyway, there's a rumor that some British princess will be the surprise guest of honor! I heard that Yolanda Amanjiwo bought five tables—cost her half a mil."

"That Amanjiwo woman can stand in her shower and tear up hundred-dollar bills all day for all I care, I wouldn't pay a cent to go to any costume ball!" Daisy huffed.

Nadine gave Daisy a pleading look. "But it's for the orangutans. Don't you care about the plight of the cute orangutans?"

"Ey, Nadine, when Ah Meng died, did you cry?" Daisy asked.*

"Er . . . no."

"I didn't either. So why on earth would I want to pay ten thousand dollars just to sit in a room full of *ang mors* eating *ang mor* food to save a bunch of Ah Mengs?" Daisy argued.

"Daisy, you just don't have the heart for animals like I do. Beyoncé and Rihanna, my two Pomeranians, bring me so much joy you have no idea," Nadine said.

Just then, a maid showed Rachel into Carol Tai's bedroom.

"Rachel, you came!" the ladies all said excitedly.

"Of course I came! Nick's told me so many stories about your Thursday Bible study, I've always been curious to attend! Sorry I'm late. I drove myself and got a bit lost trying to find the neighborhood. Google Maps didn't anticipate all the detours."

"*Alamak*, why didn't you have Ahmad drive you? He's so free shaking legs all day at Tyersall Park now that the old lady is gone," Eleanor remarked.

---

*   Ah Meng was an irrepressible orangutan that was for many years in the 1980s the star attraction of the Singapore Zoo.

"Oh, I didn't even think of it!" Rachel said.

"Well, Rachel, come meet my niece Jackie. She's a doctor that lives in Brisbane," Eleanor continued.

"Hello. It's a pleasure!" Rachel said, shaking hands with the pretty thirtysomething woman and sitting down beside her on the chaise lounge. A maid immediately thrust an oversize flute of champagne into her hands. "Ooh, I didn't know you ladies drank during Bible study!" Rachel said in surprise.

"Of course we do! After all, Jesus turned water into wine," Eleanor said. "Rachel, this is very expensive champagne from the *Dato*'s wine cellar. You mustn't waste a drop—drink it all up!"

"Twist my arm," Rachel said merrily, as Carol handed her a Bible.

"Sister Daisy is going to lead us in the Scripture reading today," Carol began, as the ladies quickly flipped their Bibles open to Proverbs.

"Yes, okay, Proverbs 31:10: 'A wife of noble character who can find? She is worth far more than rubies.' What does this mean to you all?" Daisy asked.

"The only thing that is worth more than rubies are good Bolivian emeralds," Lorena remarked.

"Well, you haven't seen my new ruby earrings from Carnet! They are drop-dead, and worth far more than my emeralds," Nadine interjected.

"Nadine, are you still buying jewelry at your age? Don't you have enough at this point?" Daisy chastised.

Nadine gave her a sharp look. "Pardon me, what do you mean by *enough*?"

Just then, an army of maids entered the room, each carrying a lacquer tray containing a bento box filled with Hainanese chicken rice. "*Aiyah*, they're too quick with lunch today. I told my

butler we wouldn't be ready to eat until one thirty at the earliest!"
Carol pretended to complain.

"Well, we mustn't let the food get cold!" Lorena commented.

"Okay!" the ladies said, throwing their Bibles aside and digging in to their individual bento boxes with gusto.

"Wait, that's it?" Rachel figured that Bible study with these ladies probably wasn't going to feature any probing theological discussions, but she was surprised it was over this quickly.

"You're very lucky, Rachel. Auntie Daisy heard you were going to come to Bible study today, so she *personally* had her cook Swee Kee make her famous Hainanese chicken rice," Eleanor explained, as she quickly shoveled a tender, juicy piece of sliced chicken into her mouth.

"Oh wow, thank you, Auntie Daisy. I've become addicted to chicken rice ever since Nick first introduced me to it! I wish we could find authentic chicken rice in New York," Rachel remarked.

Right on cue, Nadine's iPad started buzzing. "*Alamak*, I totally forgot! It's time for my daily good-night call with my grandson in London." She took her iPad out of her large Bottega Veneta Hobo bag and turned on FaceTime. "Joshie, Joshie, is that you?" A moon-faced blond girl appeared on the screen. "Mrs. Shaw, I just got your urgent e-mail. You wanted me to put—"

Nadine quickly interrupted. "Yes, yes, Svetlana, you don't have to mention anything in the e-mail! Just put Joshua on the screen."

"But we're in the middle of his bath now."

"It doesn't matter, put him on, *lah*!" Nadine insisted.

The nanny tilted her phone and a little naked toddler appeared on the screen, sitting in shallow water in the middle of an enormous marble bathtub.

"*Alamak*, what a cutie he is!" the ladies all gushed in unison.

"There's my little Joshie!" Nadine cooed.

"He's not that little. Don't you think he has an *enormous* coo-coo for his age? My boys were never that big," Daisy whispered to Lorena.

"Isn't the father Arab? Arab men are supposed to be hung like camels," Lorena whispered back.

"The father's not Arab. He's a Syrian Jew. And we shouldn't be talking about such things at Bible study!" Carol glared at the women distastefully.

"*Aiyah*, what's the big deal? The Bible is filled with penises! There are so many scriptures about circumcising your boys and all that nonsense!" Daisy said.

"You know, in Australia we don't customarily circumcise boys anymore," Jackie interjected. "It's seen as an outdated practice, and a human rights issue. Boys should be given the right to make a decision about their own foreskins."

Rachel had been enjoying her lunch immensely, but all this foreskin talk was suddenly making the glistening bits of chicken skin on her dish look particularly unappetizing. After the ladies had taken turns passing around the iPad and oohing and aahing over the chubby little toddler, Nadine ended the call as the maids brought in trays filled with sinfully delicious *nyonya kueys*.

Daisy spoke up as she ate a piece of *kuey dadar.** "That grandson of yours is just tooooo cute! I look at him and I want to pinch those fat cheeks!"

"Next to Beyoncé and Rihanna, he is the greatest joy of my life," Nadine said.

---

* A sweet rolled pancake filled with coconut palm sugar that, because of the way the pancake is folded at the ends, just happens to resemble a small uncircumcised penis.

Rachel glanced at Nadine curiously, wondering if she had heard her correctly.

"Really, Nadine, you should be in London enjoying your grandson. He's at the most adorable age right now!" Carol suggested.

"I loved my grandkids when they were at that age. After they were potty trained, but before they started getting potty mouths!" Daisy laughed.

"How about you, Rachel? When are you going to make Eleanor a proud grandmother?" Lorena asked point-blank.

Rachel saw that all eyes in the room were suddenly glued on her. "Nick and I do hope to have children someday."

Lorena cocked her head. "And when might that someday be?"

Rachel noticed that Eleanor was staring at her intently but staying absolutely silent, so she chose her words carefully. "Well, the last few years have been . . . so eventful . . . we're just waiting for the right time."

"Trust me, there's never going to be a right time. You just have to do it! I had three sons in three consecutive years. Got them out of the way in one go, *lah*!" Daisy said breezily.

"It's a lot more challenging to have kids these days than during your time, Auntie Daisy. Especially raising children in New York, you really have to—"

"So have your baby in Singapore. You can have your pick of nannies here—Filipino, Indonesian, Sri Lankan—or even splurge on an eastern European," Lorena chimed in.

"And all of us will gladly help to babysit!" Nadine volunteered.

Rachel was quietly aghast at the thought—Nadine couldn't even babysit her own shopping bags. She smiled at the ladies and said diplomatically, "Thank you for all your advice, aunties. I really will take it to heart and discuss this with my husband."

"Is it Nicky who's stopping you from having a baby?" Daisy inquired.

"Um, no, not exactly . . ." Rachel said awkwardly.

"Then is it you? Are you concerned about being not able to bear a child at your age?" Daisy prodded.

"No, that's not a concern." Rachel took a deep breath, trying not to get annoyed by all this probing.

"*Aiyah*, aunties, stop putting so much pressure on poor Rachel!" Jackie suddenly spoke up. "A woman's decision to have a child is the most important decision she can make."

"Okay *lah*, okay *lah*, we are just so eager for Eleanor to join us in the grandmas' club!" Daisy laughed, breaking the tension in the room.

Rachel shot Jackie a grateful look.

Jackie stood up and said to Rachel, "Here, come with me. Let's get a little fresh air."

Rachel put her tray aside and followed Jackie out of the bedroom. Jackie made a quick turn around the corner and opened the door to what was Carol's private prayer room. "Let's go in here."

Rachel entered and the first thing she saw was a medical examination table in the middle of the room, the kind with raised footrests found in gynecological clinics.

"You know, Rachel, I'm an ob-gyn in Brisbane, and if you have any medical concerns at all about your reproductive system, we can address them right now," Jackie suggested, flipping on a switch. The room was suddenly flooded with harsh white fluorescent light.

Rachel stared at her for a few seconds, too stunned to speak.

Jackie smiled as she handed Rachel a pale green patient gown. "Here, why don't you put this on and get on the table, and I'll perform a quick pelvic exam?"

"Um, I'm quite all right, thanks." Rachel began backing away from her.

Reaching into her pocket, Jackie pulled out a pair of surgical gloves and began to put them on. "This will just take a few minutes. Auntie Elle just wants to know how those ovaries of yours are doing."

"Get away from me!" Rachel cringed as she turned toward the door. She ran into Carol Tai's bedroom and grabbed her purse without a word.

"*Aiyah*, so fast?" Nadine commented.

"Is everything okay?" Carol asked sweetly.

Rachel turned to Eleanor, her face red with fury. "Just when I thought you might be a semi-normal mother-in-law, you go and pull this stunt?"

"What are you talking about?" Eleanor said innocently.

"You had an entire friggin' examination room set up next door! You planned this entire bullshit ambush, didn't you? Just because Nick and I haven't had any babies yet, you think *I have some medical problem*?"

"Well, you can't blame her for thinking that. We all know this isn't Nicky's problem—he's got great genes," Lorena said.

"What is wrong with you people?" Rachel seethed.

Eleanor suddenly stood up and began shouting. "What is wrong? Look at my hands, Rachel. They are empty!" She thrust her open palms out. "Why am I not getting to cradle a baby? It's been more than two years now, five if you count how long you've been sleeping with my son! So where's my grandchild? How much longer are these hands going to be cold and empty?"

"Eleanor, THIS ISN'T ABOUT YOU! Nick and I will have a child when we are good and ready!" Rachel yelled back.

Daisy spoke up in defense of her friend. "Don't be so selfish, Rachel! You and Nicky have had your fun! It's time to do your duty and give Eleanor a grandchild now! How many more years do she and Philip have to enjoy their grandchildren? The next time I see you in Singapore, I want you to be holding a big bouncy baby!"

Rachel was outraged. "Do you think it's that easy? I just snap my fingers and a baby will magically appear?"

"Of course! It's soooo easy to have babies these days!" Nadine exclaimed. "I mean, my Francesca didn't even have to get pregnant herself. She was so scared of getting stretch marks, she hired a pretty girl from Tibet to carry the baby. The day after Joshie was born she was already off to some party in Rio!"

Carol tried to step in. "Ladies, let's not get too worked up. I think we should all say a prayer together—"

"You want a prayer? I'll give you a prayer. Dear Lord, thank you for getting me the fuck out of here. Amen!" Rachel said, storming out of the room.

CHAPTER SEVEN

From Tommy Yip's daily gossip column:

Titas were atwitter last night over what happened in the middle of the spectacularly elegant party at **China Cruz's** divine mansion in Dasmariñas. Apparently, while **Chris-Emmanuelle Yam** (clad in a curvy Chloé confection) was belting out the Captain and Tennille's "Love Will Keep Us Together" accompanied by a full orchestra, a tremendous crashing noise sent the couture-clad guests rushing out of the ballroom to the grand foyer. There they found debonair **Diego San Antonio** wrestling on the marble floor with an intruder.

"It was this Chinese man, rather handsome, but obviously quite deranged. He had Diego by the collar and he kept shouting, 'Tell me where she is!'" social dynamo **Doris Hoh** (enchanting in an emerald Elie Saab) breathlessly told me. "It was surreal. Here were two men rolling around on the floor, with purple glass everywhere and a huge roasted pig right next to them!" Apparently the fight began upstairs, where Diego first encountered the intruder in China's library. A tussle began and they ended up rolling down the dramatic curving *Gone with the Wind*–style double staircase, toppling over the buffet table where a huge *lechon** was just about to be carved, and smashing into a **Ramon Orlina** glass sculpture.

"That sculpture was of my breasts. It was a beautiful masterpiece that got destroyed!" China (sheathed in a show-stopping strapless Saint Laurent) lamented. "What a waste! I was so looking forward to the *lechon*. I heard it was a special pig that had only eaten truffles its entire life and was flown in from Spain," **Josie Natori** (draped in a dress of her own design, of course) said with a sigh. Thankfully, before the intruder could do much damage to Diego's fabulous Brioni blazer, **Brunomars**—China's 250-pound Tibetan mastiff—leapt onto the intruder and according to onlookers "bit him in the ass."

But the intrepid journalist **Karen Davila** (astonishingly alluring in Armani) quashed that story. "Tommy, do your fact-checking, please! Brunomars *did not* bite him in the ass! He is still a puppy, and he leapt onto the men on the floor because he was trying to get a taste of the *lechon*! He bit the *lechon* on the ass!" Whoever's ass it was, Brunomars saved the day, because the intruder suddenly calmed down when he saw all the guests clustered around like they were watching **Manny Pacquiao** in the boxing ring. (Manny was actually at the party too, but he was in the basement having an intense chess match with China's son.) He ran out the front door without another word, jumped into a waiting black Toyota Alphard, and sped off before any of China's guards could stop him.

. . .

---

* A traditional roast pig and one of the hallmarks of Filipino cuisine.

Charlie leaned against the bathroom sink in his suite at the Raffles Makati, holding a towel full of ice to his face to soothe the swelling. How in the world had he let things devolve to this point? He had snuck unnoticed into China Cruz's party, and managed to get Diego's attention when the singing began. Diego had suggested that they go upstairs to the library to talk things over, but things became heated when Diego had refused to reveal Astrid's whereabouts.

"I can assure you, Mr. Wu, that you can search every corner of Manila and all seven thousand islands of the Philippines, but you'll never find her. If she wanted you to know where she was, she would have told you," Diego had said rather nonchalantly.

"You don't understand! If she knew what was really happening, she'd come out of hiding. The situation has changed, and there's some vitally important information she needs to know!" he had pleaded.

"Well, who put her in this situation in the first place? As far as I'm concerned, everything bad that's happened to Astrid in the past few months has had something to do with your involvement in her life. The leaked paparazzi photos. The leaked video. Your ex-wife. I'm sorry, but my only duty here is to protect Astrid *from you*."

And that's when things got out of control. He knew he shouldn't have lunged at Diego, but some visceral force just overtook his body. And now he had caused yet another scandal, this time among the most elite circles of Manila high society. And these people were sure to talk. The news would be all over town, all over Asia, and into Astrid's ears in no time. And this might make her go even deeper into hiding. Goddamnit, he had really screwed things up again.

Charlie dumped the ice from his towel into the sink and

splashed some cold water on his face. Turning off the running faucet, he suddenly heard a soft knock on the door. He walked out of the bathroom and peered through the peephole. He saw a petite Filipino girl in a gold lamé cocktail dress standing in the hallway.

"Who is it?"

"My name is Angel. I have a message for you."

Charlie opened the door and stared at the girl. She looked to be in her early twenties, with shoulder-length hair and a friendly, open face. "Sir Charlie, I have some instructions for you from my boss. Go to the ITI Private Terminal on Andrews Avenue in Pasay City tomorrow morning and take the seven-thirty flight. Your name will be on the list."

"Wait a minute, how do you know me?"

"I was at China's party tonight. I recognized you immediately."

"Who's your boss? How does he know I was staying here?"

"My boss knows everything," Angel said with an enigmatic smile, before turning to leave.

The next morning, Charlie followed the instructions that had been provided by the mysterious girl and went to the private terminal in Pasay City, where he discovered in the hospitality lounge that this was a charter plane bound for different resorts on the Philippines' southwest coast. He boarded the twin-propeller plane, which was filled with tourists eager to get their beach vacations started. The plane took off and flew low over the coast, landing forty-five minutes later at a small desolate airstrip on the edge of the sea.

It was gray and raining when Charlie got off the plane. All the passengers were guided onto a colorfully painted bus, and they were driven down a muddy track to a series of open-air wooden huts. EL NIDO AIRPORT, a charming painted wooden sign announced. A row of Filipino women stood in the rain at the edge of the hut, singing a welcome song. Charlie got off the bus and was about to follow the tourists into the hut when an athletic young Filipino dressed in a white polo tee and crisp navy cargo pants approached him, holding a large white golf umbrella.

"Sir Charlie? My name is Marco. If you'll come with me please," the man said in an American accent. Charlie followed the man down a pathway to a private dock, where an elegant Riva speedboat awaited. They hopped into the boat, and Marco turned on the engine.

"It's been a wet morning. There's a raincoat under that seat for you," Marco said, as he expertly turned the boat around and sped off onto the open sea.

"I'm fine, I enjoy the rain. Where are we going?" Charlie yelled over the roar of the wind and the splashing waves.

"We're heading twenty-five nautical miles southwest."

"How did you recognize me?"

"Oh, my boss showed me your picture. You're easy to spot in a crowd of American tourists."

"Sounds like you spent some time in America yourself," Charlie said.

"I went to UC Santa Cruz."

"I don't suppose you'll tell me who your boss is?"

"You'll find out soon enough," Marco said with a little nod.

After about thirty minutes, the gray clouds gave way to open sky and puffy white clouds, turning the color of the ocean into a deep sapphire. As the speedboat continued to zoom along the Sulu Sea, Charlie stared out to the horizon as fantastical rock

formations rose up from the water like apparitions. Soon they
were surrounded by what seemed like hundreds of tiny islands
floating on the blindingly azure waters. Each island resembled
a monolithic rock carved in some otherworldly shape, bursting
with lush tropical vegetation and sugary white beaches.

"Welcome to Palawan," Marco announced.

Charlie took in the mystical landscape in awe. "I feel like
I'm dreaming. These islands look like they don't belong on this
earth—they look like they rose out of Atlantis."

"They are more than fourteen million years old," Marco said,
as they sped past a towering rock face that gleamed in the late-
morning sun. "It's all part of a marine reserve park."

"Are most of them deserted?" Charlie asked as they passed an
island with a particularly pristine crescent-shaped beach.

"Some, but not all. That one we just passed has a great little
beach bar that only opens after sunset. They make the best mar-
garitas," Marco said with a big grin.

The Riva sped past a few other small islands before coming to
one of the larger ones. "Did you bring any swimming trunks?"
Marco asked.

Charlie shook his head. "I had no idea where I would be
going."

"There's a pair in that cabinet under your seat that should fit
you. You're going to need them."

As they rounded the other side of the island, Charlie hastily threw on the pair of blue-and-white-striped Parke & Ronen
swimming trunks that happened to fit him perfectly. Marco
anchored the boat by a rocky cove and handed Charlie a mask
and snorkel. "The tide is a bit high right now, so we're going to
be underwater just for a little while. You're okay with a bit of
ocean swimming?"

Charlie nodded. "Where are we going? Or let me guess, I'll find out soon enough."

Marco flashed his pearly whites again. "This is the only way you're gonna meet the boss." He stripped off his clothes to reveal a red Speedo underneath and dove into the water. Charlie dove in after him, and as they floated together by the side of the speedboat, Marco said, "These rocks are really treacherous whenever the waves crash onto them. Once you dive underwater, you'll see a cave opening under the rocks. We're going to swim through the opening, and you'll only need to hold your breath for fifteen, twenty seconds max."

"We're going now?"

"Wait for my signal. We'll go after this next big wave has passed. Otherwise we get smashed against the rocks. Understand?"

Charlie nodded, putting on his mask and snorkel.

"Okay, now!" Marco dove under the water and Charlie followed. They swam along the side of the jagged cliffs and suddenly the rocks opened up to reveal a large cave entrance. Marco swam freestyle without a mask, guiding Charlie along as they swam through the underwater passage.

Within a few moments, they emerged to the surface again. Charlie caught his breath and when he ripped his mask off, what he saw almost took his breath away again. He was in the middle of a calm lagoon completely encircled by towering limestone cliffs. The only entrance to this secret place was through the underwater cavern. The shallow, crystal-clear turquoise waters teemed with colorful fish, coral rock, and sea anemones, and along one side of the lagoon was the perfect hidden beach of sparkling white sand shaded by overhanging branches of palm trees.

Charlie was awestruck by the unbelievable beauty surrounding him, and he floated in silence for a few moments, looking around like a newborn child who had just entered a completely different world. Marco caught his eye and said with a nod, "Over there. My boss."

Charlie turned toward the hidden beach and there, emerging from behind a cluster of palm trees, stood Astrid.

CHAPTER EIGHT

Before Rachel was even fully awake, she could smell the coffee. The aroma of the Homacho Waeno beans she loved so much roasted, ground, and poured into a French press with boiling water. But wait a minute—she was still in Singapore, and the one thing that wasn't absolute perfection at Tyersall Park was the coffee. Rachel opened her eyes and saw her usual breakfast tray placed on the ottoman next to the tartan-covered armchair, the beautiful silver curves of the Mappin & Webb teapot glinting against the morning light, and gorgeous Nick sitting in the armchair smiling at her.

"Nick! What are you doing here?" Rachel sat up with a start.

"Um, last time I checked this was our bedroom." Nick laughed as he got up and gave her a kiss.

"But when did you get back from Thailand?"

"An hour ago on Prince Jirasit's plane. Guess what type of coffee they had on board?"

"Oh my God—I think I smelled it in my dreams!" Rachel exclaimed as Nick handed her a cup and sat cross-legged on the bed next to her.

"Mmmmm!" Rachel sighed in contentment after taking her first sip.

"I love seeing you so satisfied." Nick beamed.

"I thought you were going to stay in Chiang Mai until the end of the week?"

"You know, I went to Chiang Mai expecting to meet a guy who would lend me a few billion dollars. But what I discovered there were treasures far beyond my imagination, things you can't place a monetary value on. I was reading Ah Ma's diaries, and what I found in them was so important that it couldn't wait another day. I needed to share them with you."

Rachel sat up against her pillows. She hadn't seen Nick this excited about anything in a long time. "What did you find?"

"There's so much to tell you, I don't even know where to begin. I think the first revelation was that Prince Jirasit was my grandmother's first love. They met in India, where she had escaped to just before the Japanese invaded Singapore during World War II. She was twenty-two, and they had a passionate wartime affair and traveled through India together."

"That's not too surprising. I mean, she did entrust him with her most private journals," Rachel commented.

"Yes, but here's a surprise: At the height of the Japanese occupation of Singapore, my grandmother actually managed to sneak back onto the island with Jirasit's help. It was pure madness, because the Japanese were on a torturous rampage, but she did it anyway. And when she was reunited with her father, she found out he had arranged for her to be married to a man she had never even met."

Rachel nodded, recalling a story Su Yi had told her. "When we had tea five years ago, your Ah Ma told me that her father had specially chosen James for her, and that she was grateful for his actions."

"Well, she was actually dragged kicking and screaming to

the altar by her father, and for the first few years, she resented my grandfather and treated him abominably. After the war, she reunited with Jirasit in Bangkok and although both of them were married to other people by this point, they couldn't resist resuming their relationship."

Rachel's eyes widened. "Really?"

"Yes, but that's not even the real shocker. She found that she was pregnant in the midst of her affair."

"Noooo!" Rachel gasped, almost spilling her coffee. "Who's the baby?"

"My aunt Catherine."

"Oh my God, it all makes sense now. That's how Auntie Cat knows Prince Jirasit, and that's why she was left the estate in Chiang Mai! Are you the only one besides her who knows?"

Nick nodded. "I actually flew back to Bangkok last night and had a very interesting conversation with her. We sat in her garden overlooking the Chao Phraya River and she told me the whole story. My grandmother was in a terrible bind, of course, when she found out she was pregnant. Jirasit couldn't leave his wife—he was a prince and too bound to all the family politics, and they also had two young children—so my grandmother was faced with a choice: She could either divorce my grandfather and live as a single woman alone with an illegitimate child, cast out by society, or she could tell him the truth and beg him to take her back."

"I can't even imagine how hard it must have been for her in those days, especially for a woman of her background," Rachel mused, suddenly feeling sorry for Su Yi.

"Well, I always knew my grandfather was a saint, but I didn't realize quite how much. Not only did he take Ah Ma back, he apparently never once gave her any grief over the affair. He knew going in to this marriage that she wasn't in love with him, but he was determined to win her over. And that he did. Being the good Christian man that he was, he forgave her completely and he treated Auntie Cat exactly as he did his other children. In fact, I always thought she was his favorite."

"So you think your grandmother grew to love him then?" Rachel asked.

"According to Auntie Cat, my grandmother fell in love with him—truly, deeply—when she saw the kind of man he really was. You know, before I left her last night, Auntie Cat told me something else she's never told anyone—what happened the day that Ah Ma died. She was the only one in the bedroom with her when she passed." Nick's voice became a little choked up as he recounted his aunt's words:

When I first got to Singapore, your grandmother told me that the spirits had been visiting her. She said that her older brother, Ah Jit, had come, her father had been in the room. Of course, I thought that all the morphine she was on was giving her hallucinations. Then on the afternoon she died, I was sitting at her bedside when her breathing started becoming more and more labored. I watched the monitors, but everything seemed fine and I didn't want to raise the alarm just yet. Then suddenly Mummy opened her eyes and gripped my hand. "Be a good girl, give up your chair for him," she said. "Who?" I asked, and then I saw this look on her face, this look of pure love. "James!" she said in this joyous tone, and that was her last breath. I swear to you, Nicky, I felt him. I could feel my father's presence in the room, sitting on that chair, and I could feel them leave together.

Rachel sat on the edge of her bed, blinking away the tears. "Wow. I'm getting chills. It's starting to make sense now . . . why your grandmother was so opposed to our marrying."

"She felt that her father had been right to choose my grandfather for her, and she should have obeyed his wishes all along. *That's* why she was so adamant that I obey her!" Nick said.

Rachel nodded slowly. "Yes, and think about how she found out that my mother had an affair with a man out of wedlock, and that I came from that relationship. It must have brought back all her own fears and her guilt over her affair."

Nick sighed. "It was so misguided, but she thought she was protecting me. Let me show you something. It fell out of one of her diaries." Nick took out a small folded letter and handed it to Rachel. Embossed in red below an ornate coat of arms were the words:

WINDSOR CASTLE

My Dear Su Yi,

I cannot begin to express my debt of gratitude for all you and your brother Alexander did during the darkest days of the war. Allowing Tyersall Park to be a safe haven for some of our most essential British and Australian officers played no small role in saving countless lives. Your acts of heroism, too many to recount here, will never be forgotten.

Sincerely,
George R.I.

"George R.I. . . ." Rachel looked at Nick incredulously.

"Yep, Queen Elizabeth's father. He was the king during the war. Rachel, you won't believe some of the stories in my grandmother's diaries. You know, growing up I was told so many stories of how my grandfather was a war hero, how he saved countless lives as a surgeon. But it turns out my grandmother and her brother were also instrumental in saving so many lives. Right as the occupation was beginning, Alexander was in Indonesia officially to oversee my great-grandfather's business interests, but secretly he was helping get important people out of the country. He helped hide some of Singapore's most crucial anti-Japanese activists—people like Tan Kah Kee and Ng Aik Huan—in Sumatra. In the end, he was tortured to death by a Japanese agent trying to find out his secrets."

"Oh no!" Rachel gasped, putting her hands over her mouth.

"Yes, but as it turns out my grandmother had secretly returned to Singapore at the height of the Japanese occupation. And she had made a daring trip to see Alexander in Indonesia right before he died. She absolutely adored him, and this tragedy is what galvanized her to continue his fight. Tyersall Park became a sort of Underground Railroad for all the operatives passing from Malaysia through Singapore, trying to get to safety in Indonesia and Australia. It became a place for secret high-level meetings and a safe house for some of the key people who were being hunted down by the Japanese."

"How amazing! I would have thought that this house would be too conspicuous a place," Rachel remarked.

"Well, it would have been, but the leader of the occupying Japanese forces, Count Hisaichi Terauchi, commandeered Tyersall Park and took over the main house. So my grandmother and all the servants were made to live in the back wing, and that's how she managed to hide so many people right under the nose of the general. She disguised them as part of the staff—because there were so many of them everywhere, the Japanese troops never noticed. And then she managed to get them in and out through the secret passage from the conservatory to the Botanic Gardens."

"The one you used to sneak into the house!" Rachel exclaimed.

Nick held the letter up to Rachel. "This is not just about me anymore and losing my childhood home or my connection to the past. It's much bigger than that. This house should be a historic landmark, a heritage site for *all* Singaporeans. It's far too important to be altered in any way, and I believe conservationists would argue it urgently needs to be preserved."

"Does this mean you can block the sale to the Bings?"

"That's what I'm trying to figure out. Knowing Jack Bing, I'm sure he'll put up a fight."

"And so will your aunties. They're going to want their money from the sale. What would happen if you deprived them of what they see as their rightful inheritance?"

"What if there was another way where no one had to be deprived? I've been thinking it over for the past few days, and I think I have a plan that can save this historical landmark *and* transform it into something viable for the future."

"Really?"

"Yeah, but we're going to need people with really deep pockets to believe in us."

Rachel's mind began to race. "I think I may know just the people we need to talk to."

CHAPTER NINE

Charlie and Astrid stood on the beach of the lagoon, locked in an embrace. "I'm never going to let you go again!" Charlie sighed happily, as Astrid simply smiled up at him. They sat down on the sand, dipping their toes into the gently lapping waters, staring out at the incredible view of the towering rocks encircling this hidden place, holding hands and not saying anything.

Astrid spoke first. "I didn't mean to worry you. I hadn't realized quite how concerned you would be until I heard about the fight at China's from Diego. How's your jaw? It looks a little purple."

"It's fine," Charlie said, rubbing his jaw absentmindedly. "I haven't even thought about it once, to be honest. How could you not know I was worried? I mean, you've been missing for close to six weeks!"

"I haven't been missing. I've been on FaceTime with Cassian every other day and my family knows I'm fine. But I guess my mother never mentioned anything to you, did she?"

"No, she didn't! The last time I spoke to her over the phone, she said she hadn't heard from you and she didn't much care to. And then she banged down the phone," Charlie huffed.

"Figures." Astrid smiled, shaking her head. "I've been fine,

Charlie. More than fine, actually. I needed to take some time out for myself. You know, being here, I realized I haven't ever done that. Any trip I've ever taken has involved family, or it's been a work trip, wedding, or some other social obligation. I've never actually gone anywhere alone just for *myself*."

"I understand, I knew you needed the time alone. But I also was scared that your mind was spiraling out of control, not knowing all that's been happening back home."

"I haven't wanted to know, Charlie. And I'm not sure I even want to know now. That's the whole point. I needed to get to someplace where I could really escape and unplug from everything just so I could make sense of what was going on in my own head."

Charlie gazed at the calm waters, bluing in intensity as the late-morning sun continued to rise. "How did you ever find this place?"

"I've owned a little island here for many years. Not this one, mind you, this is Matinloc, and it belongs to the state. But I have a little spit of land not too far away. Great-aunt Matilda Leong left it to me, but in secret. You know she was a bit of an eccentric . . . she was a conspiracy theorist and she really thought the world was going to be wiped out in a nuclear war one day. So she bought a little island in Palawan and built a house. 'The ultimate safe haven,' she called it, and she wanted me to have this as a refuge of last resort. I'd never actually visited until now, and I can't believe I've waited this long."

"It's paradise here. Any minute, I expect to see a naked Brooke Shields coming out of the water!"

"You wish!"

"Actually, I have an even better vision right in front of me," Charlie said, admiring the hints of Astrid's beautiful tan body showing through her gauzy white cover-up. As if reading his mind, Astrid stood up. "Have you ever swum naked in a hidden lagoon before?" she asked, as she removed the linen cover-up.

"Um, won't Marco be back soon?" Charlie asked, a little alarmed.

"Marco's not coming back for a couple of hours," Astrid said as she slipped off her white string bikini and dove into the lagoon. Charlie reflexively looked around for a moment to make sure they were alone, took off his swimming trunks, and dove in after her.

They glided through the crystal-clear water for a while, peering at all the colorful fish darting about the coral reef, the sea anemones waving their fingers Zen-like in the current, the giant clams embedded in the sand that would open for a split second to suck in water before shutting again forcefully. They floated on their backs in the middle of the lagoon, staring up at the passing clouds, and then Charlie took Astrid in his arms, lifted her out of the water, and made love to her on the smooth glistening sand, their moans of ecstasy echoing in the lagoon as they became one with nature, with the sea and sky.

Afterward, Charlie lay on his back against the pillowy sand. He was beginning to doze off in the sun, slightly hypnotized by the palm fronds undulating in the breeze over him. Suddenly the sound of chattering voices began to fill the air.

"What's that?" Charlie asked lazily.

"Tourists, probably," Astrid replied.

"Tourists? What?" Charlie bolted up and saw a gaggle of people in bright yellow T-shirts entering the lagoon through the cave, which was only partially submerged now that the tide had gone down.

"Fuck! Where are my swim trunks?" Charlie scrambled

around, trying to find them. "You didn't tell me there could be tourists."

"Of course—this is one of the most popular attractions in Palawan!" Astrid giggled at the sight of Charlie rushing around naked on the beach, trying to find his trunks.

"Oy, mate! You looking for these?" an Aussie surfer shouted from the other side of the lagoon, holding up Charlie's blue-and-white trunks.

"Yes, thanks!" Astrid shouted back. She turned to Charlie, who was hiding behind a palm tree, still laughing. "Oh, come on out! You have nothing to be ashamed of!"

. . .

"You really *have* changed. I don't know if the Astrid I knew would ever want to make love spontaneously in a lagoon or walk around naked on a beach in front of a bunch of Australian tourists," Charlie said as they sat having lunch on the terrace of Astrid's spectacular white villa perched on the hilltop of her private island.

"You know, it might sound cliché, but getting away from it all has been a transformative experience for me. I've realized that so many of my fears aren't really my own. They're the fears of my mother, my father, my grandparents. I've just unconsciously internalized them, and I've let these fears affect every decision I make. So a few people see me naked on a secluded beach in one of the remotest places on earth. Who cares? I'm proud of my body, I have nothing to hide. But of course, some voice in my head would automatically say, 'Astrid, put some clothes on. It's not proper. You're a Leong, and you're going to disgrace the family.' And I realize that most of the time it's my mother's disapproving voice I hear."

"Your mother has always driven you half crazy," Charlie said as he piled another big helping of *guinataang sugpo* over his garlic rice.*

"I know, and it's not all her fault. She said some terrible things to me, but I've already forgiven her. She's damaged herself—look, this was a woman that was born during World War II, in the midst of the most unimaginable horrors occurring in Singapore. How could she not have internalized all the experiences of my grandparents? My grandfather was imprisoned by the Japanese and barely escaped the firing squad, my grandmother was covertly helping to organize resistance efforts while being a new mother and trying not to get killed herself."

Charlie nodded. "My mother's entire childhood was spent at the Endau concentration camp in Malaysia. Her family was forced to grow all their own food, and they almost starved to death. I'm sure that's why my mother is the way she is now. She makes her cook save money by buying the discounted, three-day-old bread from the supermarket, but she'll spend $30,000 on plastic surgery for her pet fish. It's completely irrational."

Astrid looked out onto the view of the peaceful cove below the terrace. "Scientists talk about how we inherit health issues from our parents through our genes, but we also inherit this entire lineage of fear and pain—generations of it. I can acknowledge whenever my mother is reacting out of this fear, but the most powerful thing I've realized is that *I'm not responsible for her pain*. I won't make her fears mine any longer and I don't want to pass them on to my son!"

Charlie stared at Astrid, pondering her words. "I like everything you're saying, but I gotta ask—*who are you?* It's like you're speaking in a whole new language."

---

* Fresh caught jumbo prawns in coconut milk, a Palawan delicacy.

Astrid smiled enigmatically. "I have to confess, I've been here for the past five weeks but I haven't been here alone. When I left Singapore, I went to Paris first and saw my friend Grégoire. He told me about a friend of his who was living in Palawan. That's really why I came here. I had no intention of being anywhere near Asia—I was on my way to Morocco, to a place I know in the Atlas Mountains. But Grégoire really encouraged me to see his friend."

"Who is this person?"

"Her name is Simone-Christine de Ayala."

"Is she related to Pedro Paulo and Evangeline in Hong Kong?"

"Turns out they are cousins—it's a big family. Anyway, I'm not quite sure how to describe her. Some people call her an energy worker or a healer. To me she's just a very wise soul, and she has a beautiful home on a neighboring island. We've met up almost every day since I got here and had these amazing talks. She's led me through these guided meditations that have led to some incredible breakthroughs."

"Like what?" Charlie asked, suddenly getting worried that Astrid was under the influence of some quack guru.

"Well, the biggest one is realizing that I've lived my entire life trying to anticipate the fears of my parents—trying to be that perfect daughter at all costs, never putting a wrong foot forward, never speaking to the press. And look where that's gotten me? By trying to hide behind that façade of perfection, by trying to always keep my personal life and my relationships so goddamn private, I've actually done far more damage than if I'd just lived my life the way I wanted to in the first place!"

Charlie nodded, a little relieved. "I couldn't agree more, actually. To me, it's always seemed like you've lived your whole life in the shadows. You're so much smarter and more talented than anyone's ever given you credit for, and I've always thought you were in the perfect position to be doing so much more."

"Do you know how many things I've wanted to do that have been shot down by my parents? When I graduated from college and got that great job offer from Yves Saint Laurent in Paris, they told me to come home. Then they wouldn't let me start my own fashion business—it was just too common for them. Then when I wanted to work for certain very *unfashionable* causes, like the horrific problem of human trafficking and child prostitution in Southeast Asia, they wouldn't hear of it. The only acceptable thing for Astrid Leong to do is serve on the board of certain well-vetted institutions, and even those had to be on one of the super-private committees, nothing that would put me in the public eye. It's like my family has lived for generations so frightened of their own wealth, of the fact that someone might accuse us of being rich, of being vulgar and showy. To me, it's our wealth that puts us in the fortunate position of being able to do an enormous amount of good in the world, not hide from the world!"

Charlie clapped his hands excitedly. "So come back, Astrid. Come back with me and we can do this together. I know you were in a completely different head space when you wrote me that letter, so I'm going to forget you ever wrote it. I want us to be together. I want you to be my wife, to live your life and be exactly the woman you want to be."

Astrid looked away for a moment, staring up at the beautiful white villa gleaming in the sun. "It's not that simple . . . I don't know if I'm ready to return yet. I think I need to repair myself for a while longer before I can face the world I left behind."

"Astrid! The world you left behind has changed so much.

Can I please tell you what's been happening? I think it will help," Charlie pleaded.

Astrid took a deep breath. "Okay, tell me what you want to tell me."

"Well first of all, Isabel is out of her coma, and it looks like she's on her way to a great recovery. She's suffered quite a bit of memory loss, and she has no clue what happened to her that night, but she's going to be okay."

"Thank God," Astrid muttered, closing her eyes.

"The other big thing that you need to know is that Michael has signed your divorce papers with no contest."

"What?" Astrid sat up in her chair, completely shocked. "How did this happen?"

"Well, it's quite a tangled story, but let's start with the leaked video. It turns out that Isabel was the one who had the video first, not Michael. She had us under surveillance all along. The paparazzi tailing us in India, the video of us in my bedroom, that was all her doing."

Astrid shook her head in disbelief. "How did she do all this?"

Charlie smiled. "You're never going to believe it. You know that raggy old stuffed giraffe that Delphine has?"

"Yes! The one she can't sleep without every night?"

"It was a gift from Isabel, and it turns out there was a very sophisticated camera and recording device implanted inside."

"Oh my God . . ."

"Delphine would drag the damn stuffed animal with her between both houses, so Isabel always knew my every move. And she got the footage of us completely by accident, because Delphine had slept in my room the night before you came over and left the giraffe on the chest at the foot of my bed."

"No wonder the footage was shot from such a weird angle!"

Astrid said with a little laugh. "But how in the world did she get this sophisticated nanny cam made?"

"Michael helped her. They were in cahoots all along. It came out after Isabel's suicide attempt, and the police got involved investigating the source of the video clip on her phone."

Astrid shook her head sadly. "So they ganged up . . . the two bitter ex-spouses."

"Yep. But their little partnership is also the silver lining in all this. I flew to Singapore a few weeks ago and had a nice long chat with Michael. I told him he could withdraw the lawsuit, sign the divorce papers, and go on enjoying his life as a billionaire bachelor, or he could do the following: First, he could go to jail for aiding and abetting Isabel in her illegal surveillance. Second, he could go to jail for extortion, since he stupidly sent you the video with that text message demanding $5 billion. And third, he could go to jail for being linked to the malicious leak of the video. By the time the Singapore court system is done with all the charges that I would bring against him, he could very well spend the rest of his life in Changi Prison, or worse, he could be extradited to Hong Kong and then sent to a prison camp in Northeast China, near the Russian border, where guys that look as pretty as he does end up having a very *sore* time."

Astrid leaned back into her chair, taking it all in.

Charlie grinned. "Michael has promised to never be of any trouble to you or Cassian. Ever again. So the minute you put your name on those divorce papers, you'll be a free woman."

"A free woman," Astrid said the words softly to herself. "Charlie, I love you, and I'm so grateful for everything you've done for me over the past few weeks. If I'm being true to myself—to the new me—and if I'm being completely honest with you, I just don't know if I really want to get married again right now. I'm

not sure I'm ready to return to Singapore yet. I've been explor-
ing these islands quite a bit, getting to know the locals, and I am
really connecting to this place. I think there's a great deal I could
do right here to help the indigenous people. I could really use
more time here, and what I really want is to send for Cassian.
I've seen how happy the kids are in these islands . . . their lives
are so integrated with nature, they're so free and adventurous.
They run along the narrow little prows of wooden boats like
sailors, they climb the trees like acrobats and knock down all
the ripe coconuts. They laugh and they laugh. It reminds me a
little of the kind of childhood I had at Tyersall Park. Cassian's
whole life these days is about homework and exams and Chinese
lessons and tennis lessons and piano competitions, and then
when he's not doing that he's just glued to his computer screen
playing those violent games. I can't remember the last time I saw
him laugh. If I'm going to live a new life of true freedom, I want
the same freedom for him too."

Charlie peered deep into Astrid's eyes. "Listen, I want you to
have exactly the kind of life you've dreamed about, for yourself
and for Cassian. My only question to you is: In this new life, is
there a place for me?"

Astrid looked at Charlie, not sure what to say.

CHAPTER TEN

Kitty stood in the middle of the space, staring at the exquisite alchemy of furnishings, *objets*, nature, and light. There was an elegant purity to the way everything was arranged, and the room emanated a calm and quietly invigorating energy. "This is what I want! This is how I want Tyersall Park to be," she told Oliver. They were in the midst of wandering through Kanaal, a nineteenth-century complex of industrial spaces next to a former grain silo on the Albert Canal that had been breathtakingly transformed into the atelier and private showroom of Axel Vervoordt, one of the world's most esteemed interior designers.

"We're already halfway there, Kitty. Tyersall Park has amazing bones, and it's got that perfect patina of age that no amount of money can buy. We wouldn't have to import any new floors or create new walls that look like they came from the seventeenth century. But look how this bronze ax from the Neolithic period changes the whole vibe of the room. And these simple ferns wilting beautifully on this refectory table. It's all about *placement*, and Axel is the master of all this."

"I want to meet him right now!" Kitty said.

"Don't worry, he'll be here very soon. Didn't you hear what

his assistant said? *He's having lunch with Queen Mathilde of Belgium right now*," Oliver whispered.

"Oh, I couldn't understand his accent. I thought he said he was in the middle of reading *Matilda*. I was thinking, why is this man reading a children's book when I've flown all the way here to meet him?"

"Axel's work is held in such high esteem, his clients include many of the world's crowned heads," Oliver informed Kitty as they wandered into a dramatically lit chamber that was, coincidentally enough, filled with nothing but ancient Buddha heads carved out of stone.

"Can we do this somewhere in the garden? I think it would be so cool to wander through the forest and just find a bunch of Buddha heads everywhere," Kitty suggested.

Oliver chuckled to himself, trying to imagine how Victoria Young might react to the sight of dozens of Buddhas scattered around Tyersall Park. Still, Kitty's idea wasn't half bad. Maybe the way to really launch Kitty into the social stratosphere would be to style her as Singapore's answer to Peggy Guggenheim, and have the grounds of Tyersall Park become a venue for contemporary art like Storm King in New York or the Chinati Foundation in Marfa. They could have the world's greatest artists in residence to create site-specific installations. Christo could wrap the entire house in silver fabric, James Turrell could create a light projection in the conservatory, and maybe Ai Weiwei could do something controversial with the lily pond.

In the midst of his reverie, there was a sudden flurry of activity as Axel Vervoordt entered the room, impeccably dressed in a gray suit with a black turtleneck, and surrounded by a monastic entourage of assistants. "Oliver T'sien, what a pleasure to see you again!" the legendary antiquarian said.

"Axel, the pleasure is all mine. May I introduce Mrs. Jack Bing."

"Welcome to Kanaal," Axel said, giving Kitty a courtly bow.

"Thank you. Axel, I am in awe of your creations! I've never seen anything quite like this before, and I feel like I just want to move in here right now," Kitty effused.

"Thank you. Mrs. Bing, if you enjoy what you see here, perhaps I can invite you to visit me at my private residence Kasteel van's-Gravenwezel while you are with us in Antwerp."

"You won't want to miss this, Kitty. Kasteel van's-Gravenwezel is one of the most beautiful castles in the world," Oliver explained.

Kitty batted her eyelashes at Axel. "I'd love to!"

"If I had known earlier that the two of you were coming today, I would have invited you to lunch. Her Majesty the Queen honored us with her presence today, and she brought along a most delightful couple."

"I hope you had a lovely time," Oliver said.

"We did, we did. This young couple have just acquired the most magnificent property in Singapour. It is apparently the largest private estate on the island."

Kitty's face went pale.

Axel continued. "Wait a minute—it completely escaped my mind. You're from Singapour, aren't you, Oliver?"

"Indeed I am," Oliver said, forcing a smile.

"Have you heard of this property? Apparently it's quite an architectural folly—a mixture of styles and periods, but set on sixty-four acres. Tivoli Park, I think it is called." Axel cocked his head.

Kitty calmly walked out onto the balcony of the showroom and could be seen jabbing her iPhone screen frantically.

"Actually, I believe you mean Tyersall Park," Oliver corrected him.

"Yes, that's the place! Apparently, the lady's father has given her the property as a wedding present, and she wants me to help her with the redo. It will be quite the commission."

Oliver looked out the window, where Kitty was screaming in Mandarin and gesticulating wildly into her phone. "I know you never discuss your clients, but I'm going to guess that the couple were an English lord and his Chinese wife?"

Axel smiled. "Nothing escapes you, does it? I haven't attempted anything on this scale before in Asia, and I do believe I'm going to be calling on you for some help."

"Congratulations, Axel. It would be a pleasure," Oliver managed to utter as he felt like he was going to throw up.

"Now, what can I do for you and Mrs. Bing?"

Oliver watched Kitty fling her cell phone off the balcony into the canal far below. "Oh we were just in the neighborhood. I'm about to take her to meet Dries at Het Modepaleis, so I figured we should stop by."

. . .

"He said Colette was a new woman. That she had transformed her life and he was proud of her for wanting to do something good in the world. That's why she needed a proper house in Singapore. How gullible can you be?" Kitty cried.

"Yes, let it out. Let it all out," a soothing voice above her said.

"He said that Colette had made a secret trip to see him in Shanghai. She had prostrated herself at his feet and begged for his forgiveness. Can you fucking believe it?" Kitty was lying on the massage table, her head in the face cradle, as her massage therapist Elenya placed a row of hot stones along her spine.

"Good, good. As I place this stone on your lower back, I want you to really feel it burn into your second chakra, and I want you to go deeper into your anger and release it," Elenya encouraged.

"He said, 'Do not make me choose between you and my daughter, because you will lose. I only have one daughter, and I can always get another wife.' I hate him I hate him I hate him!" Kitty screamed, tears flowing freely and dripping on the tatami-matted floor.

Suddenly the floor trembled violently, and a couple of the stones rolled off her back onto the side of the table. Oliver, sitting in an armchair next to the massage table, pulled his seat belt tighter.

"That wasn't turbulence, Kitty. That was your anger releasing into the universe. How does it feel?" Elenya asked, as she began to rub Kitty's feet with a steaming hot towel.

"It feels fucking great! I want to tell the pilots to steer this plane and crash it right into his fucking face!" Kitty screamed again, before breaking into loud heaving sobs.

Oliver sighed as he looked out the window of the spa on the second floor of Kitty's Boeing 747-81 VIP. They were over the English Channel now, and soon they would be landing in London. "I don't know if a quick revenge is the answer, Kitty. I think you need to be playing a long game here. Look at the life Jack has given you. You've got three airplanes at your disposal, wonderful Elenya here to give you hot-stone massage treatments when you need it most, and all your other beautiful homes around the world. And let's not forget about Harvard. You've given Jack a son, and as he grows up, he will begin to eclipse Colette in importance. Kitty, do you know the story of the Empress Dowager Cixi?"

"She was the old lady that died in the opening scene of that *Last Emperor* movie, wasn't she?" Kitty said in a quiet voice.

"Yes, the Empress Dowager Cixi was one of the concubines of Emperor Xianfeng, and after he died she launched a palace coup and became the true force of power in China. Cixi had a greater impact than possibly any other emperor in the country's history—she transformed it from a medieval empire into a modern nation, opened the country up to the West, and abolished foot-binding for girls. And she did all this, Kitty, even though she technically had no power at all because she was a woman."

"So how did she do it?" Kitty asked.

"She ruled indirectly through her five-year-old son, who succeeded to the throne as emperor. And after he died as a teenager, she adopted another boy and put him on the throne so she could rule through him. As the Empress Dowager, court etiquette decreed that she wasn't even allowed to be seen by men, so she took all her meetings with her ministers from behind a silk screen. You could learn a great deal from Cixi, you know. You need to bide your time and solidify your position by being the best mother to Harvard that you can possibly be. You need to be the most influential person in his life, and in time, he'll come to rule the Bing empire and you will be the power behind the throne. Throughout history, Kitty, the people who wielded the most power weren't always the ones who were in the spotlight. Dowager Empress Cixi, Cardinal Richelieu, Cosimo de' Medici. These are the people who flew under the radar in their own time, but they amassed all the power and influence through patience, intelligence, and stealth."

"Patience, intelligence, and stealth," Kitty repeated. Suddenly she rolled over and sat up on the massage bed, the hot stones rolling off her back and scattering onto the floor as Elenya scurried to pick them up. "Has the contract to buy Tyersall Park been signed yet?"

"I think the lawyers are still drafting the agreement."

"So it's not a done deal?"

"No. There's a gentleman's agreement, but it won't be official until the contracts are actually signed." Oliver wondered where she was going with all this.

"Didn't you tell me that there were other interested parties in Tyersall Park before Jack bought it?"

"Well yes, my cousin Nick was trying to buy it, but he never managed to scrape up enough money to match Jack's offer."

"How much did he need?"

"I think he was short about four billion dollars."

Kitty's eyes gleamed. "What if I became a secret investor in the house? What if I put in the money and stole this house away from Jack?"

Oliver stared at her in surprise. "Kitty, do you have that kind of money on your own?"

"I got two billion in my divorce settlement from Bernard, and I invested all that money in Amazon. Do you know how much those shares have gone up in the past year? I have more than five billion dollars, and it's just all sitting there in an account managed by the Liechtenburg Group," Kitty proudly announced.

Oliver leaned forward in his armchair. "You'd really be willing to invest all that money in a deal with my cousin?"

"You'd still get your commission either way, wouldn't you?"

"I would, but I'd just be concerned about you putting so much of your own money into one venture."

Kitty went quiet for a moment, touched that Oliver cared for her beyond her money. "It will be worth every last cent just to know that Colette doesn't get her hands on that house!"

"Well, let me make a few calls." Oliver unbuckled his seat belt and left the spa cabin. Five minutes later, he returned with a smirk on his face. "Kitty, there's been the most interesting development. I just spoke to my cousin Nicky. It turns out that Tyersall Park has been deemed a national historic landmark, and he and a group of partners are putting together a radical new proposal to challenge Jack Bing's offer."

"Does this mean Colette won't get it either?"

"Well, that's very likely. However, they are desperate for one more investor. They're short three billion dollars."

"Only three billion? Sounds like a deal."

"Should I call the cockpit and get them to turn this plane around?"

"Why not?"

Oliver picked up the phone by the console. "There's been a change of plans. We need to get to Singapore, and fast."

"Not too fast. I want to get back to my hot-stone massage," Kitty purred, as she stretched languidly onto her massage bed again.

EPILOGUE

ONE YEAR LATER . . .

"I can't wait to see the bride. I wonder which designer she chose to do her gown?" Jacqueline Ling said to Oliver T'sien at the reception before the intimate wedding ceremony. Two hundred guests invited by the happy couple's families milled about the Andalusian Cloister, enjoying cocktails and canapés while admiring the mesmerizing light installation created by artist James Turrell in the columned arcades surrounding the courtyard.

"Let's make a bet," Oliver ventured.

"The way you're rolling in money these days, I'm not sure if I want to bet against you. Congratulations on your new commission in Abu Dhabi, by the way."

"Thank you. It's just one palace for now. The princess was so impressed by what we did here that she's put me on an embarrassingly large retainer. Anyway, let's make the bet for lunch at Daphne's the next time we're both in London, and my money's on Giambattista Valli," Oliver said.

"Okay, lunch at Daphne's. Well, I wager that the bride's gown will be designed by Alexis Mabille. I know how much she adores his work."

The string quartet that had been playing suddenly stopped as the door at the far end of the courtyard opened to reveal a dashing young fellow in a tuxedo holding a violin to his chin.

"Oh look, it's Charlie Siem! He's popping up everywhere these days, isn't he?" Oliver commented as the absurdly handsome virtuoso strolled along the arcade playing Elgar's "Salut d'amour." The doors at the other end of the arcade opened slowly, and Charlie strolled through, turning around to beckon the guests to follow him as he continued to play. Outside, a pathway lit with thousands of votive candles led from the rose garden past the stunning new saltwater swimming pool lined with thirteenth-century Moorish tiles into the wooded area of the estate.

Following the musician as he ambled along merrily playing his violin, the guests oohed and aahed when they reached the lily pond, where black wooden chairs had been arranged in a crescent along one side of the pond. Hundreds of pale pink lanterns hung from the trees, cascading down branches and mixing with thousands of hanging vines that had been festooned with white dendrobium orchids, peonies, and white jasmine. A beautiful arched bridge built just for the wedding extended from one side of the pond to the other, covered entirely in different-hued roses, making the whole bridge appear as if it had been painted with impressionistic brushstrokes like one of Monet's bridges at Giverny.

After the guests had settled into their seats, four cellists placed in the direction of the four winds began to play Bach's Cello Suite No. 1 in G major as the wedding procession began. An adorable little flower girl dressed in a gossamer white Marie-Chantal gown scattered rose petals along the central aisle, followed by Cassian Teo, who ambled up the aisle in a white linen suit (but barefoot), focused intently on not dropping the velvet pillow bearing the wedding rings.

Next came Nick and Rachel walking arm in arm. Eleanor swelled up with pride as she watched Nick, dashing in his midnight blue Henry Poole tuxedo, escort Rachel, who Eleanor had to admit looked glowingly beautiful in a sublimely simple eggshell pink silk crepe gown designed by Narciso Rodriguez.

"*Aiyah*, it's like their wedding all over again," Eleanor sniffed to her husband, dabbing away a few tears.

"Minus your crazy helicopter invasion," Philip quipped.

"It wasn't crazy! I saved their marriage, those ungrateful kids!"

Nick and Rachel parted at the end of the aisle as they took their places as best man and matron of honor on opposite sides of the bridge. Suddenly, a grand piano became illuminated behind the bridge, giving the effect of floating in the middle of the pond. Sitting at the piano was a young man with slightly disheveled strawberry blond hair.

Irene Wu gasped out loud, "*Alamak*, it's that Ed Saranwrap! I love his music!"

As Ed Sheeran began singing his wildly popular love ballad "Thinking Out Loud," the groom, looking sharp in a bespoke tuxedo from Gieves and Hawkes, walked up to the middle of the bridge with the American pastor from Hong Kong's Stratosphere Church. And then as a full band assembled at the far end of the pond emerged to accompany Ed in his song, the bride made her grand entrance at the foot of the pathway.

The guests rose from their seats in unison as the proud father of the bride, Goh Wye Mun, nervously escorted his daughter Peik Lin up the aisle. The bride wore a strapless gown with a fitted white bodice and a long train skirt of ruffles appliquéd with pale pink silk roses. Her hair was swept up into an elaborate braided bun and crowned with a vintage pearl-and-diamond tiara from G.Collins & Sons.

Jacqueline and Oliver looked at each other and said in unison, "McQueen!"

As Peik Lin glided past them, Jacqueline nodded approvingly. "Sublime. Sarah Burton does it again!"

"We both lose, but we can still have lunch at Daphne's. Of course, you're treating, Jac—you've got more fuck-you money than I do," Oliver said with a wink.

Peik Lin walked up to the middle of the bridge, where she was met by the pastor, who looked a little too disturbingly like Chris Hemsworth, and the man she was about to marry—Alistair Cheng.

Nick and Rachel beamed joyously as the couple exchanged their handwritten vows, while Neena Goh, dressed in a gold-sequined Guo Pei gown with a plunging neckline, wept noisily. The Young sisters—Felicity, Catherine, Victoria, and Alix—glared at the mother of the bride with varying degrees of disapproval while shedding their own discreet tears.

"I can't believe my baby Alistair is getting married," Alix sniffed to her sisters. "It seemed like only yesterday he was crawling into my bed, too afraid to sleep in the dark, and look at him now."

"Well, the boy was smart enough to marry a woman as capable as Peik Lin! I must admit I am quite impressed with what she and Alistair have done with Tyersall Park," Felicity said.

"I'm impressed by what they *all* did!" Catherine interjected. After all, it was she who cast the tiebreaking vote between the sisters one year ago when Nick had come to them with a radical new proposal hours before they were about to sign the sales contract with Jack Bing.

The result of Nick's proposal had now come to life as the just-completed Tyersall Park Hotel and Museum, which preserved the main house as a historic landmark while breathing new life into it as an incomparably elegant new boutique hotel run by Colin Khoo and Araminta Lee. Set among nineteen acres of lush gardens in the immediate vicinity of the main house were forty guest villas exquisitely designed by Oliver T'sien in partnership with Axel Vervoordt. Beyond this rose Tyersall Village, a forty-five-acre community of sustainable housing specifically designed for artists and middle-income families, built by Goh Developments—the construction company owned by Peik Lin's family.

"I think Father would be proud of Nicky. I don't think he was ever truly comfortable coming home every night to this decadent palace, when he spent the whole day being a doctor to the poorest people on the island," Alix said approvingly. From the row behind the sisters, Cassandra Shang leaned in and whispered, "I'm told every single house in Tyersall Village sold on the first day of offering, because for so long no one with less than ten million dollars has been able to afford a house with a garden in Singapore! But apparently the people living in those big houses along Gallop Road are furious that the hoi polloi are now moving in to this tony neighborhood!"

"I don't mind what they did with Tyersall Village, but all those Buddha heads in the garden have got to go!" Victoria huffed. "I wonder if Peik Lin had anything to do with that. Those parents of hers look like they could be Buddhist."

Felicity shook her head. "I don't think Peik Lin was involved. I think the Buddhas belong to the secret investor who chipped three billion in to Nick's venture. I just wish I knew who it was!"

When the ceremony had concluded, the guests proceeded to

the wedding banquet at Alexander's, the ravishing new restaurant in what was formerly the conservatory managed by Araminta Lee's Sublime Hospitality Group. Su Yi's prizewinning orchid hybrids commanded the space, but now they sprang out of handblown glass vessels suspended from the ceiling. Lit by candlelight, the hundreds of orchids seemed to dance in the air like celestial creatures over the long wooden seventeenth-century refectory tables.

Eddie was the first to clink his wineglass and propose a toast to the newly married couple. "Peik Lin, I want to officially welcome you to the Cheng family, even though you know that you've already been welcomed into our hearts. And Alistair, my baby brother, I've never been more proud of you than I am today, and I just wanted to tell you how much I appreciate you and cherish you! I love you, brother!" Eddie said, crushing Alistair into a tight bear hug as he began sobbing into his collar.

Sitting at the family table, Astrid turned to Fiona. "Is Eddie okay?"

Fiona smiled. "He's fine. After Ah Ma died, I forced him to go see a therapist. I gave him an ultimatum—either he went, or I would leave him. At first he was very resistant, but now it's completely changed his life. And ours too. He's given up all his mistresses, he's become totally devoted to me and the kids, and he's really learning to process his feelings in a healthier way."

"Well, it's been more than a year since I've seen him, so it does seem like quite a transformation," Astrid noted, watching as Eddie continued to soak Alistair's shoulder with tears.

"You know my Eddie. Whenever he does anything, he goes all out. Anyway, how have you been? I see that island life suits you well—you look amazing!" Fiona remarked, as she admired Astrid's golden tan, naturally sun-streaked hair, and new style, which seemed like a perfect fusion of laid-back beach chic with imperial splendor. Astrid wore a simple indigo-dyed sarong-wrap dress with an incredible pearl choker that was comprised of crisscrossing vertical ropes of pearls starting from just underneath her chin and cascading down to the middle of her chest.

"Thank you."

"The choker is just *beyond*! Is that one of Ah Ma's pieces?"

"No, it's from Chantecler Capri—a birthday present from Charlie."

"I have to ask where you got that dress. It looks so refined, and yet somehow so relaxed!"

Astrid gave an almost bashful smile. "Actually, I made this dress."

"You're joking? I thought you were going to say this was Yves Saint Laurent from some obscure resort collection in the eighties."

"Nope, it's Astrid Leong Resort Wear 2016. I've learned to sew, and I'm also creating my own fabrics. This is actually a bamboo cotton, hand-dyed in ocean water."

"My God, Astrid, it's amazing! Can I buy a dress from you?"

Astrid laughed. "Of course, I'll make you a dress if you like."

"I guess you aren't bored in paradise?"

"Not at all. I'm absolutely in love with my life in Palawan, and every day's an adventure. Charlie and I have also started a school, partnered with this wonderful arts-focused school in Brooklyn called Saint Ann's. Charlie's discovered a new passion—teaching! He's leading all the math and science classes, and Cassian's one of the students. The boy's never been happier being in a classroom with no walls and a constant ocean breeze. You really should bring the kids for a visit sometime."

Charlie came strolling up with two flutes of champagne for

the ladies. "Thanks, Charlie. So are tonight's nuptials inspiring you two?" Fiona teased.

"Haha. A little bit, maybe. But right now I just enjoy living in sin with my gorgeous lover. Plus, it infuriates my parents to no end," Astrid said, giving Charlie a long, tender kiss just as her mother glanced over in their direction.

After the banquet, the bride stood on the top steps of the rose garden with her back to a gaggle of excited women ready to catch her bouquet. Peik Lin threw it up in the air with gusto, and the bouquet of lilies of the valley made an almost perfect arch, landing right in Scheherazade Shang's hands. The crowd cheered wildly as Scheherazade blushed.

Catching Carlton's startled expression, Nick said teasingly, "The pressure's on now!"

"No shit." Carlton nodded grimly, before breaking into a huge grin.

An ornate outdoor ballroom had been created on the great lawn, complete with marquetry floors and enormous standing baroque mirrors placed strategically around the perimeter so that the dancers could feel as though they were whirling through the ballroom at Peterhof Palace. As the band went into full swing and the guests took to the dance floor, Nick, Rachel, and Kitty stood off to the side admiring Colin and Araminta's two-month-old son, Auberon.

"He's sooooo cute!" Kitty cooed at the wriggling infant. "Look, Harvard, you were just like this not too long ago."

"Was I ever that little?" Kitty's three-year-old boy asked.

"Of course you were, darling! You were my little pea pod!"

"I think we should probably get Auberon home. He's getting

a bit fussy, and he'll never go back to sleep with the music," Araminta said a little anxiously to Colin.

"Okay, okay. Hate to dash off so early, guys, but Mummy calls the shots now." Colin looked around apologetically. "But hey, this evening marks an auspicious start to our venture, don't you think? Two of our partners got married in grand style, and everything went off without a hitch! Tyersall Park Hotel and Museum is going to be the premier event space in Singapore!"

"No, it will be the premier event space in all of Asia!" Kitty insisted.

"Oh, I forgot to mention—I've just received an inquiry from a certain European prince who wants to buy out the entire hotel for a week to throw a huge birthday bash!" Araminta said.

"We're attracting royalty already! Maybe the Countess of Palliser will hire it out for her next big gala," Rachel said with a slightly naughty smile.

"How is she doing, by the way?" Araminta asked Kitty. Everyone knew that Colette had been the victim of a horrendous freak accident at her Save the Orangutans Proust Ball last year at the historic Goodwood Park Hotel. Colette had insisted on re-creating the space to look exactly like the French château where the original Proust Ball took place in 1971, complete with authentic 1971 lighting. In the middle of her speech, the electrical wiring on the 1970s lamp at her podium had short-circuited, and it would have been fine if Colette hadn't been wearing her multimillion-dollar Giambattista Valli gown plated with eight hundred eighteen-carat rose gold disks.

"From what her father tells me, she's getting better every day. She's still in that wonderful facility in England, and she can speak without dribbling now, but it will be some time before she can make it to Sumatra again," Kitty said sweetly.

Harvard tugged at her sleeve. "Mother, I'm getting hungry."

"Okay honey," Kitty said. She walked with him to a quiet corner of the woods, undid the specially designed bodice on her strapless black Raf Simons jumpsuit, and took out her left breast. Kitty had become a staunch believer in attachment parenting, and as her son sucked happily on her nipple, she admired all the hauntingly lit ancient Buddha heads staring back at her, feeling extremely pleased with her one decorating suggestion. All these Buddhas would surely bring this place good karma.

On the other side of the garden, Nick and Rachel were taking a walk to see how the new development was coming along. "It's unbelievable how fast they've worked," Nick remarked as he peeked into one of the bungalows.

"Yeah, when we were back last Christmas, this was all one giant construction site, and now these beautiful little villas have appeared, looking like they've been here forever!" Rachel said admiringly as she fondled the ivy creeping along one of the reclaimed stone walls.

"You know, none of this would have happened without you. You're the one who came up with the idea of putting Peik Lin, Alistair, Colin, and Araminta together to create this dream team, and look what they've achieved. In one year, they've created this whole eco-village *and* Araminta even had time to have a baby! Isn't Auberon a cutie?"

"He's adorable." Rachel paused for a moment, as if deciding whether to say something. "I'm so happy she had her baby now . . . because he's going to be the perfect playmate for ours."

Nick looked at his wife with eyes huge as saucers. "Are you saying what I think you're saying?"

Rachel nodded, with a smile.

Nick hugged her excitedly. "When? Why didn't you tell me?"

"I was waiting for the right moment. I took the test a couple of days ago—I'm about six weeks along."

"Six weeks!" Nick sank down on a carved stone bench outside the villa. "Jesus, my head is spinning!"

"Are you going to be okay?" Rachel asked.

"Totally! I'm just overwhelmed with joy!" Nick said. Suddenly he looked up at Rachel with a jolt. "Listen, we *cannot* mention this to my mother."

"Oh, hell no!"

Nick got up and took Rachel by the hand as they strolled down the pathway back to the wedding festivities. "Maybe if Mum behaves herself, she can meet our baby at age eighteen."

Rachel thought about it for a moment. "We should probably wait till twenty-one."

Nick escorted Rachel onto the dance floor just as the band struck up a ballad. As he held her body tight against his, he closed his eyes for a moment, thinking he could almost feel the heartbeat of his child. He opened his eyes again, gazing at his beautiful wife, gazing across the dance floor at Astrid and Charlie in their blissful embrace, and gazing at last toward the great house with all the lights in its windows ablaze, alive, reborn.

ACKNOWLEDGMENTS

SPECIAL THANKS

I am deeply grateful to the following guardian angels for so graciously sharing their expertise, talent, advice, inspiration, and support during the writing of this book:

Nigel Barker
Ryan Chan
John Chia
Cleo Davis-Urman
Todd Doughty
David Elliott
Richard Eu
Grant Gers
Simone Gers
Cornelia Guest
Doris Magsaysay Ho
George Hu
Jenny Jackson
Judy Jacoby
Wah Guan Lim

Lydia Look
Alicia Lubowski
Alexandra Machinist
Julia Nickson
Anton San Diego
David Sangalli
Alexander Sanger
Jeannette Watson Sanger
Shane Suvikapakornkul
Nellie Svasti
Sandi Tan
Jami Tarris
Lynn Visudharomn
Eric Wind
Jackie Zirkman